THE LIFE & TIMES OF
ALTU-FALTU
A Fable

Author sketch: Salam Hidish

RANJIT LAL was born in Calcutta in 1955, and educated in Mumbai. As a freelance writer, he has had over a thousand articles, features and photo-features published in more than 50 newspapers and magazines at home and abroad, specialising in natural history (particularly birds), humour and automobiles.

He is the author of *The Crow Chronicles* (Penguin, 1996), a bird-based, socio-political fable, and *Enjoying Birds* (Clarion, 1998), an illustrated book on birdwatching.

He is unmarried and lives in Delhi.

THE LIFE & TIMES OF
ALTU-FALTU
A Fable

Ranjit Lal

IndiaInk

This book is entirely a work of fiction.
All the characters, events and places are fictitious, and any resemblance to places,
events, or persons, living or dead, is purely coincidental and unintentional.

IndiaInk
An imprint of RST IndiaInk Publishing Company Private Limited
B-57, New Rajinder Nagar, New Delhi 110 060, India

Published by IndiaInk 2001

1 3 5 7 9 8 6 4 2

ISBN 81-86939-09-1

Ranjit Lal asserts the moral right to be identified as the author of this work.

Illustrator: Mishta Roy
Designer: Sudhir John Horo
BuffaloDesign

Published by Tarun J. Tejpal for IndiaInk
Printed and bound in India by Thomson Press (India) Limited.

CONTENTS

Chapter 1

STILL
WATERS

Altu Faltu, the slim, lithe Rhesus macaque slipped through the narrow side entrance to the North Delhi Ridge from Rajpur Road and crouched low, his heart hammering against his ribs.

He knew that, yet again, he was about to do a very foolish thing. Eloping by full moon had seemed to be such a dashing, romantic idea at the planning stage that he had not paused to think about it at all. But now, when the time was at hand, it seemed neither romantic nor pragmatic, just extremely (and unnecessarily) dangerous. Especially since he was about to run away with the recently betrothed daughter of the most powerful Rhesus chieftain this side of Delhi. If elope he had to, so be it, but surely there were safer ways of doing so?

Now, even as midnight approached, there was so much (decidedly unromantic) moonlight pouring through the canopy of trees that it was as good as trying to elope in broad daylight. Also, he didn't like the sinister lurking shadows cast by the restless foliage — the many trembling, quivering shapes, all of which could conceal Chaudhury Charbi Raisahib's yellow-fanged thugs waiting to ambush him.

Ahead, the red-brick pathway made its way up the shoulder of the Ridge in a series of shallow steps, flanked on either side by tall columns of eucalyptus that glimmered eerily in the moonlight. A fork to the left led to the little hunchbacked bridge that spanned the still, glinting waters of the Khooni Khan Jheel, which, legend has it, was haunted by the spirits of many unhappy lovers (both simian and human) who had drowned themselves there in times past.

It was under this bridge that the petite and lovely Rani-beti, princess of the Flagstaff Tower macaques had sworn by the blood of her tail to wait for him. She had chosen this unwise spot because it had been here that the besotted (some say bewitched) young couple had carried out their ecstatic clandestine affair during the past few weeks, and it was here that they had sworn, like other lovers of the past, to drown themselves if they were thwarted.

"What better place to die together than here, where we have been so happy!" Rani-beti had exclaimed during a maudlin interlude one torrid afternoon. And Altu Faltu had only been able to nod dumbly in agreement, ignoring the small faraway voice that had wondered if he really would jump if push came to shove.

A sentry dozing on a small tree next to the entrance coughed and grunted. Altu Faltu froze, a grimace of terror stretched across his face. For an instant, he thought about abandoning the whole escapade; of fleeing to his tool-shed shelter at the Hindu Rao Ridge nearby, and taking refuge in a bottle of Phensidyl cough syrup. Of going back to his usual lackadaisical, loose-limbed life, where nothing really ever mattered too much.

But then he thought of Rani-beti, waiting for him under the little hunchbacked bridge...

Beautiful Rani-beti, with her gold-flecked eyes and strange pixie ears. Her lovely silky coat (such bliss to groom!) and delicate, supple limbs. . .

Rani-beti, favourite daughter of the mighty Chaudhury Charbi Raisahib, scion of the Flagstaff Tower macaques. Rani-beti, so recently engaged with thumping fanfare to the hulking great Bade Badtameez, self-styled nawab of the much-feared Tughlakabad clan...

Brave Rani-beti, now defying both her powerful father and fearsome fiancé, to run away with him, Altu Faltu, a two-bit awara who loafed about with the stoned Hindu Rao crowd, and spent his time smoking bidi butts and drinking bottles of cough linctus stolen from the hospital on the hilltop.

How on earth had such an unlikely alliance been forged?

The Ridge at North Delhi lies between the sprawling campus of Delhi University and the still genteel area of Civil Lines, like an enormous emerald flint-head. Its broad-end gives way to the teeming Sabzi Mandi, its northern tip tapers off near the banks of the Yamuna. Nearly 90 hectares in area, the North Delhi Ridge comprises a small, independent section of the beautiful, notorious and terribly degraded Delhi Ridge, which itself forms the tail end of the Mewat branch of the Aravalli mountains.

It was amidst the ravines and gullies of the Northern Ridge however, that the British garrison camped during the rebellion in the summer of 1857. British civilians, living in the cantonment area, where the Delhi University stands today, had taken shelter within the thick walls of the Flagstaff Tower (now flying Chaudhury Charbi Raisahib's colours) before fleeing to Meerut and Karnal. In the months of bitter fighting that followed, the Flagstaff Tower, the house of Hindu Rao (now replaced by the hospital from where Altu Faltu pinches his supplies of codeine), the Chauburja mosque, also nearby, and Metcalfe House, down by the river, became important strategic locations and the scenes of fierce skirmishes and bombardment.

At that time, the Ridge was a barren rocky wilderness, supporting a few stunted acacias and thornbushes — a region too inhospitable for any self-respecting simian family to consider settling down in. After the Mutiny however, and especially at the turn of the century, the British began afforesting the Ridge in right earnest. By the 1930s, the area was said to be crowded with leopard, chinkara, wild-boar, jackal and other wildlife.

It was around this time that Chaudhury Charbi Raisahib's grandfather, the late Chaudhury Mota Raisahib, migrated with his family from the Uttar Pradesh hinterland and established the clan at the Flagstaff Tower. Rhesus families from all over the countryside had begun flocking to the new capital, drawn by the great wealth, power, corruption, and enterprise of its inhabitants.

They called themselves Delhizens, these olive-brown, lobster-bottomed macaques, and considered themselves to be quite superior to the city's human population whose generous patronage they enjoyed (even if the occasional conflict did break out). They spread rapidly throughout the city, settling down in, and encroaching upon, colonies, market-places and parks.

Under the sagacious leadership of Chaudhury Mota Raisahib, and later his son, Chaudhury Taza Raisahib, the Flagstaff macaques remained as happy as any large joint family could expect to be. There was enough to eat and plenty of space for the clan to spread out in. When Chaudhury Taza Raisahib relinquished control of the family to his son, Chaudhury Charbi Raisahib, he was a content, happy elder, and insisted on retiring to one of the wrestling akharas that had come up on the banks of the Yamuna opposite the Tibetan monastery nearby.

But fate played a devious trick on Chaudhury Charbi Raisahib. A sudden resurgence of religious activity during the late 1980s and early 1990s resulted in an increase in patronage (some called it sponsorship) on an unprecedented scale. Delhizen-macaques everywhere, including those on the Ridge, began being plied with vast quantities of the choicest fruit and sweetmeats on a long-term sustained basis. (Of course, Tuesdays and Saturdays remained extra special). Like many others who are unable to handle sudden wealth, the members of the Flagstaff clan were unable to deal with this sudden, colossal and seemingly endless largesse. They grew fat and greedy and selfish. Worst of all, they began breeding like flies and all too soon, there were just too many of them living too close to each other for comfort. Quarrels and brawls began breaking out frequently, and Chaudhury Charbi Raisahib was hard pressed to keep his fractious family intact. Many insolent young thugs (cousins and nephews for he had no sons as yet) had formed their own gangs and were threatening to secede from the Flagstaff clan. His own younger brother, Chaudhury Harami Raisahib had, in fact, laid claim to the large feeding plinth near the Chauburja monument and its surrounding areas, and had virtually declared his independence.

Actually the Delhizen population throughout the city had increased tremendously and it was no longer as easy for a youngster to stake a territorial claim and start an independent clan as it had been in the past. Territorial disputes were commonplace, and getting uglier every time.

With the betrothal of his lovely daughter Rani-beti, to Bade Badtameez, the nawab of the powerful Tughlakabadis, Chaudhury Charbi Raisahib had hoped to make it easier for some of the Flagstaff Tower inhabitants to resettle in the vast Tughlakabad area and ease the population pressure on the Ridge. The match would also extend his own sphere of influence, and with such a powerful son-in-law by his side, the more rebellious elements in his own family would think twice before voicing their demands for independence. Also, there was nothing quite like a large, lavish wedding to bring a family together.

Another troupe of Delhizens comprising an (allegedly) semi-criminal tribe of idlers had occupied the hilly area of the Ridge opposite the Hindu Rao Hospital much to the disgust of Chaudhury Mota Raisahib. The troupe was notorious for its ether-sniffing, linctus-drinking and bidi-smoking and had degenerated completely. Alas, their indolent, iconoclastic ways had served as inspiration to many a frustrated adolescent simian, and they had ruined many a bright and promising Delhizen career and life.

Altu Faltu had been just one of their voluntary victims. He

hailed from the renowned Nicholson troupe, the family that had occupied the once-shady environs of the Nicholson cemetery opposite Kashmere Gate. Always a bit of a dreamer, Altu Faltu had 'dropped out' of the rat race before even getting into it. Instead of availing of the small territory his father had acquired for him in the neighbouring Qudsia Gardens, and settling down with a mate of his mother's choice, he had gotten mixed up with the degenerate Hindu Rao crowd and had taken instantly to their idling, vagrant ways. Easy come, easy go, had been the guiding philosophy of his life. Until that fateful evening when he had encountered Rani-beti for the first time during the feast at the Flagstaff Tower.

It had happened a few weeks earlier. Yet another banquet had been laid out by the devout for the overfed Flagstaff Tower macaques. Mangoes, guavas, bananas, grapes, litchies, papaya, pudina paranthas, jalebis, almonds, cashewnuts and other delicacies had been laid out in great profusion in the clearing around the burly Flagstaff Tower. News of the repast had spread swiftly, and Delhizens living in the surrounding areas loped in to see what they could steal. Of course, Chaudhury Charbi Raisahib had stationed sentries all around the area to ensure that not a single grape was illegally lifted. He was like that. But the guards had had their hands full with trying to maintain a semblance of law and order amongst the Flagstaff macaques themselves, and some were more concerned that they would be left out of the feasting.

And Altu Faltu had always enjoyed the gift of being

inconspicuous...

He had been idling away his time breaking empty bottles in the hospital garbage dump when he heard of the feast. It had been child's play for him to slip unseen through the undergrowth right up to the Flagstaff Tower clearing. In front of him, a rabble of Flagstaff macaques squabbled noisily and snatched fruit from one another as though they had never seen any before. It was quite easy for him to dart out of cover every now and then, palm a mango (his favourite fruit) and slip back into the bushes unseen. So much so that he grew bolder. With so many screeching simians swarming around, it was unlikely that he would be noticed as an outsider. He sauntered out nonchalantly, picked up a slice of papaya and returned to cover. Courage gave way to recklessness. On his next trip, he even dared to cuff a young brat away from the luscious langda both of them had made a grab for. When he finished with the mango, he casually tossed the seed and peels into the swarming mob.

Then he looked up (for a piece of jalebi) and saw her. Staring across a sea of bobbing simian heads, directly at him. A bunch of jade-green grapes held delicately in one paw.

He recognised her at once — who wouldn't! Next to her sat a formidable female (her mother, Bibi-Ek, he learnt later) stuffing her face with almonds. Both she and her mother were surrounded by several unsavoury looking bodyguards.

But dammit, there she was, ignoring her grapes and staring at him as though she had never seen another monkey in her life. He gave a sheepish grin and a half-shrug, poised for a high-speed take-off. But she didn't scream or swoon or warn the guards as he was sure she would do. She just stared at him, and then, to his growing disbelief, smiled sweetly back at him!

Of course, later on, when he knew how she had been dreading her forthcoming marriage and all that, he lied heroically about their first encounter.

"You looked... you looked as though you had been tied to a stake and were about to be burned!" he declared passionately. "As though you were willing me to rescue you!"

"I was!" she had replied, not entirely fibbing, and turning him to jelly.

And thus they had gazed at one another with inane smiles on their faces, as the other monkeys gobbled and fought around them. Dimly and uncomfortably, Altu Faltu recalled that the penalty for this kind of voyeurism was to be bitten to death by all the princess' outraged male relatives. Both of them wondered who would be the first to switch off the smiles and drop their eyes.

But then a violent brawl broke out nearby and the guards came thudding up, clouting monkeys left and right. Bibi-Ek and her soppily smiling daughter were hastily escorted away. And Altu Faltu melted quickly back into the undergrowth and made his way back home like a zombie, wondering what on earth had happened to him in those few (and oh, so precious) moments.

Why had the lovely princess of the Flagstaff Tower clan stared and smiled at him like that? Any normal princess should have screamed blue murder and swooned. Had she been making eyes at him?

In the time-honoured way of all criminals, he returned to the scene of the crime the following evening at the same time. If she had been so interested in him, then it was remotely possible that she might want to continue from where they had left off yesterday. The thought of flirting with the engaged daughter of Chaudhury Charbi Raisahib sent a perverse thrill through Altu Faltu. It also covered up an uncomfortable feeling he had been having that there was something more to this lurking beneath the surface like a spring-loaded net buried in the ground.

There were few monkeys at the Tower the next evening as Chaudhury Charbi Raisahib had called an important meeting of the clan elders at the Serpentine arbour to discuss the socio-political implications of his daughter's forthcoming union. And Altu Faltu's heart started pounding when, as though on cue, Rani-beti appeared again in the empty clearing, this time without her formidable mother, but in the company of several tumbling siblings.

Rani-beti had been bored stiff by the feasting at the Flagstaff Tower the previous evening. In a few weeks from now, she would be leaving the Ridge for good to live with her husband amidst the rocky, sprawling ruins of the Tughlakabad Fort. She was not looking forward to this, for she had entirely disliked what little she had seen of her massive fiancé. He had seemed to be so coarse and crude, a brute of a monkey, and allegedly had a rapacious sexual appetite. Also, she was sure she had overhead him sniggeringly refer to her as a 'sexy bit of tail!'. Besides, everyone excepting her parents knew that the Tughlakabadis were grossly feudal and medieval in their ways.

She had, at first, objected to this alliance with floods of tears and much wailing, but then had been subjected to heavy doses of emotional blackmail regarding her (robust) mother's frail heart and her family's (now grossly overestimated) sense of honour.

Eventually, sobbing, she had given in. She had felt that her own case for objection was considerably weakened by the fact that there was no one else in her life at the time.

Accordingly, she had been rather vulnerable at the time she saw Altu Faltu cheekily pinch mangoes and chuck the peels at the rabble.

A flicker of rebellion had sparked inside her against the fate that had been decided for her. Even if this cheeky Charlie was not the kind of knight in shining armour who would rescue her from the hairy clutches of Bade Badtameez, he was certainly worth a sweet smile, and making eyes at... His unkempt coat and sly movements made it clear that he was not of the Flagstaff Tower clan. The somewhat indolent and faraway look in his eyes indicated that he was probably hooked onto taking intoxicating substances. He was obviously neither powerful nor influential (despite the influence he was having on her), and probably did not come from a 'status family' either. Her mother had been gloating about that ad nauseam, ever since her engagement.

And when he had given her his self-effacing grin and half-shrug on discovering she had singled him out, she had smiled back involuntarily and then with deliberate sweetness. (Rani-beti's sweet smile had played havoc with several young hellions in the past.) If she had to go down, she thought, she might as well go down flirting outrageously — with all guns blazing so to speak. And what better choice than this awful, untidy layabout — the perfect antithesis to Badtameez! The brawl had interfered with her plans to somehow fix a rendezvous with him, and she had contrived to come to the Flagstaff

Tower at the same time the following evening in the wild hope that he would do the same thing.(Surely they had stared at each other long enough, and then, fools seldom differ...)

Then, when she saw him peering at her through the undergrowth, her heart gave a sudden lurching bump. She quickly did half-a-dozen neat somersaults and landed right next to the bush he was hiding behind. Six inches from his face, she looked into his dreamy brown eyes.

"Can I... can I meet you somewhere alone?" he had asked, adding with charming diffidence, "that's if you don't mind, of course!" Actually he hardly knew what he was saying or from where the courage had come.

She reined in the silly simpering smile that was threatening to break out and pursed her lips.

"If you want," she had replied coolly enough.

"Where? When?"

Rani-beti decided to enjoy her flirtation to the hilt. Her eyes grew large and sad.

"Meet me..." she whispered dramatically, like a tragedienne in a play, "Oh, meet me under the bridge over the Khooni Khan Jheel tomorrow, before sunset!"

He nodded and she was gone.

The Khooni Khan Jheel, where Rani-beti had promised to meet (and later elope with) Altu Faltu consists of two small, dark ponds linked by a narrow neck of water over which crouches the little bridge. It is surrounded by trees — great trembling-leafed peepuls, lovely filigreed neems, fiery gulmohurs and others. During the hottest days of summer, the Flagstaff Tower macaques used the pond as a swimming pool, though now, with October approaching, it was too chilly and humid for that.

Altu Faltu had crawled commando style through the deep, thickly foliaged gully that separated the Khooni Khan Jheel from Rajpur Road. By the time he had squirmed under the culvert adjacent to the pond, he was muddy and dishevelled, and in no state to meet a princess for a first date.

And what a princess she was!

He spotted her immediately from the edge of the culvert, sitting demurely on the girder that supported the bridge, eating a pomegranate. The rain–distilled sun, slanting through the great cathedral of trees, encased her in a halo of pure bullion: every silken hair seemed to be made of spun gold. Now and then she would look around anxiously (he thought) and pop some pomegranate into her mouth. ("You looked like you were cast in gold, and eating rubies in an emerald cathedral!" he told her later on, hoping he sounded poetic.)

He swiftly skirted the waters of the pond and clambered up to the girder of the bridge. And once again, the pair were face to face, gazing at one another, but without knowing what to say.

In all probability, their flirtation would have remained just that; a harmless matter of smiles, holding hands and small talk. They had absolutely nothing in common and the social gulf separating them was oceanic. But it is to be believed that the spirits of the many unhappy lovers (both human and simian) who had drowned themselves in the pond thought otherwise.

For Altu Faltu, ragged, and covered with decaying herbiage, and Rani-beti, cast in gold and eating rubies, found themselves being drawn towards one another by a force too powerful for either of them to resist. Within moments of meeting, they were wrapped in each others arms, as tightly as only monkeys can be (and much closer than any human embrace, which is one reason why they consider themselves superior to humans). How long they remained thus, they do not know.

They did not notice the dark moth shadow of dusk slip across the pond as the sun dipped behind the shoulder of the Ridge. They did not see the faint white mist rise from the still, deep water, covering the surface with a silvery sheen. They did not feel the faint whisper of breeze that caressed that silver mist. Had they looked up then, they might have seen the mist being stroked into the shapes of lovers in close embrace. But they were lost in their own ecstatic embrace and anyway, their eyes were shut tight.

There was really no going back for them after that first bewitching rendezvous. They met subsequently several times, each time more urgently, passionately and torridly than before. Their trysts were all too brief, for it is not easy for an engaged princess to slip away alone for long. They generally avoided talking about their future, except for the occasional passionate proclamation of drowning themselves in the lake if faced with separation. For both of them, the present was enough. They knew they were sitting on a time bomb, but were content to do so for as long as it carried on merely ticking.

When he was away from her, back in his tool-shed on the Hindu Rao Ridge, Altu Faltu often wondered if this was all a fantastic dream or hallucination brought on by sustained linctus drinking. It seemed to him that he was living two diverse lives: one, as a no-good, drug-addict loafer; and the other as the passionate, terrific and secret lover of Rani-beti, princess of the Flagstaff Tower clan.

More practically, Rani-beti knew only too well that their day of reckoning would inevitably come, when she (and not he) would have to make a terrible decision. She pushed away the uncomfortable thought by busying herself (and the irony was not lost on her) with her wedding preparations ("It felt as though I was digging my own grave!" she later told Altu Faltu.). Though she knew subconsciously what her decision would be, she was forced to act much earlier than she had wanted to.

For love is not a secret that can be easily kept.

Especially from the flickering, marble-hard eyes of Leechadji, gross, pendulous-paunched sycophant par excellence in the court of Chaudhury Charbi Raisahib. He saw the "new light" shining in Rani-beti's eyes, so (refreshingly) different from the tearful redness of the recent past. He noted her frequent evening disappearances and the flimsy excuses given for them. He followed her. And after he had spied upon the lovely princess and her ragamuffin lover, he decided to act.

He approached Rani-beti one morning and greeted her with an oily smile. "It is good to see Rani-beti so happy!" he remarked unctuously, as the princess peeled an orange, "and so well recovered from what had been upsetting her recently..."

She was on her guard instantly. "Well Leechadji, I am going to be married so I ought to be happy!" she replied with unconscious irony. Then because she knew him and his slippery, roundabout ways, "What do you want Leechadji?"

He smiled self-deprecatingly and settled his jackfruit paunch. "Oh nothing Rani-beti, nothing at all! It is only my earnest hope that the princess' happiness is due to the fact that she has decided to stop meeting that awara bandar under the bridge at the Khooni Khan Jheel every evening. It would be such a relief to know that..." He blinked his pebble eyes in mock earnest hope.

Rani-beti paled. "I asked you what you wanted Leechadji!" she repeated as steadily as she could, even though she felt as though a steamroller had gone over her stomach.

"Your parents would be very much upset if they came to know..." Leechadji sat back, his expression smug and sanctimonious.

"How would they come to know? If you tell them, I will simply deny everything and it will be your word against mine! And everyone knows you are just a vindictive old gossip and sycophant..."

Leechadji threw up his hands in mock horror and then placed them over his ears as though to block those terrible accusations. "Rani-beti didi! Do you really think I would do such a thing as carry tales about you to your parents? I only want to bring to your notice that there are other ways by which such canards are spread!"

"My parents would never believe anonymous rumours!" Rani-beti wished she felt as confident as she sounded.

"Ah, Rani-beti didi! You are so young and tender and naive! So idealistic! You should know that everyone is not like that! The elders you know, they believe such things!"

"What do you want Leechadji?" she asked again, looking at him levelly. So it was to be blackmail.

The gross, grizzled monkey folded his hands around his huge stomach and drew back his ears, recalling the scene by the bridge the previous evening.

"I would like it very much if you groomed me every evening for an hour", he said softly. "In a nice private place

I know about. We can take things from there..."

And for the first time in her life, Rani-beti struck another simian (and an elder!) with the intent to hurt. She slapped Leechadji so resoundingly that he lost his balance and fell off his branch with a yell of fright. Rani-beti didn't wait. She fled, knowing that if she didn't act fast this whole matter would blow up in her face. If her father came to know about it, he would place her under house arrest and have Altu Faltu killed. But now, more than anything else, she needed an ally — someone she could confide in, someone she could trust, someone who would convey a message to Altu Faltu that she would run away with him. For the time had come. There was no way she could flee the Ridge now without being spotted and brought back by her father's guards, for surely Leechadji would have gone and complained. Someone would have to convey to Altu Faltu what had happened...

She thought at once of her step-mother, Bibi-Do, her father's concurrent second wife. Much younger than her own mother, Bibi-Do had, some months ago, desperately requested Rani-beti to run a similar sort of errand in connection with an old flame who had turned up unexpectedly (she said) on the Ridge. Rani-beti had obliged for the sheer excitement of it and afterwards, had not breathed a word about the matter to anyone.

Bibi-Do had professed herself eternally grateful to her for that and was now more than understanding. When the young princess confessed her plight, Bibi-Do held her close and stroked her consolingly.

"If you love him so much, you must go with him!" she said softly. "You must elope!"

"How can I elope?" Rani-beti wept bitterly, the events of

27

the morning catching up with her. "I can't even meet him now! That Leechadji will have told my parents everything and I'll be locked up and Altu Faltu will be hunted down!"

"Hush! Don't you worry about anything! Now tell me, what does this bandar of yours look like and where does he live?"

A quiet gleam entered Bibi-Do's eyes. For she had just realised that if Rani-beti eloped, her own daughter Chamkili (who was a bit of a zero-watter) would probably be married off to Bade Badtameez. That would be nice for her, and a nice one to pull over the domineering Bibi-Ek. At the same time, she was exceedingly fond of Rani-beti. Sweet, innocent little thing...

His face stinging, his ego shattered, the vindictive Leechadji too had decided to act. Rani-beti's slap had rattled him badly, and the warped, scheming monkey was afraid that the princess might go and tell her parents about his filthy proposition. It would be better if he got in his story first — anything Rani-beti said after that would be likely to be construed as defence and not prosecution.

That afternoon, while Chaudhury Charbi Raisahib was enjoying his usual 'hath malish' massage at the Flagstaff Tower, Leechadji slithered up in his grovelling way. The chieftain's three wives, Bibi-Ek, Bibi-Do and Bibi-Teen sat in close attendance and glared at him. None of them liked him — he knew too many of their little secrets. Leechadji cleared his throat apologetically.

"If I may have a word with you, sire..." he began.

Chaudhury Charbi Rai, almost asleep, grunted with annoyance. "Now what is it, Leechadji?" he mumbled irritably.

Bibi-Ek hustled up. "Please do not disturb him Leechadji!" she said firmly, baring her teeth. "Whatever it is, it can wait! Chaudhury Sahib needs his rest!"

Leechadji smiled and bowed ingratiatingly. "I too wish it could have waited, madamji! But it is a matter of some grave importance! Regarding the innocent Rani-betiji!"

"Rani-beti?" exclaimed Bibi-Ek in surprise. And added hurriedly, "She is all right, isn't she? No accident or..."

"Oh no, madam! Nothing to worry about on that account. No accident of that kind! Only it has been noticed that Rani-betiji has changed..."

"Changed?"

"Er... yes, madamji. There is... how can one put it... a new light shining in her eyes..."

"New light? Don't talk rubbish Leechadji!" Chaudhury Charbi Raisahib grunted, closing his eyes as his masseur got to work.

But Bibi-Ek thought she understood. "Oh yes, of course!" she said happily. "Rani-beti's getting married after all!"

But Leechadji continued to look grave and Bibi-Do itched to whack him one as Rani-beti had done.

"You are right, madamji," he intoned sepulchrally. "But I am afraid it is not for nawab sahib Bade Badtameez that Rani-betiji's eyes are shining."

"What? What are you saying Leechadji?" The rest of them were also looking at him now, Bibi-Do fidgeting with her tail to keep her hands busy.

Leechadji nodded and sighed sadly. "I am sorry madamji, but it might come as a bit of a shock. His name is Altu Faltu and like his name suggests, he is a useless vagabond who lives with the bekar Hindu Rao troupe. Always smoking and drinking and drug taking and getting into fights. He's been seducing Rani-betiji..." There was nothing more he needed to add.

Chaudhury Charbi Raisahib reared up and sent his masseur sprawling with one brawny blow.

"What?" he roared. "My daughter being seduced by a... a...!" The oaths poured out and he bounced furiously on all fours sending tremors through the thick walls of the Flagstaff Tower that had stood firm even through cannonfire.

"...seduced by a drug addict!" Bibi-Ek repeated weakly, "My innocent little daughter!"

Bibi-Do said nothing and Bibi-Teen, her eyes as large as dinner plates, wished she could get the hell out of there in order to spread the delicious scandal. Chaudhury Charbi Raisahib regained control, his fur still standing up on end making him look twice his size.

"Where is she?" he roared. "Bring her to me at once!"

Bibi-Do decided it was time she took control.

"Bibi-Teenji, you look after Bibi-Ek!" she commanded firmly. "I'll go and look for Rani-beti!" She cast a cold, flinty eye at Leechadji. "And while you are on the subject of Rani-betiji," she said to him with steely malice, "you might like to explain why you were so forcefully grooming her at the Serpentine arbour this morning! The poor thing was in tears and said you had forced her down!"

It was a brilliant, devious lie on the part of Bibi-Do. Had Rani-beti at this time made the same sort of allegation against Leechadji, she would not have been believed. But here was Bibi-Do, an apparently independent and objective witness. Chaudhury Charbi Raisahib eyes lit up lividly. Bibi-Ek's hair

began bristling

"Leechadji! You were grooming my daughter?" Chaudhury Charbi Raisahib's voice was slow and dangerous.

"No sir! Not at all! She had... she had only got some thorns stuck in her coat and requested me to remove them for her!" Leechadji invented wildly, knowing that an outright denial would be tantamount to calling Bibi-Do a liar (which she was, and he wondered why).

Bibi-Ek snarled and drew back her upper lip. "For your sake Leechadji, I hope you are telling the truth! I shall find out, you can be sure of that. As for Rani-beti being seduced by some awara bandar from the Hindu Rao troupe, frankly Leechadji, I think you are the one who has been drinking with them! My daughter would not look at such specimens!"

"But madamji..."

"Get out of here Leechadji! I think we've had enough of you for one afternoon!" There was no mistaking the menace in Bibi-Ek's voice. Leechadji hoisted himself up and slunk off towards the trees. Bibi-Do rose to her feet.

"Let me go and look for Rani-beti," she said, and disappeared into the forest.

She knew exactly where to go. And keeping a discreet distance, Leechadji followed her, cold fury in his eyes.

"You've got to pretend that you've fallen in love with Badtameez!" Bibi-Do advised her step-daughter a few minutes later. "It's what your mother thinks, or at any rate, wants to think! It will also assuage any suspicions they may harbour to the contrary. I've settled Leechadji's hash for the time being; if he has any sense he will stay out of your mother's way for a while."

"Thank you Bibi-Do, for all you've done. But I have to meet Altu Faltu. He must know about what's happened!"

"Don't worry. I'll go and see him. But I think you should keep away from him for a few days. You never know what that hideous Leechadji will be up to next. Go spend some time with your parents. Play the darling daughter. Now are you sure you want to go through with all this? I mean, elope with this awara bandar of yours?"

"I'll go to the ends of the world with Altu Faltu," said Rani-beti, her defences completely down and commonsense temporarily jettisoned.

That evening Bibi-Do crossed over to the Hindu Rao Ridge and was directed to Altu Faltu's ramshackle tool-shed. She was not very impressed by what she saw.

Altu Faltu was lolling on a window sill, mumbling to himself, clutching a purple-labelled brown bottle in one paw. He looked thin and emaciated and lacked the tough muscular physique of most bachelor Delhizens. (Then again, maybe she was thinking about her own ex-flame...) He was also very young and not yet fully mature mentally. He yelped like a stricken puppy when he saw her.

"Who are you and what do you want?" he asked nervously.

"My name is Bibi-Do and I am Rani-Beti's step-mother," she replied. "And throw that filthy bottle away before I hit you!"

The wimp of a monkey put down the bottle and backed away. "Step-mother? You are Rani-beti's step-mother? Rani-beti! Is she... all right?"

Bibi-Do leapt up to the window sill and stared at Altu Faltu wondering what the hell Rani-beti had seen in this creature. Even Chamkili would have had better sense!

"Do you love Rani-beti?" she asked bluntly, the doubts stirring ever more vigorously.

"Do I love...?"

"And are you willing to elope with her? I said, drop that stinking bottle!"

"Elope?" he squealed. Altu Faltu's two separate lives were suddenly coming alarmingly together. "Why?" he asked, buying time. "What's happened? Is she, is she..." he tailed off in horror thinking of all the awful things that could have happened to her.

Bibi-Do went on remorselessly and dramatically, "Because if you don't elope with her, she is likely to throw herself off the Khooni Khan bridge and drown herself!"

"Drown herself?" The little monkey stood up suddenly, bristling with determination. "I will not let her drown! I will rescue her! Elope with her! Now! This minute!"

"Sit down, you silly drunken bandar, and listen to me. You are not to meet Rani-beti for the next few days. Her parents are suspicious. If they catch you, they will kill you and God knows what they will do to Rani-beti!"

"I must rescue her!" the idiot exclaimed, jumping up and down on all fours like Chaudhury Charbi Raisahib had done not too long ago. Then, suddenly suspicious, he asked, "How do you know about all this? And why are you telling me all this?"

"Mind your own business! Now, are you willing to elope with Rani-beti when the time is right?"

Altu Faltu nodded loftily. If elope was the honourable thing to do, then elope he would. He recalled those blissful moments at the Khooni Khan Jheel. If elope was the dishonourable thing to do, then too elope he would. Bibi-Do glared at him menacingly.

"Very well," she said. "I shall go and let her know. We will fix a time and place, and I will get back to you. But remember one thing: if you disappoint her, I will personally hunt you down and kill you! Do you understand?"

He looked at her through huge, frightened eyes.

"Yes... yes!" he stammered. "I will never disappoint her!"

Then suddenly, a cunning glint entered his eyes. "You said just now that you are Rani-beti's step-mother?" he asked, warily.

Bibi-Do nodded.

The little monkey snorted. "Hah! Wicked step-mother no doubt! I know all about your kind! You're doing this because you hate Rani-beti! You want them to trap us! You want to humiliate Rani-beti! I will not elope with her to have her get caught and publicly humiliated! I'd rather she went and married that Badtameez fellow!"

God, thought Bibi-Do. The silly ass was not such a fool after all and he obviously loved Rani-beti more than he knew it himself. He was also very stoned or drunk.

"Look," she said patiently. "I'll bring you a note from her. Will that convince you?"

"First bring the note!" he demanded shrilly. "Then I'll see!"

The note, written with the blood of Rani-beti's beloved tail, was brief and evocative. It said that if he loved her, he, Altu Faltu, would meet her, Rani-beti, a week from then, on the midnight of the full moon, under the bridge over the Khooni Khan Jheel. She would then elope with him.

Altu Faltu sniffed the note rapturously and nodded his

head. He couldn't believe Rani-beti had actually cut her beautiful tail to write him this note. He was overwhelmed. No monkey had done such a thing for him. His eyes brimmed.

"Tell her... tell her I will be there!" he instructed Bibi-Do grandiosely, as she looked on in amusement. "And that I will carry her away in my arms by the light of the full moon!"

The little monkey had it bad.

But now, as the appointed hour approached and the moonlight poured through the trees, Altu Faltu knew that he was about to do a very stupid thing. And he was right to be apprehensive. For the gross and pendulous Leechadji, slapped and humiliated, had spent the last week quietly following Bibi-Do.

Now, as midnight approached on the night of the full moon, he waited silently in a clump of glimmering spider lilies, by the still waters of the Khooni Khan Jheel.

In the week preceding her elopement, Rani-beti followed her step-mother's advice carefully. She was sweet with her parents and blushed and simpered (thinking about Altu Faltu) whenever Badtameez's name came up in the course of conversation. Her mother had not questioned her at all about Altu Faltu but had asked about Leechadji's alleged grooming session, to which she had responded by biting her lip and looking away. Her mother swore Leechadji would pay dearly for the indiscretion, but the huge monkey seemed to have vanished. There were several weak moments during which she hated herself for deluding her parents like this, but she remained determined not to make a clean breast of it. Instead, she hardened her heart; her parents had fixed her marriage without really consulting her, more for their own and the clan's convenience. They didn't seem to care about her happiness. She had no illusions about what her father would do if he learnt the truth about Altu Faltu. She sighed. If Altu Faltu had been a strapping, musclebound hunk with territory of his own instead of a ramshackle tool-shed and had had the glitter of greed in his eyes, perhaps it would have been different. Then her parents might have conceivably agreed to the match. But then, she would not have fallen for him in the first place.

She retired early to her brooding perch near the nursery on her last evening in the Ridge, claiming she was tired. Bibi-Do joined her and held her close for a long while.

"Everything will be all right," she assured the young princess. "I will escort you to the bridge tonight! You can't go there alone in the middle of the night!"

At around a quarter to eleven, the two monkeys slipped noiselessly to the ground and made their way along the rocky moonlit path that led to the Khooni Khan Jheel. They halted just before reaching it, under a towering clump of bamboo. Rani-beti clutched Bibi-Do's hand tightly. The time had come.

"This is it, Bibi-Do! From here, I must go by myself." She smiled weakly. "Thank you for accompanying me here and for everything else."

"Goodbye Rani-beti, and good luck! May you always be happy!"

And Bibi-Do wondered why she had a catch in her voice and a lump in her throat as she blessed her beautiful step-daughter.

She watched Rani-beti scamper along the rocky edge of the pond and settle on the girder, nervously twisting her tail and looking around her with uncertain eyes. A soft, silky breeze whispered through the casuarina grove nearby, and an ancient acacia creaked with weariness. A bullfrog began to croak.

And then suddenly that awara bandar appeared, dropping out of a tree at the foot of the bridge. He had been sitting on a low branch, waiting for the past ten minutes or so, panic welling up inside him, especially in his bladder, with every passing minute. Even so, he had paused for a minute or more after Rani-beti had appeared, just to be able to gaze upon her by the lunatic light of the full moon. Then he dropped light-ly onto the bridge.

Her vision still blurred with tears, for she was now think-ing about her own last full-moon tryst, Bibi-Do watched the besotted couple wrap their arms around one another. At last they parted aside and sat on the curved railing of the bridge, staring rapturously at each other.

The breeze changed direction and the bullfrog stopped croaking. Bibi-Do felt a sudden, chilling tremor knife through her, making her squirm as though she had been exquisitely stabbed. A terrifying premonition gripped her. Something evil was afoot, she was sure of it. One by one, the hairs on the nape of her neck began standing up and her ears flattened against her skull. A prickle of fear coursed up and down her spine, light as a feather. On the bridge, the foolish couple had gotten into yet another clinch — why the hell didn't they get away from this moon-mad, dreadful place? Surely this was not the time or place for canoodling!

Leechadji, gross and obese, his pendulous paunch swinging low, padded silently out into the moonlight and onto the bridge from a clump of spider lilies. He looked around briefly and then fixed his eyes on the enraptured couple on the railing. In a single fluid movement, he leapt onto the railing and lunged, his big feet gripping the railing mesh for support. He grabbed Altu Faltu by the scruff of his scrawny neck and tore him loose off the embrace he would so much have liked to have been in himself with one vicious yank.

"Get off her, you dirty little leech," he hissed, as Rani-beti backed away in horror and screamed. She saw the crazed, red glint in the huge monkey's eyes and she knew he was going to kill Altu Faltu. Screeching hysterically, she lunged towards him. He flung her out of the way with one hard back-handed slap growling, "Keep out of this Rani-beti, it will be your turn next!"

And Rani-beti fell.

Straight into the moon-silvered waters of the Khooni Khan Jheel. She disappeared under as Leechad, his fat paws embedded in Altu Faltu's neck, looked over his shoulder. "Bah!" spat the big monkey in disgust.

Rani-beti spluttered to the surface and looked up at the bridge. She saw Altu-Faltu, his neck laid on the railing as though on a guillotine, his body dangling over the side, thrashing weakly against the railing mesh. She saw Leechad, squatting, bulging out from the railing, his ugly paws still buried in Altu Faltu's neck. The little monkey's movements were becoming feebler as consciousness drifted away and death drifted in.

The beautiful princess of the Flagstaff Tower clan stopped struggling. Now it was only in death that she could be united with Altu Faltu again. And if it had been written in her fate to join the many unhappy lovers who had drowned themselves here, who was she to fight it? The silver-pleated waters closed over her head.

Bibi-Do shook off the trance that appeared to have overcome her and prepared to dive. But then she stopped (or was she jerked back, as some insist) and stared. Rani-beti had risen to the surface again, spotted green with duckweed. She was being propelled unprotestingly towards the shore on her back. By what, Bibi-Do could not quite make out: her vision was still blurred and a gossamer mist was sweeping over the surface of the pond.

At the same time, she heard a strangled, gurgling shout. On the railing of the bridge, Leechad had released his hold on Altu Faltu's neck and was clutching desperately at his own throat, gagging for air. Altu Faltu had miraculously fallen onto the bridge, and not in the water. Leechad swayed to keep his balance on the railing as he fought with his invisible enemy. Bibi-do watched in disbelief as the huge monkey was plucked off the railing by some invisible, invincible force, and hurled through the air, screeching with terror. He fell with a scream and a soggy thud, into the clump of lilies from where he had emerged.

The gossamer-misted waters of the Khooni Khan Jheel swirled and rippled excitedly. Gradually, they calmed down and the moon, a huge silver medallion, quivered and trembled to stillness.

Altu Faltu crawled off the bridge to where Rani-beti had been deposited on a mossy rock. In spite of his near strangulation and badly bruised neck, he felt as if he was crackling with energy; bouyant as one feels before a thunderstorm.

"Let's get out of here. Rani-beti!" he said with astounding nonchalance. "Let's elope!"

"Leechadji?" she inquired, shivering with cold and fear and relief.

"Judo!" he explained succinctly. "I threw him into the lilies!" Without knowing where the thought had come from.

"And then you jumped in and rescued me?" She had no idea how she had been brought ashore.

"Uh uh..." he said noncomittally, wondering if she would notice that he was dry.

Involuntarily, he looked down at himself. He wasn't dry — he was sopping wet! And shrouded in a chilly, silvery mist. He shivered and put his arms around her.

"Let's go!" he said.

Bibi-Do, her fur still standing up on end and tingling as though with static, made her way back to her roost, knowing full well she would not sleep that night, and would miss the strong, comforting arms of her ex-flame around her.

Spreadeagled on his back amongst the flattened lilies, Leechad groaned and fell back. A feeling of desperate loneliness suddenly assailed him, which not even an image of the saucy bandaris at the Khyber Pass Massage Parlour could vanquish.

But fortunately for him, the feeling lasted just a fleeting moment. Then he blacked out.

Chapter 2

BLACK
TUESDAY

"Aaao...aaao...aaao...!"

The loud nasal calls echoed imperatively under the brooding canopy of the Ridge, forcing the early birds to fall silent. In the trees that surrounded the nursery, the members of the Flagstaff troupe stirred restively, some grunting and coughing with annoyance. The juveniles and adolescents were the first to descend, dropping lightly to the ground and loping off nonchalantly towards the calls. The heavy grizzled elders followed more slowly, quick to cuff or lunge viciously at an upstart who had temporarily forgotten his manners.

Four men, all clad in spotless, politician white, and laden with polythene bags stuffed with fruit and fresh bread, passed through the rattling turnstile and waited briefly at the foot of the road that wound up to the Flagstaff Tower. These pious souls then entered the landscaped park area on their left, depositing heavy bunches of bananas in their wake. Three of the men fell back slightly, while the fourth and most powerfully pious came forward to meet the monkeys and personally hand out the offerings he carried, still calling sanctimoniously as though chanting an incantation. Within seconds, the Flagstaff troupe swarmed all around him and he smiled warmly at them, grateful for their benediction.

Breakfast was being served to the Flagstaff Tower clan.

It was a slightly more elaborate one than usual, because this was Tuesday, and already another couple of carloads of banana-laden souls had arrived at the gate.

But, for the rulers of the Flagstaff clan, this was to turn out to be a very black Tuesday indeed...

The monkeys poured out of the trees in an unending stream, and within seconds, fur had begun to fly as old animosities flared up and new ones were sparked and greed got the better of everyone. The guards were especially vigilant this morning, for there had been a tip-off that the breakaway group led by Chaudhury Haramisahib might attempt a raid. (They were usually given their breakfast by their own pious following on the feeding plinth near the Chauburja monument.)

Chaudhury Charbi Raisahib took his time about waking up. (He was usually awoken by the screams and shouts of the quarreling monkeys which ignited his own fabled temper like tinder). Eventually, in the company of his three wives, numerous offspring and coterie of bodyguards, he made his way in regal procession to the Bada Nashta Khana under a huge clump of bamboo adjacent to the nursery. Here, his large retinue of lackeys had already collected and tastefully arranged the choicest of the fruit and freshest of the bread that had been offered that morning.

By now, cars were pulling up in the parking lot outside, disgorging large numbers of paunchy, jowly early-morning walkers, all greeting each other with whoops and yells of holy exuberance. The monkeys usually ignored them, or glared at them with cold disdain; the people regarded them with a mumbled prayer and all due reverence.

Bibi-Ek glanced around the Bada Nashta Khana, puzzled. She knew that Rani-beti, like most princesses, liked sleeping late, but she was normally up in time for breakfast. Yet there was no sign of her here this morning. Perhaps she had over-slept more than usual. Perhaps she was not feeling too well...

Bibi-Ek summoned Bibi-Do (who was not looking at all well) with an impatient gesture. "Rani-beti has overslept," she said, "would you kindly go and wake her up?"

Bibi-Do obeyed immediately. She returned after a few minutes, a strange, haggard look on her face. "I can't find Rani-beti anywhere," she told Bibi-Ek worriedly. "I've looked everywhere!" she lied, for she had certainly not checked out Altu Faltu's tool-shed on the Hindu Rao Ridge.

Bibi-Ek's brows furrowed. "What?!" she whispered fiercely, "Are you sure you looked properly?"

"Well you can go and see for yourself!" Bibi-Do replied tartly, as Chamkili came up grinning for a good-morning hug.

"I will," grunted Bibi-Ek and vanished in one bound.

In the Bada Nashta Khana, Chaudhury Charbi Raisahib was reclining regally against a rock and condescendingly reaching out for a banana being offered to him by one of the leading pious souls (who had also recently been named as a leading proclaimed offender). The big monkey peeled the banana, took a token bite, and flung the rest away, before reaching out for another. He was sorely tempted to jump at the pious bugger and bite his bottom, but knew that it would not be a good example to set for the already rowdy juveniles gathered around. Moreover, he knew that even if he did bite the fellow, the man would be back the following morning with an even more lavish offering.

Bibi-Ek thudded up suddenly and screeched at the man, who backed off hurriedly looking like a proclaimed martyr.

"Rani-beti," she panted, "I can't find Rani-beti anywhere! She's not in her usual sleeping quarters. I've searched the nursery area and the Flagstaff Tower clearing. I even... I even looked into the reservoir."

Chaudhury Charbi Raisahib was irritated with his senior-most wife. He had just spat out the second banana and was reaching out for the rest of the bunch when she had barged in and scared off the joker he so enjoyed humiliating.

"What is it Bibi-Ek? Calm yourself!"

"I said I can't find Rani-beti anywhere," repeated Bibi-Ek even more agitatedly.

"Oh, she must be sleeping somewhere. Now come on, it is time for my morning grooming session. Kindly begin and make sure that Bibi-Do and Bibi-Teen are at hand to take over when their turn comes." Chaudhury Charbi Raisahib burped grandly, scratched himself languidly and lay back to be groomed. Bibi-Ek clasped her hands pleadingly.

"With all due respect Chaudhury Sahib, have you ever known Rani-beti to miss breakfast? She does oversleep once in a while, but she's not in her usual sleeping quarters and you know how she hates sleeping anywhere else. Besides I saw her settle down there myself last evening. Bibi-Do was with her."

Breakfast was now over and the clan members had begun dispersing amongst the trees for sessions of grooming, playing, wrestling, conspiring, gossiping, quarrelling and lazing. The guards relaxed, for it seemed unlikely that Chaudhury

Haramisahib would now launch a raid. But some of Bibi-Ek's worry had begun to infect Chaudhury Charbi Raisahib. He got ponderously to his feet and blinked.

"Where's Bibi-Do?" he demanded.

Bibi-Do sidled up to him in the suggestive way that had recently caused her ex-flame to come alight again. "You called?" she inquired huskily, as Bibi-Ek pursed her lips in disapproval. Bibi-Do had never learnt to behave decorously with Charbisahib.

"You were with Rani-beti last evening?" The question was barked out and Bibi-Do became decorous at once. "Yes sir!" she said demurely, her head lowered. "I was with her until she fell asleep!"

A hearty breakfast had driven away the earlier pangs of guilt she had felt, when Bibi-Ek had asked her to look for Rani-beti. And anyway, Rani-beti must be in seventh heaven by now and that was the important thing.

"You haven't seen Rani-beti this morning?"

"No sir," said Bibi-Do truthfully.

"Was she upset about anything last evening?" Bibi-Ek asked worriedly.

"Well, no. She was a bit nervous about her forthcoming wedding, but I suppose we all are!" Bibi-Do was fast discovering the art of diplomatic lying. She was, however, getting increasingly worried, for Leechadji had not yet put in an appearance in the Bada Nashta Khana. And he was not the kind to miss a free meal. He would have a very interesting tale to tell. If he was still alive. Too late, Bibi-Do realised that she ought to have checked this out last night, and if necessary, taken steps to ensure that Leechadji would never get the opportunity to tell his story. She been too overcome by the strange happenings at the Khooni Khan Jheel to even think about the consequences of what he might say.

Chaudhury Charbi Raisahib was getting organised now.

"I want search parties to set out immediately. Bibi-Ek, Bibi-Do and Bibi-Teen, you will each lead a group and comb the forest and park adjoining the roads leading off from the Flagstaff Tower. I will take a party and beat the wild flank that runs along the shoulder of the Ridge past the nursery. It is likely that Rani-beti might have gone off for an early morning ramble and fallen and hurt herself."

Bibi-Ek was suddenly struck by a dreadful thought. "Do you think... do you think Rani-beti could have been kidnapped?" she asked faintly, and Bibi-Do, disgracefully incorrigible even now, bit her cheek to prevent herself giggling at the thought of Altu Faltu kidnapping Rani-beti, or for that matter anyone else.

"Kidnap? Who would want to kidnap her?"

"Chaudhury Haramisahib..."

Chaudhury Charbi Raisahib began to bristle. "If that... if that no good bastard has laid a finger on my Rani-beti he shall pay!" he growled. "I will see to it personally! But let's look for her first before jumping to conclusions!"

They made their way up to the Flagstaff Tower clearing and Bibi-Ek began organising the search parties. Like ourselves, monkeys are pretty hopeless when it comes to efficient organisation. Thus the members of the troupe were milling about the clearing aimlessly, joining one group and then another, when suddenly they all froze dead in their meandering tracks.

A loud, piteous wail emerged from the verdant jungle nearby; a wail that made their flesh crawl. As Bibi-Do tensed and stiffened, the gross and pendulous Leechadji, still hidden in the foliage, prepared to make his grand entrance into the Flagstaff Tower clearing.

Leechadji had regained consciousness shortly before dawn, and for some time had lain back in his lily bed, groaning. His throat and neck were bruised and tender, his massive soft body was a mass of aches and pains. It took a few minutes for his head to clear and recall the events of the night. And when he realised that he had neither seen nor heard his powerful assailant, a tremor of fear quivered through him once more. Something awesomely strong had assaulted him while he had been throttling that wimp of a bandar. It would be prudent to remove himself from this spot lest the monster attack him again. Or had the monster been brought along by that awara bandar, Altu Faltu, as a bodyguard? A sort of simian-Frankenstein who had been fed and fattened on the strange concoctions they mixed on the Hindu Rao Ridge? At any rate, there was no sign of Altu Faltu or Rani-beti here now.

Leechadji hoisted himself up and dragged himself up the stone steps that led away from the pond. His mind was working faster now. It appeared that the lovely Rani-beti had eloped with that awara bandar — about whom he had warned her parents and been rebuffed. Bibi-Do was certainly deeply involved in the whole affair, even if he had not seen her at the Khooni Khan Jheel last night. And Bibi-Do was also a remarkably pretty little bandari...

But now it was time he broke the news to the doting parents — they must have missed Rani-beti already. He would, of course, have to suitably modify the part about him being attacked by an unseen monster. Bibi-Ek would never swallow that and might even start suspecting his involvement in Rani-beti's disappearance. Still, there were so many things he could take advantage of. It was time he reached the Flagstaff Tower and established contact. To his delight, he saw the entire clan gathered around the burly monument, milling about aimlessly. He lay down in the high grass, and dragging himself along the ground, began emitting loud and piteous wails at regular intervals.

A monkey's wail can be an extremely heart-rending sound and Leechadji ensured that his were amongst the most pathetic and penetrating. Within seconds, every simian eye in the clearing was fixed on him as he crawled out of the jungle and dragged himself painfully towards the leaders of the clan. Bibi-Do backed away unobtrusively towards the edge of the clearing in case a quick getaway was required. Leechadji prostrated himself at the feet of a horrified Bibi-Ek in the manner of some lesser ministers in the presence of their chief minister.

"Kill me!" he howled. "Oh kill me and throw my corpse to the crocodiles in the Khooni Khan Jheel! For I have failed!"

"Leechadji!" There was whiplash in Bibi-Ek's voice. "Why are you making such a spectacle of yourself? What are you shouting about? Are you drunk? At this time of the morning? You ought to be ashamed of yourself!"

"I am ashamed!" the gross fellow blubbered. He made as though to clasp her tail and Bibi-Ek flicked it away, with an expression of acute disgust. A couple of bodyguards thudded up and took hold of him.

"Arrest me! Execute me! Throw me to the leopards and the jackals! But first listen to what I have to tell you. I beg you!"

"Leechadji, we have no time for your histrionics and nonsense. Rani-beti..." Bibi-Ek stopped in astonishment. Leechadji was hammering his great fists into his flabby chest (a sight repulsive in itself) and blubbering at the top of his voice. "Rani-beti!" he howled (and Bibi-Ek prickled all over), "It's about Rani-betiji! She's been abducted and carried off!"

Chaudhury Charbi Raisahib shouldered his way past the gawking monkeys and bodyguards.

"What are you talking about? Abducted? By whom? Chaudhury Haramisahib?"

"No sir! No! Even Chaudhury Haramisahib would not stoop to such a thing! It was a gang of those drunken drug addicts from the Hindu Rao Ridge! Led by that thug Altu Faltu. I warned you about him!" Leechadji rocked back and forth, moaning as though in great pain. He thought his performance ought to get him promoted quite high up in the group hierarchy.

But Bibi-Ek's voice still hadn't lost its snap. "Leechadji! Compose yourself! And kindly tell us exactly what you know about all this!"

Leechadji calmed down with startling alacrity. He saw, with obvious satisfaction, the large mob of curious monkeys gathered around and gaping at him like people at the site of a horrible accident. (Actually, he did look like one.) He cleared his throat and blinked.

"Last night..." he began softly, so that the monkeys had to crane forward to listen, "I awoke suddenly at around eleven thirty. I was sleeping in a tree that stands just off the rocky path that runs through the wild flank from the nursery. Some unusual sound had disturbed me. I listened, and then heard it again: the click of a pebble being kicked on the path. I looked down from my roost, and to my horror saw a group of strange, evil-looking monkeys walking past stealthily. They were heading in the direction of the Khooni Khan Jheel. Four of them were carrying Rani-beti between them, holding her by the arms and legs. She seemed to be asleep or unconscious or... she was limp and did not stir or struggle. In the lead was that Altu Faltu fellow, with a bottle in one hand!" Leechadji paused, and looked around. He did so enjoy telling tales.

"Why didn't you sound the alarm Leechadji?" There was cast iron in Chaudhury Charbi Raisahib's voice.

"I thought of it sir, I thought of it! But they, those brutes had Rani-beti! If I had sounded the alarm, they would have used her as a hostage! So I decided to follow them instead!" Leechadji bit his lips and gulped, one beady eye now fixed on Bibi-Do, who was furiously biting at her tail. He was really enjoying this, and she, pretty little bandari, was plainly not.

"They halted at the bridge over the Khooni Khan Jheel. For a moment I thought they had stopped to change the carriers. But no! They laid our beloved Rani-beti down on the bridge..." Yet again he paused, and his tongue flickered out again. "Bibi-Ek, forgive me! You are not going to like this..."

"And what? What did... they do to her?" Bibi-Ek's voice was a sibilant hiss, and Bibi-Do felt quite terrible for her unnecessary suffering. 'Chamkili,' she thought, 'I'm doing this for my daughter Chamkili.'

"They laid her on the bridge, and led by that Altu Faltu demon, they began looking at her. Just looking at her, like you see some men do at courting couples in this park! Just looking! Poor thing! Perhaps it was just as well that she was unconscious. Then they began drinking something out of little brown bottles and some began cavorting around her. As though they were preparing for some hideous ritual. I knew they would probably throw Rani-beti into the Khooni Khan Jheel after they had done what they wanted with her! Many such things have happened there in the past! So I decided to attack them on my own. It was now too late to come back to the nursery for reinforcements." He blinked self-effacingly again. "I charged them as hard as I could, thinking that if I could just grab Rani-beti in my arms (Bibi-Ek shuddered) and rush away with her, shouting for help... But alas, there were too many of them for me! I knocked about five or six of them out of the way, but then ten or twelve of them sat on my chest, and four others squeezed their bony fingers into my neck, trying to strangle me! I lost consciousness. When I awoke, they were gone. And there was no sign of Rani-beti in... in the Jheel. They had obviously taken her with them. See here Chaudhury Sahib, the mark of their evil fingers on my throat!" Leechadji proffered his fleshy neck for examination and Bibi-Do wished she had a knife. One of the bodyguards examined Leechadji's neck, and nodded briefly. The bruise marks were clear.

"And exactly where did this struggle take place?" asked Bibi-Ek, who had not been able to bring herself to look into the fleshy folds.

"They... they dragged me off the bridge into one of the lily beds alongside the Khooni Khan Jheel... I don't remember exactly which one..." But now there was genuine fear in Leechadji's eyes as he remembered.

Again, Bibi-Ek summoned Bibi-Do with an imperious forefinger. She whispered something into the junior wife's ear. Bibi-Do vanished into the jungle and reappeared after a few minutes. She nodded briefly at Bibi-Ek and avoided looking at Leechadji, who had recovered now and was blinking smugly, happily surrounded by his own coterie of sycophants-in-the-making.

Bibi-Ek consulted with Chaudhury Charbi Raisahib. The chieftain turned to Leechadji.

"Very well Leechadji, we have checked out your story. One of the lily beds adjoining the Khooni Khan Jheel has indeed been flattened." Chaudhury Charbi Raisahib's blood pressure began to shoot up as he recalled the scene Leechadji had just described.

Luchcha lafanga awara hooching bandars, looking at his beautiful Rani-beti with lascivious eyes on a full moon night!

"Come on!" he shouted. "To arms! What are you waiting for? We march to the Hindu Rao Ridge! Now! If those thugs have so much as touched a hair on Rani-beti's hide...!" And Chaudhury Charbi Raisahib lost his fabled temper completely. He bounded up the Flagstaff Tower and shook the flagpole so violently, it rattled loudly. "To battle!" he raved, "To war on the Hindu Rao bandars!"

Bibi-Ek, quite used to her husband's temper tantrums, took charge. She waited for the sabre-rattling to subside and then went over to her bristling lord and master.

"We can't go to war, Chaudhury Sahib," she explained. "You forget those thugs have Rani-beti with them. If they see us marching on the Ridge, God knows what they'll do..."

"Then what do you suggest we do?" countered her husband testily, somewhat embarrassed about having lost his temper like that in front of everyone.

"I think this is a job for the Kachcha-Banyan gang," Bibi-Ek said slowly, admirably displaying that she had her wits about her even in this moment of crisis.

The Kachcha-Banyan gang (comprising its founders Shri Kachchaji and Shri Banyanji and four anonymous thugs) were employed by Chaudhury Charbi Raisahib for sensitive, discreet and very delicate assignments, usually of a rather violent nature. Now Chaudhury Charbi Raisahib saw the wisdom of his wife's suggestion.

"Tell Shri Kachchaji to report to my private chambers in the Serpentine arbour in five minutes!" he ordered. "And the rest of you..." he was shouting again, his temper back on the boil, "what are you doing gawking and loitering like those Hindu Rao loafers?! Get lost... move it!"

The guards charged the mob and the monkeys scattered into the surrounding jungle. But they were still shrill and agog with excitement. What a morning it had been!

"**R**ight!" said Shri Kachchaji, his cheek pouches bulging with mashed banana. "No problem! We go to the Hindu Rao Ridge. We bust the butt of that wimp Altu Faltu and anyone else whether necessary or not. And we bring Rani-beti back with us. No problem!" He masticated his banana squishily and pulled out the slithery skin that looked like the corpse of a long drowned reptile. He was a hefty simian, with powerful shoulders and long dirty canines. (One of which had gone missing in action making him look even more dangerous).

He smiled hideously at Bibi-Ek to reassure her. "No problem madamji. Nothing to worry about. We'll bring Rani-beti back here in no time at all. No problem!"

But there was a problem. For Bibi-Do had thrown caution to the winds and had fled to the Hindu Rao Ridge.

While Leechadji was recounting his fabulously fictitious encounter that she could not openly deny, she had wondered uneasily why he had not divulged her role in the whole business. Why had he said that Rani-beti had been kidnapped rather than that she had eloped of her own free will? He had obviously known that she, Bibi-Do, had aided and abetted the princess. But he had remained silent about it, and had blinked at her expressionlessly on the couple of occasions he had caught her eye.

Or had those been hideous winks?

She knew that it could only be a temporary silence. And then, she went pale and trembled when she overheard Bibi-Ek mention the Kachcha-Banyan gang. Come what may, she had to warn Rani-beti and that awara lover of hers that the Kachcha-Banyan gang was being sent out after them.

Bibi-Do shivered again.

Bloodhounds would have been nicer.

Altu Faltu had taken Rani-beti straight to his ramshackle tool-shed on the Hindu Rao Ridge after their hair-raising, judo-throwing escape from Khooni Khan Jheel. Safe within its musty walls, the enormity of what they had done, and the manner in which they had eloped, struck them as hard as a dozen, quick gins. A terrible trembling reaction set in like a rigour. Both monkeys clutched one another and whimpered. Altu Faltu's unexpected bravado had evaporated completely, and Rani-beti thought in dread of the terrible repercussions that would surely follow. Huddled thus, they fell asleep, shivering with damp and fear. They slept well into the following morning until the sun slanted powerfully through the tool-shed's window and into their screwed-up faces.

When they awoke, their fears of the previous night had vanished like puddles after a midsummer thunderstorm. They were together. Nothing else mattered.

Or nearly nothing else. Breakfast mattered. Their exertions of the previous night had left them both ravenous. Altu Faltu led the way to the feeding area — a pleasant grassy clearing between two small hillocks — and drew back in horror. The idlers and layabouts that comprised the Hindu Rao troupe (and who would now be the low class neighbours of Rani-beti, princess of the Flagstaff Tower clan) had long since finished with their breakfast, and had carried on with their day's routine of lolling, imbibing and hallucinating. Fruit peels and empty polythene bags lay strewn all over the clearing. Rather disconsolately, Altu Faltu and Rani-beu satisfied themselves with leaves and berries and returned still hungry (it was the first time for Rani-beti) to their little tool-shed. Altu Faltu rummaged in a dusty corner and pulled out a little brown bottle.

"Oh well," he said, trying to sound philosophical, and not quite succeeding. "Thankfully, we can always drink this!"

Rani-beti took the bottle curiously, conscious of a sudden sinking feeling in the pit of her stomach. She sniffed the contents and wrinkled up her face coughing.

"You drink this stuff?" she asked incredulously. "It stinks!"

"Oh, you get used to that," replied Altu Faltu, a shade too airily. "After a while, it's truly wonderful! Now come on, have a swig and see for yourself!"

But Rani-beti didn't. "Why do you drink this stuff?" she asked unexpectedly, and Altu Faltu thought he heard the faintest ring of steel in her voice.

Already.

"Because it makes you feel so good!" he replied with enforced bonhomie. "It can make you feel fantastic! You know, really great! Come on, take a swig and you'll see what I mean. You'll feel on top of the world; as though you could do anything!"

"It can make you do... anything?" Rani-beti inquired in the slow, dangerous drawl she had inherited from her father.

"Yes, yes, I told you that!" Altu Faltu's eyes suddenly filled with foolish tears. "Like elope with you from Khooni Khan Jheel and throw that Leechadji fellow all over the place!" He thought he sounded grand, and this was without even having had a swig. "Now come on, sweetheart — give me the bottle if you don't want any yourself!" His dreamy brown eyes were riveted to the bottle, but as he reached out for it, Rani-beti darted away.

"Altu Faltu, did you elope with me because you were sloshed to the eyeballs with this... this sewage? Because only this gave you the courage to do so? Because it propped up your flimsy, wet-cardboard ego and enabled you to do all those other things that you otherwise wouldn't have dared to do to me? Like..." her voice dropped to a dramatic whisper, "like seduce me at the Khooni Khan Jheel?"

Actually, she was a little confused about how to react to

the situation; whether to be all steel and razor or play the sorrowful martyr. Altu Faltu was clearly nonplussed by the unexpected turn of events.

"Eh?" he said blankly, still reaching for the bottle.

Rani-beti went into full-blown saint-martyr mode. She thrust the bottle at Altu Faltu.

"Take it!" she exclaimed, choking back a tremendous sob. "And if you really do love me, break it! If you can't break it, then I know what I must do!"

"What's that?" he asked, hopelessly tactless, clutching the bottle. Anger flared again in the little princess and the razor was back in her voice.

"What's that?! You actually asked me that! Well, since you are as thick as the walls of the Flagstaff Tower, let me tell you what it is! It means that you do not really love me! It means that I must go back to my family and beg their forgiveness! It means that I must marry that lout Badtameez! Or else of course, I could always go back to the Khooni Khan Jheel and throw myself off the bridge in the traditional way! Which do you suggest I do?" she finished off bitingly, but very close to being overwhelmed by a tidal wave of tears.

"What are you talking about?" Altu Faltu asked, genuinely bewildered, and rapidly unscrewing the top of the bottle. "We've only just eloped from there!" She snatched his fingers away from the bottle's neck. The tidal wave was fast nearing the shore.

"Altu Faltu," she gulped, "you have to chose between me and the bottle!"

"Why?" he asked simply, as the tidal wave burst over her. "Rani-beti, why are you so upset?"

But the little princess was engulfed in a paroxysm of

sobbing. He stared at her helplessly and automatically began unscrewing the bottle cap again. Just then a large looming shadow fell across the window. Altu Faltu looked up and his eyes widened in terror. Her flanks heaving, her face flecked with foam, Bibi-Do filled the window and blocked out the light. She was gasping for breath. She looked at him and then at the weeping princess. There was murder in her eyes as they swivelled on to him again. Altu Faltu gave a despairing squeak and hurled the bottle to the far end of the shed where it shattered against the wall. Rani-beti looked up and saw the smashed glass and spreading stain. Her sobs magically subsided and she turned to Altu Faltu, the sweetest smile imaginable lighting up her face. He was standing rigidly, gibbering something incoherent.

"Oh you wonderful, brave little bandar," whispered the princess of the Flagstaff Tower, her voice blurry with love and tears.

Then suddenly she saw Bibi-Do, filling up the window, still heaving and unable to speak.

"Bibi-Do! What are you doing here?!" Rani-beti giggled. "We've just had our first honeymoon tiff and were about to make up!"

"Flee!" gasped Bibi-Do hoarsely. "Get away from here! Now! Go! The Kachcha-Banyan gang! They've been sent after you!"

"Where...what?" The little princess was quite bewildered and Altu Faltu had recovered enough to already regret smashing the bottle.

"I can't stay!" Bibi-Do exclaimed. "Now get away from here. At once! Go!"

"But where can we go?" Rani-beti wailed, moving into

Altu Faltu's arms. He had started trembling again, and clutched her close instinctively. When he looked up, Bibi-Do had gone.

And from the distance came the blood-curdling whoops and yells of the Kachcha-Banyan gang as they vandalised their way over the treetops towards the ramshackle tool-shed on the Hindu Rao Ridge.

Within seconds, they were thumping on the roof. And then Shri Kachchaji himself — huge, swarthy and flaunting the most lurid loins imaginable — filled the window at which Bibi-Do had so recently appeared. His leering gaze fell on the frightened pair, cowering in a corner, clutching one another. He grinned, displaying his ancient, yellowing canines, and that terrible black gap.

"Wah wah wah! Look what we have here!" he said, with astounding disrespect. "Very well, Rani-beti, you will kindly accompany me — those are your father's orders!"

"I won't!" countered the plucky princess. "I've eloped of my own free will! You can tell him that!"

"Come away from that bekar bandar, Rani-beti! You might catch some foul disease from him! Come on now, I haven't got all day and you know how impatient Chaudhury Sahib gets!"

Altu Faltu seemed to have turned to stone. But an awful truth was dawning on him. He would have to let Rani-beti go, rather than risk having her injured if these brutes got rough. Rani-beti turned her face up to his.

"Take me hostage," she whispered urgently. "Tell him you will kill me if he comes any closer. Grab me around my neck and hold me in a pincer grip! It's the only chance we have!" Thankfully she hadn't at least asked Altu Faltu to indulge in any judo throwing! He came out of his trance at

59

once. He put one scrawny arm around Rani-beti's slim neck and held his mouth close to her jugular, his teeth bared.

"Stay away! Stay away! Back off! Now!" he shrieked. "Or I will bite her to death!"

"My Dracula!" murmured Rani-beti, falling back into his arms in a well simulated faint. "My darling Dracula!"

At the window, Shri Kachchaji, now joined by Shri Banyanji, paused. He was a little taken aback by the hysterical shrillness in Altu Faltu's voice, and Rani-beti's sudden collapse. These druggies were capable of anything. And he certainly did not want to take back a dead or bitten princess to Chaudhury Charbi Raisahib.

"Get away from that window!" Altu Faltu screamed again, picking up a shard of the smashed bottle and holding it at Rani-beti's throat. "Back off, I tell you!" On the roof, the other members of the Kachcha-Banyan gang had stopped dancing, hearing the shrill commotion beneath. They joined their bosses at the window sill and the six unsavoury creatures jammed the small opening, shoulder to shoulder. The door to the shed was locked, and the window was the only means of entering or leaving.

"You had better let her go now! It will be so much simpler for everyone concerned."

Shri Kachchaji spoke with the sweet reasonableness of one who is accustomed to dealing with hardcore terrorists.

"Shut up!" screeched Altu Faltu. And then, inspired by sheer panic, he added, "And listen to me! See those large piles of flower pots in the yard outside? Knock them over! All of you! Now! Or I will bite her and... and suck her blood!" he finished, baring his teeth again.

The Kachcha-Banyan gang, taken aback, looked to Shri

Kachchaji for orders. In the yard outside, several dozen brand new empty flower pots lay piled in teetering towers five feet high. "Go on!" shrieked Altu Faltu, and then bent down and bit Rani-beti gently in the neck, with a great show of ferociousness. She screeched shrilly and then moaned. "Ummm... that was quite a love bite! Now do it again!"

"Shut up!" hissed Altu Faltu, and bit her once more. She faked another blood-curdling scream.

Shri Kachchaji's nerve broke. Rani-beti, princess of the Flagstaff Tower clan, was being slaughtered like a pig before his eyes and her screams would bring every Delhizen within earshot bounding over in no time. He could be lynched for this.

"Do what he says," he ordered tersely, and the six big monkeys slipped off the window sill and heaved at the piled up flower pots. They fell over with a resounding crash that brought the gardeners hotfoot to the scene. Within seconds the Kachcha-Banyan gang were in full retreat, dodging the missiles hurled at them by the infuriated men.

"Run!" yelped Altu Faltu. "Now! Follow me!" And the limp, semi-slaughtered princess sprung instantly to life. "Where to?" she panted, as the pair hurtled through the window and scuttled between the legs of the startled men outside. But Altu Faltu was haring over the grassy slope in the direction opposite that taken by the Kachcha-Banyan gang, all of whom had now scrambled up trees to escape the wrath of the malis. He whizzed across a large park and shinned up a wall on the far side, making sure that Rani-beti was following close behind. They jumped off the wall and entered a noisy narrow street, scuttling under parked vehicles and scampering past startled people. They shot across a busy road, the thunder of traffic reverberating in their ears. Rani-beti had never been more frightened in her life, but she was too busy running for it, to think about it. And a brand new happiness was glowing inside her, even in this moment of crisis.

For once, Altu Faltu seemed to know exactly what he was doing and where he was going.

They were running more easily now, along a tree-shrouded road where the pavement was wide and relatively empty.

"Where are we going?" Rani-beti gasped again, wondering for how long she could stand the pace.

"Home!" replied Altu Faltu succinctly, as they darted across yet another nightmarish road. "To the Nicholson Cemetery!" He turned towards her briefly and gave her his shy half-grin.

"I'd like you to meet my mother," he said and was off again.

Back on the Hindu Rao Ridge, Shri Kachchaji furiously shook the branches of the tree he was marooned in, sending the leaves planing tipsily down. To be outwitted like this by a pair of nincompoop wimps! By God, they would pay for it! (Quite forgetting that one of the nincompoops was the princess of the Flagstaff Tower clan.) The gang had to wait awhile before the angry malis dispersed. Then they followed the trail of the fugitives up to the narrow street, after which it was lost amidst the medley of stinks and smells. Shri Kachchaji returned to the Serpentine arbour to report the failure of his mission.

"We had to let them go sir," he told Chaudhury Charbi Raisahib. "The little bastard was threatening to kill Rani-beti.

With a broken hooch bottle. And to suck her blood!"

"You said they fled... was he dragging Rani-beti with him? Did she resist?" inquired Bibi-Ek fearfully.

Shri Kachchaji looked as uncomfortable as it is possible for a hitman with a problem to look. "I'm afraid, madamji, she ran willingly with him." And then to ensure that he had covered his own lurid butt properly, added: "But I am sure madamji, that had we attempted to take her away forcibly, he would have killed her. You know these druggie types. Completely unpredictable!"

"My daughter!" wept Bibi-Ek. "That evil little bandar has seduced and bewitched my daughter! Who will marry her now?"

"Any idea as to where they might have gone?" asked Chaudhury Charbi Raisahib, remarkably cool in the face of this fresh crisis. Shri Kachchaji fidgeted and shrugged. "They could have gone anywhere sir. But I have sent feelers out. Sooner or later, there will be news. They can't just disappear." The big monkey frowned. "There's just one other thing, sir. As I was leaping through the trees towards the tool shed, I thought I saw a monkey leave the window sill in great haste. It had not seen us approaching, yet it fled. Unfortunately, the whole tool-shed was reeking of hooch and I couldn't catch an identifiable scent when I reached there..."

"Are you saying that some monkey from the Flagstaff was trying to warn them off?" Chaudhury Charbi Raisahib's blood pressure had begun to take off again.

"It looks like it, sir."

"Leechadji!" breathed Bibi-Ek illogically. "I'm sure it was him! That story he told us about Rani-beti's kidnapping... if Rani-beti ran willingly with that loafer bandar, as Shri

Kachchaji has so tragically informed us, why would he have had to kidnap her? All he would have had to do," she added with unmotherly bitterness, "is look at her and she would have gone running!"

"Bibi-Ek, don't talk nonsense!" Chaudhury Charbi Raisahib snapped. "Why should Leechadji aid and abet Rani-beti's elopement? He had in fact complained to us about that loafer bandar and Rani-beti, don't you remember? There's something odd going on here. Where is Bibi-Do? She was close to Rani-beti and maybe she knows something she hasn't told us!" He looked up decisively. "I want to see Bibi-Do and Shri Leechadji in the Serpentine arbour immediately. Send out the messengers."

But the big flaccid monkey and the pretty little bandari were nowhere to be found.

It wasn't Shri Kachchaji's feelers that brought the startling news to the Flagstaff Tower later that black Tuesday afternoon. It was Bibi-Teen's gossip grapevine. Of course, the news was all over the Ridge before Bibi-Teen, her hubcap eyes polished with tears, presented the news to her lord and master and his senior-most wife.

There had been great excitement at the Nicholson Cemetery that morning. The prodigal son of Brigadier and Lady Ladsahib, given up as a hopeless case by his distinguished parents, had suddenly returned home that morning, bringing with him a beautiful, tender young bride, or so they said.

Bibi-Teen looked tragically at Bibi-Ek and Chaudhury

Charbi Raisahib. "Yes," she said with a sob in her voice. "None other than our own beloved Rani-beti!" She burst into tears and went to console the stricken mother, who so far, had taken the news far more calmly than she had. "They are saying that the couple were chased all the way there by a horde of badmash bandars," said Bibi-Teen, pretending she did not know about the Kachcha-Banyan gang's failed mission. "They're saying that Lady Ladsahib was extremely upset that her son had brought home a bride without first obtaining her approval."

The barb hit home.

Bibi-Ek rose slowly to her feet, her eyes glinting. "Bibi-Teen," she rumbled ominously, "since you seem to know what everyone is saying, you can add this: you can say that if I, Bibi-Ek, ever catch Lady Ladsahib's snivelling, drunken drug addict of a son, with or without my daughter, I will twirl him round my head by his tail and fling him into the Khooni Khan Jheel! Is that salacious enough for you?"

Chaudhury Charbi Raisahib summoned Shri Kachchaji again.

"Get Rani-beti out of that cemetery," he ordered. "As quietly as possible. I want no fuss." He looked up angrily.

"Afterwards... afterwards you can make Altu Faltu disappear. For good. Now go! And don't mess up this time!"

It was threatening to be a very black Tuesday afternoon for Bibi-Do as well. Very soon after her return from the Hindu Rao Ridge, she had been accosted by one of Leechadji's apprentice sycophants.

"Shri Leechadji would like to meet you privately this afternoon in the old hunting lodge on the top of the Ridge near the Observatory," he informed her smugly and loped away indolently. And now, here she was, waiting for the obese creature, who was no doubt deliberately keeping her waiting. She unhappily wondered what devious suggestion he would come up with.

At last, he oozed his way through the narrow doorway of the moss-covered ruin.

"Ah, Bibi-Do! I am so happy you could make it," he gurgled, squashing her slim hand in his fleshy paws and pressing them to his lubricious lips. She tried snatching it back, but he held fast and hitched himself closer, till she could feel his foetid breath hot on her cheek. "So cosy this is, don't you think? Just the two of us in this historic old hunting lodge high up on the Ridge. So romantic! And we have so many things of mutual interest to talk about." He leered at her and winked.

"Let me go!" she demanded breathlessly, "or I will complain to Chaudhury Sahib!"

"You will, eh?" He pulled her closer and dropped his voice to a liquidy whisper. "And will you also tell him that you personally arranged for the elopement of his beloved daughter, Rani-beti? With that useless, drunken bandar? You were so busy all of last week, running up and down the Ridge with their love letters!"

"I don't know what you are talking about!" she said, a shade too quickly. "Now let me go will you!"

"Oh, so you don't know what I'm talking about! Well I do! You see, Bibi-Do, I've been following you around a bit. Couldn't help overhearing all that nice step-motherly advice you gave Rani-beti on how she could deceive her parents. She was so sweet to them all of last week. And you were the last one with her before she eloped..."

"You can't prove anything!" fumed Bibi-Do, giving herself away completely. But she was more shocked by what Leechadji was attempting to do to her paw with his mouth. He gave her a fleshy squeeze and sneered. "Not perhaps in a court of law, but there's enough, I would think, for Chaudhury Charbi Raisahib and Bibi-Ek to believe me! You see Bibi-Do, or can I call you Baby-Do now? — my story worked out. I did warn them about that loafer bandar and Rani-beti. And my warning turned out to be justified. Hey presto — they eloped! And did you know that Shri Kachchaji reported seeing a monkey flee from that bandar's tool-shed this morning, just before he got there? That wouldn't have been you now, would it, Baby-Do? Though I do recall that you did disappear from the Flagstaff clearing pretty quickly once it was suggested that the Kachcha-Banyan gang be called in to bring Rani-beti back..." He sniggered and snuggled closer. "I rest my case, Baby-Do," he said softly.

"What do you want?" she asked dully, echoing Rani-beti. The fleshy monkey put his hairy face alongside hers, his chins quivering. "Thisss!" he said obscenely, "I want you to groooom me Bibi-Do, gently, every day. And then massage me thoroughly." He put his flabby arms around her. "Embrace me, Baby-Do! Embrace me!"

Later she wondered if she would have had her inspiration had he not put his arms around her. She stared into his small, pebble eyes.

"Get your filthy paws off me, Leechadji!" she snapped with sudden, shark-toothed menace. "You do remember what happened to you the last time you put your filthy fingers around a monkey's throat?" She lowered her voice to a hiss. "Last night, at the Khooni Khan Jheel..."

Even she was startled by the big monkey's reaction. He jerked violently away from her, literally throwing her away from him, and bounded for the doorway. His pebbly eyes were dilated with fear and he blinked rapidly. "What... what are you talking about?" he stuttered hoarsely.

"You tell me," she countered, completely in command now. "Those fingers around your throat... yanking you through the air..."

"How do you know all this?" This time it was the dry-voiced Leechadji who had given himself away.

She shrugged. "I know," she said simply. "I was responsible. I have... protection!"

He looked around fearfully. There had always been something strange and fey about Bibi-Do. An unnatural shimmer about her, an unnatural sway about the way she walked.

She gave a brief, high-pitched laugh, wondering whose ghost she had usurped. It was for a good cause anyway. Leechadji, now in the doorway of the hunting lodge, with the verdant Ridge all around him and the vast blue sky above, was summoning fresh courage.

"I can still tell Chaudhury Sahib about your despicable role in Rani-beti's elopement. You can't stop me," he said stubbornly.

"Can't I?" She gave another brittle, venomous little laugh. "And how would you tell Chaudhury Sahib anything with your tongue pulled out and twisted up into knots?"

The panic was back in Leechadji's eyes and he felt his throat gingerly. "Okay," he said, "let's strike a deal..."

"I'll strike a deal!" Bibi-Do snapped, wondering for how long she could carry on this charade. "You are to stay away from me and will remain silent about what you know. Rani-beti has gone with someone she cares for, and anyway it's none of your business. Do you understand?"

He nodded. Bibi-Do regained the swing in her walk and the arch in her tail. "And if I were you, I would stay away from the Khooni Khan Jheel!" She fired this parting shot and walked past him into the sunny, golden afternoon.

Later that evening, she didn't have much difficulty in convincing Chaudhury Charbi Raisahib and Bibi-Ek that Rani-beti had completely pulled the wool over her eyes regarding her secret affair with Altu Faltu.

"Those in love," she submitted humbly (and more knowingly than Chaudhury Sahib suspected), "can be very devious indeed. I only wish Rani-beti had taken me into confidence! I could have advised her, talked to her, persuaded her..."

And Bibi-Do, more devious than Rani-beti ever was, dabbed her eyes and sighed.

Even Leechadji wriggled out of his tight corner without too much difficulty. When Bibi-Ek confronted him with the fact that it was obvious that Rani-beti had gone willingly with Altu Faltu, and had not been abducted, he quickly admitted that perhaps he had misinterpreted what had happened the previous night. Yes, perhaps Rani-beti had been carried off willingly, and Altu Faltu had brought his gang of thugs for his own protection. Perhaps the cavorting and staring he had seen had been part of some tribal victory dance or ritual...

"At any rate, we shall know the truth soon," declared Chaudhury Charbi Raisahib grimly. "The Kachcha-Banyan gang should be back with Rani-beti from the Nicholson

Cemetery soon. Just wait till I get my hands on that insolent, disobedient little monkey!"

But Chaudhury Charbi Raisahib was not to lay a hand or an eye on his beloved, insolent daughter, Rani-beti, that evening or for many more evenings to come. For the events that took place at the Nicholson Cemetery that evening gave the whole matter a dreadful and very serious dimension indeed.

The Nicholson troupe at this time consisted of about forty to fifty individuals of all ages and sizes. Led by the military minded Brigadier Ladsahib and his wife, the siren-voiced Lady Ladsahib (who called her husband 'Ladlooji' in private and sometimes in public), the troupe had inhabited the cemetery since around the same time that Chaudhury Mota Raisahib had taken possession of the Flagstaff Tower.

The leaders of the Nicholson troupe had, over the decades, tried to develop and maintain a military tradition in honour of the audacious generals who lay buried beneath their home. But it was an uphill battle, Brigadier Ladsahib had to admit, for the Delhizen macaque, especially in these modern times, was inherently not a very disciplined creature. The Brigadier's biggest personal failure however, had been his son, Altu Faltu, who had turned out to be a good-for-nothing layabout. Instead of accepting the small piece of land he had annexed for him in the neighbouring Qudsia gardens, and settling down with the mate Lady Ladsahib had chosen for him, a smaller, uglier clone of herself, Altu Faltu, always given to day-dreaming, had stormed off in a petulant huff one evening, shouting strange things about wanting to discover his own identity. All he had discovered was the stuff the notorious Hindu Rao troupe imbibed, sniffed and smoked all day, and he had converted almost instantly to their wastrel ways.

The Nicholson Cemetery is bound on three sides by busy roads. On its fourth side, it borders the Oberoi Apartments residential complex, from which it is separated by a tall, pale green wall, topped with lashings of barbed wire. And it was in this complex, barbed wire notwithstanding, that the Nicholson troupe carried out their military exercises. As the Brigadier maintained, it kept them all in fine fettle, mentally and physically.

Every now and then, the troupe, led by the conscripts of the elite First Rhesus Infantry, would launch devastating raids on the complex. They would annexe car roofs and bounce on them victoriously, chew up the wipers, rip out the rubber beading, and would then (figuratively speaking) twirl their moustaches in the mirrors. They would systematically behead the flowers in the gardens, demolish vegetable patches, bite through TV cables, shred the newspapers and professionally cut the telephone lines. On one memorable occasion, as part of a Special Military Exercise, they had even taken possession of a vacant apartment, just to show that it could be done.

Of course they faced retaliatory measures. The furious residents pelted stones, aimed catapults and airguns, shook their fists and set off fireworks. Occasionally they called in trappers, and on a few occasions the First Rhesus had lost several of its more foolish and greedy conscripts. But a "healthy tension" was always maintained, which the Brigadier said served as a "vital tonic" for the well-being of the troupe.

He had, in fact, personally led a spectacularly successful raid the previous Sunday. Conscripts of the First Rhesus had slipped over the high green wall commando style, early in the morning. Several car roofs had been badly dented. Telephone wires had been cut and a large satellite dish torn out of its moorings. The good Brigadier himself had slipped into an apartment and extensively redecorated the living room while the occupants had watched fearfully from halfway up the stairs, believing him to be in the pay of the demolition squad of the municipality. He had then removed a piece of extremely expensive and frilly black underwear hung out to dry, and had presented this to Lady Ladsahib as the spoils of war. She had tried it on gleefully and then discarded it after having rendered it even more frilly. Her two daughters had then fallen upon it and had done a disgraceful cabaret act with it on the wall while their parents were not looking.

The repercussions of this raid were inevitable. Two mornings later, on the same black Tuesday, two sly men glided into the complex in a cycle-rickshaw. They quietly buried nets in the ground at the base of the tall green wall, and scattered sweet delicacies and nuts over the tamped soil. To escape recognition, the head trapper draped himself in his wife's sari and held the ghungat alluringly across his face at all times.

But the sentries appointed by Brigadier Ladsahib were not fools to fall for such despicable subterfuge. Their hard eyes had seen everything. They emitted their staccato coughing barks as warning and informed the Brigadier immediately. He called an emergency General Body meeting of the troupe.

"A Red Alert has been sounded," he barked. "The wall of the Oberoi Apartment complex is out of bounds for all. The trappers have been called in once again. No monkey is to sit, lie, groom, walk or go anywhere near that wall until further notice. Dismissed!"

Even as he gave the order, their echoing enticing calls drifted over the high green wall. "Aaao... aao... aaao...!"

As usual, a few dare-devil adolescents had not been able to resist the temptation of "walking the wall" to tease the trappers and impress their girlfriends. But then, the sudden and unexpected return of prodigal Altu Faltu, along with a remarkably pretty little bandari had completely diverted the attention of everyone. For most of the day, the wall remained deserted.

A youngster, stammering with excitement tore across the cemetery to the top of the cemented-up well where the Brigadier and Lady Ladsahib were being groomed.

"Sir... sir... sir... madam... madam!" he squeaked, dodging an outraged batman who made a grab for him. "Sir...sir . . madam! Altu Faltu... Altu Faltu... he's come back!"

"What on earth are you gibbering about, you bad-mannered little nitwit?" inquired Lady Ladsahib coldly, and then to the lunging batman, "Bring him over here, will you?"

"Lady sahib! Lady sahib! He's come home! Altu Faltu's come home! He's on the wall! He's on the wall!"

"I thought I had given orders that the wall was out of bounds!" growled the Brigadier. Lady Ladsahib grabbed the excited messenger by the forehead. "What do you mean Altu Faltu has come back? Explain yourself, you little nitwit!"

"Yes, yes, madam! He's come back! He's on the western wall! They've all gone to see him! I came here to tell you!"

The dowager shook the little monkey. "You mean my son Altu Faltu has come home? Ladlooji did you hear that?"

"Hurrumph!" grunted the Brigadier disgustedly. "He's probably dead broke, dead drunk and here for a handout! What does he want now?"

"Where is he?" Lady Ladsahib clasped her hands, tears brimming over. In spite of everything that had happened, Altu Faltu had always been a favourite with her (he had a way with women...). Of course, he was a silly little fool who didn't know what was good for him and had messed up his life.

"He's on the western wall madam, with a friend!"

"A friend?" Lady Ladsahib's voice suddenly became as cold and sharp as an ice tong.

"Yes ma'am!"

"A girlfriend?" She released the messenger's head from her grip.

"I... I don't know ma'am. I think so! I'll call them here if you like."

"Do that!" Lady Ladsahib's voice snapped like a gin trap. She turned to her husband. "Imagine! He's gone and brought home some flea-infested hussy! The cheek!"

"He was always a useless little bugger!" muttered the Brigadier.

A large, excited crowd of monkeys was now approaching them from across the cemetery in complete disorder. The Brigadier watched their progress with increasing disgust. "Look at them!" he shouted, "After all that marching and training to conduct themselves in an orderly fashion, they go and behave like locals swarming about the Inter State Bus Terminal!"

"Does anything happen in an orderly fashion when your son is involved?" asked Lady Ladsahib acidly. So Altu Faltu had brought home a mate without consulting her about his choice. She gave a regal sniff. She would see the little trollop off in a hurry — she was not Lady Ladsahib for nothing.

But the Brigadier was quick to notice that the little

74

bandari accompanying his useless son was stunningly pretty and had golden eyes.

Altu Faltu and Rani-beti clambered up to the platform and Altu Faltu grinned rather inanely at his parents.

"Hello ma! Hello pa! How are you? Er... this is Rani-beti!" he said by way of introduction. "Rani-beti, my parents..."

"Rani who?" inquired Lady Ladsahib frigidly. The little trollop was squatting shyly next to her son.

"Rani-beti," repeated Altu Faltu, and then, remembering that his mother was a great one for family lineage, he announced proudly, "She's the daughter of Chaudhury Charbi Raisahib, grand-daughter of Chaudhury Taza Raisahib, great-grand-daughter of Chaudhury Mota Raisahib. A real princess actually!"

"A princess, eh?" said the Brigadier thickly, not really listening. "And does the princess' parents know that she is running around with a layabout like you and do they approve of it? You have their blessings?"

Altu Faltu's face clouded over. "Er, no sir... that's why we came here. They were actually chasing us, you see..."

"Chasing you?" the good Brigadier exploded, his face turning purple.

"Er... yes. You see, we have er... let's say eloped! From the Khooni Khan Jheel last night..."

"Eloped?" squealed Lady Ladsahib. She had been too busy examining the pretty little trollop from head to toe to pay any attention to what Altu Faltu had been saying. But the dreaded word "elope" had come through loud and clear.

"Eloped?" roared the Brigadier.

Lady Ladsahib fanned her face faintly. "But... but..." She looked at Rani-beti keenly. "My dear, what did he say your name was?"

"Rani-beti, ma'am, of the Flagstaff Tower clan."

"Oh my God!" moaned the dowager. "But weren't you the one who was recently engaged to that Badtameez fellow of Tughlakabad (she made it sound like Thuglakabad)? Chaudhury Charbi Raisahib's daughter? We were invited to a very lavish party at the Flagstaff Tower..."

"That's why we eloped, Mother!" explained Altu Faltu helpfully as his mother put her face in her hands and moaned. The Brigadier had begun to bluster.

"Are you trying to tell us," he inquired throatily, "that you have eloped with the recently betrothed daughter of Chaudhury Charbi Raisahib of the Flagstaff Tower, and were chased after by him? Is that correct?"

"More or less," admitted Altu Faltu. "Not exactly by him. By his goons."

"She will have to go back home immediately!" ordered the Brigadier.

"What?" yelped Altu Faltu. "But you can't do that!"

"You heard me! I will get some of the officers to escort her back home! I'll deal with you later Altu Faltu!"

"But sir," said Rani-beti in her gentle way (like a soft lamp coming on, thought Altu Faltu), "I don't want to go back home. I want to be with Altu Faltu..."

"You want to be with Altu Faltu?" echoed the Brigadier incredulously. "You must be out of your pretty little head!"

What on earth did this slim, lovely thing see in the twit that was his son? "Besides, what you want or don't want doesn't matter in this case. You are engaged to that Badtameez fellow. Dammit, we attended your engagement party!"

"Why doesn't it matter?" asked the princess quietly, as Altu

Faltu gazed at her in admiration.

"Eh? Why doesn't what matter?" The Brigadier looked blank. He was used to giving orders, not to being asked impertinent questions.

"Why doesn't what Altu Faltu and I want matter?" repeated the princess, colour creeping into her face.

"Because... because you are too young for all these things to make such decisions!"

"But father, we have eloped by mutal consent!" said Altu Faltu earnestly, joining the fray. "I am the eloper and she is the elopee. . ."

"Eloper? Elopee?! Will you shut up, you young pup!" spluttered the Brigadier.

A plaintive wail crept into Rani-beti's voice as she launched another line of attack. She had picked up a trick or two of emotional blackmail too. "But sir... you can't send me back! My family, they would... they would..." A sob shook her slender shoulders.

The Brigadier looked embarrassed. "Now don't cry... it's no use. You're engaged to someone far more deserving than this useless bounder. You've had your little fling. Now it's time to go back home and that's all there is to it!"

"You... you don't understand, sir!" wailed Rani-beti piteously, as Altu Faltu put his arms around her protectively (Lady Ladsahib flinched). "I can't go back now! After this, my engagement is as good as broken! My family and the Tughlakabadis would never accept me back! My father would prefer to kill me..."

"What nonsense!" But the Brigadier didn't sound too convinced. He had heard a thing or two about the peculiar customs of some of the local simian tribes. Rani-beti was gulping down her sobs.

"You see sir, it's an old family tradition I have broken. I have dishonoured the family name! I am a disgraced person! A fallen simian! I will be ostracised and maybe even lynched..."

Lady Ladsahib eyed the sobbing princess with renewed, shrewd interest. Many, many years ago, she had taken a similar line with the Brigadier's old fogey (and battle-axe wife) and he had been putty in her hands ever since. The Brigadier had begun to splutter now, the chivalry in him rising rapidly to the top. "Nonsense, my dear," he said, "no one would want to lynch you!"

The runaway princess clasped her hands pleadingly. "You see sir, in some ways, we are a very old-fashioned family. I will...will probably be thrown into the Flagstaff Tower and starved to death! That's the customary punishment for the sort of thing I have done!"

Lady Ladsahib raised an eyebrow. The little princess was laying it on a bit thick, she thought. But the Brigadier was falling for it, hook, line and sinker.

"Ahem... very well my dear. Under the circumstances, I will have to grant you and Altu Faltu asylum here. Till things settle down a bit. Then we'll see what's to be done. Come, come, dry your eyes now and do stop crying!" He never could resist a damsel in distress.

Altu Faltu clapped his hands in delight. His father gave him a disgusted look. "As for you," he said, "you've been nothing but a load of trouble!"

Lady Ladsahib took the hand of her princess daughter-in-law-to-be. "Come my dear, and let me show you around!" She beamed. It was all right after all. Her Altu Faltu was not as much of a fool as everyone had thought.

He had in the end, chosen a girl just like his mother...

But he really ought to have been less foolish later that evening. The young couple had slipped away from the rest of the troupe and had clambered up the forbidden wall, hoping to get a few moments of privacy. (All day, Rani-beti had been looked at, examined, groomed, licked, questioned, touched and hugged by various members of the troupe, and it had been a bit overwhelming). Altu Faltu had also thought it would be fun to tease the trappers — of whose invidious presence they had been warned — for Rani-beti's entertainment and his own edification.

So he pretended to be lured by their beseeching "Aaao... aaao... aaao!" calls (which made Rani-beti a little homesick); he came off the wall and snatched a few peanuts from their hands, then danced away, bared his teeth and gibbered in mock rage. Up on the wall, Rani-beti giggled and laughed and clapped her hands, her golden eyes shining. For the first time since their arrival at the cemetery, they were quite alone and it was bliss. The rest of the troupe had gone off to the front of the cemetery for their evening's quota of bananas.

But they were not as alone as they thought they were. For the members of the Kachcha-Banyan gang had stationed themselves on the terraces and balconies of the apartments overlooking the cemetery and had kept them under surveillance since early that afternoon. Now at last, their perseverance appeared to be paying off.

The foolish young couple had turned up alone on the

wall and that idiotic Altu Faltu had left a giggling Rani-beti by herself. Shri Kachchaji gave a signal and the gang fanned out, making for the extreme ends of the wall. They shinned up it and swiftly closed in on either side of the unsuspecting princess. As Altu Faltu tugged cheekily at the leading trapper's gunghat, Messers Kachchaji and Banyanji materialised silently on either side of Rani-beti.

"Time to go home, Rani-beti," Shri Kachchaji said firmly, and took the princess's arm. She screamed and bit him instinctively, pulling free desperately.

"Help!" she screamed. "Altu Faltu, help me!" She leapt off the wall, into the complex grounds, hoping to land in her lover's arms. Instead there was a sudden thwanging snap and then Rani-beti was struggling in the mesh of a monstrous net, screeching with panic.

The head trapper discarded his sari in a trice and leapt forward with a cry of triumph. He plucked Rani-beti up by the scruff of her neck and pinioned her arms and legs behind her. Altu Faltu had fled up the wall instinctively on hearing Rani-beti's first scream. Now, sitting alongside an equally aghast Kachchaji, he watched with numb horror as the trapper held up the hysterical princess as though she were a sacrificial offering. He then bundled her into a sack, grinning viciously; the long wait had paid off at last. There was a sudden commotion further down along the wall and Altu Faltu saw one of the Kachcha Banyan gang members struggling in another deadly net.

The screams had brought the sentries of the Nicholson troupe galloping up, and they hurled themselves at the stunned members of the Kachcha-Banyan gang, with angry grunting whoofs. And for the second time that day, the Kachcha Banyan gang found themselves in full and ignominious retreat.

It had been a very black Tuesday for them as well.

Up on the wall, Altu Faltu stared hypnotically at the wriggling sack into which Rani-beti had been bundled.

"I'm coming!" he screamed. "Rani-beti I'm coming!" And braced himself to jump. But just then, a powerful paw gripped him by the back of his head and hauled him off the wall into the cemetery. He turned and found his mother looking at him out of terrible, stricken eyes.

"No, Altu Faltu! No!"

"Let me go! Will you let me go!" he screeched and then bit her hard. She gave a gasp of pain and surprise and lost her grip. But by the time he had stormed back up the wall, it was too late.

The trappers and their sacks were gliding around the corner at the far end of the road in their cycle rickshaw. By the time he had scampered all the way to the main gate, there was no sign of them.

He returned blindly to the wall where now, the whole troupe had gathered, gibbering with anxiety and excitement. His mother was sobbing, and the Brigadier was trying in vain to comfort her. He stared at them wordlessly for a moment and then walked off tiredly towards the western boundary wall.

He was going back to his ramshackle tool-shed on the Hindu Rao Ridge to get utterly, comprehensively and completely smashed.

As he left, he heard the metallic mewing calls of the peacocks in the cemetery raised in lamentation.

Chapter 3

THE
DRUMS
OF WAR

They waited in the Serpentine arbour as the great cloak of dusk engulfed them in its blanket shadow: Chaudhury Charbi Raisahib, scion of the Flagstaff Delhizens; his three worried wives, Bibis Ek, Do and Teen, and the gross, obese Leechadji, who had been right about his promotional prospects. Since his extraordinary performance at the Flagstaff Tower that morning, he had been elevated to the rank of Personal Assistant to Chaudhury Charbi Raisahib, even though both Bibi-Ek and Bibi-Do had objected vehemently to the appointment.

The 'Serpentine' at the Ridge consisted of a series of brooding, contorted ponds linked together by narrow channels of water. The area around it was as densely vegetated as that around the Khooni Khan Jheel nearby. It rustled and creaked with towering thickets of bamboo that leaned and crowded over it, and was intricately plaited with creepers and vines that could tangle up a careless monkey and strangle it too. It was roofed delicately with a wide-spreading fretwork of neem, jacaranda, acacia, lagaestromia and jasmine. The Ridge rose steeply along one side of this twisted water-filled gully while a rocky pathway ran crookedly around it. Four small, humpbacked bridges, again identical to the one at the Khooni Khan Jheel, connected the paths to the arbour where Wandering Jew had been confined to neat beds and the shade was deep and cool even during the most torrid of summers. A small, thatch-roofed cement platform had been built in the heart of the arbour, and here, in this Diwan-e-Khas of the Flagstaff clan, the four eminent Flagstaffers waited for their absconding princess, Rani-beti, to be brought before them for explanation, chastisement and justice.

A choleric white-breasted waterhen startled them all with its sudden hoarse "Kwaark! Kwarrk! Kwarrk!" call, sounding as though its neck was being slowly wrung. A grey partridge let off its warning "Trrlll...!" alarm and took off with a 'bhrrr!' of blurring wings. A squirrel shrilled in blind panic.

Two of the Ridge's most notorious Delhizens suddenly materialised on one of the bridges and crossed over to the arbour. Shri Kachchaji and Shri Banyanji had arrived at last to report on the outcome of their mission at the Nicholson Cemetery. Shri Kachchaji rocked on his lurid haunches and blinked uneasily. Chaudhury Charbi Raisahib glared at him in the fading light.

"Well, Shri Kachchaji, where is Rani-beti?" His voice was harsh and Bibi-Ek paled, seeing the set expression on Shri Kachchaji's face.

"I am afraid we lost her, sir," the big monkey said in a low voice.

"Lost her? What do you mean lost her?"

They were all staring at him now, and Bibi-Ek had begun

to whimper.

"They got her sir, before we could do anything..."

"Who got her? What are you talking about Kachcha?"

"Trappers sir..."

"Trappers? What trappers?"

Shri Kachchaji took a deep breath. "It happened like this sir... Those Nicholson bastards and that Altu Faltu fellow had been eve-teasing Rani-beti all day. We saw it all from our surveillance posts. They were making fun of her and pulling her tail and passing lewd remarks. They insulted her and the honour of the clan. She was crying most of the time and trying to escape from their clutches, but to no avail..."

"And you watched all this and did nothing?"

Bibi-Ek's voice was an incredulous whisper and she had trebled in size. Bibi-Do gripped her arm fiercely, disbelief writ large on her face.

Kachchaji continued in his low, sullen way.

"There was nothing we could do. She was in alien territory. And she was surrounded by about ten guards at all times. They would have killed her had we tried anything. We had chalked out a rescue plan for the night however — we thought we would pull her out after dark..."

"What happened?" Chaudhury Charbi Rasisahib's voice was like granite.

"Well sir, they hounded her into the traps, that's what happened. We had noticed the presence of trappers in the residential complex that adjoins the cemetery. They had buried nets into the ground and baited the area with delicacies. At around 6.30 p.m., a group of those Nicholsonites, led by that Altu Faltu fellow, dragged Rani-beti up to the wall. They were laughing at her, pinching her and doing other obnoxious things. Then they pointed to the sweets lying in the traps and asked her to get some for them. When she refused, they just took her by the arms and swung her over the wall straight into the traps. We leapt to the rescue but were too late — in fact, one of our own fellows, Pehelwan, was himself captured..."

Kachchaji looked up tensely. Would they bite? Would they swallow the story and accept the explanation? Bibi-Ek had collapsed weeping and was being consoled by Bibi-Do. Bibi-Do herself was bristling with anger and shock for she was sure that Kachchaji had been lying. But was angry with herself too, for the guilt he had again aroused in her. Bibi-Teen stared out of her huge saucer doll's eyes. "They're all like that!" she exclaimed with well simulated bitterness, shaking her head tragically. "First they seduce you, and then when they've got what they want, they hound you to death. Poor Rani-beti!"

"Oh shut up, Bibi-Teen," snapped Bibi-Do viciously, as Bibi-Ek wailed, "my Rani-beti, my Rani-beti, my Rani-beti!" and beat her breast.

Chaudhury Charbi Raisahib cast a hard look at Shri Kachchaji. "Shri Kachchaji," he said carefully, trying to keep his temper in check, "this morning you reported that Rani-beti was held hostage by Altu Faltu when you went to rescue her from the Hindu Rao Ridge. Then you told us that she fled willingly with him to the Nicholson Cemetery. Now you are telling us that she was being harassed by Altu Faltu and his family and thrown into the traps by them..."

Leechadji intervened smoothly. He had sensed a kindred soul in Shri Kachchaji and saw no harm in making an ally of him now.

"Ah, Chaudhury Sahib! You know how it is with the young! When they think they are in love they are blind to

85

reality! And this sort of thing happens in the best of simian and human families. The blushing, innocent bride is first seduced, and then harassed and got rid of when they tire of her, or if she has not brought them enough dowry...Though I must admit that I am surprised by the behaviour of the Nicholsonites. To behave so cruelly with the sweet, innocent Rani-beti so soon! But they say a streak of lunacy runs through the clan..."

Shri Kachchaji nodded gratefully in surprised agreement, but Chaudhury Charbi Raisahib cast his P.A. a flinty look.

"I am not concerned with what happens in the so-called best of simian or human families as you might like to think they are, Shri Leechadji. I just find it difficult to believe that Rani-beti could get entangled with such a sly, two-faced bastard, and did not see through him. I suspect her reason and judgement may have been influenced by the filthy drugs the little bastard might have forced her to take!"

The anger frizzled him up again as he thought of his beautiful truant daughter with the golden eyes and pixie ears. If what Shri Kachchaji had reported was true, this was an extremely serious matter. The Nicholson troupe had insulted the great Flagstaff clan and had committed the grossest of outrages. An unprovoked act of aggression and violence on one of the most innocent (not really) and lovely of the troupe, and his daughter no less. They had behaved like hoodlums and terrorists and barbarians. But first, before he swore revenge and eternal enmity, there was another more immediate matter to take care of. Justice had to be dispensed to the Kachcha Banyan gang for this, their latest failure.

"Shri Kachchaji and Shri Banyanji! You and the members of your team are hereby expelled from the precincts of the

Northern Ridge until such time as you bring Rani-beti back. I don't care what you have to do to bring her home." He turned to his fat P.A. who was nodding sanctimoniously. "Shri Leechad, you will arrange a summit meeting with that fat-arsed Brigadier of the Nicholson troupe for noon tomorrow at the Mutiny Memorial. This is a very serious matter involving the clan's honour and may well mean war. I will address all members of the Flagstaff troupe at the Tower at 5 p.m. thereafter. In the meanwhile, I hereby impose the Order of Silence on the Ridge..." He broke off to bob his head warningly at Bibi-Teen who met his gaze with all innocence. "Not one word of what has passed here is to be repeated to anyone! Is that clear?"

They nodded and Kachchaji, with his partner, slunk off to plan yet another rescue mission. Bibi-Ek, still weeping inconsolably, was led away towards the nursery by Bibi-Do and Bibi-Teen.

"Rani-beti will be all right." Bibi-Do assured the sobbing senior wife. "You know human beings never harm our species. They revere us!"

But Leechadji had sidled up, his eyes malicious, and Bibi-Do stiffened.

"Ah, Bibi-Do, you are so right!" he taunted slyly, "maybe they do not kill us outright! But they are known to conduct the most hideous and cruel experiments on us. Head and brain transplants! Pumping us full of painful slow-killing viruses and nuclear radiation. Subjecting us to solitary confinement and sleep deprivation... Ah! But what am I saying! Bibi-Ek you mustn't upset yourself so!"

And the vindictive old monkey slipped quickly away into the darkness before Bibi-Do could summon her djinns, happy with his pound of flesh.

That night Bibi-Do could not sleep. She had not, for one moment, believed Shri Kachchaji's story of the alleged harassment of Rani-beti at the hands of Altu Faltu and the Nicholsonites. But she knew instinctively that he had been telling the truth regarding the fact that Rani-beti had been captured by trappers. Guilt and remorse made her toss and turn all night for she felt herself to be responsible for Rani-beti's fate. Yet she had a burning desire to find out exactly what had happened that evening in the Nicholson Cemetery and what had become of Altu Faltu. Her natural simian curiosity would not let her rest.

Early next morning she set off for the cemetery. She had barely sat herself down on the pale green wall when one of the guards came bouncing up.

"What do you want? Don't you know you're trespassing?" he said belligerently, and then, seeing that she was young and shapely and it was almost October, more politely, "Can I help you, madam?"

"I want to see Altu Faltu," she replied, giving him a smouldering look. "I believe he returned home yesterday..."

"Altu Faltu?" The guard grimaced. They all wanted to see Altu Faltu. What they saw in him, he couldn't for the life of him fathom. "I'm afraid Altu Faltu's not here anymore. His... er, girlfriend, got caught by some trappers yesterday and he went off in a huff." The guard eyed her appreciatively and shifted closer. But suddenly she was gone and he hadn't even asked her her name or where she had come from.

Bibi-Do was making it at all speed to the ramshackle tool-shed on the Hindu Rao Ridge. Her eyes were smarting with anger.

There, on the mud floor of the shed, surrounded by a welter of little brown bottles, sprawled Altu Faltu, moaning, snoring and twitching. Bibi-Do loomed over him, grabbed him by the neck and shook him as a terrier would a rat. Altu Faltu lolled in her grasp like a rag doll, the whites of his eyes glimmering through almost-closed lids. With strength born of sheer rage, Bibi-Do hoisted him over the window sill and dragged him by the tail to the large stagnant water-body near-by that, despite its corrupted state, reflected a sky of the deepest, purest blue. She gripped his head in both her hands and immersed it into the still water. A kingfisher exploded like a turquoise firework, but Bibi-Do concentrated grimly on the task at hand. Suddenly Altu Faltu spluttered and struggled. She lifted his head so that only his flaring nostrils and eyes breasted the water. His eyes were glassy, but cleared slowly to their usual dreamy brown.

"What... what...?" he spluttered and coughed, thrashing wildly with his arms and legs.

"I told you that I would kill you if you did not look after Rani-beti!" She said it in such a matter of fact tone that it made even Altu Faltu's linctus-saturated blood freeze. He struggled ineffectually in her grasp and the water slopped over his face.

"I couldn't help it!" he wailed. "They caught her and took her away! They wouldn't let me go after her!"

Bibi-Do held him by the forehead till he had explained, as coherently as he could, what had happened. Wet, bedraggled and unhappy, he looked a pathetic wreck.

"So you just came here and got drunk and stoned?" she said grimly, and pushed him under once more, in sheer disgust.

"What could I do?" he blubbered, almost as disgustingly as Leechadji had at the Flagstaff Tower the previous morning. She shook him again, hoping to clear his drug-fogged mind.

"Somewhere," she enunciated slowly and clearly, "somewhere Rani-beti is alive! And probably hoping, believing that you will come looking for her. Waiting for you! Instead you are lying here, dead drunk and wallowing in self-pity. And you said you loved her! You make me sick!"

"What can I do?" he wailed pathetically, and this time she could not resist slapping a rapid tattoo onto his face.

"Find her, dammit!" she hissed, her face close to his (his breath nearly made her pass out), her canines bared. "Find her, or else I swear that your skinny, pathetic body will be found floating in this stinking, foul blue pond!"

"Find her? But where?"

"You have the whole of Delhi to look in," she replied spitefully (but sick inside herself), "and maybe the surrounding countryside too!"

"Will you help me Bibi-Do?" he appealed pathetically, and once again she wondered what on earth Rani-beti had seen in this witless, spineless wonder. "I will not!" she declared vehemently, "This is something you have to do on your own! Dammit, you are supposed to be in love with her!" For an awful moment Bibi-Do wondered whether Shri Kachchaji had been right after all. Had Rani-beti fallen for a no-hoper who did not care for her after all? If so, she, Bibi-Do had made a terrible mistake and poor Rani-beti was paying the price for it. She clung to a straw: the twit had wailed something about not being permitted to go after Rani-beti when she had been captured. Something about being held back by his mother. Perhaps all this was just the shock... She yanked him out of the water. He crouched miserably before her, sopping and trembling. There came a sudden crashing and smashing sound from the direction of the toolshed. Instinctively, both the monkeys ducked for cover, and making their way through the undergrowth, approached the toolshed.

The Kachcha Banyan gang were at it with a vengeance. Altu Faltu was now number one on their list of those to be interrogated, and it appeared that he had given them the slip again. So they proceeded to wreak their rage on his shed. (The greedy little bastard had even polished off all his bottles!) By the time the malis had come running (they had been delayed as they had been taking tea) there was very little left of the tool shed and its contents.

"They are coming after you!" Bibi-Do breathed in a diabolical whisper that made Altu Faltu squeak and jump. "At least they will have broken all your bloody bottles!" She grabbed him by the ears and stared menacingly into his eyes. "One week," she hissed sibilantly. "You have one week to find Rani-beti. Next Wednesday you will bring her to me at the old hunting lodge on the top of the Ridge. If you fail, or try to run away, I will hunt you down and kill you." She paused as though in thought, and continued softly. "I have my ways, Altu Faltu... you recall what happened to Leechad at the Khooni Khan Jheel that night?" She thought his eyes would fall out and wondered if the djinns would mind being commandeered a second time.

"That... that... judo?" he stammered.

She shook her head. "No, not judo, Altu Faltu, but jadu!

Magic! Black magic! Now go!" she commanded, "go and find Rani-beti!"

He opened his mouth like a goldfish, but she bobbed her head fiercely and charged him. He fled like a skimming stone.

The Mutiny Memorial, a fluted, eight-sided Gothic structure, resembles a church tower that has been abandoned by the rest of the church. It was erected by the British thirteen years after the revolt of 1857, to commemorate their dead; a plaque added later, in 1972, equally commemorates the rebels who died fighting for freedom. The memorial is located in a quiet, shady park (where quiet, shady deeds are known to be done) on the Hindu Rao Ridge, halfway up the hill overlooking the old bastion of Mori Gate from where rebel cannonfire had once roared. The structure, now rather defaced, lies a stone's throw away from the Hindu Rao Hospital, and Altu Faltu's now wrecked tool shed.

As a site for a summit meeting between the two most powerful Delhizen macaques of the area, it was ideal. The steeple slanted upwards in a series of fluted steps, each ringed with a narrow plinth and adorned with ornamental spires. The tiny gallery located just beneath the top of the main spire offered privacy, a position of power and status (equally shared) and a view of the surrounding territories.

At 1155 hours on the stipulated day, Brigadier Ladsahib, accompanied by his aide-de-camp, Colonel Kela, and six bodyguards, marched up to the plinth of the Memorial. They were met there stiffly by Chaudhury Charbi Raisahib, who had brought along Shri Leechad and his own guards. The guards were ordered to remain at the base of the monument while the leaders conferred on top.

Chaudhury Charbi Raisahib broke the steely silence.

"Shall we ascend?" he said coldly, his face set and hard. Brigadier Ladsahib nodded equally stiffly. The two huge macaques hoisted themselves up the steeple in a series of swift, powerful bounds, arriving at the top almost simultaneously. Both were rather huffed by the effort but tried not to show it. Colonel Kela skimmed up to his position on the gallery beneath with the ease born of regular exercise and grinned at Leechad who struggled up, panting and cursing.

At the summit the Brigadier inclined his head again.

"Should we proceed, Chaudhury Sahib? But before we go any further, I would like to register my official protest against the lack of a documented agenda for this meeting and its unduly short notice. Now to what do we owe the pleasure of this sudden, secret meeting?" He raised his eyebrow haughtily and folded his hands in his lap. Of course he knew why the meeting had been called, but proper form had to be maintained. Chaudhury Charbi Raisahib, however, was in no mood to observe niceties.

"We owe this meeting to the elopement of your son with my daughter, Rani-beti, sir!" he riposted angrily. "I would have you know that the Flagstaff clan and myself hold the Nicholson troupe and yourself responsible for the capture and abduction of my beloved daughter, Rani-beti, by trappers, while she was in illegal custody at the Nicholson Cemetery yesterday. And also for the unspeakable torture, molestation and humiliation she was subjected to by your son and his friends while being held there against her will. I demand that she be immediately rescued and returned herewith, unharmed. I hold you personally responsible for that!" And Chaudhury Charbi Raisahib glared and bobbed his head angrily.

The Brigadier glared back.

"And I, sir, refuse to accept that responsibility! Your daughter was most unfortunately captured because she was terrorised and panicked into the trappers' nets by the hoodlums you had sent to kidnap her. I would like to remind you sir, that your daughter came to us of her own free will and was in fact, fleeing from your hitmen at the time. She was welcomed by us as one of our own and given asylum. The thugs you had employed to kidnap her illegally entered our territory and were duly driven away by the guards responsible for maintaining the integrity of our borders. Unfortunately and most stupidly, your hoodlums panicked your daughter into the nets of the trappers, in their clumsy attempt to kidnap her!" Brigadier Ladsahib sat back smugly after this long and (he thought) powerful delivery. But Chaudhury Charbi Raisahib was accepting none of it.

"The delegation I had sent to the Nicholson Cemetery to peacefully persuade my daughter to return to her rightful home was attacked savagely without provocation by your guards, sir!"

"Nonsense Chaudhury Sahib! They had grossly violated our borders!"

"In fact, one respected member of the delegation was himself captured by trappers in his gallant attempt to rescue my daughter after she had been thrown into the nets by your goonda son and his friends!"

"My son would have also been captured by the trappers,

had my wife not forcibly held him back in time!"

"Speaking of your son, sir," and Chaudhury Charbi Raisahib nearly spat out the word, "I have reason to believe that he and his hooligan friends forcibly drugged my daughter and then held her hostage when I had sent the delegation to rescue her from his den of vice on the Hindu Rao Ridge. He held a broken bottle to her throat and threatened to drink her blood!"

"Altu Faltu is incapable of holding a peanut hostage, let alone your daughter!"

"I repeat sir, I am holding you responsible for Rani-beti's safe return. If she is not returned unharmed to the Flagstaff Tower within one week of this meeting, you will have to face the consequences!"

"Are you trying to threaten me, sir?" The Brigadier's eyes bulged and he shot up the spire and shook it violently to let off accumulated steam. Chaudhury Charbi Raisahib waited for him to come down and bobbed his head rapidly. He leaned forward threateningly.

"I am giving you an ultimatum, sir! If my daughter is not returned within one week, be prepared to face the military might of the invincible Flagstaff Tower clan!"

"A declaration of war? Is that it sir?"

"The Flagstaff clan will not stand by and see its honour besmirched and its daughters molested and humiliated!"

"May I remind you sir, that your daughter and my son came fleeing for their lives to the Nicholson Cemetery, chased by your hoodlums? I was honour-bound to offer them asylum, and we Nicholsonites do not compromise in such matters. The Declaration of Simian Rights..."

"My daughter was drugged sir, drugged by your son and

held hostage! I repeat you have one week to ensure her safe return to her rightful home!"

"As far as your daughter is concerned sir, her rightful home is now the Nicholson Cemetery or wherever she chooses to make it by the side of my son!"

"Then sir, be prepared to face the consequences!"

"And you sir, to pay the price for any foolhardy actions! Any attack on the integrity of our borders will be repulsed with memorable force!" The Brigadier slipped one below the belt: "In any case, going to war will not bring your daughter back!"

"It may not! But honour shall be satisfied!"

"So this is about so-called honour is it? Rather than for love for your daughter! I didn't think the Flagstaff clan was quite so medieval!"

And now it was Chaudhury Charbi Raisahib's turn to lose his temper. For a moment, it seemed as though he was about to attack the Brigadier and fling him off the gallery; fortunately better sense prevailed and he remembered the conventions of summit diplomacy. He leapt up the steeple and shook the lightning conducter loose and flung it down violently. His face was as lurid as his loins.

The Brigadier sat back, scratched himself and yawned. "There is no point continuing this discussion if you are going to behave in this infantile manner," he smirked, quite forgetting his own little tantrum. "I suggest we adjourn this discussion and resume talks when you are in a more amicable and coherent state of mind!"

Chaudhury Charbi Raisahib glared at him, his fur rising fast. "No talks!" he spluttered, finding his voice at last. "No more talks! If my daughter is not at the Flagstaff Tower one week from today it will be war! Good day, sir!"

And he turned his back on the reclining Brigadier, arched his tail and plunged headfirst down the steeple at a dangerous speed. Leechadji slithered down clumsily after him.

Still on the summit, the Brigadier exulted briefly in what he considered had been a verbal triumph, but then turned grim. The prospect of war with the powerful Flagstaff clan seemed inevitable if the Chaudhury's daughter did not turn up within the stipulated period. But there was no question of the Nicholsonites sending out search and rescue parties for her. It had been the Chaudhury's men who had been responsible for her capture. Of course, now that she was a Nicholsonite by marriage (or whatever her relationship with Altu Faltu could be defined as), it could equally be held that it was in fact the responsibility of the Nicholson troupe to search for and rescue Rani-beti. But the Chaudhury's attitude to the whole affair had made it impossible to accept that, and the Brigadier too had his pride. He climbed down the steeple and called out to his aide.

"Colonel Kela, on the double now! We have work to do. A military campaign to plan. We may have to prepare to face a siege."

Later that afternoon, the Brigadier began plotting his strategy in earnest. He knew that the Flagstaff forces would heavily outnumber the Nicholsonites. But he also knew that the attacking force would not be likely to launch an offensive from the three sides of the Cemetery that faced the road:

that would be foolhardy and too dangerous. So, only the long pale green wall that bordered the residential complex would have to be defended. But even so, for how long could the small if well-trained Nicholson force hold the huge army of the Flagstaff clan at bay? Brigadier Ladsahib paced up and down the cemented-up well top, deep in thought. He knew that there had been trouble brewing on the Ridge; he knew that various rebellious princelings had been making mutinious noises and demands for independence. Perhaps this was an avenue worth exploring. He summoned Lieutenant Hazari Kaan, the head of his intelligence network.

"Hazari Kaan, what's the latest on the state of fraternity between Chaudhury Charbi Raisahib and his brother Haramisahib?" he inquired, an idea glimmering.

Hazari Kaan raised an eyebrow. "Haramisahib sir? Well sir, it is common knowledge that the brothers are at daggers drawn. Harmisahib wants to secede with a lot of territory. He's already claimed the Chauburja area as his own and has launched several raids on the Flagstaffers. They say he's gunning for the Flagstaff Tower itself!"

"I see. Well, thank you very much and keep me updated about the position. Now send Colonel Kela to me!"

Cononel Kela listened respectfully as the Brigadier outlined his plan.

"What we do is simple really! We forge an alliance with Haramisahib. If he agrees to assist us in beating off Chaudhury Charbi Raisahib, we help him oust his brother from the Flagstaff Tower. From the entire Northern Ridge in fact. Ah, if this works out, Chaudhury Charbi Raisahib may be in for an unpleasant surprise when he attacks us. Now take this message to Chaudhury Haramisahib, will you Colonel Kela..."

Chaudhury Charbi Raisahib had returned to the Serpentine arbour and was also discussing strategy with his recently appointed P.A., Shri Leechad. He knew full well that going to war with the Nicholson troupe would not bring back Rani-beti, but was still quite confident that the Kachcha Banyan gang would find her eventually. One thing however, was almost certain. Whether they did or, God forbid, did not, Rani-beti could not now be married to Nawab Bade Badtameez. If Badtameez ever found out — and he was bound to sooner or later — that Rani-beti had been with someone else, and someone like Altu Faltu, there would be a hell of a scandal. And he could not afford to offend the powerful Tughlakabadis. Perhaps Badtameez could be persuaded to marry that other, if dimwitted, daughter of his — Bibi-Do's favourite — Chamkili? She was pretty enough. He would speak to Bibi-Do about the matter at the earliest.

Actually, the idea of going to war against the Nicholson troupe did not seem to be such a bad one at all. The more he thought about it, the more it appealed to him. There was nothing like a war to unite a divided clan; to rekindle the fierce flame of patriotism. There were other advantages to be gained too, especially in a winning war, as this one surely would be. As he told Leechad, "If we annexe the Nicholson Cemetery and drive out that troupe, we would have so much more territory to spread out in!"

But it was Leechad who had the real brainwave (or so they thought). "Why don't you have a formal rapprochement with Chaudhury Haramisahib sir?" the wily simian suggested. "If he can assist us in our campaign against the Nicholson troupe, we can let him have the Nicholson Cemetery for himself, to rule as an autonomous area. It will get him out of here and confine him to a place where he will be more or less isolated and can pose no threat. And we'll be rid of him from the Ridge for good!"

Chaudhury Charbi Raisahib was greatly impressed. It seemed to be an excellent idea. "Brilliant, Leechad, brilliant!" he congratulated the fat, smirking monkey. "Now will you kindly take a letter to my dear brother Haramisahib, along with a crate of those delicious out-of-season alphonso mangoes we recently received..."

Early that same evening, Chaudhury Charbi Raisahib summoned Bibi-Ek and Bibi-Do to the Serpentine arbour.

"Bibi-Ek," he began, coming to the point immediately, "I am afraid that in the light of recent developments, we will have to break the engagement of Rani-beti with Nawab Bade Badtameez. Even if Rani-beti returns home in the near future..."

Bibi-Ek looked up tearfully. "Do you know where she is? What has happened to her?"

"There is no news as yet, I'm afraid. But it is really too early to expect any. I am sure the Kachcha Banyan gang will rescue her shortly. But you will agree with me, Rani-beti cannot marry Badtameez now, under any circumstances."

"I don't care about Badtameez. I only want my Rani-beti back!"

"We all do Bibi-Ek, we all do! But we cannot ignore our greater responsibilities and obligations to society. We will appear to have let Badtameez down. Our name will be mud!

The clan's image irrevocably tarnished! I have therefore thought of a way out. Bibi-Do, I assume you will have no objection if I offer Chamkili's hand in marriage to Badtameez in lieu of Rani-beti's?"

Bibi-Do looked away, feeling absolutely wretched now that the moment of victory had come. She could not savour it, not with Rani-beti taken by trappers and gone missing.

"No sir," she said in a low voice, clutching Bibi-Ek's hand tightly. "Not at all. I would be honoured!"

"Very well. But now we shall have to inform Badtameez!"

"What reason are you going to give for breaking off Rani-beti's engagement?"

Bibi-Ek's question was a choked whisper, and Bibi-Do felt as if her guilt would strangle her. Even Chaudhury Charbi Raisahib appeared troubled by the question. It was Leechad who broke the silence, licking his lubricious lips.

"Let us first rule out what we cannot say," he began smoothly. "We cannot tell the truth of course; that Rani-beti has been seduced by and run off with a drunken bekar bandar and foolishly got herself captured by trappers. Badtameez would think that all our princesses are... like that, and refuse to marry even Chamkili!" He was enjoying himself hugely again, stringing both Bibi-Ek and Bibi-Do with the same bow as it were. "We cannot say that Rani-beti has... er... left for her heavenly abode. There would be considerable embarrassment caused when the Kachcha Banyan gang turn up with her." He looked at them one by one, completely unperturbed by the emotional holocaust he was causing. "We could perhaps say that Rani-beti has had an unfortunate accident and can be of no use to His Highness as a wife... or mistress... or for that purpose thereof." Hideously smug, he ground on. "Perhaps we could say that she's lost her mind or memory... Though no, that may not deter a feudal playboy like Badtameez. No, I think the physical thing is best."

"You bastard!" Both Bibi-Ek and Bibi-Do spat out the words together, their eyes smouldering with rage. Chaudhury Charbi Raisahib felt his fur rise and controlled himself with difficulty. It scoured deeply, like acid, but he realised all the same that this was the only feasible way they could save face in front of Badtameez.

"Very well," he agreed heavily, "we shall inform Badtameez that Rani-beti is no longer a... a viable proposition as a bride. I hope he accepts Chamkili though."

"If the Nawab Sahib is agreeable, for when do we fix the wedding?" In spite of everything, Bibi-Do could not help feel a flicker of excitement. She was always quick to recover from a traumatic situation.

"For the same day as we fixed Rani-beti's wedding."

"But sir, you are planning to go to war on the Nicholson troupe..." Leechad reminded his boss.

Chaudhury Charbi Raisahib smiled grimly. "Yes," he growled, "but it will be a quick ethnic cleansing operation. Should not last more than a day. We storm the Cemetery and drive the troupe out on the roads and under the buses." He glanced at Bibi-Ek, his face furrowed. "At least we can avenge Rani-beti's misfortune, even if we cannot rectify it." He signalled his wives to leave and beckoned Shri Leechad. "Any response from Chaudhury Haramisahib?" he inquired. Leechad shook his head. "No sir, nothing as yet." And the gross monkey sighed. "Poor Rani-beti!"

Chaudhury Haramisahib, younger and delinquent brother of Chaudhury Charbi Raisahib, lay sprawled in shameless abandon on the large cement feeding platform near the Chauburja monument while a coterie of saucy little bandaris from the Khyber Pass Massage Parlour worked him over expertly. His majordomo, Tedi Poonch, hovered nearby, hoping to receive a stray pinch, squeeze or nibble.

"Suddenly," murmured Chaudhury Haramisahib, almost to himself, and Tedi Poonch hitched himself closer the better to hear and hopefully, bump a little bandari. "Suddenly there appears to be a great deal of concern for my leadership and well-being amongst the neighbouring clans. First I get this love letter from that fart of a Brigadier at the Nicholson Cemetery, wondering if I would be interested in taking over the Flagstaff Tower and the rest of the Northern Ridge. Merely in return for assisting him in fighting off my dear brother Charbiji who has been beating war drums and casting covetous looks at that godforsaken cemetery." He flipped open the 'love letter' and read, sotto voce, "'Together we can work to rid the Ridge of the ineffectual leadership of Chaudhury Charbi Raisahib and install you in his place. If you are agreeable to this in principle, we can work out the details of the campaign...'" Tedi Poonch nudged a bandari and got clouted on his ear.

Haramisahib yawned and went on with his monologue. "And then I get a flattering visit from the most hideous Macaca mulatta in all of history, bearing a crate of the most fabulous alphonsoes I have ever seen. Along with a conciliatory message from my dear, estranged elder brother! Saying that it is high time we put aside our petty differences, bury the hatchet, and unite to fight that fart of a Brigadier and drive him out of that godforsaken cemetery. In order to ensure that the bloodlines in the area remain noble and are, I quote, 'not contaminated by that impure clan'. Which has also, incidentally besmirched our family's honour — some matter of an unfortunate elopement involving his daughter. Imagine Tedi-Poonch, the family's name has been tarnished! Anyway, if I agree to assist him militarily, and we drive out the pompous Brigadier and his foul-blooded troupe, the whole godforsaken Cemetery becomes my territory, ghosts and all! Well Tedi Poonch, which offer shall I accept?"

"Whichever offers the best return on investment sir," replied Tedi Poonch automatically, skillfully sandwiching a dishy little bandari between himself and Haramisahib.

"You see, Tedi Poonch, this puts me in a dilemma of sorts! On the one hand is my dear brother wanting to kiss and make up and offering me a ghost-infested cemetery as a present. On the other, I have this pompous ass of a Brigadier offering me the entire Northern Ridge if I would just stab my brother in the back! Such nice simians we have in the neighbourhood!"

"So have you decided what to do sir?"

"Of course I have. Since they are both offers I can hardly refuse, I have delightedly accepted both of them!" He pinched a bandari till she squealed. "Now my dears, thank you very much and scuttle off. I have work to do and plans to make..."

Some twenty-five kilometres south of the Flagstaff Tower sprawled the massive stone citadel of Tughlakabad; certainly one amongst the most forbidding fortresses in all of India.

The enormous impregnable edifice was built by the terrible Ghiyas-Ud-Din Tughlaq between 1321 and 1325 on the spur of a rocky escarpment and was surrounded by not only a deep moat, but also by a (now dry) large lake. The burly rampart walls, thirty feet thick in places, straddle a perimeter of around eight and a half kilometres and rise between fifteen and thirty metres into the burnished Delhi sky. In its day, a barrack-township flourished between these frowning walls; today only dust devils and ancient legends haunt the place. Legends about huge underground tanks filled with molten gold; of secret tunnels burrowing all the way to Agra; of poisonous wells and dungeons so deep only the ghosts of those thrown inside them making their way out again; and of powerful curses deeming that this magnificent fortress city would be ignored by all excepting shepherds and their goats. The marble tomb of Ghiyas-Ud-Din Tughlaq, still well preserved, lies adjacent to the main structure, protected by its own moat and linked to it by an umbilical causeway. By some strange coincidence, the ruined hunting lodge on the Ridge where Leechadji had tried to blackmail Bibi-Do was built in 1353 by a descendant of Ghiyas-Ud-Din: Feroz Shah Tughlaq. Inside the massive walls the rubble lies strewn everywhere — boulders as big as houses, massive bastions that have begun to crumble and cave in, and walls that have avalanched down in sections.

If you stand atop one of the great rumbling turrets and gaze northwards, a chill of apprehension may creep up on you. For now, this giant and forbidding fortress seems to be under relentless attack and siege itself, threatened by the dreadful phalanxes of apartments built by the Delhi Development Authority, which inexorably inch closer and closer to its shattered walls. How the mighty are fallen! If the Angel of

Death had been kept at bay successfully by the walls of this fort — as some say had been the intention — there is no keeping at bay the more invidious Angel of Development.

Already, as far as the Delhizen macaques were concerned, the fort and the wooded park nearby had been ruthlessly encroached upon, or in the journalist's lexicon, 'land-grabbed'. The much feared freebooter and self styled 'Nawab', the terrible Bade Badtameez, and his horde, had descended from the north one brilliant winter morning, and without warning, had fallen upon and decimated the peaceable troupe that had inhabited the area for as long as anyone could remember. The old, with their slow, peaceful and cultured ways, had given way to the new; the brash, savage and crude. Badtameez and his horde, originally from the ghastly small towns of neighbouring Haryana and Uttar Pradesh, had long heard of the great wealth and power of the capital city, and had lusted after them. Badtameez had in fact been extremely surprised by the ease with which he had annexed this, its supposedly most formidable fortress. And now he wanted the others. The strategy he had devised to take the rest of them was simple (simplistic many believed). If he could obtain a stranglehold on the high ground of the Northern Ridge, he could eventually work his way in a pincer movement into the city, closing in on the Red Fort (and thereby the Walled City), the Feroz Shah Kotla and the Purana Qila, one by one. With these major fortresses under his control he could then launch an assault on the most prestigious citadel of them all — the palatial Rashtrapati Bhavan and the Presidential Estate, driving the troupe in power (lazy and apathetic, so he had heard) into the wilds of the Central Ridge.

Already it seemed as though the stars were colluding with

him. He had barely settled into Tughlakabad (which he was considering renaming Badtameezgarh) when he had been offered the Northern Ridge on a platter as it were: his hand in marriage to the daughter of the territory chieftain. One look at the lovely Rani-beti had settled the matter beyond all doubt. Apart from the territorial conveniences of such a match, the lovely princess had aroused his (already excessively developed) playboy instincts as no luscious bandaria had done before, not even his current chief mistress and concubine-keeper, the voluptuous Suna Hai.

Rather on the lush side, Suna Hai had, in fact, spent the last twenty-four hours cradling a delicious secret from the Nawab and was absolutely revelling in anticipation. Almost as soon as the Order of Silence had been imposed on the Northern Ridge the previous evening, she had learnt of the terrible events concerning Rani-beti. (A tribute no doubt to the efficacy of Bibi-Teen's Gossipnet.) Now she was gleefully waiting for the right moment to break the news to the Nawab. If anyone deserved to marry the Nawab, it was herself, and certainly not some self-styled princess from the wilds of the Ridge, whose only claim to fame was golden eyes and pixie ears.

Nawab Bade Badtameez was, at that moment, in his usual fashion, chasing half-a-dozen comely bandaris round and round the dusty forecourt of the great fortress, roaring with crude laughter. The pretty little monkeys fled from him, squealing, their giggles not unmixed with a note of fear. Badtameez liked it that way, especially when he could discern more terror than glee in a bandari's squeal. He would single her out and chase her relentlessly until he caught her, half crushing the little thing under his bulk.

"I am the great red Indian loin!" he would roar, and his acolytes and sycophants, who were only allowed to watch, would cheer and jeer crassly.

Suna Hai watched now through narrowed eyes as Badtameez frolicked in the dust with six nubile young things. Then she rollicked over to him and grabbed him by an ear. Only she was permitted such liberties yet, but who knew what would happen once the delectable Rani-beti arrived...

"Ah, Nawab Sahib," she whispered theatrically, "would you like to spare a moment to listen to the most salacious slice of gossip between here and the Flagstaff Tower?" Her eyes glinted with malice.

"And what may that be, my Suna Hai, or are you simply jealous of my luscious little peaches?"

She pulled the battle-crumpled ear harder and rolled her eyes in mock amazement.

"But don't tell me you haven't heard, Nawab Sahib! It's all over the place! That Rani-beti creature of the Flagstaff clan... suna hai she has..." She broke off and squealed as Badtameez grabbed her roughly by the head, his fist like iron.

"What about her, Suna Hai?" he grated, his anger sparking like a struck flint.

She pouted mutinously. "I thought you knew," she fibbed with saccharine malice, "that the cheap little floozy has run off with a drunken bekar bandar and gotten herself caught by trappers. Suna hai she was carrying on with him even after her engagement to you. The nymphomanic strumpet!"

Badtameez flung away his chief mistress who shrieked and fled. Screeching with anger, he tore up the huge stone steps to the top of the massive turret and clutching one of the great rocks, tried shaking it loose from its eternal moorings. Then he bounced around the turret wall three times, a ball of furry rage, raising a cloud of dust. He came to a halt facing his now silent clan, squatting terrified at the base of the turret, waiting for the tantrum to subside.

"Nawab Bade Badtameez has been insulted!" he shouted, "He shall not rest or sleep until this monumental insult has been avenged. He shall have Rani-beti! He shall have the Northern Ridge! He shall have the whole of Delhi!"

Two mornings later, a messenger arrived from the Flagstaff Tower bearing grave tidings. Chaudhury Charbi Raisahib, Honourable Chieftain of the Northern Ridge and Great Governor General of the Flagstaff Tower, presented his compliments, and was grieved to announce that his beloved daughter Rani-beti, recently betrothed to His Highness Nawab Bade Badtameez, had been seriously injured in a fall and had been rendered incapacitated for life. Her engagement to the Nawab, was therefore, most regretfully cancelled. However, her charming sister, Chamkili of the glittering smile, would be more than honoured to take her place if His Highness found her suitable.

Badtameez's eyes were slitted and cunning as he gave his reply to the messenger.

"Tell Chaudhury Sahib that the Nawab is extremely pained to hear of what has befallen Rani-beti. Alas, such matters do not lie in our hands. The Nawab accepts the gracious offer of the hand of Chaudhury Sahib's other daughter, Chamkili of the glittering smile. There is no need to change the date of the wedding: the night of the coming full moon. And tell the Chaudhury Sahib to expect a barat of one thousand bandars!"

He waited for the messenger to leave and then called Suna Hai.

"Suna Hai, most cuddlesome of my concubines! Summon my lovely damsels at once! For I now have to announce and celebrate my engagement to the chaste and lovely Chamkili of the glittering smile, second and virginal daughter of Chaudhury Charbi Raisahib, chieftain of the Flagstaff Tower clan!" He broke off into gales of wild laughter.

Suna Hai sidled up and began to groom him.

"Nawab Sahib," she purred, stroking him the way he liked, "suna hai this Chamkili thing is a bit of a... what do you call it... zero watter...?"

And continued to groom him lovingly.

Chapter 4

SLOWLY
SLOWLY CATCH
THE MONKEY

Rani-beti, pixie-eared princess of the Flagstaff Tower, would probably have required intensive psychiatric counselling for the rest of her life had her commonsense survival instincts not quickly taken over following her capture on that black Tuesday evening. After the sari-clad chief trapper had pounced upon her and pinioned her, he had so vindictively flaunted her in front of Altu Faltu's panic-stricken face that a lesser simian (let alone human being) would have had a dangerous attack of hysteria on the spot. The man had then bundled her into a dusty gunny bag wherein she had screamed for help before instinct took over and she fainted. Curled up foetally, she regained consciousness for brief periods, only to be petrified by the incessant roaring and shrieking (of peak hour traffic) that assaulted her from all sides. She screamed again once, when the sack containing her was lifted clear and tossed onto a hard cold floor. She wriggled a bit, her body bruised and aching. Then she passed into a stupor once more.

Moments later, or so it seemed, she was jolted awake again. Another hideous, slewing journey began, another trip into bedlam. The contraption she was being transported in this time (an autorickshaw) bucked and shuddered so much that it was impossible for even her teeth to chatter properly. Again, the traumatised princess simply passed out.

The sound of gruff human voices awoke her and then hard, bony fingers closed over her trembling body. She was dragged out into the blinding sunlight and cast onto a rough cement floor. The powerful reek of strange and unknown simians assailed her tentative nostrils. A new fear flamed through her. She rolled over onto her back and shut her eyes, her heart beating as rapid a tattoo as Bibi-Do had rapped across Altu Faltu's face that same morning. Very slowly, she opened her eyes and peeped through slitted fingers. High above, a sloping corrugated roof blocked out the sky and the trees. Sunlight flooded in from one side, where a wire mesh stretched upwards all the way to the roof. On the other side was a blank stained cement wall, with a mezzanine row of small cells.

She was obviously in an enclosure of some kind.

Caged.

But what caught her attention immediately was the soft but excited murmur of simian voices. There were monkeys very close by! Painfully she sat up and looked around. At one end of the cage, a huddle of fifteen or twenty Rhesus regarded her in that unsettling, blinking, bobbing way that monkeys have. Occasionally, they would whisper amongst themselves. Most of them were young like herself — in fact there was only one large grizzled and wise-looking elder in the group, which she thought was distinctly odd.

He now made his way towards her with grave dignity and

a presidential smile. But she was not to be fooled or taken in! Gibbering and whimpering, she fled to the far corner of the enclosure. Even so, he continued padding towards her, in much the same manner as Leechad had done on the bridge over the Khooni Khan Jheel. Now some of the others too had started towards her, exchanging glances amongst themselves.

The golden-eyed princess of the Flagstaff Tower and coura-geous 'elopee' of the wimp Altu Faltu braced herself for this, the final indignity and trauma: to be raped and ravished by this silken-footed elder and then, turn by turn, by his lank-limbed acolytes closing ranks behind him.

But equally she waited, with a grimace of distaste, to bite his walnuts off, for she was not Rani-beti, daughter of Chaudhury Charbi Raisahib and lover of Altu Faltu for nothing!

Halfway across the sunlit cage however, the grizzled elder stopped and squatted on his haunches. And appraised her gravely.

"Good morning!" he said in a voice so paternal, it made her hair stand on end. "And welcome to the National Centre of Simian Edification and Entertainment. My name is Professor Guruganthalji and I am Director here."

She blinked. "This is the what?" she asked faintly.

He smiled kindly. "The National Centre of Simian Edification and Entertainment at the National Zoological Park, New Delhi," he repeated slowly.

"The zoo?" she whispered, her heart sinking. "Oh no!"

"You'll be starting off as Apprentice Simian Grade IV on a provisional basis..."

"Apprentice Simian? What's that?"

"Trial monkey..."

"I'm afraid I don't understand. I'm not an Apprentice

Simian or Trial monkey. I'm Rani-beti, daughter of Chaudhury Charbi Raisahib of the Flagstaff clan and... wife of Altu Faltu of the Nicholson troupe..." She broke off weakly and looked around. Here, she was nothing but a zoo monkey. The shame!

"Ah, don't worry my dear! Here, you are one of us," said the elder creamily.

"But... but I still don't understand!" The panic welled up and she looked around wildly. But then, good sense and breeding prevailed. She took a deep breath. "I don't understand. I was abducted last evening. Trapped in a net and brought here... like some wild animal. And now you're telling me that I'm an Apprentice Simian. I'm Rani-beti, a princess!"

He nodded sympathetically. (They all had delusions of grandeur, didn't they?) "I know, I know. But you've now become a participant in the great National Simian Rehabilitation Programme."

And suddenly it all became too much for her. The princess of the Flagstaff Tower broke down and sobbed with uncontrollable abandon.

"There, there, my dear. You mustn't cry like that," admonished the paternal Professor. "Tabli, go get her something to eat. Then take her to my cell to rest." He wrapped a comforting arm around her and she was too wrought to even attempt to pull away. "Perhaps you would like to spend some time at the Displaced Simian Trauma and Rehabilitation Centre, next door. I am Director of that too."

"Noo..." wept the golden-eyed princess. "I just want to go back to the Ridge and be with Altu Faltooo."

But she let herself be led to the Professor's little monastic cell, and slept.

She awoke several hours later, much refreshed and calmer. As she opened her eyes, she was greeted by the somewhat reverent sight of Professor Guruganthalji squatting silently in the path of the single beam of sunlight that slanted through the cell's narrow window. His hands were folded across his belly, his heavy shoulders were hunched, and he blinked pensively every now and then.

The events of the immediate past washed over her again like a breaking wave and the little princess whimpered in distress. The big silent monkey turned and smiled at her kindly.

"Ah, feeling better now? Rested? Good! Now perhaps, if you feel like it, you can tell me all about it."

The query was gentle; the voice so compassionate and persuasive and she wanted so badly to talk and talk and talk about this terrible tragedy that had so destroyed her happiness (really, to scream and pull the fur off all those who had done this to her but she was a princess after all...).

Tentatively, haltingly, she began, and suddenly it all came out in one big cathartic rush. The kindly Professor listened intently, contributing only the occasional sympathetic murmur or encouraging noise when emotion and sentiment overcame her.

"...and now, here I am, locked up in a cage, a zoo animal, and will never see Altu Faltu again!" the princess concluded tearfully, swallowing back huge sobs. And lest she seem ungrateful (she was at their mercy after all), added somewhat incoherently. "I mean all of you have been very sweet and kind to me and I thank you with all my heart, but a zoo cage is no place for a royal princess. I don't think I'll be able to take it!"

The Professor smiled what she was soon to dub his private, beatific smile and nodded. "Ah yes, Rani-beti. At the moment you rightly feel you may not be able to take it. But you will gradually learn that appearances can be deceptive. And that under the skin, we are all the same. Let me introduce you to some of the others now."

She followed him out of the cell into the sunny, wire-meshed enclosure and sat demurely by his side as he made the introductions.

"Ah, this is Tabli, whom you met before. She's a Senior Assistant Simian. And this is Tabla, Executive Cage Manager. You others come on and introduce yourselves." One by one, they stepped forward.

"Hello, I'm Ghungroo... I used to dance..."

"Jalebichor."

"Jamun."

The names flowed over her until she completely lost track of who was who. It didn't seem to matter though they all seemed so friendly and eager to please. And considering their circumstances — they were all zoo monkeys after all — were incredibly cheerful. A couple of reckless looking bounders swung down from a dead branch (all the branches in the enclosure were dead and leafless, she noticed); "Langoti!" barked one as he whizzed by; "Yaar!" snorted the other and bounced against the wire mesh. "Also known as the Chalta Phurta twins," they both chimed and jangled the mesh.

"Enough of that!" admonished the good Professor and turned to her again. "Now my dear, let me show you around your new home."

It was far more terrible than she could ever have imagined, and worse, there appeared to be no hope of escape. Three large enclosures formed a rough 'U' linked by a meshed-in gallery that ran alongside the outer bend of the 'U'. While the inmates of the National Centre of Simian Edification and Entertainment (NCSEE) seemed quite happy with their humiliating status as zoo animals, the monkeys next door, at the Displaced Simian Trauma and Rehabilitation Centre (DSTRC) were certainly not: a more miserable, unhappy and depressed (if honest) bunch of monkeys, Rani-beti had not seen. As the good Professor explained to her (and she wondered whether there was a message in it for her): "You see, some monkeys, after they have been recruited," (he wouldn't say caught, she noticed), "never really reconcile themselves to their situation. They have nervous breakdowns and other behavioural problems, and have to be segregated."

But it was the inmates of the enclosure farthest away that interested Rani-beti the most; from where, most of the time, the sounds of healthy simian activity and interaction emanated loudly. There was grunting and hooting and time and again, the wire mesh jangled harshly as some heavy weight bounced off it. To her surprise, the Professor grimaced in disgust.

"Oh, that lot! Profligates! Wastrels! They're known as the Bhangra Bandars. Spend all their time making an exhibition of themselves. You know, indulging in obscene acts — peep shows and flashing — anything to draw a crowd. They have brawls all the time. Nothing but a nuisance. Of course, we here have nothing to do with them. Just ignore them."

But in the days that followed, Rani-beti could not help noticing that the Bhangra Bandars were also the fattest, sleekest and most robust of the lot of them. And if their raucous parties were any indication, they certainly had the most fun — as far as it was possible for zoo animals. But even better, they never gave up on escaping and the keepers had to be exceptionally careful while cleaning their enclosure. Their spirit gave her hope (how the good Professor would have been horrified!).

Actually, the Bhangra Bandars had been recently subject to a hostile takeover of sorts. On the same morning that Rani-beti had been brought to the NCSEE, Pehelwan, thug of the Kachcha Banyan gang (who had been captured at the same time as the princess) had been unceremoniously jettisoned into the Bhangra Bandars enclosure. Here, his previous experience as a ruthless street-fighter stood him in good stead, and he was soon in total command of the motley bunch. It wasn't very long before Pehelwan learnt about the whereabouts of Rani-beti. He also knew that she had no knowledge of his existence or his past association with the Kachcha Banyan gang. Which suited him perfectly.

"Slowly slowly catch the monkey!" murmured the new boss of the Bhangra Bandars, lolling in the laps of three dolly bandaris, daughters of the deposed chief. And abandoning himself to their largesse, began plotting his own private headhunt.

It took Rani-beti several days to settle into her new, constrained way of life — though she thought the inactivity would kill her. Two swings and a leap was all you could manage in the enclosure — if the area was clear and Professor Guruganthalji not looking. She missed Altu Faltu and the great rambling Ridge tremendously. Also, she couldn't for the life of her understand how ostensibly intelligent, sensitive and sophisticated monkeys like Guruji and the rest could take to captivity so placidly and even contentedly. She had a shrewd suspicion that some of them were certainly unhappy. Tabli twitched and blinked constantly, Tabla would occasionally chase his tail mindlessly, muttering to himself.

Then there was their relationship with human visitors, of which Guruji was so proud. He believed that they were truly educating and entertaining the dumb human masses outside. Frankly, Rani-beti found nothing educative or edifying in spending the day dodging sticks and stones and refusing lit cigarettes and razor blades. If the monkeys grimaced their distaste, the public did the same; if they jangled the mesh, the public would lean across and bang sticks against it; if they scratched themselves, the public would imitate them and hoot with mirth. It was galling in the extreme. Out there on the Ridge, the relationship had been so much more proper. There, the public had by and large respected them and offered them out-of-season fruits and delicacies.

Speaking of which, the food she received here was another sore point. As Apprentice Simian Grade IV, she was entitled to only the most mildewed and over-ripe fruit and vegetables. In a fit of royal pique one morning, she had flung her peanuts (and something much worse) at the wire mesh, screaming, "Peanuts are for monkeys, I'm a princess." Half hoping her tantrum would rouse Guruganthalji out of his somnolent benevolence. No way.

"Patience, Rani-beti, patience! You must have patience," he exhorted when he came to know that the princess was dissatisfied with her peanuts.

Guruji, the princess concluded somewhat sulkily, was always sitting on his fat arse and gassing about lofty ideals and principles and theories, and rarely about the hard-bitten realities of life. There was no question that he was boss at the Centre. He exerted his authority, however, in a strange, seemingly benign (perverted, she thought) way. He would never fizz up and bounce and charge like her father did, but would rock back on his big haunches, blink pensively, look martyred and in an injured tone of voice, patiently rebuke an offender. His bottom line was always the same. He would shrug his shoulders and say disparagingly: "Well, if you feel that way, perhaps you would be happier with the Bhangra Bandars." Sometimes, Rani-beti wondered why monkeys like the Chalta Phurta twins hadn't taken up the offer. The other thing she noticed was that all the activities at the Centre revolved around Guruji. You could not play and chase and swing because Guruji was invariably meditating (dozing really, she thought uncharitably, if accurately); you could only eat after he had, and any kind of 'normal' simian behaviour was frowned and looked down upon as 'junglee'. The females at the Centre spent nearly all their time assiduously grooming Guruji, with expressions of such beatific bliss on their faces, it made her want to scream. They also disappeared frequently into that little monastic cell, singly or in groups, to emerge looking as though they had seen a holy vision. And yet, nearly all of them twitched and squinted and had nervous tics and sucked their tails...

But in all honesty, she had to admit, that to her, Guruji had always been (so far) kind and caring and had not probed too much. And more than anything else, he had been there to give her solace when she had needed it the most — and had said the words she had so much wanted to hear.

"Do you think I did the right thing by eloping?" she asked imploringly. Adding, with hands dramatically clutched to her little bosom, "And causing so much uproar in my family?"

Of course she was dying for absolution.

He raised his eyebrows and scratched his wise old balls meditatively. "You acted according to your principles," he replied gravely. "I see nothing wrong with that. Of course your principles may be different from those of others, but that is another issue altogether."

She was calmed, but not entirely, because he seemed more intent upon examining his balls than her problem. Then Tabli materialised to see what was wrong, bending over him solicitously.

Sometimes, however, the sadness inside her could not be quelled. One such evening, with a huge lump in her throat, she approached Guruji.

"Is there any way by which I — we all — could get out of here?" she asked tremulously, yanking her tail. (God, now even she had started doing this.)

"You mean escape from here, my dear?" The Professor gave a short laugh. "There are a hundred ways by which you could escape from here. The question is, what would you be escaping from?"

She opened out her arms expansively. "From... from all this," she spluttered, "from this cage!" She jangled the mesh to make her point.

"Rani-beti, Rani-beti, Rani-beti!" There was gentle regret in his voice, tinged with hurt. But he had begun to scratch his balls again — did he always do this while philosophising, she wondered. He went on. "I didn't imagine you would be unhappy with us." He lay down, as though with great effort, and three slim female acolytes slipped over to groom him.

"Have you ever thought or realised that you might find more happiness and freedom here," (He was now lying in gay, shameless and free abandon alright.) "in this cage, working jointly for the upliftment of human and simian-kind, than by swinging in the trees with Altu Faltu or some other lover? Till now you have lived an extremely privileged and spoilt life, if I may say so, as your Guruji of course." (Look who's talking, she thought disrespectfully — he had three of them leaning all over him and was grunting with pleasure.) "Anything you wanted was yours for the asking. All you ever did was take, take, take. And now, this is your big chance to give something back! To do some real good! Haven't you seen how happy we make little children and all those young men who think they are us?"

But were his eyes suggesting something very different, she wondered, and why had the three little bandaris made space between them for a fourth? To be safe, she looked at the sky.

"But Guruji, don't you think, that if we were free, out there on the Ridge for instance, we would serve as better examples to humankind? They would see us as we really are. I remember on the Ridge, how much they respected our family members. Here, they see us locked up in cages, and that seems to bring out the worst in them."

Guruji, gloriously, blissfully spreadeagled by his acolytes, skilfully switched track.

"No, Rani-beti. I don't think that is correct. They behave the way they do because symbolically they are seeing themselves in cages too! Most of their lives are as confining as ours appears to be. They may be outside the bars, but most of them have neither the time nor the freedom to go tree-swinging on the Ridge, metaphorically speaking, of course. When they see us, they actually see themselves — locked up and frustrated by life. And it is our duty to assure them that the image that they see is not as fettered as it appears to be. That there is freedom in so-called captivity."

Rani-beti did not think so at all, but didn't argue the point. Already her discussions with Guruji were raising murmurs of shock at her out-spokenness amongst some of the others. But the princess grew increasingly restive and fidgety — and to her horror, discovered that she had developed a nervous tic too. And then at last, the new boss of the Bhangra Bandars made her an offer she could not refuse.

One morning, Langoti slipped up to her in his laconic way and dropped the bombshell.

"Rani-beti, you know Yaar and I do some moonlighting for the Bhangra Bandars now and then. Well, they have a new boss now, a big fellow called Pehelwan..."

"Langoti! You don't interact with that disgusting bunch!" But she didn't sound quite as appalled as Guruji would have expected of her.

Langoti made a face. "Well, they get fabulous things to eat. And between you and me, they're not half as bad a bunch as Guruji makes them out to be. Anyway, the point is, this big dad Pehelwan wants to meet you!"

"Meet me? Why?" She was astonished.

"Who knows! According to the grapevine though, he's

thinking of offering you a position."

"A position?" She was horrified but also curious and excited.

"So, will you see him? And if so, when?" asked Langoti, in his blunt, head-on way.

"Um… okay! I suppose there's no harm in simply meeting him. This evening, if it's convenient. And Langoti, don't tell anyone about it, will you?"

That evening, when Guruji had retired for his evening grooming session, Rani-beti slipped along the outer gallery and knocked on the door of the Bhangra Bandars' enclosure, her heart thudding. Soon she was sitting demurely before the thug of the Kachcha Banyan gang who had now made it big and was revelling in every moment of it.

For, given the circumstances, Pehelwan had really done well for himself. After having taken over the Bhangra Bandars he had revamped the 'system' so that they now drew far larger crowds than ever before. They indulged vigorously in 'interactive entertainment' with the public, including in their repertoire such daring acts as chewing up tubelights, and others of a shockingly orgiastic nature. And Pehelwan realised that he was as much of a showman as a hitman and enjoyed himself to the hilt. Of course, he was still very much a gangster, and there was, at the top of his agenda, a job to be completed, a reward to be won. Now he looked at the pretty little princess in front of him and grinned sardonically. But remembered his manners.

"Ah, good evening miss! Do make yourself comfortable. Arré Banniaji, bring our guest a bunch of cherries. And tell those fools outside to keep the racket down." He turned to the princess and smiled again. "Now then, my dear, shall we get down to business? Good! I see you are currently with that stuffed oaf of a Professor and his bunch of goody-goody psuedos. Not much good it seems to have done you my dear! You look pale and emaciated, if I may say so!"

"They have been very kind to me," the princess averred primly.

"Ah, I'm sure they have! But not as kind and generous as I can be, my dear."

"Meaning?" she asked frigidly.

"Meaning that I am offering you a position here. All you have to do is wiggle your bum a bit for the public — a little cabaret number while the rest of us cheer and hoot. And maybe get chased coyly around the enclosure by some of our handsome young studs. Anything to keep the crowds coming. In return, you get the best of everything. Like these cherries. Also a cosy place to snuggle in at night, and positively no interference in your private life and certainly no moralising and hectoring! How does that sound, eh?"

She was astounded, mortified and outraged.

"Me? Do a cabaret?" she squeaked indignantly. "Just who do you think you are talking to? One of those Khyber Pass bandaris?"

"You can call it classical dance, if you like," he responded, without batting an eyelid. "But it has to be the sort where you jiggle your hips, pout coyly and waggle your bottom."

"I'll have you know there's more to life than waggling your bottom for a bunch of cherries!" she countered hotly, biting into a delicious one nonetheless. "And I'm quite happy, thank you, with Professor Guruganthalji. We do very good... er, significant work there. Not cabarets." She tried to sound acidic, but it didn't quite come off.

"You must be bored half to death! A pretty little princ... er, bandari like you!" He bit back the 'princess' just in time.

"Well, I have been accustomed to more freedom," the princess admitted, as usual, talking too frankly with those she knew too little about.

"Really my dear? Where are you from?" A gleam had entered his eyes.

"My name is Rani-beti! I'm princess of the Flagstaff Tower clan. Daughter of Chaudhury Charbi Raisahib."

"Of the Northern Ridge?" he enquired, leaning towards her and taking her paw. "A princess, eh? Would you believe it!"

"Yes, the Northern Ridge! Do you know it?" She was suddenly homesick again, but felt a clutch of excitement.

"Of course I know the Northern Ridge! Spent many happy months there before I took up this assignment here. Can't say I knew the Chaudhury Sahib personally though, of course I had heard of him. A great simian!"

Still clutching her hand, he leant back reflectively and delivered his bombshell. "I did know a fellow on the Hindu Rao Ridge though. Chap called Altu Faltu..."

"You knew Altu Faltu!?" Was that what he had really said?

"Yes," the big fellow replied laconically. "Not a very big guy, and always day-dreaming as though he was a poet or something, but, by God, he could hold his liquor!"

"Yes... yes, that's him, Altu Faltu! I'm... er, married to him!" she stammered incoherently, hardly able to control her excitement.

"You... you married him? Well, well well! But then what are you doing here, my dear? Is Altu Faltu here too? No, I would have heard if he had been." He looked at her interrogatively, concern in his voice (sounding almost like Guruji). The tears flooded her eyes.

"I... I got trapped during our honeymoon and was brought here," she choked, and once again let herself be comforted by a strange male simian. He stroked her head as she sobbed.

"There, there, my dear! Don't cry like that! Now listen to me! You come here and start work and we'll figure out a way to get you out of here and back on the Ridge with Altu Faltu in no time at all!"

"What? What? But then who'll do your cabarets?" she wailed, so overcome that he wondered if he had gone too fast.

"It's like this... I... er... owe Altu Faltu a favour. He saved my skin once. This would be a nice way of cancelling that debt. Now tell me, my dear, when can you join us?"

"I... I don't know," she whimpered forlornly. "I'll have to tell Professor Guruji first. Give me a few days."

"As you wish, my dear, as you wish."

Slowly slowly catch the monkey... The uncouth thug of the Kachcha Banyan gang had come a long way indeed. And had ambitions of going much further.

Rani-beti spent all of the next day trying to screw up the courage to break the news to Guruji. She knew she would have no peace of mind until she did. Sometimes she wondered about Pehelwan and his glib manner. But he had mentioned Altu Faltu by name (and had described him quite accurately) and for her, that was enough. At last, that evening, she went up to the grave Professor.

"Guruji sir? I would like to speak to you," she began hesitantly, "privately in your cell if you don't mind."

His pebble eyes widened a fraction and he made an expansive gesture. "Not at all, Rani-beti, not at all. Now tell me what is bothering you."

He settled comfortably near the window, in the path of his trademark sunbeam and smiled in his kind, messiah-like manner. "Now what can I do for you, Rani-beti?"

"I'm very sorry, Guruji, but I've decided to leave." She'd put it very badly, she thought.

"Leave? What do you mean? You can't leave here..." He obviously didn't understand.

"Guruji, I've been offered a very good position with the Bhangra Bandars," she admitted in a low voice. And then confessed all in a rush. "You see, their new boss Shri Pehelwan knew Altu Faltu and says he will be able to organise my release."

Guruji pursed his lips, smiled enigmatically and drummed his fingers a bit, then sighed.

"I see," he said at last. And then, very gently. "And you believed him? This Pehelwan thug?"

"He described Altu Faltu very accurately to me, Guruji. Said he had met him on the Ridge."

He looked at her indulgently. "Rani-beti, my dear, you are so charmingly naive! Of course this Pehelwan fellow may have known Altu Faltu, but how do you knew he intends to organise your release?"

"He says he owes Altu Faltu a favour."

"And you believed him! Rani-beti, Rani-beti, Rani-beti!" Guruji's voice had slipped into its sugar-cream baritone.

"I wouldn't like to belittle anyone, but you know the reputation the Bhangra Bandars have..."

She looked away. "I know," she said in a small voice. "But it is a risk that I have to take."

"You know, you are doing a lot of seriously good work here, Rani-beti." (Strange, she thought, he had never mentioned this before!)

"I'm sorry, Guruji. I know that all of you have been very good to me and all that — and I'm very grateful. But I just have to take this opportunity."

He was staring out of the cell's little barred window, into the purple twilight beyond, deep in reflection.

"Rani-beti," he said suddenly, and so softly, she had to strain to hear him. "How would you define selflessness?"

Oh God, no! she thought. Don't let him beat me over the head with that. And tried to frame an answer.

"I suppose... I suppose it involves giving things up... making sacrifices for others..."

He nodded approvingly. "Very good, Rani-beti, very good! But that's not enough. Being selfless means that you are also willing to give yourself up — body and soul — to someone deserving, or to some noble cause, as some of us are trying to do here."

And then her incorrigible tongue ran away from her. "Ah, then Guruji, I too have been selfless!" she exclaimed. "I gave myself up body and soul to Altu Faltu and a more deserving cause you could not find! I was trying to get him off drinks and drugs..."

But Guruji was not impressed. He shook his head.

"No, Rani-beti, you know that's not true! You gave yourself up to him because you were in love with him! And such love is selfish. Indeed, it is the most selfish thing of all! No Rani-beti! In such a case, pure selflessness would mean giving yourself up body and soul to a stranger. Or even, for example, to the Centre here or myself!" His voice was grave and sincere, the tone implying that he was offering her a favour. A kindness. She was completely taken aback.

"To... to give myself up to you?" She played for time, hoping to wriggle out of this increasingly intractable conversation. "But Guruji, I know you. You are no stranger!" She tried to laugh it off but did not quite succeed.

He was still staring out of the window.

"Yes, Rani-beti! I do realise that. But perhaps that would make it easier for you. So would you like to attempt it?"

"Attempt what?" she asked, hoping that Tabli or someone would come waltzing in and rescue her.

"Do you think you could be selfless enough to give yourself up to me, body and soul, here and now?"

He purred the offer like a saint, turning slowly to face her, a beatific smile lighting up his face. He looked as though he were blessing her!

"I... don't know," she squeaked helplessly, momentarily outgunned.

"Well, would you like to find out?" he asked, his voice as sweet and warm as hot butter and honey. He drifted to the door and closed it gently. Then, he opened his great hairy arms to her. "Shall we?" he whispered wetly.

"What? Here? Just now?" she squealed, shrill with panic.

"Yes, Rani-beti, just now. Don't you see, this is a heaven-sent opportunity for you to test yourself. To see whether you have the courage. For if you are able to give yourself up to me, body and soul, here and now, while still harbouring intense personal and selfish thoughts about Altu Faltu, well that would be the ultimate test of your selflessness, wouldn't it? The ultimate sacrifice! Proof that you have gone beyond the pettiness of love. Also, I would then no longer have to worry about how you make out with the Bhangra Bandars. For I will know that in spite of your apparent selfishness, deep inside, you are pure and completely selfless!"

He had clasped her hands now and drawn her close, as though preparing her for a religious ritual. "Come to me Rani-beti, my dear," he crooned, "Groom me, my dear, grooom me...!"

Almost exactly the same words in exactly the same salacious, lubricious tone of voice that Leechad had used in the Serpentine arbour a million mornings ago!

As the scales fell from her golden eyes, Rani-beti snatched her hand away and wriggled free. And scampered to the far corner of the cell, where not many mornings ago she had slept, curled up innocently beneath his apparently benevolent gaze (voyeur!). She then prepared to play the devil's own game with him, her guru! She faced him, a distraught tragedienne princess at bay, the gold-flecked eyes brimming with fabulous pearly tears. She looked like some angel about to be martyred (she hoped).

"Guruji," she sobbed. "Oh, Guruji!"

"What is it Rani-beti, what is it?" he asked, surprised. His voice was so furry with concern it made her want to throw up.

"Can't you see? Don't you understand?"

"See what? Understand what?" He, Director of the National Centre of Simian Edification and Entertainment was hopelessly bewildered.

The princess let a little wail escape. "Oh, can't you see? I don't love Altu Faltu! That was just a silly, adolescent crush!"

"You don't love Altu Faltu?" he repeated blankly.

The princess shook her head vehemently. "You!" she choked. "I love you!"

Stunned, his mouth fell open. Rani-beti was now in full throttle.

"Yes! I love you! I love you! I love you!" She spoke with such fierceness it actually made him a little afraid. He recovered quickly, and loped in close, hope gleaming. But she danced away, light as a ballerina.

"But then... why don't you and I...?"

She shook her head vehemently again and slipped further away.

"No!" she hissed sibilantly. "Remember what you just told me about selflessness! To give myself to you, oh Guruji, would go against your principles! I couldn't do that to someone I love!"

The cunning bitch! Ever since he had set his feckless pebble eyes upon her, he had wanted her. But he did not want to take her in the crude, vulgar manner that say, the Bhangra Bandars might have done. He wanted to have her his way. To lure her into a web of sweet talk and noble philosophy. To manipulate and control her mind. To make her feel enormously privileged and eternally in his debt — for allowing her to come to him. And she had craftily wriggled out of it by throwing his own spiel back at him! Now she had slipped away to the door, and turned to stare at him, her huge globular eyes still glimmering.

"I think it would be better if I took up this offer from the Bhangra Bandars," she said in a small husky voice, filled with infinite sweetness. And slipped out before he could answer.

Guruganthalji lost no time in taking the first bite of his revenge though. The next morning, he called a meeting of all members of the Centre to announce the news of Rani-beti's resignation. He squatted gravely at the entrance of his cell, while Rani-beti squirmed with embarrassment. The monkeys listened raptly. Such a thing had never happened before.

"Dear friends and colleagues," intoned Guruji, as though beginning a remembrance service. "It is with regret and sadness that I have to tell you that our newest and most promising recruit, the princess Rani-beti, has decided to leave us for what she believes is a better prospect." He paused as an excited murmur rose and died like a sighing wave. "Yes, Rani-beti has decided that she has a better future with the Bhangra Bandars." This time an excited chatter broke out and Rani-beti felt hot and cold all over.

Guruji went on relentlessly. "Yes, Rani-beti has decided she will be better off doing cabarets with the Bhangra Bandars rather than helping us here with whatever little contribution we can make towards the betterment of human and simian-kind. Of course, we must respect her decision and wish her all the best in her new position. Let us hope she finds the satisfaction and happiness she is seeking and has been unable to find with us." He turned towards her and smiled. "Rani-beti, my dear. If you are ever unhappy with the Bhangra Bandars and wish to return to us, do not hesitate. Our doors are always open to you!" He then actually embraced her in front of all

of them! At the same time, Tabli came forward shyly and spon-
taneously, and in all innocence, offered her a bunch of bright
yellow bananas — the best she had ever had at the Centre.

Certainly, all was not shame and disgrace and unspoken
disapproval.

"Good for you!" murmured Langoti, with genuine delight,
and squeezed her hand. "Congratulations!" added Yaar,
thumping her lightly on the back. Then Ghungroo came up
to her with pleading eyes.

"Rani-beti, will you please... will you please put in a good
word for me when you've settled down a bit? I want to join
the Bhangra Bandars. I want to dance, Rani-beti, I want
to dance!"

She nodded dumbly and pushed past the excited, gibbering
crowd to the common gallery. And though she was glad to be
out of the Centre, with all its sanctimonious goodness, she
wondered uneasily about what lay ahead. Sure, Pehelwan had
talked about Altu Faltu as though he had known him well...
but he had been so glib and slick about it...

And suddenly she wished with all her heart that that silly,
witless fool that she loved, Altu Faltu, would swoop down
miraculously and carry her off to freedom.

Little did she guess that Altu Faltu was soon to attempt
something far more astonishing than just that...

Chapter 5

A LITTLE KINDNESS FROM STRANGERS

But what indeed of that witless wimp Altu Faltu? What had that no-hoper lover of Rani-beti been up to all this time while his beloved princess languished at the National Centre of Simian Edification and Entertainment and then rehearsed cabarets for the reprobate Bhangra Bandars?

After having watched his precious tool-shed being demolished by the Kachcha Banyan gang, and been subsequently charged at by the bristling Bibi-Do, the hapless little monkey had fled down the hilly winding road that bisected the Hindu Rao Ridge, and had found himself on Rajpur Road once more — the same, long road skirting the Ridge along which he had eloped with Rani-beti just two moonlit nights ago.

He paused for breath in a mango tree in the garden of one of the large houses on the road and took stock of his situation. It was not an enviable one. Rani-beti had gone and he would probably never see her again. He was a ruthlessly hunted simian and obviously could no longer remain in the area

— for either the ferocious Bibi-Do or the professional Kachcha Banyan gang would seek him out and kill him. There was, of course, no question of his being able to find Rani-beti (if she were still alive) in the week's time that Bibi-Do had granted him. Neither would he return home to the Nicholson cemetery.

He was, he thought piteously, a bereaved, bereft and belea-guered little monkey whom no one wanted or loved, except-ing perhaps Rani-beti if she were still alive, and whom almost everyone else was looking to kill.

In brief, he needed a drink.

But there was no way by which he could get one from his regular suppliers — the Kachcha Banyan gang would have staked out all the outlets at the Hindu Rao Hospital good and proper. Whimpering disconsolately, Altu Faltu set off along Rajpur Road towards Khyber Pass, taking care to keep a healthy distance between himself and the dark, brooding Ridge on his left. The saucy little bandaris at the Khyber Pass Massage Parlour, located at the northern-most tip of the Ridge, would certainly have some ideas about where one could get a drink.

They did. They clicked their tongues sympathetically at his plight (he said that the Kachcha Banyan gang were after him over an unpaid debt, as though they did not know the truth), and stroked and hugged him in an entirely sisterly fashion. In matters of love, they automatically sided with the jilted or broken, and had often been called upon to patch a shattered heart and prop up a collapsed ego. Knowing Altu Faltu, they directed him to the Tibetan eating houses at Majnu Ka Tila down by the river nearby.

"Chhang," chimed one of the saucy little bandaris with the

conviction of one who knew. "It's the best thing in the world to drown your sorrows in!" And added helpfully: "If you need company, I'll be happy to come along!" (The poor fellow had such dreamy hazel eyes...) But Altu Faltu's dreamy hazel eyes glazed over.

"No," he said petulantly, "I want to be alone!"

The saucy little bandari, who had begun falling for this woebegone monkey, shrugged. "Okay, okay suit yourself. No need to bite my head off. Go feel sorry for yourself alone if you think that will make you feel better!"

Majnu Ka Tila was the site of a Tibetan refugee camp that had been set up during the early Sixties and which flourished (according to some) on the pale, butter-coloured barley-based Tibetan beer known as chhang. Slightly bitter to taste, it is a cunning drink. It slips down quickly and innocently by the tumblerful, and then slyly makes you broody and introspective, before suddenly turning you embarrassingly and volubly personal and confession-prone. Too much, too soon, can also send you scurrying for the lavatory.

The dark, dingy eating houses and 'bars' at Majnu Ka Tila serve this seemingly innocent beer with steaming dumplings, noodles and fried rice. Freelance vendors peddling dark, ready-to-eat hearts, lungs and other parts of goats weave their way between the rickety tables hawking their wares. But it is really chhang which controls the hearts and minds of the custom here, lightening burdens and purses.

Exhausted rickshawallas, roving-eyed truck drivers, labourers, students, policemen (in lungis of course), journalists, prostitutes, pimps, politicians (small local ones), philosophers, philanderers, barbers, butchers, crooks, conmen, clerks and beggars; all these and more cluster around the unsteady tables where the centre piece of attention is the large plastic pink, green, yellow, blue or red jug, filled to the brim (and ever being refilled) with the pale yellow beer which, in the good old heady days, cost three rupees a refill.

Here they drink deeply, reflect deeply, sigh deeply, pontificate deeply, belch deeply, yawn deeply, sleep deeply and hope to forget, forget, forget...

To this motley clientele came the witless wimp Altu Faltu. It had taken him several hours to locate the place and he was an exhausted, footsore, thirsty and depressed little simian when he reached it at last, late in the afternoon. He edged warily along the thatched roofs of the dingy bars, looking down curiously into the narrow, flyblown alleyways where heaps of soggy barley hummed with drunken bluebottles. Hospitality was extended to him soon enough by a sodden cycle rickshawala who felt inexplicably sorry for the sad faced monkey who had suddenly appeared at the window sill. He also wanted to make sure that he was not merely seeing things.

Alas, even in this time of deepest and darkest (manic, he would insist) depression and personal loss, Altu Faltu clutched the proferred plastic mug in both hands and downed the contents in one deep, shuddering draught. The sodden rickshawalla brightened up and prodded his bleary neighbour. Within minutes, Altu Faltu was being offered mugfuls of chhang left, right and centre by the admiring clientele and smiling hostess, who welcomed his kindred soul to their collective burping bosoms.

Of course, it went to his silly little head! He literally began to swagger after his fourth or fifth mugful. He would grab the brimming mug and carry it skillfully to the roof, quaff back the contents and throw it down empty to the raucous rabble cheering him on. Very soon, heaven be blessed, he had completely forgotten about Rani-beti's capture, the Kachcha Banyan gang, Bibi-Do, and the fact that he was a ruthlessly hunted simian on the run.

It obviously didn't last! Suddenly, it all came back like some hideous ghost from his father's cemetery. It was confession time. Altu Faltu emitted a gigantic belch and staggered off the roof desperate for the company of a fellow monkey (bitterly regretting his rejection of the saucy little bandari) to whom he could pour out the passionately maudlin contents of his heart, soul and very being. He lurched his way out of the alleys and down along the river bank, before entering a quiet grove of stately eucalyptus. Awkwardly, and nearly falling over a couple of times, he shinned up to a convenient branch and squatted miserably there. Through the filigree of silver-grey leaves, he could see the river — dark, glutinous and oily, brightened up only by the occasional marigold wreath floating sadly down-stream. A few greedy gulls dived for scraps at the base of the ghat steps; an ancient wooden boat, sea-blue and red, creaked at its moorings.

Altu Faltu blinked his dreamy brown eyes in sudden sur-prise and sat up very straight. An enormous aged monkey was sitting on the prow of the boat mumbling to himself. Altu Faltu shook his head to clear it of the fumes of chhang. The huge old monkey remained as he was, hunched over the prow of the sea-blue and red boat.

Was he the boss of the local troupe? He looked far too old for that and Altu Faltu had not noticed any monkeys in the area. A sage? A philosopher? Friend? Guide? He would have to find out. At any rate, here was at least someone he could talk to, even if he did turn out to be deaf and senile.

Galvanised and emboldened by the chhang, Altu Faltu slipped down the tree and scampered erratically over to the boat. He gauged his distance and leapt, meaning to land airily on the stern. But the mooring rope tripped him up neatly and he somersaulted once before landing headfirst with a splash into the filthy holy river. The boat bobbed unperturbed and the big monkey took no notice at all as Altu Faltu spluttered and splashed. The shock and chill of the water cleared his head (momentarily at least) and he paddled vigorously to the side of the calm boat.

"Help me up dadaji!" he blubbered, and extended his hand. The elder seemed to notice him for the first time and peered myopically down at him. Altu Faltu saw a deeply etched face afuzz with grey, eyes pearled with cataract, and was nearly sent reeling into midstream by the gush of chhang-laden breath that the "dadaji" exhaled into his face. This dada was truly an ancient old soak. But he seemed to be a pleasant old soak, for a slow, sweet smile (where had he seen that smile before?) had lit up the carunculated old face.

"Beta!" exclaimed the elder fondly, in a hoarse whisper. "You have come at last! They have sent you! But why are you swimming here — the water must be cold and it is filthy!"

"Eh?" spluttered Altu Faltu, as the filthy muck slopped into his mouth. "Dadaji, grab my hand and help me up!"

Casually, the elder bent over, gripped Altu Faltu's out-stretched hand and effortlessly flicked the little monkey into the boat as though landing a sardine. The bottom of the boat was afog with chhang fumes.

"Ah, beta! They have sent you at last," the elder repeated, sitting back and beaming, his hands clasped in delight.

"Er... yes, dadaji," Altu Faltu replied, thinking it would be best to humour this formidably strong old fogey.

"You are a beta, aren't you?" enquired the old king kong, suddenly suspicious, and leaning forward to take a good look at the bedraggled wreck he had rescued. "And not another beti? Come here and let me have a look. My eyes are no longer as sharp as they used to be." A gnarled hand beckoned imperiously and Altu Faltu went up to the big monkey obediently, wondering what he would do if old king kong decided to sodomise him. His fears were nearly realised in the next second. The big dadaji peered closely and then grabbed at him, making him squeal and leap back in alarm. The old crock grinned.

"It's all right beta, I was only checking! So your father has sent you to me for my blessing!"

"My father? Has what...?"

"He might have let me know that he had had a son! Why did he keep you a secret from me for so long beta? I might have died not knowing..." He had begun mumbling to himself.

"I was a secret?" asked Altu Faltu, totally bemused, the chhang making his mind wander again. "A secret son?"

"Only daughters!" the old bugger barked suddenly, thumping his fist on the side of the boat, and making it rock. "Just imagine! My son, my first-born eldest son, inheritor of my great empire, only capable of producing daughters! Bah! The shame of it! Every year he has daughters, daughters and more daughters! A dozen by now. Sweet girls no doubt, but all of them daughters. And my other son, a rascal from the moment of his birth, whom I disown and spit upon even today — he has sons! As many as you could want! Bah!" He shook his head disgustedly, and to his astonishment, Altu Faltu saw a couple of large tears roll down those ancient furrowed cheeks.

"But what I don't understand, beta," he continued, "is why he kept you hidden from me for so long?"

Then the old fogey, who was thoroughly plastered (any fool could see that, especially Altu Faltu) began to nod slowly as though he had seen the light.

"I think I understand..." he mumbled, again more to himself than to Altu Faltu, "I think I understand why your father kept quiet about you for so long. He was ashamed! And now, sensing that I do not have much longer to live, he has sent you to me at last, for my blessing!" The tears were flowing freely now, and seeing them, Altu Faltu felt a lump rise in his own throat, and remembered his own tragedy and predicament.

"Ah, dadaji, but you are so lucky! At least you have a son and a disowned son and a dozen grand-daughters every year! Look at me! I... I have nothing!"

"Beta!" There was shock in the hoarse voice. "What are you saying! What do you mean you have nothing? You have everything you could possibly want!"

"The love of my life...!" exclaimed Altu Faltu gesticulating dramatically with both arms, "The most beautiful golden-eyed, pixie-eared monkey in all the world! Gone! Taken! Snatched cruelly..."

"She went with another?" interjected the elder gently.

"No!" Altu Faltu's vehemence rocked the boat and a gull screamed in protest. "Trapped! Taken by trappers! On our honeymoon, no less! And now they are hunting for me high and low and here and there and everywhere," he declaimed, becoming increasingly incoherent.

"Trappers eh?" whispered the elder knowingly, and sighed, exhaling chhang all over Altu Faltu again. "I have had many memorable encounters with trappers in my day. Even chased them down roads and knocked them off their bicycles. So that is why you have sought me out. To get my blessing and ask my advice about trappers. Aaao beta, stop whimpering and come with me. We'll have some chhang and I will tell you how I deal with trappers!"

The sun was slanting blood orange over the river waters as they made their way back into the maze of alleys at Majnu Ka Tila. Evidently the elder was a much respected regular here, for he stalked regally through the narrow lanes, his tail arched high, an expression of acute condescension on his face. Wet and bedraggled, Altu Faltu scampered by his side like a sodden dishcloth. They ducked into a small back room, lit by a couple of flickering candles. On a trestle table, a huge deckchi of chhang frothed gently.

"She's gone," lamented Altu Faltu again, after yet another tumblerful. "And I'll never see her sweet face again!"

"Then forget her," advised the elder who had also helped himself liberally and was now noisily smacking his lips. "Forget her."

"Never! I will never forget her!" Altu Faltu stamped his foot petulantly.

"Then beta, you will have to find her, no?" The elder belched delicately.

"Where?" wailed Altu Faltu, and hiccoughed back like a pistol shot.

"Everywhere beta! She may be anywhere!" announced the elder gravely. Adding, "She is of a good family I hope?"

"Oh God!" moaned Altu Faltu.

"You know, you look and sound just like your father, beta," remarked the elder unexpectedly. But Altu Faltu couldn't care less whom he looked or sounded like.

"I don't give a damn about whom I look or sound like," he replied ungratefully. "I just want to find her!"

"Then you must go and look for her, no?" the elder prompted again, "And not waste time drinking chhang and moaning. But you have my blessings, beta! Now tell me about this trapping..." A glint had entered the old monkey's eye and he leaned forward keenly.

"Tell me beta, were you actually present at the scene when your beloved was trapped?"

"I was! I was going to leap to her rescue when my mother grabbled me and forcibly held me back!"

"Ah, mothers! What they will not do for their sons! Even destroy them if they think it is for their own good! But tell me beta, what were these trappers like?"

"Oh they have been seen in the area before. The chief trapper wears a sari..."

"Ah, the old sariwalla! Still up to his no good tricks! Beta, I know that one: a sly, scheming jackal. Smells like one too. But a dangerous one that. He would have taken your beloved to wherever he would get the best price for her. Perhaps the market at Jama Masjid, or a circus, or God forbid, a laboratory, or the zoo. But you'd better start searching quickly, for there are many handsome devils that are locked up in captivity and your beloved might soon find it difficult to remember you if she remains locked up with them for too long!"

"Rani-beti will never forget me!"

The elder looked up slowly from his tumbler.

"Rani-beti? Did you say Rani-beti?"

"Yes! My beloved! My abducted beloved! She would never forget me! Ah dadaji, I am sorry, I forgot to introduce myself — I got upset and carried away. My name is Altu Faltu..."

"Your name is Altu Faltu and your beloved is Rani-beti? Am I hearing you correctly beta, or have I consumed too much chhang?"

"I am Altu Faltu. I know that. And my beloved is Rani-beti. I know that too. . ." Altu Faltu sounded as though he were trying to convince himself. This old bugger was confusing him so.

"And your father?" asked the elder. "Who is your good father?"

"My father? My good father is a pompous old fart called Brigadier Lad Sahib!" retorted Altu Faltu with astounding disrespect.

"Lad Sahib? But my son is no Lad Sahib! My son is Chaudhury Charbi Raisahib, chieftain of the Flagstaff Tower clan! Then... then you are not the secret bastard son of Charbi as I have been thinking all this time!"

"No! But come to think of it, dadaji, Charbisahib does look like you and Rani-beti smiles just like you too," prattled Altu Faltu with astonishing gumption, all credit to the beer though. "I should have guessed who you were!" He had not quite realised how potentially dangerous his situation could turn out to be. The elder was evidently still figuring the matter out.

"And you are beloved of Rani-beti, who is my favourite and most precious jewel of a grand-daughter!"

"Precious jewel is right dadaji! Did you know she is made of pure gold and eats rubies while sitting in emerald cathedrals," waxed Altu Faltu, getting completely carried away. "And who now lies trapped, trapped, trapped!" he bawled, suddenly losing control and bursting into tears. He sniffed loudly and gulped. "Who are you dadaji?" he asked, bemused, foolish and drunkenly forgetful till the last.

"Who am I? By God beta, you must have drunk a lot to be able to look me in the eye and ask me that question! Or else, wah, what courage you have! I am telling you that Chaudhury Charbi Raisahib is my eldest son who only has daughters and no sons, not even bastard ones like you; and you are telling me that I look like Charbi and smile like golden Rani-beti, and yet you are asking me who I am! Arre budhoo, I am a monkey's uncle, who else!"

"Whose uncle?" asked Altu Faltu gloriously befuddled.

The grand old simian sat up creakingly, as straight as he could and burped like a drum roll of thunder.

"Beta, I am Chaudhury Taza Raisahib, respected father of Chaudhury Charbi Raisahib, chieftain of the Flagstaff Tower clan, now living in self-imposed exile," he declared patiently and with shining clarity.

"Oh," mumbled Altu Faltu, hazily aware that yet again he had made a faux pas but not quite clued in as to its nature and extent. "Then that makes you Rani-beti's grandfather!" he deduced brightly.

Then and only then did the implications begin to sink in like lead in his belly.

"Oh no!" he squeaked dismally. Trust his luck! Of all the thousands of Delhizens in the city, to have unerringly sought out none other than Rani-beti's formidable grandfather for friend, philosoper and guide! To whom he had already unburdened the contents of his heart and soul. Talk about fraternising with the enemy! This enemy would no doubt kill him for dishonouring the clan and deflowering his precious grand-daughter. These old dada chieftains were notoriously feudal in their ways and this ancient king kong was also at least ten times as strong as he was.

He began to edge nervously towards the door, wondering whether he ought to dart in, blow the candles out and escape in the darkness. To his surprise, he saw that the old crock still wore an extremely benign expression on his face and was not bristling with outrage as he would have expected any self-respecting grand-father of Rani-beti to have been.

"Wait!" the elder commanded calmly. "Even if you are Altu Faltu, you are still beloved of Rani-beti, isn't that so? That makes you a potential grand-son-in-law! Well, if that Charbi can't have a son or even a bastard son, at least he can have a son-in-law. You have my blessings beta, jeete raho!"

"How can I jeete raho?" wept Altu Faltu bitterly, promptly helping himself to another glassful of chhang. "When my beloved Rani-beti lies captured by trappers, God knows where!"

"Then beta, as I have been telling you again and again, it is your duty to go and look for her." The grand old Chaudhury drank deeply. "Rani-beti is far too pretty for her own good and may easily be led astray!"

Altu Faltu had nearly fallen asleep.

A puzzled expression entered the Chaudhury's rheumy eyes. He gazed at the nodding Altu Faltu wonderingly, as though struggling with some great doubt. At last he spoke.

"Tell me beta," he probed gently, "if you are Altu Faltu and beloved of Rani-beti, then who is Nawab Bade Badtameez who is betrothed to Rani-beti?"

"Badtameez?" squealed Altu Faltu, jolting awake as though he had been kicked in the stomach. He gave a hollow laugh and dived into the beer. "That... that... er... broke off! That thug... that Badtameez fellow insulted Chaudhury Charbi Raisahib!" Altu Faltu gestured expansively with his arms and knocked over his glass. "Yes, it was all over the Ridge! Badtameez wanted a huge dowry and insulted Chaudhury Charbi Raisahib who cancelled the engagement!" How brilliant he was, he thought, how pat. He wished Rani-beti had been here to appreciate his quickfire genius. The old Chaudhury looked puzzled.

"Ah, but it is so strange that Charbi did not inform me about it! Perhaps he thought I would be upset. But then, I suppose it is none of my business anymore, now that I have taken vanvas and exiled myself. Why should they bother about a senile old clod like me anyway?"

True, he had come out of exile briefly once, to attend the lavish party that had been given to celebrate Rani-beti's engagement to Badtameez. But that had only been an evening's interlude and he had not particularly enjoyed it. He had taken a deep and abiding dislike to that sniggering hulk Badtameez, and had blessed his grand-daughter's obviously ruffian fiancé very ungraciously. He had made his feelings clear to his son and had stalked back to his akhara on the river bank and had forgotten all about the matter. It was no longer his business; he no longer belonged to the clan.

Chaudhury Taza Raisahib's akhara lay just a few hundred metres downstream of Majnu Ka Tila, and here, the grand old simian had settled down comfortably. Every morning after he had exercised and been groomed (by a live-in-companion and retired madam from the Khyber Pass Massage Parlour — he had outlived all of his wives), he would make his way through the eucalyptus grove to his favourite watering hole at Majnu Ka Tila, where he would be greeted with smiling hospitality by its proprietress. Here he would steadily imbibe the delicious butter-yellow beer until everything became gloriously hazy and benign. Then he would ruminate on the prow of the ancient creaking boat, munching peanuts, belching massively, and mumbling reminiscently about the grand old days when he had ruled at the Flagstaff Tower. He knew he had been a sagacious and successful leader, and his only disappointment had been the fact that his eldest son and first-born, Chaudhury Charbi Raisahib, appeared incapable of siring sons, whereas his younger son, the rascal Haramisahib, whom he had disowned (for attempting to seduce Bibis Ek, Do and Teen and impregnating nearly all the saucy little bandaris at the Khyber Pass Massage Parlour), had produced them in plently. But now, the chhang helped him forget what was forgettable and remember what was memorable, and he was quite content.

In the evenings, the grand old Chaudhury would shamble back to the akhara and consume the generous meal left for him by the respectful pehelwans. He would watch with interest their grunting bouts and exercises, before retiring for the night to the experienced arms of his mistress.

Today, it had all been so different! This strange, skinny weakling of a monkey had been suddenly thrown up by the river, and had matched him tumbler for tumbler without turning a hair. Apart from appearing slightly sleepy and repetitious, the little fellow had shown virtually no signs of going under. (To tell the truth, the old Chaudhury himself was in quite a state of fuzzy logic by this time.) And the strong-drinking weakling had turned out to be none other than the beloved of his precious grand-daughter Rani-beti! It did seem a bit odd that Charbi had accepted such a malnourished looking monkey as a match for Rani-beti, but it was none of his business, and perhaps Charbi too had been impressed by the little fellow's capacity. At any rate, he was an improvement on that unsavoury hulk Badtameez, and that was a good thing.

"So this means you are both beloved of, and betrothed to, Rani-beti?" he inquired, wanting to get matters clear in his head once and for all, and at the same time not offend Altu Faltu.

"Yes, dadaji," replied Altu Faltu truthfully. "Now will you please tell me how I can rescue her from the clutches of those evil trappers? I will be beholden to you!" And there was no mistaking the note of urgent appeal in the little fellow's voice.

Thus, Altu Faltu, bekar bandar of the Hindu Rao Ridge, pulled off his monumental bluff with none other than Rani-beti's formidable grandfather. He had no idea how long his story would stand, and really, if he had been in the least bit pragmatic, should have cut his losses and fled immediately. But he had taken an instant and instinctive shine to this ancient old soak; besides, that old perverse tendency of his to flirt with the enemy had flared up again, provoking him to walk the tightrope once more. Besides, the old fogey could probably give him some very sound advice, that he desperately needed on how to go about looking for Rani-beti.

He was right about the Chaudhury being able to advise him, and (for once) he was lucky. For Chaudhury Taza Raisahib was a simian of experience and had dealt with many a crisis in his time. He was no philosphical theorist waxing eloquent about the joys of liberty within four walls and behind iron bars. He was a grizzled, hard-headed old pro who knew the ropes and who was only too happy to take Altu Faltu under his wing and guide him step by step. Thus, the rootless, aimless, bekar bandar of the Hindu Rao Ridge found his bearings at last, and began his long and arduous search for his beloved golden princess who ate rubies in emerald cathedrals.

"The Jama Masjid pet market! That's where you should start," instructed the old Chaudhury, following this up with detailed directions and the names and addresses of contacts and of likely hotspots where Rani-beti might have been taken.

Altu Faltu soon discovered to his horror that life was red in tooth and claw and not the stuff of linctus-inspired daydreams, as he'd imagined nearly all his life (i.e. until Rani-beti had come into it). It was something he would have preferred not to have discovered at all, but for the fact that he had to do everything he could to find Rani-beti, and if this was to be a part of that, then so be it.

So he plunged into the clamourous labyrinths of the Walled City for days on end and was appalled by much of what he found. There were monkeys (but alas, no Rani-beti) and other animals and birds — sick, unhappy and frightened — stuffed into tiny airless cages piled tiers high. On several occasions, he was nearly captured himself and soon developed hyper-sensitive reflexes. Very early on, he had fortunately discovered that fortifying himself with chhang before he set out could be extremely dangerous, for it impaired the reflexes. He sneaked into several circus shows in town and was sickened to the core by what the animals were forced to perform. Every tattoo of a bandarwalla's dug-dugi sent him scurrying to the source, hoping wildly that he would find Rani-beti — even though it was unbearable to think of her as a bandarwalla's nautch girl dancing to his tune. The witless wimp of the Hindu Rao Ridge grew up very quickly indeed, as he skedaddled and snooped around narrow bylanes and cave-dark shops, was spat upon by mangy cats, chased by mongrels and stoned by rehriwallas whose peanuts he had pilfered from their carts. The old Chaudhury's specific instructions and directions prevented him from going to pieces completely and he worked his way through their plan of action as grimly as if his life depended on it (which in a sense was true of course). He kept his head which, for him, was quite an achievement. But he didn't find Rani-beti.

Defeated and dispirited, he returned to the old Chaudhury's akhara and shook his head with hopeless grief.

"It's no use Chaudhury Sahib," he wept, "I've combed the Walled City. She's not there. I've lost her. I've lost my Rani-beti!"

Bibi-Do's dire Wednesday deadline had of course long come and gone. But Rani-beti was still missing and with every passing day, his chances of finding her became more remote.

"Try the zoo," suggested the old Chaudhury after he had thoroughly debriefed Altu Faltu to ensure that he had indeed exhausted all the possibilities in the Walled City. "That old sariwalla had contacts there. He used to use the zoo as a holding spot. He might have taken Rani-beti there. But beta, I must warn you — this is our last real hope. If she is not at the zoo then I am afraid we will have lost her..."

He couldn't bring himself to tell Altu Faltu what the old sariwalla's third option might have been: to clandestinely sell Rani-beti to any of the research and medical laboratories that used monkeys for experimental purposes.

Altu Faltu set off early the very next morning, the directions given by the old Chaudhury bright as a beacon in his head. He scuttled along the ghats and bustees and parks that lined the banks of the Yamuna, past the glowering grimness of the Rajghat Power Station, and under the Inderprastha bridge, over which traffic thundered incessantly. He was terrified by the roar of the Inderprastha Power Station nearby.

As he scampered across a railway line, he began looking for a tree from which he could take his bearings as the old Chaudhury had advised him to do. ("When in doubt, climb a tree and look around!") There was a column of tall eucalyptus lining the road, and Altu Faltu shinned up one of these, like a sailing ship's lookout monkey. And there, due west, as the Chaudhury had said, was the glowering eastern facade of the Purana Quila, where he was to head. He crossed the terrifying Ring Road and fled across the railway tracks and clanging container depot adjacent to Pragati Maidan. At last, he crouched at the base of the great wall and, taking a deep breath, began scaling it with elastic agility. Within the walls of the fort lay a large, calm park, studded with monuments and palms. Altu Faltu struck off southwards along the battlements and at last espied what he had been told to look out for: the southern gateway of the fort. He scrambled over the rubble of tumbled walls, and at last passed through the magic gateway. In front of him lay spread out his final destination: the National Zoological Park. A lake glinted gold in the evening light and large noisy-winged birds flapped about, squabbling and trying to settle on the acacias that shrouded the islands. Roads and pathways wound their way mysteriously through the trees, and the distant coughing grunt of some large carnivore made his hair stand on end. He shivered, suddenly aware that he was bone weary (and there was no chhang at hand!). It had been a long tiring day, full of noise, smoke and helter-skelter scampering. Altu Faltu retreated through the gateway and found himself a snug niche in the great wall — rudely evicting a roosting blue rock pigeon and helping himself to its eggs. Then, he slept.

Somewhere in the sprawling grounds at the foot of these

walls, hopefully, was Rani-beti. She simply had to be there. Tomorrow, he thought, as his eyelids drooped, tomorrow he would enter those grounds and seek her out. Now, now he simply had to sleep...

But alas, Altu Faltu was not alone...

About half an hour after he had bid goodbye to the old Chaudhury, a band of hefty Delhizens had descended on Majnu Ka Tila and sought the elder out. They were goonda types, the old Chaudhury knew at once, though they addressed him with all due respect and courtesy.

"Babuji, good morning," greeted the leader. "My name is Shri Kachchaji and this is my partner Shri Banyanji. We are private investigators who have been commissioned by your most honourable son Chaudhury Charbi Raisahib of the Flagstaff Tower to locate a dangerous drug-dealing vagabond called Altu Faltu. It is in connection with the tragic disappearance of the Chaudhury's beloved daughter Rani-beti. We have specific information that this Altu Faltu ruffian may be in this locality. He has a predisposition for intoxicating substances you see."

Actually Kachcha was furious. For the past so many days, the trail of Altu Faltu had lain stone cold. The little bugger had simply vanished from the Ridge area (where there was now a more dangerous stew bubbling). He had — after his disastrous meeting with Chaudhury Charbi Raisahib and his wives at the Serpentine arbour — recovered some ground with the chieftain by claiming that he had a detail (Pehelwan actually) close on Rani-beti's trail, and it would only be a matter of time before she was recovered. But Altu Faltu's slick disappearing trick had really cut him to the quick and his reputation was now at stake. (For this was the second time that the wimp had given him the slip.) And then, just early this morning, the saucy little bandari he had been patronising at the Khyber Pass Massage Parlour had yawned, stretched, kicked him in the groin and mumbled in her sleep...

"Oh Altu Faltu!" she had moaned. "You do have the most dreamy hazel eyes!"

The rest had been easy and the saucy little bandari had a dreamy black eye for her indiscretion. Now, to Kachcha's amazement, the old bugger here was smiling knowingly.

"Oh, so you are looking for Altu Faltu! Too bad, you've just missed him!"

"He was here?" barked Kachcha, nearly collaring the old bugger.

"Yes, he's been staying here for the past several days. Searching high and low for his beloved Rani-beti. I have been helping him of course, but we have had no luck so far!"

"Helping him?" Kachcha's jaw dropped.

"Yes, the poor heartsick fellow was in quite a state, I can tell you! Though why it's taken you fellows so long to offer your assistance is something I would like to bring up with my son, even if it does mean that I have to come out of retirement again!" The old Chaudhury was quite indignant. He had occasionally wondered why Altu Faltu had had apparently no contact with the clan on the Ridge (he was a son-in-law after all), but had flatteringly assumed that it was because they knew that he was in good hands, being guided by him, Taza Raisahib. The ruffian was looking at him askance.

"Us? Help that bekar bandar, Chaudhury Sahib?" Kachcha scratched his head vigorously, utter disbelief in his voice. "We have been instructed to deal with him with exreme prejudice!"

"How dare you call Rani-beti's betrothed a bekar bandar!" Now it was the old Chaudhury who nearly collared Kachcha.

"Chaudhury Sahib! That... that fellow abducted and eloped with Rani-beti who as you know is engaged to marry the Nawab Bade Badtameez of the Tughlakabad clan. We have to recover Rani-beti and Altu Faltu as soon as possible. Now where has that little bastard... that Altu Faltu gone to?"

"Altu Faltu eloped with Rani-beti? Then I have been deceived! That badmash told me that Rani-beti's engagement to that Badtameez bastard was cancelled..."

"He lied to you Chaudhury Sahib. Another one of his heinous crimes! Now where has he gone?" Kachcha was almost frothing at the mouth.

"He dared pull the wool over my eyes! Me! Chaudhury Taza Raisahib! But he seemed such a sweet and harmless fellow..." The old Chaudhury drank deeply to get used to the idea that he had been made a fool of by the little wimp of a bandar he had pulled out of the river.

"Chaudhury Sahib, do you know where he has gone?" Kachcha was almost crying with frustration.

"The zoo... I sent him to the zoo," replied the Chaudhury absently, still grappling with his dismantled ego.

Kachcha and his gang bounded off without even thanking him. The gnarled old Chaudhury sat hunched over the prow of the creaking old boat, lost in thought and deeply troubled.

Somehow, he could not help feeling that he had betrayed his new young friend. True, Altu Faltu had deceived him, but there had been a pathetic sincerity about him. The little fellow had gone looking high and low for Rani-beti for days on end. And there was no mistaking the desperation in his eyes when he returned empty-handed from his search of the Walled City. That was true love, make no mistake. No! He had done wrong by telling those ruffians where Altu Faltu would be. For this, he owed the little monkey (if he survived — for they had mentioned something chilling about dealing with him with extreme prejudice) a very big favour. If he could not pay his debt in this life, it would remain a sin he would have to pay for in his next. Again, he shook his head sorrowfully and wondered how he could set the balance straight with the little bandar he had just betrayed. He knew for a fact that the little wimp was more deserving of his precious grand-daughter than Nawab Bade Badtameez would ever be. But then, he was out of power and his son was in power, so it was his son's business to form and decide on alliances and marriages. Not his.

Fleet of foot and well experienced at travel, the Kachcha Banyan gang first espied their quarry as Altu Faltu peered westwards from the top of the eucalyptus tree, looking for the walls of the Purana Qila. It was easy following him after that, and keeping watch while he slept.

"We do nothing!" declared Kachcha. "Let him take us to Rani-beti. Let him seek her out for us. Then we'll have them both! Slowly slowly catch the monkey!" he gloated, unaware that he was echoing the anthem of two of the great minds in the zoo whose quarry had also been the golden-eyed, pixie-eared princess of the Flagstaff Tower.

Chapter 6

TIGER
BY
THE TAIL

Altu Faltu awoke early the next morning, chilled and numbed by his cold fortress bed. On a nearby ledge, a dozen blue rock pigeons gurgled and burbled fatly and tightly, carnally communal as always. Lonely and jealous, Altu Faltu lunged at them, sending them clapping into the sky in panic. He then proceeded to breakfast rather vindictively on the six oval white eggs they had left rolling forlornly behind.

The pigeons' clap-winged panic aroused the members of the Kachcha Banyan gang, including the guard whose shift it had been. Instantly alert, they jerked and bobbed into readiness. They fixed their hard pebbly eyes on their slight and lonesome quarry. There would be no easy getaway for Altu Faltu this time.

In the meantime, Altu Faltu had slipped through the southeastern gateway of the great fort and was surveying the zoo grounds spread out beneath him. Somewhere here, Ranibeti languished behind bars, no doubt being molested by foul-fanged thugs and harrassed by uncouth visitors. She simply had to be here! He had no idea how he would free her when he found her; his first task was to locate her.

The zoo grounds were deserted at the moment, though in

just a few hours, the Sunday hordes would begin to pour in.

As expertly as any cat burglar, Altu Faltu shinned down the forbidding massif with quicksilver elegance, and plunged into the thick tangled undergrowth at its base. Burrowing through the thorny, contorted bushes and vines, he emerged into the open at last, dishevelled and scratched from head to toe. Still up on the fort ramparts, a cool Kachcha spotted the slight figure emerge from the undergrowth and gave the signal. More expertly than cat burglars, the members of the Kachcha Banyan gang slithered down the great stone walls and melted into the undergrowth without a sound.

Altu Faltu crossed a pathway and found himself at the edge of a moated enclosure. Inside this, a few black monkeys wearing silver-grey capes hunched dispiritedly with their backs to him, facing the sun as though in homage. Altu Faltu positioned himself opposite the monkey closest to him and cleared his throat.

"Uncleji!" he hissed across the moat. "Uncleji!"

Slowly, majestically the rare lion-tailed macaque turned around to face him, as a king might for a peasant. Altu Faltu bobbed his head excitedly.

"Uncleji! Good morning! Can you kindly tell me where they keep captured monkeys in this place?" he whispered furtively. The once regal lion-tailed monkey, now distinctly frayed around the edges, stared at him with bitter contempt.

"In case it has escaped your attention," he said, with slow biting sarcasm, "they only keep captured monkeys in this place!" He spat into the moat and slapped his forehead. "Hai! But what am I doing talking to a low caste rhesus first thing in the morning! Hai! I will have to take a holy ablution in the sacred waters of this moat to wash off the pollution! Begone you... you chooda! How dare you creep behind my back and address me thus! May your vile, blasphemous tongue be severed for your sins! Go sacrifice yourself to the leopards to absolve yourself, if you have the slightest shred of decency and self-respect. Begone!"

By now, the others had turned to stare hostilely at Altu Faltu. Then, as the speaker gargled his mouth with dirty water from the moat, chanting incantations between mouthfuls, they turned their backs upon him and continued their worship of the sun.

A gang of crows had spotted the commotion and winged over to investigate. "An escapee!" cawed the leader gleefully, "Get him!" Repeatedly they dive-bombed the surprised monkey, forcing him back into the undergrowth and almost into the brawny arms of an implacable Kachcha. But Kachcha kept his head and froze and Altu Faltu never knew a thing.

He was able to emerge only after what seemed like hours, when the crows finally lost interest and went after more rewarding game. For now, the first of the visitors had begun trickling in, clutching their wafers, peanuts and children.

Looking repeatedly over his shoulder, Altu Faltu scampered across the road and took cover in a small, shady copse opposite the enclosure of the surly black macaques. In front of him rippled the large shallow lake with its island full of terrifying and stupid looking birds. They had small, domed heads, little, protuberant eyes and filigreed black and white plumage touched up with fluffs of rose-pink. They flapped about in disarray and clattered their huge yellow swordbills — with which they could no doubt easily skewer a careless monkey. Small flotillas of ducks bobbed on the water, occasionally taking off in a flurry of needless panic, infecting him with fear and making him look around wildly. Behind him sprawled a large shadowy enclosure, which appeared to be deserted, but he couldn't be too sure and had no intention of finding out. To his right, about two hundred metres away, reared the gaunt walls of the Purana Quila from where he had emerged.

But where was he to go from here?

Suddenly, on an eddy of breeze, Altu Faltu got a chilling, terrifying whiff of a predator! And a supreme predator at that! Altu Faltu froze, his eyes rolled, his nostrils flared and twitched wildly. Again — the powerful, petrifying reek of big cat on the fresh morning breeze! An ancient primordial fear coursed through him like a flame, loosening his bowels; it was the sort of fear he had sometimes experienced when he had experimented with drugs during his Hindu Rao days.

Willy-nilly Altu Faltu knew what would happen next, and that he would be powerless to prevent it. And within seconds, he was struck! Like an allergy, the dreadful perversity that tempted him to flirt with the enemy flared up and took as firm a grip on him as any ambushing leopard. He jumped down from his tree and scuttled along the embankment, ignoring the great whooshing wings of the swordbilled storks flapping over his head. He swerved sharp right at the far end of the lake and went over a tiny bridge in a twinkling. The life-threatening reek became stronger and more alluring, almost overpowering him. But a surviving iota of good sense and self-preservation made him dive into a hedge at the last possible moment. From this position of safety, Altu Faltu peered with delicious exhiliration into a small, heavily barred pen where a striped flame-orange giant padded up and down relentlessly, whoofing to itself.

Tiger!

This was the greatest enemy of them all! One so great that it usually regarded hunting monkeys as being beneath its dignity — leaving them for the more lowly leopards...

Oh yes? He'd show the pompous beast a thing or two or his name was not Altu Faltu! Great huffing, bewhiskered fool, grimacing and grunting to itself, and padding round in circles like a buffalo around a well!

Altu Faltu darted out of cover and squatted on the thick, shiny barrier rail outside the cage. He waited until the tiger had padded to the far end of the cage and was just about to turn around.

And then, drawing in a deep, deep breath, this bekar little bandar blew the longest, wettest and rudest raspberry he could manage at that great and noble beast.

The tiger turned fluidly and in one lithe bound lunged at the bars, rearing up with a deep-throated snarl of rage. Altu Faltu tumbled off the barrier rail and fled helter-skelter, screeching with the most joyous, intoxicating terror imagin-able. It had been worth it! It had been worth it!

From the embankment opposite, the Kachcha Banyan gang looked on dubiously.

"What the devil does he think he's playing at?" muttered Kachcha. "Giving himself cheap thrills like that! Bah!"

"He's mad!" averred Banyan with convinction. "Off his rocker!"

"Come on, let's keep him in sight," ordered Kachcha, and noticed just the slightest hesitation on the part of the gang members to comply. None of them would have dreamt of sitting on the barrier rail outside the tiger's cage, let alone blowing raspberries at the brute before breakfast! Such things were simply not done!

Altu Faltu had come to rest in a grassy clearing nearby, having discovered a packet of channa spilled by a visitor. Suddenly all the hot adrenalin charging through his system had evaporated. Soberly he flicked the soggy gram into his mouth and pondered his next move. How on earth was he to find Rani-beti in this place? Both the natives and the tigers were unfriendly! He wished Rani-beti had been around to watch him rag the tiger — it had been so much more exciting than teasing the surly old sariwalla. Who, damn him, had been the cause of all his problems. But now, now he had to find Rani-beti in this huge sprawling place and didn't have a clue where to begin looking.

What would the old Chaudhury have done in his place? Altu Faltu frowned. The old Chaudhury would have... would have followed the zoo visitors of course! Visitors to the zoo invariably made a beeline for the monkeys' cages — any fool knew that — so really all he had to do was to follow them. He was brilliant! (And again, Rani-beti was not on hand to appreciate it!)

But before he could put his brilliant plan into action, Altu Faltu was brought up short by shrieks and screams that rose to a crescendo and abruptly broke off. They could only mean one thing: somewhere not too far away, a right royal simian brawl was in progress. Yes, somewhere nearby, there were monkeys in violent disagreement! And Rani-beti could well be in the middle of it, or God forbid, the cause of it!

He scuttled off towards the sound of the screams at such speed that the Kachcha Banyan gang might well have lost him had Kachcha not guessed where he was heading. They caught up with him near the crocodile's pen, peering intently at a long row of cages from where, periodically, the screams and shrieks emerged.

From his position of cover, Altu Faltu surveyed the general layout and the row of cages carefully. With a cunning born of one who has had many a narrow escape in the gullies of the Walled City, he darted unseen to the rear of the cages. Deftly, he scrambled up to the roof and then peered hopefully down at the hapless monkeys inside.

They were all strangers.

Foreigners even, he suspected.

Some had peculiar faces and even more peculiar bottoms. Some were painted in the most lurid colours and patterns. Some were bald and didn't have tails. And none of them spoke the language! They shrieked and screamed and jumped up and down and waved their arms about like monkeys all right, but none of them made any sense at all. A big silvery-white fellow with a coal black old man's face, and long, long curling tail, spotted him and set up a great hullabaloo and soon the entire row of cages reverberated with simian cacophony.

Icily, he ignored the racket, and thoroughly — as the old Chaudhury had instructed him — worked his way over the cages, peering into them and dodging the filthy missiles and angry fists of the desperate inmates. All to no avail. Forget about Rani-beti, none of these simians were even of his own species.

But a little distance away stood another row of cages. Also stuffed with monkeys, only these did look more like he did. He was getting warm! And then, at the fag end of the row of cages (as it always happens), Altu Faltu saw a large, crowded room full of rhesus!

At last, monkeys that spoke the language!

Alas, what vile and foul language!

They spotted him instantly on their roof, and screeched and cursed and leapt up with blazing eyes and bared fangs. They would have dragged him through the mesh and torn him to shreds if they had been able to.

"Come in here!" a demented old fool screeched, "And we'll hang, draw and quarter you and have you for breakfast!"

A very beautiful young female standing soulfully beneath him looked up and clasped her hands imploringly. "Oh, why, why must you come here and torment us so with your freedom?" she cried. "Go away, you evil little monster! Go away!" Then her expression changed. Her voice became husky, her body swayed seductively, and her eyes glittered with cunning. "Or else, come in here and see what I can give you," she suggested archly.

Altu Faltu slipped down from the roof and squatted on the barrier rail (it was becoming quite a habit, he thought). Inside, an old crone had begun beating her flaccid breasts and banging her head against the wire. "Beta! beta! beta!" she screamed and then rolled about, her limbs jerking violently. Another young mother was beating up the pathetic bag of bones that passed for her baby. "Drink!" she wheedled, "Drink, drink, drink up your milk my little one or I'll beat your brains out!" Several of the males had huge bloody chunks bitten out of their flanks, and savaged, ragged ears. Their eyes glittered murder as they watched and stalked each other constantly.

Altu Faltu saw all of this and felt his heart fall down a deep, black well — down, down, down, and there was no splash at the end of its fall. He peered hopefully, and yet with great dread, into the cageful of mad monkeys, wondering what he would do if he found Rani-beti in such a state.

Nervously, he inched along the barrier rail towards one

end of the dreadful madhouse, where he had noticed an old, wrinkled female sunning herself just inside the wire mesh.

"Mataji," he said softly, humbly. She stared at him unseeingly. "Mataji, where do they keep newly caught monkeys?" he asked. "Before... before they go mad? Can you tell me please?"

She nodded her head slowly, knowingly — and then just kept on nodding it. He was afraid she would nod off. "Mataji!" he hissed urgently, "Where do they keep newly caught monkeys of our kind? Please tell me! I need to know!"

"The Displaced Simian Trauma and Rehabilitation Centre and the National Centre of Simian Edification and Entertainment," she chanted unexpectedly and rather incoherently, in a voice that had not been used for years. "That's where you must go! Beyond the enclosure of the parrots and pheasants, at the far end of the zoo. But don't tell anyone that I told you!"

The beautiful young female had sidled up along the wire mesh in a manner that forced Altu Faltu to avert his eyes or else be unfaithful to Rani-beti. "Look at you," she whispered huskily and Altu Faltu could see that she was even more beautiful than Rani-beti, if any monkey could be that. "Just look at you! Flaunting your gorgeous good self in front of my grandmother. Just what will she think!" She giggled and wriggled her nubile little body against the mesh." But you can flaunt yourself in front of me. I don't mind! Really, you belong here, inside with me..."

"The Displaced Simian what?" asked Altu Faltu, trying desperately to concentrate on what the old crone had just recited and ignoring this searingly beautiful nymphet.

"Why does no one come looking for me?" screeched the nymphet, spreading herself against the mesh. "They tell me I am very beautiful, so why doesn't anyone come looking for me? I am here! You have found me!"

Altu Faltu fled. But wondered. What would he do if it turned out that Rani-beti was like this? He prayed he wouldn't have to find out.

The old crone's directions were rather vague and it took him a considerable amount of time before he approached what he hoped was his final destination. By now, the crowds had swelled considerably too and he had to exercise the utmost caution to remain undetected. More expert at this sort of thing, the Kachcha Banyan gang shadowed the unsuspecting Altu Faltu without trouble. It was only at around three that afternoon that Altu Faltu heard, once more, the screeches, screams and grunting coughs of his own kind. Then he spotted the huge, enthusiastic crowd clustered around one end of a large 'U' shaped enclosure. A wide-limbed peepul gree grew conveniently by the rivetted crowd. He climbed halfway up the trembling-leafed tree and peered through the screen of flickering leaves into the enclosure.

And what he saw made him wish with all his heart that he had indeed discovered Rani-beti in that cage full of mad monkeys he had left behind earlier that day. Even if she had been as mad as the beautiful nymphet who had slithered up to him in that shamelessly provocative way. For that would have been infinitely less shocking and heart-wrenching than what he had just discovered inside this wanton, sinful enclosure...

Ever since she had signed on with the Bhangra Bandars, Rani-beti had decided to make the best of what she knew was an exploitative job. If she cooperated with this glib Pehelwan fellow, he might be more inclined to keep his promise to her. Also, by doing her job well, and appearing to enjoy it thoroughly, she would show that Professor Guruganthalji that she was perfectly happy in her new situation. He would hate to know that! Mud in his eye!

Pehelwan had watched her rehearse with a professional eye, and grinned as an anxious young female, who wanted a break, popped grapes into his mouth.

"You know my dear, you've got to put more 'oomph!' into your performance," he commented as the golden-eyed princess swayed and wriggled her slim hips.

That cut her to the quick! She would show this two-bit smart alec what she, a princess, was capable of! And abandoning her inhibitions completely, she put so much 'oomph!' into her act, she became a star overnight. A far cry from the intense, intellectual princess who had, just recently, so hated "posturing" for the crowds. Now she wiggled and waggled and gyrated her hips with all the elastic abandon of a professional freestyle belly-dancer. And much to her astonishment (not unmixed with horror — for was she not being corrupted into a wanton woman thus?) she discovered that she was actually thoroughly enjoying herself. At first, she had danced with her eyes shut, averting them from the leering, heaving masses outside (at least her revulsion for them remained intact!). But the sharp-eyed Pehelwan noticed this immediately and knew that the princess's eyes were not closed in bliss.

"Keep your gorgeous golden eyes wide open when you dance, sweetheart, and don't grit your teeth so," he instructed.

"You've got to give those animals out there the come hither look, know what I mean?"

And so she had simply imagined that she was dancing for Altu Faltu and Altu Faltu alone, and her gold-flecked eyes sparkled and danced with a magical allure that drove the audience wild. She had also persuaded Pehelwan to sign on Ghungroo, and the little dancing monkey had taught her all the steps she had known from her circus days. (Where she had been an excellent exponent of Rap-Bharatnatyam, or rather Rappanatyam as they called it.) Fabulous, neck-snapping percussion was provided by none other than the twins Langoti and Yaar, now moonlighting full time. And sadly, Tabla and Tabli, who had been formally trained for this, could only drum their fingers clandestinely in frustration as they watched with envy, still stupefied by the dreadful moral thrall of the good Professor Guruganthalji.

And so Rani-beti and Ghungroo's Rappanatyam performances soon became a must on the agenda of every zoo visitor, the piece-de-resistance and high-point of the trip. The two little bandaris were wined and dined right royally by their Board of Directors, who profited hugely (and fatly) from their success, as every conceivable luxury and delicacy was provided for by their thrilled fan following. (The zoo-keepers, who boasted that they had trained the bandaris of course took a hefty cut.)

Their Managing Director, however, ex-hitman and showman Pehelwan, found himself dancing on the horns of a dilemma. He had originally planned to break out with Rani-beti at the first available opportunity and take her back to her father on the Ridge. Naturally, he would claim the sole and full credit for her return and deny any effort by the rest of the

Kachcha Banyan gang. The Chaudhury chieftain would reward him well — make him Head of Security perhaps — and who knew what that might lead to. He might even end up marrying one or two of the Chaudhury's daughters and that would put him in the line of succession to the Flagstaff itself! Certainly the possibilites seemed limitless.

On the other hand, here he was, albeit in captivity, already living it up like a millionaire monkey and playboy showman. He had steered scrupulously clear of Rani-beti in this regard though, and had ordered the other young studs in the enclosure to do likewise, for he wanted no complaints of misbehaviour and molestation when he returned her to her father. The little princess and her dancing partner had become the most popular item in the zoo, and were being showered with the good things in life. And he Pehelwan, ex-anonymous thug of the Kachcha Banyan gang, had been responsible for it all and was running the show. He had a good thing going, so why spoil it?

But he knew that the golden-eyed princess was cooperating so sweetly only because she was expecting him to escort her into the skinny arms of that bekar bandar of hers. In fact, she had asked him several times about when they would be breaking out, and he had had to stall her.

That Sunday morning however, the double-dealing thug arrived at what he thought was a perfect solution. Yes, he would break out of here with her and take her back to her father on the Ridge. He would spin the Chaudhury chieftain a yarn about how he had dramatically rescued Rani-beti from a potential gang-rape scenario (everyone knew what that fat Professor and his acolytes did to each other). But, he would whisper regretfully that in spite of his efforts, she had become tainted and could not possibly be married to Nawab Bade Badtameez or anyone like that. And out of the sheer goodness of his heart, he would offer to marry her himself, for had he not at least protected her from total dishonour?

Pehelwan lay back and allowed yet another black grape to be dropped into his mouth. Yes! Then, as Head of Security, he would take an immediate controlling interest in the Khyber Pass Massage Parlour and make Rani-beti dance there as she was dancing here!

Of such things are day-dreams made!

He immediately informed the princess of the break-out plan. "When they come to feed us next," he told her, "when they pour pomegranate into our palms — we shall bite them and run! Be ready and be quick!"

Enormously excited by the prospect and motivated to the hilt, Rani-beti and Ghungroo (who had caught her partner's infection) danced that Sunday afternoon as they had never danced before. As Langoti and Yaar beat a snappy tattoo on the hollow deadwood drums, the petite little bandaris wriggled and gyrated and pouted with a seductiveness that would put to shame all the highest paid Hindi film artistes clubbed together! The huge holiday crowd stomped their feet and bayed and swayed and did much worse than that. They showered the dancing damsels with cashews, pistachios, and almonds (and of course, peanuts from the parsimonious). Langoti and Yaar snapped and rippled their fingers into a blur and Rani-beti and Ghungroo danced their pert and peachy little bottoms off as Pehelwan lay back like a pasha and smirked and smirked and smirked.

Of course, they were all blissfully oblivious to the great mystic waves of disapproval that emanated from the adjoining enclosure where Professor Guruganthalji silently damned the dancing princess to hell and beyond and shook his head in tragic regret at this great debauchery while his acolytes tried their best not to watch and clap to the hip-swinging rhythms of Langoti and Yaar.

"Oooh my poor hips!" moaned Rani-beti as she took a breather at last on her favourite perch from where she could look straight into the green depths of the wide-limbed peepul outside. She was still panting but her gold-flecked eyes were shining. Soon, very soon she would be out of this place. She gazed into the emerald depths of the tree (which always reminded her of the Ridge) and once again found herself suddenly drowning in a pool of dreamy, brown eyes that could only belong to one bandar she knew from a long, long time ago...

"Altu Faltu!" she squeaked unbelievingly, pinching herself hard. "Is that you?"

He said nothing but nodded dumbly. And then whispered, "Yes!" except that she did not hear him because the crowd was baying for an encore...

Altu Faltu's heart was falling, falling, falling again, down an eternal black well. There was no splash at the end of it.

"You're doing a cabaret?" he whispered hoarsely, more to himself than to her as the crowd stomped and chanted and steamed.

Rani-beti!

His Rani-beti!

Doing a vulgar, shameless, wanton, carnal cabaret!

For this hooting, whistling rabble!

With the same expression of sheer bliss on her face that she had while canoodling with him and only him!

Here! Not minding in the least, those lascivious, leering louts in her enclosure, egging them on with that thousand-volt sparkle in her eye that he had once known only too well.

To say nothing of the heaving, panting crowd outside, showering her with pre-shelled pistachios and rose petals!

Having the time of her life!

The utter, utter, degrading, terrible shame of it all!

No!

This was not the Rani-beti he had known under the bridge of the Khooni Khan Jheel. The sweet, innocent, naive Rani-beti who had been cast in spun gold and who ate rubies in emerald cathedrals!

This was a wild, wicked, wanton woman! More wild and wicked than all the bandaris at the Khyber Pass Massage Parlour, thought Altu Faltu in an ecstasy of sorrow, quite forgetting that they had held and hugged him when he had been down and out! More wild and wicked than the beautiful crazed nymphet in that cageful of mad monkeys. This was not the Rani-beti for whom he had suffered and sacrified so much — those terrible, terrible withdrawal symptoms, those grim, dangerous searches in the Walled City. For whom he had given up drink (well, almost) and drugs and his halcyon days on the Hindu Rao Ridge. His precious tool-shed, where you could always find a handy bottle. The Rani-beti for whom he had sold a dangerous cock and bull story to her own grandfather, just so that he could find her!

Rani-beti, who now did cabarets that would make any self-respecting trollop, strumpet or poodle blush!

God knows what she did in between cabarets!

Altu Faltu's eyes blinked rapidly. He could not bear it. He had to get away. Far, far away. He dropped from his branch onto the shoulder of a startled visitor, jumped to the ground and was off and running.

The keen-eyed Kachcha made up his mind — and his move. All day, they had traipsed after this exasperating little bastard and now at last it was paying off. He had indeed led them to the missing princess of the Flagstaff Tower. Which princess, was for the time being, safe behind bars and in the protective custody of his trusted lieutenant Pehelwan, who albeit, was behaving in a decidedly peculiar manner — reclining back and having cherries dropped into his mouth by a dishy little thing.

But now! Now it was time to put away this bekar little bandar who had twice given them the slip and was a right royal pain in the arse. And who had just taken off like a bat out of hell.

"After him," he ordered. "Get him!" And grunting ferociously, the pack charged, scattering visitors left and right. Altu Faltu took one look over his shoulder and put on a panic-charged burst of speed. The Kachcha Banyan thugs thumped after him, nearly running full tilt into a small open-backed truck that was driving slowly towards the enclosure where the little bandaris danced.

For success alas, always has a way of attracting the evil eye.

The wily old sariwala had secretly watched many a performance of the famous Rappanatyam duo, in the company of several unsavoury circus types. Now a deal had been struck and he had (sans sari this time) come to collect his property in order to make the delivery. Hefty kickbacks had ensured that there would be no objection from the zoo keepers. (And anyway, Rani-beti at least had been housed at the zoo as a temporary measure in the first place.)

Still squatting on her perch, and wondering where the hell Altu Faltu had so suddenly vanished, Rani-beti did not notice the small open-backed truck pull up outside the building. She did not notice the keepers wave the crowds away on the pretext that a dangerous animal had escaped. She only looked down when she heard a wheedling human voice call, "Aao! aao! aao...!" A man was inside their enclosure, offering her a palmful of pomegranate. His face appeared dimly and dangerously familiar but she could not place it. Quickly she glanced around for Pehelwan. Four keepers were blatantly bribing the Board of Directors of the Bhangra Bandars, as well as its Managing Director, with fruit and sweetmeats. Oddly, there was no sign of Ghungroo, Langoti or Yaar.

The little princess made up her mind in a flash. She would bite this hand that offered her these rubies (as Altu Faltu had so often called them) and flee — she had noticed that the door to the enclosure was ajar. Somewhere outside was Altu Faltu, she was sure of that. She no longer needed Pehelwan to escort her anywhere. She lunged for the outstretched palm. From behind his back, the wily old sariwalla expertly flicked out a net with his other hand. Within seconds, the little princess was bundled screeching into a small wooden travelling cage on the back of the truck, where she found Ghunghroo, Langoti and Yaar already installed, staring at her out of big, frightened eyes. She heard Pehelwan's raging screeches as he realised he had been tricked and the shouts of the keepers. Then the engine roared and the truck lurched into motion.

From the National Centre of Simian Edification and Entertainment next door, Professor Emeritus and Founder Director Guruganthalji sat back and watched the little princess being carried away, as Tabli groomed him with averted eyes. He had his beatific, messianic smile plastered on his face and he nodded his head with slow satisfaction. There was justice in the world after all; that sin-filled princess had got what was coming to her at last. For the first time in her life, Tabli wanted to hit him. Instead she buried her face in Tabla's shoulder and wept.

As he charged down the main thoroughfare with the Kachcha Banyan gang in full cry behind him, Altu Faltu thanked his stars for the rigorous training the old Chaudhury had given him. "When pursued, make for cover or any place where you can lose or confuse your enemy," he had said. And Altu Faltu thought at once of the great, rustling forest of undergrowth at the base of the old fort's walls. If he could reach it, he could easily lose his pursuers there, hide out till nightfall and then make his escape to who knows where.

The problem was reaching the fort walls before the Kachcha Banyan gang reached him. He veered off sharply to the right and leapt to the roof of the parrots' enclosure.

They set up a deafening cacophony and he felt the wire mesh jerk violently as the Kachcha Banyan thugs followed him up. He ducked into the dim interior of the enclosure, where the birds' screams were even more shrill, hoping to take advantage of the sudden darkness. But he found himself trapped as the shrewd Kachcha quickly sealed both the entrance and exit.

"We have him now," the big monkey gloated, baring his teeth in triumph. "I'm going in to get him myself!"

But the sudden and frightening appearance of these bristling thugs and the terror-stricken screeches of the birds caused panic amongst the human visitors.

"Bhago!" they screamed, "Pagal bandar! Mad monkey! Run!" And stampeded out, as Altu Faltu scuttled behind them, using them for what cover they were worth.

Then he was out in the open again and running for his life. He raced along winding pathways and grassy clearings, sending picnickers sprawling, leapt over a narrow channel and headed towards a small belt of trees at the base of a hillock. And nearly twanged headfirst into the wire mesh frontage of yet another cage that had been grafted cunningly onto one side of the hillock. Up he shinned, hand over first, right up to the bouncy wire mesh roof. Then he paused to take his bearings. He had no idea where he was, though he was vaguely aware of the shrill lamentations — "hai! hai! hai!" — of the high caste lion-tailed macaques in the enclosure beneath. But then, glory be! There, through the dense foliage at his right, reared the massive stone walls of the lost fort, not fifty metres away! He had made it!

Almost!

Three Kachcha Banyan thugs suddenly loomed over the rim of the enclosure's roof, setting off a fresh wail of lamentations, and bounced towards him, great bristling balls of fury. He had been cut off! He took another flying leap and found himself haring along the embankment path alongside the lake where the big birds flapped. Banyan was close on his tail when he suddenly jinked left and then right and shot over the small bridge like a pebble from a catapult. Once more, he streaked a beeline for the structure that housed the great striped cats that did not deign to hunt his kind.

Again, he was not rationally aware of what he was doing or where he was heading, and this time, the panic had completely blocked off the overpowering stench of carnivore which even now was bringing members of the Kachcha Banyan gang skidding to a halt on the far side of the bridge.

Altu Faltu skimmed up the structure without a second's hesitation, fled across the roof and dropped down on the other side into a large natural enclosure, moated on one side. A tree stood in the middle of the enclosure and he was up this in a trice.

The big striped cat sleeping beneath it didn't even flick its ears.

Shaking from head to toe, Altu Faltu sat on a branch and tried to control his breathing. Somehow, amazingly, it appeared that he had shaken off his pursuers. He clutched a branch and closed his eyes. As the fear subsided, he heard shouting in the distance. Then his nostrils flared involuntarily, sucking in the terrorising reek, and the panic was back in a great tidal wave that threatened to engulf him and knock him off his perch. He grabbled a nearby branch to keep his balance and tried breathing deeply and evenly.

But just then, there was a mighty, explosive crack right beneath him. And he was falling, falling, falling — as his heart had fallen already twice that day. Tumbling down, down,

down, taking a dusty confetti of heart-shaped leaves and small twigs with him.

He thumped face down, limbs astraddle, onto a warm steel-muscled body, his breath going out of him in a great whoosh. Instinctively, he clutched at the body as he had clutched his mother's breast or back for most of the first year of his life. But this was not Lady Ladsahib's snug belly or back! For the monster it belonged to erupted with an earsplitting roar and reared straight up into the air. And from the corner of his eyes, Altu Faltu saw, with utter and total horror, the deadly black flames fanning across the rich sunset body, and he felt his nostrils sear with the hot, hot reek of tiger! tiger! tiger!

He shut his eyes and gibbered, plunging his fingers deep into the animal's great neck (as Leechad had done to him for other reasons) knowing that he was safest in this most dangerous of positions. The tiger took off with an explosive roar, racing in great bounds along the narrow tamped pathway that ran around his enclosure, down past the green duckweed moat and along the high barred sides.

He had been snoozing comfortably under the tree when something small and bony had fallen with a thump on his neck and clung on. He raced in blind panic around his enclosure a dozen times, trying to shake the stubborn creature off.

And thus, there, for all to see, was wonderwimp Altu Faltu, benighted lover of Rani-beti (cabaret dancer!) riding the tiger, his lips drawn back in a rictus of terror, but riding the tiger by God!

The tiger now realised what he ought to have done in the first place. He sprang into a grassy clearing in the centre of his enclosure, skidded to a halt, and dignity be dammed, rolled over onto his back. In the nick of time, and only because he possessed a monkey's reflexes that had been honed to perfection by the old Chaudhury, Altu Faltu leapt well clear. The great cat was on his feet in a trice, snarling and swirling to meet and slaughter his unknown enemy. His great cord-like tail thwacked down at Altu Faltu's feet and in an instant, the cheeky little boozer had grabbed it with both hands and was clinging on to it for dear life.

And wonderwimp, powerwimp Altu Faltu now had a tiger by the tail!

The maddened beast twisted around, his great mouth agape, ivory fangs gleaming, and roared a blast of hot carnivorous air into Altu Faltu's face, who nearly passed out as a result. The tiger lunged with a blood-curdling growl but his tail (with limpet attached) whisked just out of reach of those terrible canines. And then, like some mongrel chasing its tail, the great beast whirled like a dervish, round and round, raving and roaring impotently. Dizzily Altu Faltu saw the world whirl past in merging shades of blue green and brown and wondered how long he could hold on like this. For the tiger had begun to tighten his pirouettes. The burning jade eyes, the merciless flattened ears, and the great cavernous mouth drew closer, and the frightful growls turned his belly to jelly. Just as he felt that he was going to black out, the little monkey bent down and bit the great cord tail as hard as he could — biting the bullet so to speak before the great mouth engulfed him.

Like a whip being cracked, the tail straightened out, and wonderwimp, powerwimp, superwimp Altu Faltu found himself sailing through the air over the green duckweed moat and landing softly, softly in the middle of the mehendi hedge running alongside the enclosure. He was just about to pass out when he saw, with disbelief, a sly, dangerous face from his past looking down at him with open-mouthed astonishment.

But this time it was the wily old sariwalla who screamed and fled.

He, and the keepers who had assisted him in the recapture of Rani-beti and the others, had been driving out of the zoo when panic-stricken visitors had informed them of the great monkey chase. They had spotted the Kachcha Banyan racing after Altu Faltu along the embankment and towards the tiger's enclosure, and had followed them in the truck. They had watched, astounded and awed, as wonderwimp, powerwimp, superwimp Altu Faltu went through his paces with the most fearsome tiger this side of the Sunderbans! And then, the awesome little monkey had taken off and flown right over the moat, and had landed in the hedge under the sariwalla's nose like a calling card from the Gods! The sly old trapper's nerve broke; he turned and fled to the truck.

He let in the clutch with a bang, the truck bucked and bolted and the wooden cage slipped off its flat bed and crashed onto the road, depositing Rani-beti, Ghungroo, Langoti and Yaar, tangled but unhurt onto the tarmac.

They too had watched, with their hearts in their mouths, Altu Faltu's mighty battle (for what else could it be?) with the tiger, from the back of the truck. And even though she could not clearly recognise the jerking marionette of a monkey, first clinging on the tiger's back, and then to his tail, Rani-beti had known instinctively who it was. She clasped her hands, her eyes abrim and shining.

"That's him!" she had exclaimed in a trembling voice filled with pride, "I know it! That's my Altu Faltu!"

And now, here he was, her Altu Faltu staring down at her from his bed in the mehendi hedge, wondering if he was dead or alive or in-between. He looked at Rani-beti, now sitting up in the middle of the road, gazing at him wondrously, her golden eyes full. Cabaret and every sinful, shameful thing that went with it momentarily forgotten, he plunged into her arms, vibrating like a tuning fork as the roars of the manic tiger still reverberated between his ears.

But a gabbling round-eyed crowd was gathering excitedly around the monkeys sprawled in the middle of the road. Some had seen the whole incredible performance and were prostrating themselves left, right and centre. Others were hearing heavily embroidered versions of it, and everyone seemed to know that something miraculous had happened in the tiger's den.

Langoti collected his wits. "Come on!" he shouted. "We've got to get out of this place!"

And then they were up and running again...

Hot in pursuit of Altu Faltu, the Kachcha Banyan gang had been brought up short when the little bastard had fled towards the tiger's enclosure. They had watched with amazement as he dropped down from the tree onto the great beast's neck.

"By God!" muttered Kachcha unbelievingly. "The little wimp has gone for the tiger!"

"Taken him by the throat," added Banyan in hushed tones.

They stared glassy-eyed as Altu Faltu rode the raging tiger and then bit the great animal's tail like a mongoose dispatching a snake. To think that they had harboured ambitions of capturing this wonderwimp monkey! One who thought nothing of leaping onto a tiger's back in broad daylight and taking it by the throat. And then by the tail, for God's sake! Was there nothing he respected or held sacred?

Suddenly, they had no stomach for the chase anymore. The eager, rushing crowds had obscured their view of the great romantic reunion between Altu Faltu and Rani-beti. In fact, they had lost sight of Altu Faltu after he had apparently soared through the air like a hawk over the moat. They had paid no attention to the truck parked on the road or to the sly sariwalla — who would, with Altu Faltu peforming in the tiger's den?! And now, they wished themselves elsewhere.

Kachcha sensed that the will of the gang was going to pieces. He had to take control before they completely lost courage.

"We go back to the enclosure and take the princess," he ordered. "Now! Before the wimp gets to her. Let's go!"

Kachcha bounded off, unaware that the superwimp was now vibrating like a struck bell in the arms of the princess right in the middle of the road, surrounded by an admiring throng.

A raving, frothing Pehelwan succinctly informed them of what had happened at the corporate headquarters of the Bhangra Bandars. Kachcha gritted his teeth. Yet again, this bekar little bandar and his damned princess had escaped. Someone would have to suffer for it. Anyone.

"Break open all the cages!" he ordered viciously, and the Kachcha Banyan gang went to work with a will. There were no human witnesses around, for they had all gone running towards the tiger's den. Within minutes, the stunned inmates of the National Centre of Simian Edification and Entertainment, the Displaced Simian Trauma and Rehabilitation Centre, and of course the shareholders and

Board of Directors of the Bhangra Bandars Pvt. Ltd., were faced with a very daunting prospect.

That of instant, unlimited personal liberty.

Director and Professor Emeritus Guruganthalji looked on with bitter impotence as the great institutions he had so carefully built up and nutured crumbled inexorably before his eyes. One by one, the inmates scampered out to freedom, under the watchful supervision of the Kachcha Banyan gang.

At last he was left alone. He snarled. There was no doubt in his mind that that corrupt, nymphomanic, self-styled princess Rani-beti had been responsible for all this. He swore to avenge himself for all the humiliations she had heaped upon him. But now, there was no point in remaining here, in this silent and empty place (besides which, those great louts were beckoning him out rudely). He stalked out, free for the first time in his life. But with a heart full of molten rage, and a mind screaming with all the terrible things he would like to do to the little golden-eyed princess who had given him his liberty.

Chapter 7

SEEKING
SANCTUARY

There can be little doubt that Altu Faltu and Rani-beti, and probably even the others, would have been taken into immediate venerating custody by the crowd outside the tiger's pen — perhaps even deified — had it not been for the quick wits of the Chalta Phurta twins, Langoti and Yaar. Langoti took one look at Rani-beti and Altu Faltu locked in embrace on the tarmac and the crowd closing in with wonderous devotion in their eyes and yelled at them to run! run! in a tone that could not be disobeyed. While he led the way, Yaar brought up the rear, hustling them along like a sheepdog and keeping them tightly bunched.

At last they had come to rest; deep in the heart of the rustling forest of acacia that crowded against the base of the walls of the fort, some distance beyond the zoo gates and opposite the small glinting lake where the paddle boats wandered aimlessly. The twins pulled up in a small, well-protected clearing and took stock of the situation. They were delighted to be free again, but could the same be said of their companions?

Both Rani-beti and the little tiger-fighting monkey with her (presumably the legendary Altu Faltu), sitting some distance away at the edge of the clearing, appeared to be in a state of deep shock; grappling with an emotional trauma of epic dimensions. It was clear that they would be of little practical use for the rest of the evening. As for poor Ghungroo, she too appeared to be completely overwhelmed by the rapid pace of events. The little dancing monkey now squeezed herself between the twins and just trembled.

Langoti and Yaar exchanged glances over Ghungroo's head. Both were plotting rapidly and in tandem, nodding their heads as the plans clicked into place.

"We stay put here tonight, and move out at first light tomorrow!"

"Before the search parties get organised."

"What the hell do you think he was trying to prove, fighting that bloody manic tiger?"

"God knows! Trying to impress her, I suppose. They say love is a funny thing!"

"How did he know she would be there to watch the show? I tell you though, he impressed me all right! Biting the tiger's tail like a mongoose dispatching a snake!"

"Some little guy that!"

"Where do we head for tomorrow?"

"I was thinking of the New Delhi Ridge. Classic fugitive country that, and smack in the middle of town. Over 850 hectares of forest and park to get lost in. No one will ever find us there!"

"But dangerous country too! And rough! Remember we

have a princess in our midst."

"Ah, yes, but she has that little bugger as a bodyguard. He rode the tiger, dammit! Who the hell would dare to tangle with him? She's quite safe!"

"Okay, so we find ourselves a cosy little niche on the Ridge then. What route do we take?"

"From here across to the High Court, then onto India Gate, down Rajpath to Rashtrapati Bhavan, Teen Murti, then Willingdon Crescent and Sardar Patel Marg..."

"Hmm... it's quite a long way. It'll take us a couple of days at least!"

"At least! There are several glorious gardens en route, many of which will be coming into flower."

Their eyes gleamed. Langoti got to his feet.

"Right! I'll inform the princess and her hero about the plan." He propped Ghungroo against Yaar's shoulder and approached the besotted couple. To his surprise, he found them sitting hunched apart, with their backs to one another.

"Er... excuse me! I hope I am not interrupting anything important," he began diffidently. They looked at him wordlessly and shook their heads. He shrugged. "Very well. We camp here tonight. Leave at first light tomorrow. Yaar and I have thought it best that we go underground in the New Delhi Ridge, at least until the hue and cry dies down. It's quite a vast area and no one will find us there. Is that okay by you two?"

They nodded silently. Langoti looked askance at Rani-beti and then at Altu Faltu. The princess smiled somewhat grimly.

"Ah, yes, I'm sorry I forgot to introduce you. Langoti, this is Altu Faltu. Altu Faltu, this is Langoti — and that is his twin Yaar over there with Ghungroo."

"Glad to meet you," mumbled Altu Faltu, sounding not in

the least bit so.

"Er... you too, I mean me too!" Langoti shuffled and raised an interrogative eyebrow. "Er... sir, you were terrific down there, slamming that tiger! Tell me, do you that sort of thing very often?"

But the great little tiger-slamming hero was clearly not in the mood to talk. Langoti shrugged again, and turned to Rani-beti.

"Everything okay, Rani-beti?" he inquired.

"Why shouldn't it be?" There were icicles in the princess' voice and frost in her eyes. Langoti backed off hurriedly.

"It must be true love," he told his twin over Ghungroo's sleeping form. "They've been with each other for not even ten minutes after months of separation and there's already a royal tiff brewing! I'll bet my life on it!"

Yaar nodded. "Yup, you can feel it in the air! Those vibes! And all that taut, twanging tension. Just hope it blows over by tomorrow! I can't stand bitching couples!"

They looked at the pair of legendary lovers. Still sitting hunched and apart, with their backs to one another, exchanging rapidfire accusations in low sarcastic tones.

"Wonder what's biting them?" murmured Langoti, yawning. "They were busy enough canoodling in the middle of the road outside the tiger's pen, I tell you! Literally had to prise them apart like a pair of limpets. And look at them now!"

"We'll find out soon enough," his twin remarked. "Bah! Love and lovers! Not worth the bother I say!"

And resting his chin on Ghungroo's forehead, he was asleep in a jiffy.

Altu Faltu had been gloriously happy for a few brief golden moments. Dying (he was sure) heroically there, in the middle of the road, in Rani-beti's lap, after having done battle with the tiger. Actually, he remembered very little about what had really happened in the tiger's enclosure, except that it had been full of hot hurricane roars (that had done dreadful things to his bowels), huge gleaming canines, and dizzying, jarring motion.

But then, before he could die thus, nobly and greatly, in his faithless lover's arms, some bloody little monkey had screamed run! run! run!, put the fright of God into him and he was running full tilt again. But this time there was Rani-beti scampering alongside and some stranger shoving him from the rear shouting, "Go, go, go!" He had obeyed blindly, only because it was such a relief to be led instead of having to plot routes and strategies and run in strange country, all at the same time. They had come to a halt at last, in this well-concealed clearing, panting and gasping.

Rani-beti had turned towards him at once, her eyes soppy and shining, with that look in her face that had always turned him to jelly.

And Altu Faltu had discovered that he was still a rabidly jealous and conservative little monkey who had not forgiven or forgotten a thing, despite that wonderful little interlude in the middle of the road outside the tiger's den. For hadn't he also just seen virtually the same expression on Rani-beti's face, the same invitation in her eyes, as she had danced so shamelessly for those sweating, howling hordes?

His dreamy brown eyes shuttered over.

"Oh, Altu Faltu," Rani-beti whispered, and opened out her arms for the great reunion embrace.

"Go save it for the cabaret!" he sneered bitterly, and turned his back on her.

"But... but I was dancing for you!" she replied, shocked and then suddenly aware of how improbable that would sound.

"And for a thousand leering louts! Not to mention those great hulking studs in the enclosure with you! Hooting and whistling! Thanks anyway, I appreciate it!"

"I was dancing only for you! I made myself imagine that only you were watching!"

"Well, thanks again! You can see how it's turned me on!"

"Altu Faltu! I don't understand! What's the matter with you? Aren't you glad to see me after all this time? Aren't you thrilled that we're together again at long last? Though how..."

"What's the matter with me? Hah! I like that! I really do! I search for you high and low in those terrible gullies, I get sick with worry, I give up the bottle, I get chased all over the zoo, I risk my neck with that rabid tiger, and what do I find at the end of it all? You doing cabarets that turn the entire population of the city into lathering masses of lust, howling and moaning outside your cage! And you ask me what the matter is with me, and why I am like this!"

"I only danced because that Pehelwan fellow..."

"Ah, so now there's a wrestler on the scene too! Doing cabarets for a lout called Pehelwan? Good grief! And what were you doing with this Pehelwan champion in between cabarets, dare I ask?"

"Eating cherries and plums," she batted off in a moment of aberration. His eyes popped. Then he recovered his sneer.

"How wonderful! And romantic! Lying back and dropping glistening cherries into one another's mouths. What a cosy time the pair of you must have had! Why the hell didn't you bring him along with you or has he gone picking cherries?

Will he join the party later?"

"Altu Faltu, will you shut up and just listen for moment?
That Pehelwan fellow told me that he knew you, that he had
met you on the Ridge and that you had saved his life or
something. He promised he'd take me to you if I danced a bit
for his outfit!"

"And you just believed him? And danced like that? For any
old thug? A wrestler — not even a film producer!"

"Well, he took your name and described your capacity with
the bottle pretty accurately. That was enough to convince
me!"

But he ignored the sarcasm and plunged on heedlessly.

"Well, I don't know any Pehelwan wrestler, and even if I
did, I certainly would not have saved his life. And pray —
what else did he make you do? Or am I prying? None of my
business what the fabulous princess and cabaret dancer Rani-
beti does in her spare time...?!"

"Altu Faltu! I thought you trusted me!"

"Oh, I did, I did! Until I saw you revolving your hips and
bottom in that obscene fashion! And enjoying yourself
thoroughly, you were! I saw the look of sheer bliss on your
face, make no mistake! So don't try to deny it! You were not
doing it under duress!"

The princess' eyes flashed.

"Yes dammit!" she snapped. "I enjoyed dancing! It was
therapeutic, so there! It helped me forget where I was and
made me think of you. Which was a waste, I now see. Perhaps
I ought to have thought more about those handsome studs in
my enclosure. At least they cheered me on! Maybe I would
have enjoyed myself even more. And for your kind information the dancing was not obscene! It was post-modern-

classical stuff which you wouldn't have heard about because you've spent your life sozzled to the gills with cough syrups! And, by the way, what the hell were you trying to prove playing footsie with that tiger? Who were you showing off to? And where have you been all these months?"

"I was at Majnu Ka Tila," he let slip unguardedly.

"Majnu Ka Tila? Where the scum of the city go to get drunk? My word! Congratulations! How wonderful for you! A change, I suppose from your stinking tool-shed. You must have met some really nice Delhizens there. I hope you haven't caught anything nasty — though I suppose you could always go back to your stinking tool-shed and drink up your bottles of medicine!"

"The Kachcha Banyan gang destroyed the tool-shed," he complained, fatigue catching up with him rapidly. The princess remained merciless.

"Well, good for the Kachcha Banyan gang then! That's the first constructive thing they've done!"

"They were chasing me all over the zoo!"

"Such a pity they did not catch you then, no?"

But Altu Faltu was hot on another trail of thought.

"They must have followed me here! Or found out some-how that I was here... Of course! Your bloody grandfather! He must have told them! The slimy old informer!"

She stared at him astonished.

"You must be mad!" she said with conviction. "Blaming your troubles on my poor grandfather! Playing footsie with that tiger! Those filthy, rotten drugs must have gotten to you!"

But Altu Faltu was staring tragically into the gathering dusk. Bitter, betrayed, hounded, chased, persecuted, accused, cursed, double-crossed...

"And those saucy little bandaris at the Khyber Pass Massage Parlour!" he spat with such venom and vehemence that it surprised her. "They must have told the Kachcha Banyan gang that I was at Majnu Ka Tila!"

"Did you just say 'saucy little bandaris at the Khyber Pass Massage Parlour'?"

The steel in the princess' voice rang clear and cold and her eyes glittered dangerously. "So you've been frolicking with the saucy little bandaris at the Khyber Pass Massage Parlour, have you? And entertaining them at Majnu Ka Tila! And you dare to lecture me about the decency and indecency of my classical Rappanatyam peformances!" She groped around for something to throw at him but could find nothing.

"Rani-beti! I did not frolic with the saucy little bandaris..."

"Just snuggled up to them and had a jolly little orgy together, then? To celebrate my capture perhaps?"

"Rani-beti! I swear I did not do anything like that. You can ask them if you like!"

"Ah, yes of course! And I'm sure they'll tell me the truth, the whole truth and nothing but the truth, so help them God! Which saucy little bandaris are going to have the guts to admit to my face that they had an orgy with you?"

"Rani-beti, you've got to believe me! I did not have an... an orgy! I swear nothing like that happened!"

The fire in the princess' eye died down and she took a deep breath. "All right," she relented at last, "I'll believe you if you believe me — that I danced for only you!"

It was a fair enough deal and he really had no choice but to agree. "Okay," he said ungraciously, but nodding. "It's a deal!" He would, of course, somehow find out for himself if this was indeed the truth. But later. For the fatigue was suddenly overwhelming — it had been a very, very long day indeed for him. He glanced over his shoulder at Rani-beti.

She was looking at him covertly through one gold-flecked eye, swearing to herself that she would find out what the little bugger had been up at the Khyber Pass Massage Parlour, if it was to be the last thing she did. But now she was just too tired and cold to think about anything.

And the two exhausted little monkeys crawled into one another's arms and passed out instantly.

The truce was holding.

The first of the winter fogs came down that night, acrid and sulphurous, muffling the world with its great soft paw. And offering Rani-beti and Altu Faltu a rare bit of total privacy, of which they were blissfully unaware, wrapped up fast asleep in one another's arms.

It was still murky dark when Langoti awoke shivering and shook his twin and Ghungroo. "Get up," he urged. "It's time we were going. Ghungroo, go and wake those two. Hurry!" The little dancing monkey, bemused and very sleepy, obeyed.

"Rani-beti!" she hissed at the furry monkey ball, wondering where one began and the other ended. "Wake up!"

But it was Altu Faltu who responded with a startled yelp, thinking that the Kachcha Banyan gang had caught up with him.

"Who are you?" he asked Ghungroo, wondering where this pretty little monkey had sprung up from. The Khyber Pass Massage Parlour?

"I'm Ghungroo, sir. Rani-beti's friend. We dance together."

"Rani-beti? Where is Rani-beti?" he squealed, and then realised that he was clutching on to her for dear life. "Ah, yes... I remember now." He shuddered.

"Come on, sir. Langoti says we must be leaving immediately!"

"Langoti? Oh, yes of course. We're just coming!"

"We're waiting just there," Ghungroo indicated, as she turned away and withdrew discreetly into the fog.

He shook his sleeping princess gently. "Rani-beti, wake up! We have to be going."

She awoke slowly and langorously, in true princess style. Actually she had awoken much earlier than any of them and had lain cuddled in Altu Faltu's arms, pretending to be asleep. She had stifled a giggle when he had yelped at Ghungroo; in spite of his heroics with the tiger, it appeared that he had not changed much.

"Umm..." she moaned softly now, snuggling closer. "Altu Faltu, is that you? Where have you been for so long?"

Langoti and Yaar kept the little group tightly bunched, allowing no stragglers, for it was all too easy to get lost in the opaque cotton-wool murk. They sneaked down the path that skirted the lake where the paddle boats wandered, then darted across a broad, deserted road. The sodium vapour street lamps shone eerily, like so many lined-up dying suns. Occasionally the twins would huddle for a brief conference and then look around carefully as though to ascertain their bearings. Eventually they turned left onto a tree-shrouded road, where the fog was not so thick, and speeded up the pace.

But they were completely defeated by the opaque fog-bound spaces around India Gate. Clinging to one another like mountaineers, they somehow straggled their way up to the controversial empty canopy near the monument. "There's no way we can go further," said Langoti definitely, peering into the gloomy opaque curtain around them. "It's too dangerous. We'll have to wait till it thins out a bit."

They huddled closely together for warmth as the great fog blotted out the world.

"I can't see the end of my nose or even feel it in this cold," Rani-beti complained, clinging to Altu Faltu.

"I say, that was some fight you had with the tiger," remarked Yaar, making polite conversation before Langoti could nudge him warningly. "Slammed him all over the enclosure, you did."

"I did? Uh, yes of course." Altu Faltu still had a very dim recollection of what had happened in the tiger's enclosure the evening before. Even thinking about it now made him queasy in the stomach.

"Do you often... er, get into fights with big cats?" Yaar persisted curiously, ignoring his twin's jab in the ribs. Ghungroo was staring at Altu Faltu with reverence, and Rani-beti, basking in reflected glory, obviously hero-worshipped him.

Altu Faltu cleared his throat. "I er... don't get the opportunity to fight them very often," he replied outrageously. "But yes, I do like testing my skills to the utmost. You know, walking on the wild side, sticking my neck out right to the cutting edge as it were. It tones up the system, don't you think?" He said it with modest diffidence and Rani-beti simpered proudly. But who could deny the element of truth in what the bekar little bandar had said?

"Well, we are very glad to have you with us," remarked Langoti, a trifle laconically. "I doubt there are any tigers or leopards on the New Delhi Ridge, but it's a rough place all right. Lots of fundamentalist tribal bands in the interiors, or so I've heard. The clans that live on the borders of the Ridge are a posh lot though. Think no end of themselves."

"They're always being lavishly entertained by the people living around the area; you know, throwing big bashes on the lawns of the houses on Sardar Patel Road and Chanakyapuri," added his twin, his eyes gleaming happily. "And there's this other lot who hang around the various temples in the area. All pious and sanctimonious, yet ever ready to stab each other in the back..."

"And those Willingdon Crescent types! You know, who live on the Presidential Estate. Baboons! Absolute baboons the lot of them. Most of them are unauthorised squatters. And the rest! You want to pick a few vegetables from a garden, or mangoes from a tree, and my God, do they give you the runaround! Apply here, go there, get this permission, sanction from there, clearance from elsewhere, no objection certificates, death certificates. 'No, sorry, not today, come tomorrow'. Of course if you give them what they really want, you can get all your permissions in thirty seconds flat, no questions asked. Corrupt to the eyeballs, they are!"

"How do you know all this, Langoti?" Rani–beti asked curiously. The twins laughed. "Well, let's just say we are not known as the Chalta Phurta twins for nothing," Langoti grinned.

"Do you think all these corrupt, horrible monkeys will give us trouble?" piped Ghungroo worriedly.

"No, I doubt it. Not when they know we have the great Shri Altu Faltu with us. The one who took the tiger by the tail!"

"And how will they know what Altu Faltu did to the tiger, pray?"

"Rani-beti, you might be a princess but you're so naive!" Langoti looked shocked. "The news must be all over town by now."

Yaar nodded seriously. "Yes! That you, Rani-beti, a princess, no less, were stranded in a tiger's pen, with the beast crouched over you jaws agape. And that Altu Faltu, of simple simian stock, leapt to your rescue without a thought for his own safety. How he bit the tiger in the tail and rode the rabid carnivore to exhaustion, before carrying you back to safety with one mighty leap over that crocodile infested moat!"

"But that's not true!" protested Rani-beti, shocked. "I was not inside the tiger's pen. Outside perhaps..."

"Near enough," replied Langoti nonchalantly, "And let's say there are precedents..."

He turned respectfully towards Altu Faltu. "Er, sir, you wouldn't have any souvenirs from your encounter with the tiger, would you?"

"Not really... a few bruises maybe." For some reason Altu Faltu seemed embarrassed. Then he put his hand behind his ear and pulled out something. "I have this," he admitted. A spiky tuft of wire-like hair from the great tiger's neck that had come away in his clenched fist. "I was going to have this woven into a bracelet for Rani-beti," he added, colouring.

"Excellent! Excellent!" Langoti sounded enthusiastic. "You do that sir, so that Rani-beti can show it off proudly to all the world!"

The sky had lightened to ash-grey in the east, and somewhere the sun was trying very hard to burn through.

"Come on, the light's improving. Let's get going!" Langoti took Ghungroo by the hand and leapt off the canopy as the others followed.

And so they fled down the wide imperial streets of New Delhi, keeping as much as possible under the cover of the great belts of trees that had been planted alongside them. Ghungroo was chased briefly by a dalmatian, who Langoti and Yaar promptly saw off. They gazed in wonder as the imperious dome of Rashtrapati Bhavan loomed up in the distance, and at North and South Blocks, where, as Langoti irreverently recounted, VIP simians loafed and screamed all day, slurping tea and throwing files at one another. Late that afternoon, they entered an enormous tree-shrouded estate where the Chalta Phurta twins called a halt.

"Teen Murti House!" Langoti announced grandly. "Happy hunting grounds for us in the past. We even stayed here for a while."

"Can't we settle here then?" asked Rani-beti, who was tired.

Yaar shook his head. "Too many gardeners," he explained. "It's all right for a quick dash through the rose garden, or a frolic on the lawn when the storm lilies bloom, or going berserk amongst the dahlias, but nothing more long-term or permanent."

"Want to have a look-see?" invited Langoti, itching to have one himself. But safe in the lap of the huge banyan they had sheltered in, Rani-beti shook her head.

"No thanks," she said. "You go ahead. I'll stay here. Altu Faltu will look after me."

"Okay. Come on, Ghungroo. Let's give you a guided tour of this place." And taking her by the hand, the twins scampered off. Rani-beti turned to Altu Faltu, her eyes serious.

"Altu Faltu, can I ask you a question?"

"Yes, of course!"

"Altu Faltu, what were you really trying to do in the tiger's enclosure yesterday? You looked as though you were trying to get yourself killed."

He said nothing — and everything.

"Altu Faltu, don't you ever try anything like that again. Not for me, not for anyone!"

"Okay," he whispered, playing the tragic hero to the hilt. "But when I saw you dance..." He shrugged eloquently.

She hugged him. "Where have you been all this while?" she asked softly.

And so he told her how he had gone looking for her all over the place, and how, by sheer chance, he had rescued her grandfather from drowning in the river ("I'm afraid, the old fogey drinks a bit," he explained apologetically). And she told him how she had pined for him, and had been taken advantage of ("No, not in that sense of the word, I was too insignificant for that!") by the Professor, and how he had sold her off to Pehelwan ("For just a fistful of peanuts, that's all I was worth!") who had made her dance, while promising to reunite her with Altu Faltu.

"What do we do now?" she asked. "Have you thought about our future?"

"No," he admitted. "I've just been thinking about finding you. I suppose we should go along with those two. They seem to know their way around."

"Mmm... yes. Sometimes a little too well. But they play the drums fabulously and can be great company."

So they went along with the Chalta Phurta twins, searching for a hideout cum residence. The twins' original plan of going underground in the sprawling New Delhi Ridge didn't seem to be working out. The border areas of the Ridge, including the parks, schools and temples that encroached upon it, were pretty much occupied and certainly not private enough. The thorny, desolate interiors of the Ridge, where the partridges screamed and the monitor lizards sunbathed on the hot, mica-bright rocks, they didn't like at all. They were city-bred Delhizens after all and this harsh rocky country disturbed them. (The Northern Ridge by comparison, was so much more 'civilised' and landscaped.) Besides, what could a monkey do in such a place except comb the burrs out of its coat and pluck the thorns from its paws? They had met a few bands of wild tribal monkeys who had glowered at them warningly before vanishing into the forest. Then, one morning, they had been chased through the ravines near the abandoned shooting range by a gang of hoodlum langurs who had obviously not heard (or cared) about Altu Faltu's terrible reputation. Even Langoti and Yaar had been unnerved.

But just when things seemed really bleak, they had an incredible piece of luck. They were returning one evening to Teen Murti House, which had become their temporary headquarters, dog-tired and disconsolate, shuffling down the service road alongside Sardar Patel Marg, when Altu Faltu noticed a dark narrow lane branching off in the direction they had to take.

"This looks like a short cut," he remarked, and the others followed him without argument. The lane grew narrower and more rutted, and was flanked on either side by houses tucked well back into foliage. It ended at a large padlocked gate set in a high brick wall festooned with lantana. They shinned up to the top of the gate and looked inside. A huge, deserted-looking estate sprawled in front of them, untended and overgrown. It was surrounded on all sides by dark and handsome trees; impressive stands of shisham, neem, peepul, banyan and kikar. A squat, yellow, oblong-shaped house stood on one side of the driveway, its wide verandah nearly smothered by lantana. It overlooked an expanse of tall golden grass which at one time must have been an immaculate turf. Very promisingly, there was no sign of man or dog.

"It's beautiful!" exclaimed Rani-beti, clasping her hands and balancing on the gatepost.

Cautiously, in the ebbing light, they reconnoitered. Behind the house lay a large well-tended vegetable patch, two garages and a shed with a corrugated iron roof. A light shone out of the single window of the shed. Langoti shinned silently up to the window sill, peered inside, and then joined the others in the vegetable patch.

"Caretaker," he whispered indistinctly, stuffing his face with cauliflower and pointing towards the shed.

"No problem," said Yaar, who naturally had checked it out for himself.

The house itself was vacant. Its walls were cracked and peeling, the verandah looked in danger of collapsing under the weight of the lantana. It was built around a large courtyard, deep in dead leaves. Peepul saplings sprouted from the walls, sending cracks zithering down like streaks of black lightning. The tang of lantana was sharp in the air, and moths blurred furrily everywhere.

"The Villa Lantana!" declared Rani-beti romantically. "Where we will begin a new, free life!"

"Why do you think it is lying abandoned?" Altu Faltu asked Langoti as nonchalantly as he could, uneasily remembering Bibi-Do and her djinns at the Khooni Khan bridge.

"Legal dispute," replied Langoti decisively, looking around. "Long, drawn-out, bitter litigation is the only reason why a property like this could be left vacant."

"Suits us then. It'll remain empty for twenty-five years at least."

"After which we can always appeal!"

They celebrated that night by running rampant in the vegetable patch. The caretaker, they discovered the next morning, was a toothless old man armed with a huge bamboo who was completely ineffectual. He made a token protest about their presence, then accepted them with good grace. He was all alone and therefore glad of the company and entertainment they provided. Within days he had begun feeding them.

Word of the Villa Lantana occupation spread swiftly in the neighbourhood. The posh, elite Delhizens of Sardar Patel Marg and Chanakyapuri were agog. Even the bureaucratic 'baboons' living on the Presidential Estate nearby took time off from their internecine intrigues to be curious. They had all heard of the dramatic rescue incident at the zoo. Now it was being said that the exotic princess involved, as well as her gallant consort, had moved into the neighbourhood with a small retinue of camp followers. This they had to see.

The big bibijis with their ill-behaved broods began dropping in. They wheezed and gushed and oozed all over Rani-beti, bringing presents of fruits and flowers. So sweet she was, no, this strange little rajkumari, whose past they were determined to dig up. The big dada males swaggered up too and eyed Altu Faltu askance, wondering if this skinny wimp could really have disembowelled a tiger as everyone was saying. But they had seen for themselves the slim fiery-orange bracelet on the wrist of the princess. There was no doubt about its origin and authenticity. So they treated the little monkey with respect and reserve.

Of course the Chalta Phurta twins had provided a suitable covering-story for the celebrities in their charge.

"You are Rajkumari Rani-beti of far away Neemrana," they earnestly briefed Rani-beti. "Your mother, the late Maharani, was abducted by trappers while she was pregnant with you and incarcerated in the Delhi zoo, where you were later born. During a zoo breakout, you escaped but were chased into the tiger's lair from where you were herocially rescued by Altu Faltu. Naturally, you fell in love. I think that will keep those quivering bhenjis satisfied for a while. Got it?"

She got it easily, because she had actually begun to believe that Altu Faltu had rescued her from the tiger's jaws. As for Altu Faltu — he never felt even the faintest twinge of guilt for being treated like a hero under false pretences. He just sat back and lapped it all up. He leered condescendingly at the big dada males, glad-eyed their nubile daughters (when Rani-beti was not looking), and was utterly charming with the big, broad bibijis. The Chalta Phurta twins revelled in their role as celebrity managers and Ghungroo (whom they both adored) had become Rani-beti's lady-in-waiting.

It was not long before the celebrity couple's social life became hectic. Rani-beti and Altu Faltu had become the Delhizen couple to entertain and be entertained by. The invitations poured in thick and fast.

But it was to be but a brief, golden interlude. The past was already hot on the runaway couple's trail...

For the big bibijis had spread the word about their charming if enigmatic new neighbours. And the news filtered into the exalted ears of his most respected holiness, Swami Palang Todeji, of the newly established Harbandar Ashram in Lodhi Gardens.

Swami Palang Todeji had made his appearance in Lodhi Gardens some weeks previously, and in this short span of time, had attracted a considerable following of adoring female acolytes. They said there was something magical in his manner; in the gravity of his voice, the gentleness of his gestures and the patient, empathetic way in which he listened to even the most hysterical female before giving his blessings. He was accompanied everywhere by six swarthy disciples with virile names and amongst them were Swami Kachcha, Swami Banyan and Swami Pehelwan.

In his previous incarnation, Swami Palang Todeji had been of course, the good Professor Guruganthalji. He had felt the need for personal reincarnation ever since that slut of a princess Rani-beti had demolished his life's work at the zoo. It had not taken the shrewd professor long to realise that the lout Kachcha, like him, had a score to settle with the princess. For both of them, it was now a simple matter of vendetta, and they were united by it as swiftly as Altu Faltu and Rani-beti had been united by love.

It was Swami Kachcha who brought the news. "It must be

them, it can be no one else," he declared hoarsely, his eyes gleaming.

"Khamosh Kachchabeta. Let me think." Swami Palang Tode sat in silence for a considerable period of time. And then he appeared to attain nirvana. His entire (enormous) being appeared to glow and levitate.

"Yes," he whispered. "This time we shall have her and her consort. Now Kachchaputtar, send the good disciple Suna Hai to me."

"That voluptuous, rich female who is supposed to be a chief concubine at Tughlakabad?" asked Kachcha in his coarse manner.

"The same. She is here to learn of a way to win the permenant favour of her lord, the Nawab Bade Badtameez. What I have in mind may help her considerably in her quest. And also take care of little Rani-beti."

At the Villa Lantana, Rani-beti and Altu Faltu were entertaining yet another insufferable pair of social climbers. This couple's big boast was that they lived in the airconditioned grounds of the British Embassy. Ghungroo was dancing in the big tawny lawn and the Chalta Phurta twins were providing the percussion just like in the old days.

"Congratulations, my dear," gushed the big matron. "I see you are expecting a happy event."

Her gross mate yawned and stifled a belch. "This unrest on the Northern Ridge," he said thickly. "What do you think of it Altu Faltu, eh?"

"Unrest? On the Northern Ridge?"

"Haven't you heard about it man? Some sort of family squabble blown out of proportion. These old, feuding tribal families you know. Always at each other's throats. I really think we should just march in and take them in hand. What do you say, eh?"

Later, when they had gone, Rani-beti turned to Altu Faltu with stricken eyes. "I want to go home, Altu Faltu," she said. "I want to find out what's been happening on the Ridge. And I want to have my baby there."

"You can't possibly go to the Ridge in this condition!" He was horrified by the thought. "Besides..."

"That unrest he mentioned. Altu Faltu, do you think it is because of what we did?"

"I doubt it." But he sounded as though he didn't quite. Then he brightened up. "Look Rani-beti, we've been invited to a flower-party at the Mughal Gardens by the Presidential Estate clan. What do you think of that?"

But overwhelmed by a sudden surge of homesickness, Rani-beti was far away, in the verdant fastness of the Ridge where she had been born and where she was determined to have her baby.

Chapter 8

TURMOIL
IN
THE NORTH

Back on the Northern Ridge, a series of seismic events had taken place over the past several months, rocking the entire region and shaking the very walls of the Flagstaff Tower.

Chaudhury Haramisahib, the younger, freebooter brother of Chaudhury Charbi Raisahib, who had been 'propositioned to' (as he put it) by both his elder brother as well as Brigadier Ladsahib, had waited for his brother's deadline to Brigadier Ladsahib (for the return of Rani-beti) to expire before making his move. Bearing a big bag of pistachios (which he had received from the Brigadier as a token of goodwill) he approached the Serpentine arbour one grey and wintry evening for the great fraternal reunion meeting that had been planned. His aide, Tedi Poonch, accompanied him. On the cold cement plinth that comprised Charbi Raisahib's prestigious Diwan-e-Khas, the Flagstaff chieftain waited with his three wives and the obese Leechad.

The guards allowed Haramisahib over the humpbacked bridge with a smart salute and then the two bitterly estranged brothers were face to face for the first time in years.

"Charbi!" exclaimed Haramisahib, in an emotion-choked

voice. "It is good to see you brother!"

"And you," replied Charbi Raisahib. "You look well."

"A token of goodwill..." Haramisahib proffered the pistachios. "The best, from Afghanistan." He blinked and his Adam's apple bobbed "Thank you." And the two estranged brothers embraced.

Bibi-Teen sniffed rapturously.

"We've been behaving like two bloody fools for too long," Haramisahib admitted, allowing a catch in his voice. "How I wish the respected Chaudhuryji (their father) had been here to witness this. He would have been so happy."

"He will hear about it. I will see to it. Anyway the past is past. Let us look to the future now." Pensively, the elder Chaudhury cracked a nut and cocked his head to one side. "So you are willing to support me against this bastard Ladsahib?"

"It is my duty. He has insulted the family name. And abducted your beloved daughter and my precious niece. I will fight by your side to the last drop of my blood. My troops are at your command."

"Perhaps I have misjudged you in the past, Haramisahib."

"And I you. I always thought of you as a stuffy jellybrain."

"And I took you to be a pushy bastard who would stop at nothing."

"To imagine that two blood brothers could think such evil of each other." Haramisahib shook his head ruefully and clicked his tongue.

They laughed, if humourlessly. And Bibi-Do felt a sudden chill shoot up and down her spine.

"And how are your various sons?" enquired Charbi Raisahib, sotto voce.

"My sons? Hereafter, my sons are your sons!" declaimed

Haramisahib with simple eloquence.

"Thank you. The gesture is appreciated. Now Haramisahib, we have a battle to plan." Chaudhury Charbi Raisahib waved an arm and his wives melted away into the foliage.

"Ah, yes. To oust the bastard Brigadier and his impure bloodlines."

"Yes. My plan is simple. I propose a pre-dawn blitzkrieg on the Nicholson Cemetery from over the Oberoi complex wall. We drive them out of the Cemetery onto the roads. The traffic will do the rest."

"When do you propose attacking?"

"Just before dawn on the earliest date we are ready. The Brigadier has been formally intimated that a state of war exists between the Flagstaffers and Nicholsonites. I propose that our forces sneak into the Oberoi complex late the evening before and bivouac on the apartment terraces. At first light, we pour over the wall like the hordes of Genghis Khan and take them by surprise."

"Magnificent. It's a masterplan." Again Haramisahib embraced his brother. Then he squinted and pulled his lip. "There is one small detail that needs to be ironed out though..."

"What's that?"

"You propose a pre-dawn attack. But there is not much traffic on the roads at that hour and it is likely that the fleeing Nicholsonites will be able to escape unscathed across to the Qudsia Gardens and Nicholson Park. They will thus have the opportunity to regroup and launch a counter-offensive, and perhaps even to enlist the support of some of the Walled City clans. We could, of course, launch our attack later, at around 0930 hours, when the morning rush hour peaks. The Nicholsonites will suffer heavy casualties on the road and be too shocked to retaliate. But I doubt very much that our presence on the apartment terraces will go unnoticed by the residents for so long. And once they raise a hue and cry, the vital element of surprise will be lost."

"Hmmm... So what do you suggest?" Chaudhury Charbi Raisahib didn't like his battle plan being shot down like this by his younger, upstart brother, but was an astute enough leader to recognise its flaws.

Haramisahib's eyes glittered and he cleared his throat diffidently. "What I have in mind is this. You attack the Cemetery simultaneously from the Club Road, Boulevard Road and Alipur Road sides with great ferocity. The Nicholsonites won't be expecting to be attacked from the road fronts and are likely to flee towards and over their fourth front — the Oberoi complex wall. Where I will be waiting with my forces. Thus we box them in and finish them off. You divide your force into three battalions; one can conceal itself in the ISBT (Inter State Bus Terminal) nursery on the corner of Alipur Road, the second can bivouac in Nicholson Park across Boulevard Road, and the third can hide in the park at the intersection of Boulevard Road, Club Road and Court Road. My men will camp overnight on the terraces of the Oberoi apartments." Haramisahib rocked back on his haunches. "Well, how do you like it? I call it the Trident Attack Plan (TAP)."

And Chaudhury Charbi Raisahib had to admit that the Trident Attack Plan certainly seemed more effective than his. He conferred (for the sake of form) with Leechad for a few minutes and then nodded. "Okay," he said, extending a hand. "The plan is acceptable to us. But if I am to launch a three-pronged attack, I will have to take a much larger force than I had planned on. Anyhow, that should not be a problem."

Because now, with Haramisahib reconciled, there would be no need to leave behind a large force to guard the installations on the Ridge. He put a hand on his brother's shoulder. "After the battle, I shall hand over the Nicholson Cemetery to you, to rule as you please. But now, Haramisahib, if you will join me for a banquet at the Bada Nashta Khana... Bibis Ek, Do and Teen will be delighted."

Late that night, Brigadier Ladsahib was roused from sonorous slumber by the Captain of the Guard. Chaudhury Haramisahib (belching and farting fatuously after the banquet) required an immediate audience with him. The matter could not wait. Needless to say, the Brigadier did not keep the flatulent Chaudhury waiting.

On the day before the Great Nicholson Battle, Chaudhury Charbi Raisahib handed over the administrative affairs of state to his three wives to handle in his absence. In all likelihood of course, the battle would be over by mid-morning the following day, and he would be having a celebratory luncheon at the Bada Nashta Khana with Haramisahib. But still, proper procedure had to be followed. Bibis Ek, Do and Teen groomed their warlord husband silently, each wondering if this would be for the last time ever, for no matter what anyone said, war was war. And Bibi-Do's conscience continued to trouble her like a stubborn ulcer.

Then the Chaudhury dropped an unexpected, chauvinistic bombshell. "I am leaving Leechadji here, to look after you," he decreed. "Let it not be said that Chaudhury Charbi Raisahib left his wives unprotected."

"We can look after ourselves," Bibi-Do protested, thinking that if they did need protection, it would be from Leechad.

"Leechadji will stay here with you, and that is that."

Leechad exhaled hugely with relief and leered at Bibi-Do.

The reconciled brothers conferred briefly to synchronise their battle plans late that afternoon. Then Chaudhury Charbi Raisahib saluted his moist-eyed wives and marched out of the Ridge at the head of a splendid red-arsed army of one hundred and fifty fighting bandars. At the Chauburja Gate, the army split up into three battalions. The Pehelee Behtereen Bandar Battalion, under the command of the Chaudhury himself, crossed over to the Hindu Rao Ridge and then, via the Mutiny Memorial, made their way down to Boulevard Road. This they crossed successfully, with great skill and courage, and soon infiltrated the leafy if sleazy environs of the Nicholson Park. The Doosri Behtereen Bandars, led by the mighty General Zabardast, marched down Rajniwas Marg onto Alipur Road, and headed south towards Kashmere Gate. Warily they sneaked into the small nursery that stood at one corner of the infamous ISBT-Kashmere Gate intersection, cheek by jowl with the Cemetery itself. The Teesri Behtereens, led by General 'Muscles' Mushtanda, crossed

Rajniwas Marg, and arrogantly making their way through the Lieutenant Governor's estate, arrived in the park that lay just west of the Cemetery, bounded by Club Road, Court Road and Boulevard Road. By dusk, all three battalions were in position. Chaudhury Haramisahib was to take his army of freebooters onto the terraces of the Oberoi complex only at dusk, to avoid detection. Thus, the Nicholson Cemetery was to be surrounded and ripe for the rout.

At 0645 hours the next morning, Chaudhury Charbi Raisahib signalled his battalion into action. One by one, the elite troops crossed the southern lane of Boulevard Road and regrouped on the central verge. Just across the road they could see the long front wall of the Cemetery and the redbrick guardhouse with its black iron gates. Oh yes, Chaudhury Charbi Raisahib was determined to drive his centre prong of the Trident Attack right through the Brigadier's front door. This was a battle of honour.

He waited for a gap in the traffic, that was surprisingly heavy even at that hour, to lead the charge. A series of trucks thundered past and then the road lay empty. Chaudhury Charbi Raisahib emitted a sharp staccato bark that echoed flatly like the crack of a rifle and darted across the road. His troops loped swiftly behind him, in single file. In the nursery, about one hundred metres to the right of the black iron gates, General Zabardast, who had been listening hard, heard the bark and signalled the Doosris into action. About four hundred metres to the left, General Mushtanda's spotters espied the Pehelees dart across the road and gave the signal. "Let's go!" grunted the General, and they were off.

But to their utter surprise, all three prongs of the attacking battalions found themselves under a hammer-blow counterattack by the enemy! Chaudhury Charbi Raisahib had barely scaled the guardhouse roof when he was ambushed with a blood-curdling yell by none other than the Brigadier himself. His troops, swarming up behind him, were similarly and swiftly being given bloody noses and much else by the Nicholsonites, who thumped out of the trees or dodged out from behind the tombstones. General Zabardast, who had scaled the Cemetery wall from the nursery end, found himself under devastating attack by the enemy who had made good use of the trees that abutted the wall at this point. General Mushtanda broached the western wall easily and found himself in a section of the Cemetery that was still in use. Well-tended, this section lies at an appreciably lower level than the older, historical section. As the Teesris rushed towards the eart</ern bank that divided the two, the Nicholsonites charged out at them from behind the tall weeds and elaborate statuettes, shoving them into open graves.

There could be no doubt about it. The Nicholsonites had been tipped off! And had quite successfully blunted the first thrust of the great Trident Attack Plan.

Above the shrieks and screams of the warring monkeys, the warning bells jangled in the Chaudhury's head — too late. There was now no time to think about what had gone wrong. He had a full-scale battle on his hands. Not a simple ethnic cleansing operation.

Angry simian feet thudded up and down the front wall of the Cemetery. Screams rose to a crescendo, then got choked off with ghastly gurgles. The undergrowth flailed and thrashed, and the dust rose over the fighting bodies. Curved yellow canines flashed like sabres in the sun, ripping great rents into flesh and staining the marble tombstones red. High up in the trees, the terrified peacocks stood up and screamed their clarion trumpet blasts, spurring the fighters on. Here too, in the leafy reaches, infants clung to their mothers' breasts and gibbered with fear. Above, hundreds of kites wheeled and circled, troubled and restless. There was no peace even here, in this final resting place.

Brigadier Ladsahib's strategy was simple. He had known exactly from where the Flagstaffers would attack and had concentrated his defences at those points. His countervailing battalions had been issued terse orders: they were to beat back the enemy as best they could, using their surprise to advantage, and on no account were they to allow the three attacking battalions to unite and fight as one unit. If the Flagstaffers were successfully 'islanded' he knew he still had a chance. Especially with assistance promised, and yet to be rendered...

He saw with pride that the Flagstaffers were indeed being gamely held at bay at the two flanks. But the centre prong of their attack, led by the Chaudhury himself, was now beginning to gain ground. The enemy was advancing in a grim wedge along one of the Cemetery's main pathways, lunging viciously at anything in their way. Heavily outnumbered, he was being forced to retreat towards his cemented-up well, which was his personal headquarters. This, of course, he would defend to the death.

Appalled by the number of casualties the Pehelees had taken so early in the battle, Chaudhury Charbi Raisahib saw the Brigadier clamber up on to the well, and realised at once that the key to victory in this battle lay in its capture. He also knew that the Nicholsonites would defend this to the last, and inflict heavy casualties on his forces. A single cornered monkey, fighting for his life, could easily account for four of five of the enemy. That was an unacceptable kill ratio.

But just behind the vital well stretched the strategic 'fourth front', the long Oberoi complex wall, upon which, not so long ago, Rani-beti and Altu Faltu had had their fateful dalliance. The wall over which, any moment now, Chaudhury Charbi Raisahib expected his brother to come storming, at the head of his troop of rowdy freebooters. As he advanced towards the Brigadier's headquarters though, he could not help thinking that Haramisahib — true to type — was playing his cards a little too close to his chest. It was high time he showed his hand.

He would have been appalled to know that exactly the same thought was passing through the mind of the beleagured Brigadier.

"You see, the beauty of my plan is this," Haramsahib had explained to him gleefully. "I have assured my stupid brother that I will lead the assault from the Oberoi complex wall. When the Flagstaffers see us coming, they are bound to relax unconsciously, and not fight as hard. And they will certainly not expect to be taken by the throat by us, and assaulted! They will be tired, my troops will be fresh. They will be confused, we will be precise. We will cut them to ribbons and drive them onto the roads like the wind drives dead leaves before it."

But now, when the hour was at hand, there was no sign of Haramsahib or his big wind. Grimly, the Brigadier prepared himself for his final fight. What really pissed him off about the whole thing was that it had been sparked off by his nincompoop son, who at this moment was probably sprawled dead drunk in some ditch, instead of fighting valourously at his side.

Like a slowly tightening noose, Chaudhury Charbi Raisahib's Pehelee Behtereens surrounded the cemented-up well and drew close. The Chaudhury cast a quick look around to check on how the other two battalions were doing. General Zabardast had made some progress and with him, the Doosris were now heading determinedly towards the well. But General Mushtanda appeared to be having a rough time — somehow the Teesris had got bogged down in the low ground and open graves and were having to fight every bitter inch of the way.

The Chaudhury prepared for the final rush. There was no question of asking the Brigadier to surrender — ethnic cleansing was ethnic cleansing, and like any cleansing operation had to be done thoroughly. He raised this arm to give the signal when someone jerked his elbow violently and clutched him hard around the waist. He spun, snarling. And nearly bit her head off before he realised who she was.

It was his daughter, Chamkili of the glittering smile, but now foam-flecked and gabbling with fear. Was she a fluffhead to land up like this in the midst of all this mayhem, and was Bibi-Do out of her mind! He shook her roughly. "What the hell are you doing here?" he roared. "Do you want to be killed? Go home, go home, go home!"

Wild-eyed and dishevelled, Chamkili just kept on screeching. And then, in a sudden deathly lull, he heard clearly what she was screaming over and over again.

"Chacha Haramisahib has attacked and captured the Flagstaff Tower and Serpentine. Bibis Ek, Do and Teen have been taken prisoner, and also Leechad. There are soldiers all over the Ridge. Do something papa, please do something!"

He held on to his swooning daughter and snarled angrily.

He knew he had been tricked. Out-thought and outgunned. Right royally. If he disengaged the Nicholsonities now, and returned at top speed to the Ridge, it would be construed that he had fled the battlefield. No chieftain of the Flagstaff could survive that. Yet there was no question of his remaining here. His primary duty was to defend his territory and protect the honour of his wives. Come what may, he had to get back to the Ridge, double-quick.

"General Zabardast!" he bellowed. "Over here sir, on the double!" Some distance away, the gallant Zabardast aborted the capture of a small but vital tree and galloped over.

"There's been trouble on the Ridge. Haramisahib's staged a coup. I'm going back there with the Pehelees. You take command here and mop up this operation."

He was gone, with his shaking daughter and the best battalion, even before the hapless Zabardast could take in the news. From the well-top, Brigadier Ladsahib watched in astonishment. He grabbed his chance.

"The Flagstaffers are fleeing!" he screeched. "The Chaudhury has turned tail. Come on men, let's break their balls! Break their balls!"

His high-pitched, demented screech, ringing victoriously, washed over his desperate troops like an infusion of fresh blood. The great battle-chant went up:

"Make them swing! Make them fall! Make them break their bloody balls!"

And the Nicholsonites mounted a fearsome counter-offensive, as fearsome as any the fabled Brigadier-General would have been proud of. At the western end of the Cemetery, General Mushtanda looked up on hearing the great roar, and saw to his horror what appeared to be the

Pehelee Behtereens in full, galloping retreat. A tremor of disbelief shuddered through the rank and file of the Doosri and Teesri battalions, as they too took in this unsettling, frightening sight. A fearful chatter arose:

"The Peheless have fled! Is the Chaudhury dead?"

But both Generals Zabardast, and 'Muscles' Mushtanda were simians made of steel.

"We fight to the last bloody bandar!" Zabardast roared, unwittingly admitting in that brave cry that they were no longer the aggressors, but the defenders (or as Altu Faltu might have said, the "aggressees").

It was also the last thing he said. He had in fact, just taken a running leap at the well and had acquired a hand-hold on its rim when he was ambushed. From the tree that looked over it, a huge, screeching monkey jumped on — and broke — his neck. The formidable Lady Ladsahib, who had been watching the proceedings from the higher branches, had decided to join issue.

And then the fire went out of the bellies of the Flagstaffers. Suddenly, what had been promised to them as a picnic, an easy orgy of killing and raping, had turned into an unbelievable nightmare. They were being felled left and right. Their Supreme Commander had either been killed or had fled with the best battalion. A General lay dead on the ground, his neck snapped by an ox of a female who had jumped out of a tree. They now no longer believed in the principles underlying this battle. To several of them, it now seemed as though the Chaudhury had tried to resolve a personal ego problem by going into battle. They faltered as the Nicholsonites surged. And shocked by the sudden disappearance of the Chaudhury, and equally sudden fall of Zabardast, General Mushtanda ordered an immediate tactical retreat.

But there was to be no easy retreat for the Flagstaffers. Howling their wanton battlechant, the Nicholsonites (who had been outnumbered one to five) chased them out of the Cemetery and onto the roads, now thundering with peak hour traffic. The Flagstaffers were getting a dose of the very medicine their Chaudhury had prescribed for his enemies.

Leechad made his move shortly after Chaudhury Charbi Raisahib had marched off the Ridge at the head of his troops in defence of the clan's honour and glory. Obsequiously, he approached Bibi-Ek at the Flagstaff Tower.

"Is there anything I can do for you, Bibi-Ek?" he began deferentially. The troubled dowager silenced him with a glare.

"What do you want, Leechadji?" she asked.

Leechad clicked his tongue and shook his head ruefully. "A sad, bad business this. Such a pity it had to come to this. A pity that Bibi-Do did not know any better..."

"Bibi-Do? What has Bibi-Do got to do with this?" Bibi-Ek looked up, curious in spite of herself. She knew that Leechad was up to something invidious but...

He shrugged. "Oh, you know, filling Rani-beti's pretty head with all that romantic nonsense. Encouraging her to run away with that drunken bekar bandar."

"What are you talking about Leechadji? And don't try your evil, scheming ways with me. Don't you dare slander Bibi-Do. I won't stand for it."

"I'm not slandering her. But it is common knowledge that

Bibi-Do encouraged Rani-beti to elope. Loaded her up with a lot of sentimental rubbish about following the dictates of her heart, and how true love only comes once and so on."

"Why would Bibi-Do do such a thing?" Somehow, she had to ask.

Again the gross creature shrugged as if to indicate that the answer was obvious to anyone who cared to think about it a bit.

Eavesdropping avidly, Bibi-Teen chimed in excitedly. "It must have been because of that Chamkili!"

"Shut up, Bibi-Teen!"

But Bibi-Teen would not shut up. "Bibi-Do always wanted Chamkili to be married off as soon as possible. Preferably into a high-status family. And now, thanks to the elopement, Chamkili's got engaged to Nawab Bade Badtameez in place of Rani-beti." She was jumping up and down with excitement. What a glorious family row this was promising to blow up into.

"If all this is true, Bibi-Do has a lot to answer for." Bibi-Ek was grim and ominous and double her size, though half her anger was directed against herself, for allowing Leechad to upset her like this. But she had to get to the bottom of this. She looked up decisively. "Where is Bibi-Do, Leechadji? Tell her I wish to see her immediately."

But Bibi-Do was nowhere to be found. For she was scouring the high ground of the Ridge, searching for that drunken bekar bandar whose deadline for the return of Rani-beti had long expired.

It was only early the next morning that Bibi-Ek confronted her in the Serpentine arbour, where they had decided to have their daily administrative meetings (for the tenure of the war). Just about the same time that Chaudhury Charbi Raisahib was leading his troops into the Battle of the Nicholson Cemetery.

"Good morning, Bibi-Do. I would like to have a word with you, if you don't mind."

"Certainly Bibi-Ek. What about?" And Bibi-Do could feel the ballast settle in her belly. Feigning sleep nearby, Bibi-Teen strained her ears till they stuck out perpendicularly from her head. Concealed beneath an umbrella plant near the water, Leechad put his hands across his belly and gloated. This was going to be good.

"Bibi-Do, I have specific information that you assisted Rani-beti to elope. Is this true?"

"Bibi-Ek! Must you listen to every bit of garbage and rumour that blows around this place?"

"Is is true, Bibi-Do? I know that you and Rani-beti were very close. You even spent that last evening with her."

"Bibi-Ek, you know what that Leechadji tried to do to Rani-beti. How can you believe anything he says after that? You know how vindictive he can be."

"Just answer my question, Bibi-Do, that's all I ask. As senior-most wife of the Chaudhury I command you to. Did you, or did you not, have anything to do with Rani-beti's elopement with that useless drunk?"

She leaned heavily over the more petite Bibi-Do. Bibi-Teen quivered with delicious anticipation.

A flash of defiance sparked through the Chaudhury's romance-prone second wife. "Oh, stop throwing rank at me Bibi-Ek!" she snapped. "You're heavy enough as it is. And yes, if you must know, I did help Rani-beti elope."

"Why?" Bibi-Ek was icy cold and all steel.

"Because she loved the fellow, that's why. Maybe that's something you will never understand."

"And it was not because you wanted your flea-brained Chamkili to marry Badtameez instead, I suppose?"

Bibi-Do flinched as the shot hit home, but stuck to her guns.

"I love Rani-beti as much I love Chamkili," she said levelly, "and you know that Bibi-Ek. It was clear to me that Rani-beti was desperately unhappy being engaged to Badtameez. This was even before she met that bekar fellow. Then of course she did, and fell in love with him. If I had not helped her, your beloved daughter would have thrown herself into the Khooni Khan Jheel. I talked her out of it once..."

"What you have done, Bibi-Do, is to commit treason. You have acted against the interests of the Flagstaff clan. Our name is mud because of what you have done. You had no business to interfere with Rani-beti's marital arrangements. If Rani-beti had been unhappy, she would have come to me. And now, thanks to you, she's been taken by trappers..."

"I know, and I'm sorry about that. But Rani-beti did come to you when she was unhappy and you promptly began the emotional blackmail routine with her."

"How dare you say that Bibi-Do! You wanted Rani-beti out of the way to enable Chamkili to marry Badtameez. You ruined my daughter's future..."

"Did you ever listen to Rani-beti, Bibi-Ek? You were too busy gloating about your nawabi son-in-law to-be. Throwing grand parties. While all the time, the poor thing was being con-sumed by unhappiness." Bibi-Do bobbed her head excitedly and wagged a forefinger in Bibi-Ek's face. "You are to blame, Bibi-Ek. If only you had listened to her and not rammed the engagement down her throat, she might not even have fallen in love with that bekar bugger. It's all your fault and you're trying to blame me now."

Under the umbrella plant, Leechad blinked with mock horror, thrilled to his evil core. Bibi-Teen, forgetting about feigning sleep, was sitting bolt upright, completely transfixed. The quarrel raged on.

"It is none of your business how I deal with my children. And none of your business, Bibi-Do, to interfere in their lives. The Chaudhury will hear about this when he gets back, make no mistake. This time you have really overstepped yourself. You've caused a war, Bibi-Do, a war! And God forbid anything happens to the Chaudhury — I will kill you if anything does, you can be sure of that."

"It is every bit my business to prevent a princess of the Flagstaff clan from committing suicide just because her own mother is so damn insensitive that she can't see her daughter's great distress. Or else doesn't care about it because she's too busy throwing parties and clambering up the social ladder like a monkey up a cocunut tree." Bibi-Do knew very well that she was on very loose gravel indeed but there was nothing left now but to have it out. Bibi-Ek was three times her size and shaking with anger.

"Bitch!" she hissed.

"Whore!"

"Slut!"

There is no telling what might have happened (and Bibi-Teen had begun backing away rapidly) had not the sound of a muffled commotion from the bridge made the two furious wives break off.

"Ladies, ladies, ladies! Please, there are ladies present!" The voice was somewhat familiar and rich with amused irony.

Chaudhury Haramisahib leapt lightly onto the cement

platform in the Diwan-e-Khas and pushed between his bristling bhabis. Leechad and Bibi-Teen could only gape.

"What are you doing here, Haramisahib?" asked Bibi-Ek, taken aback and snatching her hand away, which he had already kissed.

He grinned. "Ah, yes. I have to formally inform you that I have taken over the Northern Ridge. Charbi is no longer in charge here. You lovely ladies will naturally get absorbed into my harem. I am sure we will all have great times together."

Haramisahib had planned his coup with meticulous, evil genius. He had inducted his four loutish sons and other rebellious princelings into the plot, promising them independent fiefdoms on the Ridge if they helped him oust his brother. He had watched, with great glee, Charbi Raisahib march pompously off to war, and had camped quietly on the Hindu Rao Ridge that night (instead of the Oberoi terraces). He had marched on the Ridge the moment he got the news that Charbi Raisahib had engaged the Nicholsonites.

On the Ridge, the Chauburja Gate was the first to fall, followed rapidly by the University Gate, the Flagstaff Tower, the Khyber Pass Gate, the Nursery Gate and the two Rajpur Road Gates. Resistance had been minimal. Most of the troops, and certainly the best of them, were away fighting the Battle of the Nicholson Cemetery. Chaudhury Haramisahib had just stormed over what had been left behind, and now, flushed with victory, he had entered the sacred precincts of the Diwan-e-Khas just in time to stop his two grande-dame bhabis from hurling themselves at each other.

"Ladies... If you will now permit me to escort you to the Flagstaff Tower. I am afraid I shall have to confine you there temporarily. For your own protection, of course."

They had no choice. The rebels were pressing rudely all around them.

"You too fatso!" Haramisahib prodded the stunned Leechad. "You are going to look after the ladies and ensure they don't tear each others' eyes out."

"Charbi Raisahib will tear you and your hoodlums to pieces when he gets back from the battle," spat Bibi-Ek contemptuously. "You'd better get out while you still can, Haramisahib. Double-crossing traitor!"

"Bibi-Ek, Bibi-Ek! Don't work yourself up so. I'm afraid you will just have to accept the facts. Charbi is not going to come back to the Flagstaff, now or ever. I have it all nicely planned out. Now come along. I have a lot of work to do still."

The sombre procession made its way up the shoulder of the Ridge onto the long metalled road that skirted the reservoir and led to the Tower. The prisoners could see that Haramsahib had been speaking the truth: the uncouth rebels lounged insolently everywhere.

But the grim little cavalcade had also been spotted by Chamkili. She had been foolishly mooning away her time at the Khooni Khan Jheel, thinking romantically about Badtameez, when she had heard the sounds of monkeys fighting. She shrugged her pretty shoulders. Monkeys fought all the time. But it would be better if she were closer to her mother... She nearly bumped into the little procession as it made its way up the euca-lyptus shrouded pathway that Altu Faltu had used on the night of his elopement. She ducked behind a large rock just in time.

"...A brilliant campaign, if I may say so myself," her uncle Haramisahib was saying, escorting her mother and two step-mothers solicitously up the steps. "Send the pompous Charbi marching off to war, to settle a matter of honour, and take the

Ridge myself. The Flagstaff Tower, the Serpentine, everything between the Chauburja and Khyber Pass, mine, mine, mine! With hardly any bloodshed. And you lovely ladies as part of my harem."

For several minutes after they had gone, Chamkili just crouched behind that rock, too petrified to move. Gradually it dawned on her what she had to do. She slunk off through the undergrowth, taking care to keep away from her uncle's patrolling soldiers. Perhaps she was not quite the zero-watter she had been made out to be, and certainly displayed exem-plary courage that morning as she scampered straight into the raging heart of the Battle of the Nicholson Cemetery, to give her father the terrible news.

Chaudhury Haramisahib incarcerated his bhabis in the Flagstaff Tower and issued a short statement to the stunned civilian population comprising mainly females, juveniles and infants indicating that he was now in charge on the Ridge, and that Charbi Raisahib was deposed. He then marched swiftly back to the Chauburja Gate with a strong force. He knew that news of the coup would reach his brother quickly, and now he had to move fast to deliver the coup de grace.

A small green traffic island stands just off the Ridge, at the intersection of Rajpur Road, Rajniwas Marg and Chauburja Road, well wooded with trees. Here now, Chaudhury Haramisahib and his rebels waited, bristling and eager for action. Haramisahib had guessed that that Charbi would come tearing over the Hindu Rao Ridge down to Chauburja Road, and would pause to regroup on this very island, before mounting his assault on the Ridge. And he anticipated cor-rectly. Sure enough, Charbi Raisahib came hurtling down the hill, his dazed Pehelee Behtereens strung out behind him, wondering what the hell was going on. As the chieftain and the front runners paused on that island, to catch their breath and allow the rest of the battalion to catch up, Haramisahib and his rebels hurled themselves out of the trees, grunting, snarling and biting mercilessly. The hapless Pehlees, still panting from their long run over the Ridge, were driven willy-nilly into the dangerous intersection, now frenetic with traffic. Utter pandemonium followed as the retreating Pehelees encountered those still coming down from over the hill. Eventually, the crack battalion was forced back up the Hindu Rao Ridge, with Haramisahib and his cohorts in hot and screaming pursuit.

The filthy, stomach-shaped blue pond on the Hindu Rao Ridge, where Bibi-Do had once nearly drowned Altu Faltu, is part of a composite water body that runs right round a rocky escarpment. At its southern end, the pond is connected by a narrow channel, to a larger, deeper water-body further down, reed-fringed and swampy. A narrow culvert links this rocky 'island' to the rest of the Hindu Rao Ridge — most of it land-scaped parkland. Altu Faltu's notorious tool-shed stands at the island end of the culvert, surrounded by trees, and at the edge of a patch of undulating grassland, beyond which the rocks rear up, winking with mica. The channel becomes deeper and more polluted as it circles around the eastern side of the island, again linking up the blue pond and swampy lake. On this side, sewage from the built-up area beyond feeds continuously into it. South, at the far bank of the swampy lake, the gorges and thornbrush give way to the sloping turf of the Mutiny Memorial Park.

It was on to this rocky escarpment of an 'island' that Chaudhury Charbi Raisahib and the (leftover) cream of the Pehelee Behtereens were chased by Haramisahib and his rogues. Haramisahib skidded to a halt at the park side of the culvert and quickly ordered his men to surround the water-body. He then prepared to cross over, a wolfish smile on his face.

But now it was the Flagstaffers who were at bay and fighting for their lives. Haramisahib's first charge was ruthlessly repulsed and he found himself sprawled in six inches of mud, bleeding. Again and again he ordered his men over the narrow culvert, and again and again, the Flagstaffers stoutly defended their end. His casualties mounted alarmingly and he could see that some of the rebel princelings were becoming nervous. Livid and dripping, he called a halt. "All right," he conceded savagely, "if they want a siege, we'll give them a siege. We have them surrounded. Let them rot in the swamp." And leaving behind a strong picket in the charge of his son Haramsala, Chaudhury Haramisahib left for the Flagstaff Tower.

Extracts from the 'Siege Diaries' of Sir Chaudhury Charbi Raisahib.

'What a terrible day! It could have been worse but for the spirited defence the Pehelee Behtereens put up to keep the traitors at bay. But we are marooned on a rocky 'island' of sorts, that stinks, and are in a state of siege... Harmisahib will pay dearly for his treachery... There have been some deserters from our side — rats deserting what they think is a sinking ship. Mostly in response to Harmisahib's rebels shouting at us across the culvert about the futility of our position. Bah! In a way, it is good they have gone, only the strong will be able to survive the kind of ordeal we are in for... Chamkili is with me, weeping most of the time.'

'Early this morning General Mushtanda and three others were chased into camp from over the culvert. When he had calmed down, he informed me of the debacle that had taken place after my departure from the Cemetery yesterday. This setback will have to be avenged, as well as General Zabardast's death. After the retreat, the remnants of the Doosri and Teesri Behtereens were engaged by Haramisahib's sons in the Mutiny Memorial Park (we heard the battle) and driven across the road into the Walled City. Mushtanda escaped, hoping to meet up with me on the Ridge, but bumped into a patrol on the Hindu Rao Ridge, who chased him here... It is immensely ironical how history has turned upon itself in this, the Second Great Siege of Delhi.'

'The troops are bearing up well in spite of the considerable hardships and freezing foggy weather. General Mushtanda's arrival has been a boost to morale. Chamkili too has stopped crying (thank God) and started smiling. She is keeping herself busy looking after the sick and wounded. I hope the Bibis have somehow managed to temporarily postpone the wedding. I am deeply embarrassed by the inconvenience caused to Nawab Bade Badtameez. First Rani-beti, now this. We have to regain our family honour.'

'The enemy made a concerted effort to cross the culvert but we saw them early and successfully repulsed the attack.

They lost four, we had one slightly injured. We have a 24-hour guard manning the culvert... The water here is bad; several of my men are nauseous.'

'We are subsisting on the sort of thorny stuff that only goats can eat. From the top of the escarpment, the Ridge looks so green and calm... Apart from keeping a sharp lookout for the enemy on the culvert, there is nothing much we can do. There is no way in and out of this place except by that route. Perhaps we will have to start thinking about a lightning offensive.'

'General Mushtanda and three others tried slipping out under the cover of the early morning fog, but unluckily stumbled into a picket at the other end and were chased back here. For some reason, Chamkili was in tears all the while they were gone. We must get a couple of the men out of here. If they can make it to the Walled City, they may be able to regroup the rest of the Behtereens and organise a relief party.'

'There is a small rickety gardener's shed on our side of the culvert, which we have occupied. It seems safe and provides some protection during the freezing nights. Some of the men appear to be weakening thanks to the terrible diet, bad water and damp winter fogs. No one complains.'

'Have to admit that Harmaisahib's strategy appears to be working. We have been bottled up here for too long now. General Mushtanda is champing at the bit while Chamkili hangs on to his arm and simpers. Sometimes she frets for her mother. I worry about what's going on at the Ridge and with the Bibis. Leechad is an astute strategist and ought to be able to organise something.

'I suspect Haramisahib will make his move sooner or later. It is stupid to deploy so many troops to guard so few (fifteen now) of us... Mushtanda wants to swim across the large swampy lake. "If I can just make it to the Mutiny Memorial Park, I'll be able to get into the Walled City without a problem," he says. But he'll freeze before he's halfway across the water, and knows it. So far I have forbidden him from trying anything of the sort.'

'Haramisahib has suddenly withdrawn all the guards from the paths surrounding the water. Only the guard picket at the other end of the culvert remains. The guards shouted that a 'Grand Orgy' was being organised by Haramisahib to celebrate his great victory, and that we were cordially invited. Bah!'

'A heavy rainstorm flooded part of the grassy meadow. There's mud everywhere, and everything's a mess. Several of the men are now coughing badly. I think I may have to reconsider Mushtanda's offer. We can't carry on like this for much longer. The men are definitely weakening and will not be able to withstand a charge in the near future. It promises to be another freezing night...'

That was, in fact, the last entry made in the 'Siege Diaries'. The following extracts from Lady Bibi Teen's equally remarkable 'Flagstaff Journal' links up with it and eloquently describes the events that took place in the Flagstaff Tower during those terrible days.

'We have, all three of us, and that dreadful Leechad, been held in our very own Flagstaff Tower. A small corner has been allocated to each of us. I sit at the deep-slitted window and gaze out at the flickering eucalyptus. I find our predicament extraordinary and extremely ironical. Over one hundred years ago, the stout walls of this Tower sheltered foreign (British) women and children from so-called rebels. Today, we are being held prisoner here, by actual rebels and mutineers, who have taken what is rightfully ours. History has repeated itself in such a perverted manner that it seems more like journalism.'

'Bibi-Ek and Bibi-Do are still at daggers drawn, and have not spoken to each other since their quarrel at the arbour. They both ought to realise that had they not been fighting like fishwives that morning, we might have seen Haramisahib coming and been able to escape.'

'There is very little chance of escaping from the Tower. The guards are everywhere, and all four access roads are heavily patrolled. Fat Leechad sits inside with us and leers. Lately he's been sucking up sickeningly to Haramisahib, who in turn is trying to win us over with flattery. So polite and courteous you want to throw up. Make no mistake, he's up to something.'

'Very gleefully Haramisahib informed us that he has got Charbi and some of the others in a state of siege in a stinking rocky section of the Hindu Rao Ridge. (At least he is alive!) Then he made a pass at Bibi-Do who, very creditably (for her), rebuffed him.'

'We are all getting quite sick and depressed being confined within these stout round walls. Haramisahib allows us only ten minutes outside every morning, and that's not very pleasant because his guards lounge and stare insolently. They really are an uncouth lot.'

'Leechad has turned over to the enemy good and proper. His shameless and persistent flattery seems to have paid off. The only saving grace is that he's no longer confined to the Tower, so we are spared his disgusting company. Bibi-Ek does not look well and has stopped eating. Bibi-Do seems to be nursing some deep grievance. The worst, from my point of view, is that there is no one to talk to. Hence this journal.'

'Ghastly day. Haramisahib made another pass at Bibi-Do and then Leechad tried the same thing when he had gone. Both reeked of liquor. Today a pass, tomorrow gang-rape?'

'Leechad informed us that Haramisahib expected Bibi-Do at the Serpentine arbour this evening. Later, four goons turned up and forcibly took her away. Bibi-Ek broke her silence and screeched, "Leave her alone, you bastards!" but to no avail. Leechad just stood by and smirked. He has his knife in both of them and enjoys twisting it.'

'Haramisahib and Leechad turned up drunk and demanded that we groom them on the platform outside in full view of the troops. Is this how they get their kicks? They didn't know that we could be the most savage groomers on the Ridge. Haramsahib got up quickly, muttering that we ought to take lessons from the Khyber Pass bandaris. Bah! He's sworn to get even. He's hobbling a bit and gave Bibi-Do very dirty looks. Later, Bibi-Do told me that she had nearly succeeded in turning him into a eunuch that evening. The most positive outcome of all this is that Bibi-Ek and Bibi-Do are now on monosyllabic terms.'

'Leechad very gleefully informed us that a 'Grand Orgy' is to be held at the Serpentine arbour soon. All the rebel princelings have been invited. "And you three beauteous bibis are to be the Ladies of Especial Pleasure," he said, and licked his lips. We have to do something.'

'Bibi-Ek has suggested a fantastic plan not only for our escape, but also for the recapture of the Flagstaff Tower by Charbi Raisahib. It is a terrible, audacious, if unoriginal plan, in which Bibi-Do's role is paramount, and almost sacrificial.

I too have a very important role to play. Bibi–Ek appears to have confined her role to plotting.'

'We've begun putting our plan into action. I smiled sweetly at the guards, as though involuntarily, much to their open-mouthed amazement. And started small talk with my personal guard. The fool's eyes nearly popped. So far, we have maintained a frosty silence with these traitorous hoodlums. Bibi-Do has started giving Leechad sidelong glances full of forbidden longing. Wonderful actress she is, or? Am I just being bitchy?'

'The guards must be bored silly. They just cluster around me for gossip all day, ogling openly. Very pathetically wiping my eyes, I admitted that I was being starved of stimulating company and conversation, as neither Bibi-Ek nor Bibi-Do were especially congenial. And that I was dying to know what was happening in the big, wide world outside. The fools opened the floodgates! Said that Charbi Raisahib was still being held in a state of siege on the Hindu Rao Ridge, near some stinking tool-shed and swamp. And that Haramisahib had planned his final offensive after the Grand Orgy. Hinted that we would be taking part in the offensive too, as bargaining chips. The bastards.'

'Bibi-Do has progressed from smouldering looks to accidental touches. Leechad seems surprised and a little suspicious, but is enjoying himself nonetheless. While Bibi-Ek looks on with the sternest disapproval, I pretend I'm trying hard not to giggle as Bibi-Do flirts.'

'Amazing what a little girlish innocence and flattery can do, especially with these lout-heads. Got all the necessary information regarding the number and position of guards. Bibi-Ek was very pleased with my efforts. Bibi-Do is seducing

Leechad fantastically. By God, if that's how she goes about it, it's no wonder she enjoys the reputation she has. Leechad looks dazed, bemused, but leers triumphantly at the same time. He can't take her out alone — as he is dying to — because he knows that Haramisahib still has his eyes on her, and the Ridge is crawling with his cohorts who would report any hanky-panky immediately.'

'Leechad turned up this afternoon and both Bibi-Ek and myself pretended to be fast alseep. There was much passionate whispering and tender grooming. (Bibi-Do has certainly vindicated herself, poor thing!) Leechad can hardly contain himself. I fear the poor bastard is seriously in love with her. He squashes up to her, throbbing and throaty, it's a wonder she doesn't throw up. When he left, she told us that he would be coming again tonight. So tonight's the night! Bibi-Ek took her by the hand and said, "You've done well, Bibi-Do, and made good, at least partially, some of the wrong you have done!" Sanctimonious bitch. This is probably the last entry I make in this journal.'

That was indeed, the end of Bibi-Teen's 'Flagstaff Journal'. As planned, the lovesick Leechad turned up at the Flagstaff Tower that night at the appointed hour. Outside, in the cold, the guards snored vacuously. Leechad had taken good care to ensure that. Now he just hoped that Bibi-Do had done the same for the two other amazons she shared the Tower with. He remembered, for a moment, the terrifying djinns she had summoned up so many nights ago, and smiled indulgently.

Tonight, she would be summoning up djinns of a very different kind! For he had won! After so fiercely rejecting his advances (was this because she had found him irresistible right from the beginning?) she had succumbed completely. She had been his most satisfying conquest yet. Of course, Rani-beti would have been one better. That afternoon, she had been putty in his hands.

He slipped the key into the padlock, and gently pushed the door open. She came to him at once and pointed silently to the two huddled figures on the floor. She smiled. "They won't awake if the Tower falls on them," she whispered and drew him close.

She lay down giggling as he sank flabbily on top of her, trying to control his panting. Through slitted eyes, and with considerable relief, she saw Bibi-Ek rise ghostlike and monstrous behind him. She took him by the shoulders and pushed him upright, so that he was squatting on top of her, and moaned languourously, "Leechad, oh Leechad!"

Bibi-Ek clenched both her hands into a single hate-filled fist, raised it high and brought it down with a sickening thud on the back of his neck. He collapsed like a flaccid sack of jelly on top of Bibi-Do, squishing the air out of her. She wriggled free from beneath him. "Thanks," she panted. "For a dreadful moment I thought you really had fallen asleep." And Bibi-Ek nodded expressionlessly. It had crossed her mind that an unbridled night with Leechad was just what Bibi-Do really deserved for all the trouble she had caused. It would have been poetic justice. But there was no time for that now.

She took charge swiftly. They bound and gagged the unconscious Leechad and made for the door. Bibi-Teen's eyes were still the size of grapefruit. Silently they slipped into the

238

freezing, clear night and fled down the short road that led to the University Gate. The guards had left their positions and lay huddled around the embers of a dying fire nearby, fast asleep. It would be a long run from here, up and down the twisting roads of the Ridge, but they fled as swiftly and urgently as Altu Faltu and Rani-beti had fled from the Khooni Khan Jheel on that moonlit night. And Bibi-Do of course, knew exactly where to go...

Thanks to Bibi-Teen's ability to chat up the enemy, they even knew exactly how many guards to expect at the culvert picket. Luck was with them, because on this, one of the coldest nights of the season, only two of the full compliment of six were still awake. And keeping watch entirely in the wrong direction. They dealt with them in the same ruthless manner Bibi-Ek had just dealt with Leechad. Then, in the brittle starlight, Bibi-Ek edged gingerly across the culvert, trying desperately to catch the attention of the guard at the other end and not make him raise the alarm at the same time. He had spotted them all right, and was alert and upright, bobbing his head in disbelief.

For Chaudhury Charbi Raisahib, on guard duty himself that night, could not believe what he was seeing. The looming shapes of Bibis Ek, Do and Teen, crawling stealthily over the culvert, and signalling him frantically, to keep shut, keep shut, keep shut. While in the little tool-shed behind (and unknown to him), Chamkili of the now-beatific smile lay wrapped up deliciously asleep, in the strong hairy arms of General 'Muscles' Mushtanda.

But there was no time for a sentimental reunion now. Succinctly Bibi-Ek informed the Chaudhury of her diabolical plan and he never even noticed that Mushtanda had Chamkili with him when he went to rouse him. The enervated and dispirited Flagstaffers surged to life. They crossed the culvert, and sped back towards the Ridge, retracing the steps the three gallant wives had so recently taken. The rebel guards at the University Gate had still not moved a muscle. Silently the ousted Flagstaffers loped up the road leading to the Tower. Bibi-Ek unlocked the doors. And then Chaudhury Charbi Raisahib was back again in his home and castle.

"You've done well!" he congratulated his wives. "Now get some rest. We'll take over from here." His eyes gleamed. There were fifteen fighting monkeys in the Tower now, the battered, loyal remnants of the splendid Behtereens. With them, he waited now, to re-enact yet another version of the Trojan Horse episode.

Bound and gagged on the floor of the Flagstaff Tower, on what was supposed to have been his night of bliss with Bibi-Do, Leechad surfaced to a nightmarish scenario. Of bristling, rough-looking Flagstaffers surrounding him. Then, Chaudhury Charbi Raisahib was looking down at him.

"Congratulations Leechad. You have done well. Do you have anything to say for yourself?" (Very briefly, Bibi-Ek had informed him of Leechad's floor-crossing.) The big monkey, flat on his back, did some fast thinking.

"Chaudhury sahib, thank God you're here! You are back where you rightfully belong! The Flagstaff flag can fly from the Tower once more!" He would have grovelled had he not been bound.

"So you went over to the enemy Leechad. You know what we do to traitors..."

"No, no sir! The Bibis are mistaken. It was all an act. Part of my plan."

"What plan?"

"I had to pretend I had switched sides, sir!" he gabbled. "I had to get Haramisahib to trust me. And in the end he did, because he gave me the keys to the Tower."

"I see. Then why did the good Bibis knock you out and tie you?"

"Sir, I can only think that they got taken in by my act. They too believed I had turned into a traitor. You see, sir, I could not reveal to them my true plan, for fear that they might inadevertently spill the beans." His voice dropped to a whisper. "You know sir, how Bibi-Teen loves to talk. And alas, sir, and in utter confidence, and begging your forgiveness for being the bearer of distressing news, I have to tell you that Bibi-Do and Chaudhury Haramisahib spent a lot of time alone together in the Serpentine arbour..."

"What exactly was your plan, Leechad?" asked the Chaudhury, refusing to be distracted by his second wife's alleged peccadillos.

"My plan sir? It was to rescue them, of course. To escort them to safety to your hideout, and then lead you here. It has er, worked, but not exactly in the way I had planned. Perhaps the Bibis were a little hasty and panicked when they heard me enter. Before I could divulge to them the true purpose of my visit."

Chaudhury Charbi Raisahib's eyes glinted with contempt. There is no doubt that Leechad would have been executed in the time-honoured way of death by drowning in the reservoir. (The last execution had caused an outbreak of jaundice in the entire Civil Lines area.) But he wriggled free of his bonds and escaped in the confusion of the Trojan Horse Charge, and made it — ironically — to the rough country of the Hindu Rao Ridge, hiding out in the same rickety tool-shed that had first served Altu Faltu so well, and then the besieged Chaudhury.

The doped guards around the Tower were rudely awoken by the incoming 8 o'clock shift. After kicking two of them over, a newly arrived guard peered through the barred iron door of the Tower. He saw the three huddled figures on the floor and moved away. All was well. Had he waited for his eyes to get used to the dimness, and looked carefully around, he might have seen the others, crouched against the wall, and along the ledge that ran halfway up the Tower.

Half an hour later, the Captain of the Guard organised a search patrol. "There is no sign of that fat Leechad," he said. "Go find him. He brings the ladies their breakfast and escorts them for their airing. It is getting late now."

The news of Leechad's apparent disappearance eventually reached Haramisahib, disporting himself with some of the Khyber Pass bandaris in the Serpentine arbour. Of late, he had been receiving disquieting reports about the fat monkey, pertaining to his over-frequent visits to the Tower and excessive attention to Bibi-Do. He had recently noticed a strange leery expression in the smug monkey's eyes. A dreadful suspicion entered Haramisahib's head. Had the obese bastard deluded him? Was he secretly carrying on with Bibi-Do? If he was…The personal, political and military implications of such a liaison could be disastrous.

"Have you checked the Flagstaff Tower?" he barked.

"Er, yes sir. One of the guards looked in. The ladies are still asleep."

Then the Captain of the 8 o'clock Guard came bouncing up, still furious. "Sir, I would like to officially complain that the midnight to 0800 hours shift were all found sleeping at their positions when we went to relieve them this morning. Even now, they are all moving about in a rather dazed manner. It appears that they have been drugged, sir."

"Drugged?" Haramisahib jerked up. Something was wrong. Leechad missing, the guards doped… But the prisoners were still inside, so this didn't seem to be an escape plot. What then? Had Leechad doped the guards to enable himself have a little undisturbed orgy in the Tower with the Ladies of Especial Pleasure?

"I'm going to the Tower!" he snapped. And taking a small detail of troops, he scrambled off.

It was Bibi-Teen, on the lookout at the window sill who saw them coming and bobbed the warning. In the short, fierce skirmish that followed, Haramisahib was lucky to escape with his life. And this time round, there were deserters from his side, including all those who Bibi-Teen had so sweetly befriended and had such scintillating conversations with. But while Chaudhury Charbi Raisahib was successful in recapturing the vital Flagstaff Tower and a large area around it, including the University Gate and Khyber Pass Gate, he was not able to regain the beautiful Serpentine arbour. Also, the large area bound by the Nursery Gate and the Charbuja Gate including the Bada Nashta Khana and the Khooni Khan Jheel remained in the hands of the rebels. A new line of control was demarcated along the spine of the Ridge, where the thorny wild flank gave way to the landscaped park regions. Haramisahib had lost a lot of territory, but Charbi Raisahib had not regained all that was rightfully his. The struggle continued all through that winter, and into the following spring, with fierce skirmishes erupting every now and then, and neither brother gaining or losing significantly.

And rent by civil war, the Ridge remained in a state of tension and turmoil.

In spite of which, life went on. The Nicholsonites, of course, had celebrated their great victory with a week's feasting and dancing, with Lady Ladsahib lording over everyone in style. Later however, the Brigadier's Chief of Intelligence, Lieutenant Hazari Kaan informed the Brigadier of the events that had taken place on the Ridge. His face darkened.

"That treacherous bastard Haramisahib," he swore. "He used us both! Made us look like fools. I will avenge this humiliation even if it means I have to enter into a treaty with Chaudhury Charbi Raisahib." Some thought that the Brigadier was overreacting. For had the Nicholsonites not been tipped off about the Trident Attack Plan, and had Chaudhury Charbi Raisahib not gone charging off to the Ridge in the middle of the Great Nicholson Battle, the outcome of that battle could have been quite different. Hazari Kaan tried to soothe the Brigadier's ruffled fur.

"Perhaps sir," he suggested meekly, "it would be better if we let the brothers keep fighting with one another, without interfering. Eventually they are bound to weaken one another. Even perhaps to the point when it may make sense for us to mount a millitary operation against them. Both to avenge the elder Chaudhury's attack as well as the younger one's treachery. They are already divided, maybe all we will need to do eventually, is to rule..."

After consolidating his position at the Flagstaff, Chaudhury Charbi Raisahib immediately sent word to Nawab Bade Badtameez, apologising for the inconvenience and indicating that the wedding of His Highness to Chamkili could now take place as per his convenience. The reply from the grim fort of Badtameezgarh (formerly Tughlakabad) was gratifying. The Nawab would be setting forth for the Ridge shortly, with a barat of one thousand bandars. Word would be sent to the Flagstaff Tower exactly when to expect the guests.

Chamkili paled when she heard the tidings and fled to her mother. "I don't want to marry Badtameez!" she wept. "Not anymore. I want to marry General Mushtanda."

Listening nearby, Bibi-Ek smiled with sad malice as she caught Bibi-Do's troubled eye. Then her face clouded over as she thought of her vanished daughter Rani-beti. Even the Kachcha Banyan gang had disappeared.

To Chamkili's tearful despair, Bibi-Do would not hear her protestations. General Mushtanda was firmly and politely informed that he should stop escorting Chamkili around and was soldier enough to oblige. He was tiring a bit of the glittering smile anyway. Sure, she would have been a good catch, but somehow, the shapely Bibi-Do seemed so much more alluring...

None of them had the faintest idea of the terrible surprise that Nawab Bade Badtameez had planned to spring on them on the occasion of his marriage to Chamkili of the glittering smile.

Chapter 9

MORNING DARSHAN AT HARBANDAR ASHRAM

The Lodhi Gardens are certainly the most prestigious amongst Delhi's public gardens; if you are rich, famous, bureaucratic and overweight, and live in Central Delhi, that's where you go every morning and evening to vigorously atone for the sin of being fat in a thin country. The gardens, built around the solid, solemn tombs of the Sayyids and Lodhis, are beautifully laid out with pleasant undulating lawns, tall, dark and handsome trees, rainbow beds of flowers (especially in February and March) and a curving waterway where king-fishers flash and egrets fish.

When Swami Palang Tode, (né Professor Guruganthalji) first decided to set up the Harbandar Ashram in these lovely gardens, a vicious dogfight broke out between the ranks of the rich, famous and bureaucratic, as had in the past over the issue of whether pet dogs ought to be allowed in or not. Those who considered themselves to be liberal, progressive and 'west-ernised', were horrified by the sudden arrival of a group of

twenty-odd red-bottomed monkeys (what would the diplo-
mats think?) and immediately called for firecrackers and the
services of the famous sariwalla monkey-trapper. Those of a
more conservative bent of mind passionately advocated the
great traditions of non-violence and kindness to animals,
while actually regarding the arrival of the monkeys as a good
omen, and an opportunity for them to atone for sins much
worse than being fat, by offering the animals bribes of bananas
and disco-papaya. Eventually a compromise was hammered
out at the Secretariat of the World Wide Fund for Nature
(WWF-I) located next door; if the monkeys behaved themselves, they could stay (and were not to be fed); if not, they
would be evicted.

What happened was that Swami Palang Tode and the other
founding members of the Harbandar Ashram stunned everyone by their display of immaculate manners. Putting his vast
experience in homo-simian relations (acquired at the NCSEE)
to good use, the Swami himself soon acquired a reputation
as a wise, sagacious and genteel simian, whom it was well
worth driving a long way to meet. (His sneering condescension towards the human species had been misinterpreted as
sublime benevolence.)

What was even more astonishing was the manner in which
he conducted his group. Every morning Swami Palang Tode
would hold an hour-long darshan for visiting simian acolytes.
He would squat regally on the long low wall that abutted the
rose garden, flanked by his colleagues, Swamis Kachcha,
Banyan and Pehelwan, and give benediction to the monkeys
sitting quietly between the beds of roses. (Have monkeys anywhere been known to behave thus?) Most of the 'visitors'
comprised of fat bibiji simians living in the surrounding

colonies who were tormented by tyrannical husbands, were dying of boredom or wished to do some good work before their time was up. One by one, under the watchful gaze of the Kachcha Banyan priesthood, they would shuffle up to Palang Tode to seek solace and blessing — and a stroke on their heads.

These morning darshans so impressed even the most liberal, progressive and 'westernised', that all talk of expelling the monkeys from the gardens evaporated. Instead they were soon being plied with baby corn, asparagus, broccoli and artichokes, brought all the way from Mehrauli smallholdings, and being offered Coke and Pepsi (in cans of course) and Kit Kat. Wreaths of big lemon marigolds and fragrant jasmine were placed around the monkeys' necks as they came up to accept these offerings. The wandering chaiwallas would line up glasses of hot sweet tea on the wall and be delighted and grateful when the monkeys slurped up the beverage.

After the darshan, Swami Palang Tode would make his way conspicuously through the flower beds (he could hardly be expected to walk over mere grass), his tail arched high and stiff, to his personal quarters: the tomb of Sikander Lodhi, which stood in the middle of an elevated, walled-in-garden studded with trees, and which overlooked the waterway. Here he would retire for the morning while his personal attendant, the Cheli Tabli, would supervise (under the eagle eye of the Kachcha Banyan swamis), the entry of those who had been granted private audience with him on that day. Each visitor would be made to wait on the grave in the tomb, from where the Swamiji himself would escort them up to the niches in the upper sections of the tomb, where it was dark and private and where secrets and confessions could be spilled.

Certainly, for him, it was a big step-up from the days when

he had run the NCSEE at the Delhi zoo, and frankly the Swami had only Rani-beti to thank for it. For which godman, no matter how rich, influential or crooked, has managed to shanghai such a prize piece of real-estate in the heart of the capital, in order to set up an ashram? But Swami Palang Tode did not see it like that. He felt no debt of gratitude was owed to Rani-beti for giving him his freedom, and consequently all this. Instead his desire to wreak vengeance on the little princess for bringing down his zoo institutions and shattering his ego continued to burn as brightly as the halo that burnished his head when he sat down in the path of a slanting sunbeam, as was his wont.

After the debacle at the zoo, the Kachcha Banyan gang had reunited with their captured field-agent Pehelwan and had quickly realised that their best bet lay in joining forces with this wily, syrup-tongued old cock, who had such an incredible modus operandi with the opposite sex, not to mention a personal vendetta against their quarry. Ex-Managing Director of the Bhangra Bandars, the showman Pehelwan, had also pragmatically, though temporarily, jettisoned his ambitions of marrying Rani-beti and running the Khyber Pass Massage Parlour, and had quietly rejoined his old gang. Actually, he hadn't done badly at all — having progressed from hitman to showman to godman in a matter of months. (Though some may argue that there is no difference between the three.)

At any rate, for Swami Palang Tode and the Kachcha Banyan swamis, Lodhi Gardens was a paradise where they could freely preach the art of attaining and spreading peace, bliss, mental and physical nirvana, and plot their revenge on the little princess who had indirectly been responsible for it all.

Now, the Swami's most-recent rich and famous disciple,

the lush Cheli Suna Hai, Chief Concubine at Badtameezgarh, clambered up the steps and addressed Swami Kachcha who had seen her coming.

"You sent word that Swamiji wishes to see me?" she inquired humbly, touching her nose to the ground, her roseate bottom raised temptingly.

"I may have," he replied in that enigmatic way godmen have, "Or on the other hand, I may not have."

"Would you kindly tell him that I am here?"

"I could tell him that, or I could tell him that you ignored his wishes. It depends on me."

"I will make it well worth your while to tell him that I have obeyed him. Half-an-hour's exclusive 'haat malish' in the casurina grove after I have met him, including the exquisite hot finger treatment in special areas…"

"Fifteen minutes now, and fifteen minutes afterwards."

"As you wish, Swamiji."

Ever since the Nawab had become engaged, first to Rani-beti and then to her sister Chamkili, the lush Suna Hai had known no peace. Her roguish, insouciant public reaction to the event disguised the fact that she had been deeply upset and embittered. If there was anyone worthy of marrying the Nawab, it was herself. For years she had sacrificed everything for his pleasure. She had supervised and trained his concubines as though they had been her daughters, brought up dozens of illegitimate offspring, and had made sure that his thrice-daily massage and lice-picking sessions had remained absolutely exquisite affairs. And now he was marrying some pea-brained little twit who would threaten her status of being the only bandari allowed to tweak his battle-scarred ears. There was, of course, a more basic and ancient fear underlying this: she knew that despite her superb massage skills, she was getting on a bit, becoming slow and heavy, and that the Nawab liked his bandaris to be young, succulent and tender. Like that Chamkili creature would undoubtedly be.

Troubled and insomniac for many a night, she had at last sought succour at the Harbandar Ashram, having heard of the legendary healing touch of the great Swami Palang Tode. She had taken leave of Badtameez citing special arrangements she had to make in connection with his forthcoming wedding and he had let her go, albeit reluctantly.

The Swamiji had listened to her with his customary gravity, and nodded empathetically from time to time. A single, trademark ray of sunlight lit up his great head and just gazing upon his calm countenance had brought her an immediate sense of serenity. Here was someone to whom she could easily confide her innermost fears and feelings. Who reminded her in some way of her great shaggy father, long gone. She might have seemed to be a tough, leathery madam from the outside, but she privately believed, that from the inside, she was a soft, sensitive simian with a heart of gold. A heart which now was in danger of being trampled upon and torn asunder by the cretin princess Chamkili of the glittering smile.

"You must meditate deeply about what you think is troubling you," the Swamiji had advised her. "I will too, and together we shall arrive at a solution that shall bring you everlasting tranquillity."

So she had 'meditated' conspicuously within his sight while he had nodded encouragement and smiled gently. But alas, her meditation had brought her no peace, only turmoil. It was only his smile that gave her strength and sunshine.

"Swamji will see you now beti," Swami Kachcha informed

her as they both returned from the casuarina grove. There was a snigger in his manner and a swagger in his walk which was not surprising considering his background and what he had just done to her in the soft bed of fallen casuarina needles.

She waited on the cold, stone grave, and he was suddenly with her, smiling benignly. "Aao betiji, let us go upstairs," he invited, caressing her with his voice. "I hope you have found some inner peace."

"Swamiji, these days I find peace only in your presence." (They all said this.) "When I am away, there is only turmoil boiling in my bosom, like magma in the core of the earth. When I return to Badtameezgarh, there will only be more boiling magma. And when the Nawab marries that Chamkili creature, I fear I will erupt like some terrible, avenging volcano!"

"Shanti beti, shanti! It seems to me that you care a great deal about the Nawab Sahib."

"More than he appears to care about me!" She could not keep the bile and bitterness down.

"Hush Suna Hai, beti. You must not speak so of your lord. You must realise that when a great bandar like him marries, it is often for reasons other than love or desire."

"You mean he may not love or desire this Chamkili creature? But I can tell you for sure that he greatly desired her sister, Rani-beti, to whom he was previously engaged, but who ran away with some awara. He lusted after her Swamiji, more than he has ever lusted after me or any of his bandari concubines."

"She must have been a very seductive thing. But I do feel that your Nawab Sahib is not marrying for love or desire — why should he when he already has someone like you by his side? Besides, leaders like him are far too noble to marry for something so trivial. There are probably reasons of state." And the monumental insult, served up with flattery, went unchallenged.

"Rani-beti and Chamkili are daughters of the chieftain of the Flagstaff Tower clan," Suna Hai admitted grudgingly, clinging to a faint new hope. "And the Nawab Sahib does want a power base in that area."

"So you see Suna Hai, he is obviously not marrying for love, but more out of a sense of duty. Your fears are groundless. This is a political alliance."

"But how can I be sure that I am senior-most in his affections?" she persisted petulantly. "I am Chief Keeper of His Concubines, but he spends more time with the others than with me. And when this Chamkili..."

"...Surely Suna Hai, that is an indication of how highly he regards you and your work? It would be so humiliating for you if he were to seek succour from outsiders, instead of the concubines you have trained so well. He respects your professionalism, and what greater compliment could you ask for?"

"True Swamiji, and thank you for your graceful words. You have made me feel immeasurably better. But I still fear that when this Chamkili arrives, I will be displaced. I may have massage skills which this cretin will not develop in a million lifetimes, but I no longer have the looks or figure that makes him 'mast', and pant and drool at a hundred paces." (Alas, she could not know that Palang Tode himself was fast approaching that state and moved into the shadows.)

"You are a voluptuously beautiful and sensitive bandari, Suna Hai. Both in body and soul. So gentle. So deep. Even if hurt."

"Thank you, Swamiji."

"Perhaps it would make you feel better if you were able to demonstrate your love in a more powerful and poignant way?"

"I would do anything to please the Nawab. To make him feel that he cannot do without me."

"Actually beti, there is something you can do. Something that will demand a huge sacrifice from you. But if you go through with it; it will become clear, to yourself, to me, to the Nawab, to the whole, wide world, that your love for him is as true and limpid and everlasting as the love that built the Taj Mahal."

"What must I do, Swamiji? What sacrifice must I make? I will leap into my own funeral pyre if I have to!" Her pulse was drumming and the sacrificial love-light shining from her eyes. This sulphurous madam was indeed a disgraceful softie.

Swami Palang Tode leaned back and half closed his eyes. The crunch was coming.

"You say the Nawab was bitterly disappointed, even angry, when his engagement to the seductive Rani-beti was cancelled?" he asked quizzically.

"Yes."

"And it was cancelled because Rani-beti ran away with another?"

"That is what I have heard from extremely reliable sources. Her family of course denies that, and claims that she has been severely injured in a fall."

"At any rate, it is clear that the Nawab can now never marry Rani-beti?"

"Yes, that is so. Marriage is out of the question."

"But there is no reason, theoretically speaking of course, why Rani-beti, if found and healthy, could not become one of the Nawab's concubines?"

"What?" She was utterly shocked. She blinked rapidly, scratching her head in agitation.

Palang Tode held up his hand and smiled sublimely. "Beti, just think about it. If you can somehow present the Nawab with Rani-beti as a wedding gift — the crown-jewel of his concubines, he will know without doubt that your love for him runs deeper and more passionately than the deepest, most tempestuous ocean."

"Present Rani-beti as a wedding gift! A jewel amongst his concubines!" She was absolutely flabbergasted. "But... but how am I to do that?"

His smile grew radiant. And like a godman producing sacred ash out of thin air with a wave of his hand, produced instead a princess for the Nawab.

"You leave it to me, Suna Hai beti," he said softly. "According to my information, Rani-beti has been invited to the annual Mughal Gardens Mela that is organised by the Presidential Estate clan. I want you to meet her there and persuade her to visit the Ashram. Once she is here, I will speak to her and make her see the terrible error of her ways. And convince her that her rightful destiny lies at Badtameezgarh, as the Nawab's prize concubine. If she is reluctant, Swamis Kachcha, Banyan and Pehelwan will be only too glad to escort her with you back to Badtameezgarh."

There was something chilling, even venomous about his manner, but Suna Hai was still too stunned by the idea itself to sense it. Certainly this seemed to be a unique (masochistic, most would say) way of expressing her love for the Nawab. But he was addressing her again and she turned her attention upon his now becalmed countenance.

"Beti, there is one more thing you must realise."

"What is that, Swamiji?"

"I have thought about this deeply and it pains me. It seems to me that the Nawab Sahib's love for you is of the purest, most unselfish, glorious kind. He is vastly generous and totally open with his affection, and showers you and his concubines with it. But alas, your love for him appears to be of the possessive, selfish kind. You cannot bear the thought that he might actually come to love this Chamkili cretin more than yourself. Even if it is going to make him happy. As for his concubines, deep down, you resent them. But as that is the way of the world, you have accepted it. Even so, you need to be in control and so have striven to become his Chief Concubine. In this position, you can control and measure the quantity and quality of the pleasure the Nawab receives. Suna Hai beti, this is not merely a measure of your love for the Nawab, but is more so a measure of your lust for power over him. And on the other side of such love dwells hate, which is the boiling magma that is bubbling in your bosom." He shook his head sadly, took her hand and began to stroke it.

And thus chastised by the great, gentle godman, Suna Hai could only lower her eyes, nod humbly and begin to weep. "Actually, it is worse than that Swamiji," she confessed, choking back sobs. "Of late I have also ensured that newly recruited concubines are never too pretty or attractive lest he develops a special passion for them. I have expelled those with whom he had formed a dangerous attachment on the grounds that they suffered from dangerous infectious diseases."

"Which is why, Suna Hai, I am asking you to present Rani-beti to him as a wedding gift. It will be a sterling test of your love and courage, and a step towards salvaging your ravaged conscience. But beti, you will have to go a step further to truly achieve absolution. You will have to learn to give your love selflessly too, for only then can you be truly happy."

"Forgive me Swamiji, I do not understand."

Again the beatific smile, as Palang Tode moved in for the kill. "As you must learn to let the Nawab love selflessly, as he does — yourself, his concubines and in due course, Chamkili, without you becoming jealous or angry — so must you also learn to dispense your own love with equal selfless generosity. And I mean love, not merely massages. You can be sure that there are enough souls bereft of love who will be eternally grateful for your largesse. Don't think for one moment that the Nawab will resent your doing this — indeed he would expect nothing less from you, his beloved Chief Concubine."

"But I doubt very much..."

"Suna Hai, beti! You have doubts! Doubts because your love is still selfish. You think and fear that the Nawab may not approve of your giving your love to others. But it is only because that is still how you feel about him doing so."

She struggled with it. She imagined Badtameez's great rage if he caught her with any other male monkey — surely he would chop her into pieces and feed her to the pariah dogs! Or would he? So far, it hadn't happened because he hadn't caught her. And he hadn't caught her because she had been very careful. Or was it so? Could it be, as Swamiji was saying, that he had expected her to slip behind the big boulders at Badtameezgarh with those lobster-arsed hunks, most of whom had been his trusted lieutenants? She had obliged them, in order to cosset their egos and eke out the little resentments they may have been harbouring; basically, to ensure that the power structure remained stable. A smug nobility meant there were fewer chances of a bloody coup d'etat in the middle of the night. She had played the private Mata Hari. But she had never thought that Badtameez might have realised just this, perhaps she had underestimated his intelligence. Perhaps he had seen her go off with those hulks and deliberately ignored it, knowing why she was doing it.

But these dalliances had never meant anything to her, even if some of them had been physically pleasurable. It was certainly not love she had dispensed to those lizard-eyed petty chieftains, who had come fawning up to her when the Nawab's back was turned.

She looked up shyly, embarrassed that a hard-bitten concubine as herself should be blushing so. "How can I learn to give my love selflessly?" she asked, pitching headlong into the pit he had made her dig for herself. He was wearing his most saintly expression now, and his tongue flickered across his wet lips.

"Let me show you how, voluptuous Suna Hai," he burbled, "Oh let me show you how…"

And alas, the battle-axe Chief Concubine and veteran of love, lust and orgy fell straight into the gossamer net (and hairy embrace) of Swami Palang Tode, and never even realised it. Not even when he began to live up to his self-given name with astounding vigour and indelicacy.

Once a year, when the flowers were at their most glorious, the faceless 'baboons' inhabiting the Presidential Estate threw a grand mela, or fiesta or cocktail — call it what you may — at the Mughal Gardens, to which every Delhizen who was any Delhizen was invited. And if the Lodhi Gardens were considered to be the capital's most prestigious public gardens, the Mughal Gardens were certainly the most prestigious 'private' gardens in the entire country. Ostensibly, the purpose of this mela was to enable Delhizens to celebrate the onset of spring and the advent of the new generation of babies, generally born towards the end of March and beginning of April. More crucially however, the purpose of the mela was to demonstrate to Delhizens one and all, that the Presidential Estate clan still held sway over the First Garden of the country, thus reinforcing their ultimate superiority.

Most proud self-made Delhizens found themselves on the horns of a dilemma when confronted by the gilt-scripted invitation. If they did not attend, it was assumed that they had not been invited, which in turn meant that they were no longer considered a part of the Delhizen elite, which was a social disaster that had a cascading effect on subsequent invitations elsewhere. But if they accepted and attended, it implied that they were acknowledging the overall superiority of the Presidential Estate clan — a bunch of faceless, nameless 'baboons' known only by their designations.

At the function, the invitees would first gather in the gardens in the Estate and then make their way towards the gorgeous main venue. (Note: Only a general account of what took place can be given here, as specifics pertaining to hours, locations and the flower-beds in question come under the purview of the Official Secrets Act.) Here, the tempo would pick up and the group would begin to disperse between the flower beds. The dazzling colours, the heady perfumes, the thrumming of the bees, the liquid melody of the birds and the magnificent ambience would go to their heads like buckets of pink champagne. The deflowering and feasting would commence: fistfuls of rose petals stuffed into cheeks, sunset-shaded nasturtiums eaten en masse, honeysuckle sucked dry, and the big shaggy dahlias, like so many multicoloured suns, beheaded just for the heck of it. As the party got going, petal and flower fights would break out, degenerating into all-out orgies, amidst screams and shrieks of delight. All too soon, the Delhizens would go completely berserk — much to the smirking delight of their hosts — and would lay waste months of painstaking work in a matter of minutes. Many of the invitees took this as an opportunity to get their own back at the Estate clan for past harrassments, though frankly, the Estate clan didn't give two hoots about what happened to their prize and pristine garden. They weren't paying for the damages, and that's where the buck stopped. By the time the orgy of deflowering was over, the Gardens would be in ruins, the gardeners in tears, and the commandos itching to squeeze the triggers of their submachine guns. Of course they never did, and the sticks and stones they hurled at the Delhizens only excited the guests further.

This time, several of the notable Delhizen clans from the northern part of the capital did not attend the Mughal Gardens Mela because of the bitter civil war on the Ridge. Nor did the powerful and dangerously ascendant chieftain Nawab Bade Badtameez, though his Chief Concubine, the luscious Suna Hai did grace the occasion. The most celebrated guest however, was the enigmatic princess Rani-beti from Neem Rana, and her strange, skinny consort Altu Faltu, who had valorously rescued her from the slavering jaws of tigers and thereby won her hand. The revered Swami Palang Tode from the Harbandar Ashram had put in a brief appearance, more, it was said, so as not to embarrass his hosts by not turning up at all.

Rani-beti sat in the middle of a bed of magnificent ivory roses, each bloom the size of a goblet, and meditatively nibbled at the velvet-smooth petals of one. On the grass nearby, Altu Faltu was surrounded by an admiring throng of the Estate clan, and was regaling them with yet another version of his great tiger hunt. (The number of tigers involved had now increased to three and included a tigress with newborn cubs.) Several times during the course of the proceedings, Rani-beti was called upon to hold up her slim wrist, so that their admirers could examine the fiery orange bracelet she wore, woven out of the hair plucked out from over the tiger's heart. Ghungroo and the Chalta Phurta twins (who hitherto had only gate-crashed occasions of this kind) were fast turning into the life and soul of the party: Ghungroo had begun dancing in the middle of a bed of giant floppy pansies, as the twins drummed out their magic rhythms and the Delhizens stamped and swayed. Bored and a little unhappy, Rani-beti wondered when the revelry would end and they could go back home to the Villa Lantana.

Then a big, grizzled female, who must have once been very beautiful, approached and sat down beside her.

"Halloji," she said, and smiled dazzlingly. "My name is Suna Hai. I just wanted to compliment you: you looked so beautiful just now, sitting here amidst these roses."

"Thank you," Rani-beti replied, a little surprised. It was the sort of thing she would have expected from a stud wanting to pick her up. "I'm Rani-beti from Neem Rana." She glanced at Suna Hai; the face seemed familiar, hadn't she seen it before? But where? So much had happened during the last several months; she had met so many strangers. She summoned up a smile.

"Haven't we met before sometime?" she asked. She was right. They had met before: at her long-ago engagement party thrown in honour of her forthcoming marriage to Badtameez.

But Suna Hai shook her head. "I don't think I've had the pleasure," she lied, on instructions from Swami Palang Tode. "I'm a sanyasin at the Harbandar Ashram. You may have heard about it. And about our guru, Swami Palang Todeji?"

"Er, a little. Not very much..."

"A most enlightened and wonderful simian. So full of goodness and love. A saint, really." (Though it is debatable whether Rani-beti would have considered his 'Selfless Love Programme' saintly.)

Suna Hai pursed her lips and raised an eyebrow delicately. "Forgive me Rani-beti, but when I spotted you at first, you seemed to look so preoccupied and worried. Like some beautiful tragedienne sitting there amidst the blooms. Is something troubling you? Of course, it is probably none of my business, but being with Swamiji at the ashram has made us so sensitive to the signs of suffering in others, that I couldn't help noticing. Is anything the matter?" Certainly the good swami had coached her well in playing his game.

"Er, no... yes," stuttered Rani-beti, surprised and a little nonplussed. "But it is a personal family matter really."

Why, she wondered, was this vaguely familiar female being so inquisitive? Why were they all like this? Always poking and prying and asking loaded questions like, 'He is your husband-ji, no? So sweet and brave, no?' Still, at least this one had not asked her any such questions. As yet.

"If there is something that is bothering you, why don't you see Swamiji about it?" The ravaged dowager was now speaking earnestly, while stuffing her cheek pouches full of rose petals. I am sure he will be happy to help you."

"Surely he is too busy for such trivial matters?"

"Well, yes, he is busy. I will grant you that. But he may not think the matter to be as trivial as you think. And yes, I could possibly fix something for you — if you feel like it. I'm only suggesting this because, just recently, Swamiji helped me out of a great personal crisis. His advice was so sound, so full of wisdom. I found so much peace of mind, so much shanti. For the first time in my life, I knew contentment."

"Really?" A flicker of interest lit up briefly in Rani-beti's eyes. Perhaps this Swami Palang Tode fellow could give her some advice and consolation after all. She was now aching to visit her home on the Ridge, to meet her family, especially Bibi-Do, and above all, to make up and forget the terrible past and have her baby in the Serpentine arbour where she had been born. But she knew that she could be endangering her own and her unborn baby's life if she ventured near the Ridge — the Flagstaffers were still notoriously feudal in such matters. Even if her father forgave her, which was doubtful, the other outraged males in the clan would bay for her and her baby's blood. Altu Faltu had probably been right to forbid her to go. "I can go there myself and do a recce, if you wish," he had courageously offered, but she had refused, terrified that she would lose him again. He'd be dead meat if he were found on the Northern Ridge, regardless of what he might have done to an enclosure full of tigers. But now, her new friend was addressing her again.

"I see you are expecting a happy event. My congratulations. But it is very important that you remain joyous and radiant while in such a condition. Otherwise it can cause all sorts of psychological problems to the baby. Is this your first one?"

"Yes."

"Ah, then it is doubly important." But now, Suna Hai was suddenly having second thoughts herself, followed by very evil ones. Presenting the Nawab with a slim, sexy princess as a wedding gift concubine was one thing, but presenting him with a heavily pregnant one was quite another and open to interpretation and misunderstanding. Judging by the look of things, the wedding date and the princess' date of delivery appeared to be perilously close to one another. She lidded her eyes... If Rani-beti was to lose her baby she would regain her svelte figure and there would be no nuisance brat either...

The princess was saying something to her now and she switched on her bright smile.

"Maybe you are right, Suna Haiji," she was saying. "There is a personal matter that is worrying me and I wouldn't like it to affect my baby in any way. Perhaps if I could talk to the Swamiji, it would help."

Suna Hai's smile grew dazzling. "Of course it will!" she cried. "I can assure you of that."

"When would it be convenient?" the princess inquired meekly.

"Why don't you come to the ashram in the morning, the day after tomorrow? You may have to wait a bit, but I will see that I fit you in. I'm handling the Swamiji's schedule these days, so there should really be no problem."

"Thank you so much. I will be there."

"Good, then that's fixed. Er, there's just one thing. It would be better if you came alone, Rani-betiji."

"Oh! But I don't think Altu Faltu would let me come

alone. The ashram is a long way off and I'm not very familiar with the roads."

"Well, at any rate, don't bring him along. Just for this first meeting. You see, Swamiji feels that he must see, talk to, and experience an individual completely alone the first time — as an individual. What you tell him must in no way be influenced by the presence of those — especially family members — who usually are a part of the problem. You, as an individual are of paramount importance — your fears, your feelings, your desires, hopes and joys. Once he has imbibed and assessed the nature of the problem, he may probably want to meet your dear husbandji. And then, perhaps the two of you together." She looked rather pointedly at Rani-beti's stomach, and added, "If that is the nature of the problem, of course."

Rani-beti blushed furiously. "No, no, it's nothing like that," she intervened hastily. "Actually it's rather more complicated, really. Will it be all right if I brought an uninvolved companion then? That little dancing monkey out there — my friend Ghungroo?"

Suna Hai glanced at the gyrating Ghungroo and thought, 'Well why not?' She could even be a bonus gift for the Nawab; a little nautch bandari. "Certainly," she smiled. "So I will be expecting you. There is a little stone guardhouse near Gate Number Three of the Lodhi Gardens. I'll be there at seven thirty in the morning."

"We'll be there too," promised Rani-beti, her heart already lighter within her.

She broached the subject with Altu Faltu later that evening at the Villa Lantana. "I met the British Embassy female at the Mughal Gardens," she said. "She's invited Ghungroo and me for an overnight 'At Home' in the Embassy grounds tomorrow. A kitty party. You wouldn't mind if I went, would you?"

"I thought you couldn't stand the virago," Altu Faltu remarked, surprised, but then checked himself. Lately, Rani-beti had become a rather sad and depressed little monkey, suffering from acute homesickness. But since the Mughal Gardens mela that afternoon, she had cheered up considerably. He thought he'd better humour her now.

"Sure you can go. It would probably do you a lot of good. You know, to mix around a bit in the sort of society we have now become a part of, and that kind of thing."

There was, of course, no way Rani-beti could have told him the truth. She knew how rabidly jealous he could be, and that he would immediately be suspicious if informed that Swami Palang Tode insisted on meeting her alone. Either he would want to come along, or would refuse to let her go. This seemed to be the more practical way. Ghungroo, with whom she had already discussed the subject, had been absolutely thrilled.

"What?! Leave these three fellows here to fend for themselves and go and meet some handsome Swamiji? How utterly divine!" She had been practical too. "The Lodhi Gardens are a long way off, Rani-beti. I suggest we leave here early tomorrow afternoon. We should reach there by the evening and can spend the night at the India International Centre which is next door. It is comfortable and the food's not bad, so the Chalta Phurta twins tell me. Then we can easily be in time for your appointment with the Swamiji. Gosh, this is exciting."

"It's odd, you know," Altu Faltu remarked to Langoti the

next afternoon, after they had seen off the two little bandaris. "Rani-beti couldn't stand that female when they dropped in to see us — now she can't seem to wait to meet her again."

"In her condition," snorted Langoti in his laconic manner, "expect the unexpected. Don't be too surprised if they both turn up in half-an-hour, disgusted by the whole idea."

But Yaar was having nothing of that. "Come on, you two," he shouted. "Let's go and have a ball at the Taj Palace and Maurya. It's been bloody ages since we had a night out on the town!"

Rani-beti and Ghungroo were tired and footsore by the time they slipped into the lovely garden of the India International Centre, late that evening, but glad that their journey had been uneventful. Much refreshed by the next morning, they helped themselves to some king-sized dew-fresh roses, before slipping across to Gate Number Three of Lodhi Gardens, looking anxiously around for Suna Hai.

"There she is!" whispered Ghungroo excitedly, clutching Rani-beti's arm and pointing to the small lookout-post jutting out of the old guardhouse. Sure enough, the big, ravaged madam was squatting there, composedly picking the fleas off her coat. She saw them and smiled.

"Halloji, good-marning, and welcome to the Harbandar Ashram. I hope you had a pleasant journey. Come along, this way please, follow me." They kept to the shrubberies and undergrowth, for the gardens were noisy and crowded at this hour, and it was all too easy to be run over by a jogger or chased by a dog. They stopped at last, beneath a flamboyant wig of magenta bougainvillea.

"You'll have to wait awhile, I'm afraid," Suna Hai informed them." Swamiji will see you once the crowds thin out. They tend to disturb those whom he is trying to calm and pacify and reach. Stay in these trees and I'll come to collect you as soon as he gives the word."

For over an hour they waited, as the gardens gradually emptied. Then at last there were only the tombs left, rising solidly out of the thinning mist. Suna Hai materialised silently at their side.

"Swamiji will see you now," she whispered with hushed devotion, and they jumped. "Ghungrooji, will you wait here please while I take Rani-beti inside? Later the Swamiji will give you his blessing too."

Suna Hai led Rani-beti over an artless, misaligned bridge and then up a few steep stone steps. They entered the small walled-in garden, which was broody and rather untidy, Rani-beti thought. The trees stood around like sombre sentinels, the grass was littered with leaves, and the tomb itself made you hesitant. Up in the thick branches of the trees, the Kachcha Banyan swamis kept very still indeed, and watched. Suna Hai led Rani-beti inside the massive stone tomb.

"Make yourself comfortable, my dear," she said rather ghoulishly, indicating the gravestone. "Swamiji will be with you in a moment." And left the little princess alone.

Rani-beti glanced around her a little nervously. The dome was high and dark, the stone cold and hard, and the shadowy walled-in garden with its bluish grass-mist and thick-trunked trees, somewhat claustrophobic. A faint chilly current wafted through the tomb, making her shiver. Then she heard the rough shuffle of simian feet, the dry rustle of hard pads descending rough stone steps. She turned towards the sound, her heart suddenly fluttering.

Professor Guruganthalji, alias Swami Palang Tode, emerged out of the very walls as it were, stepping out of a stairway sunk into an alcove in one of the entrances. He turned towards her, his head as always, illuminated by a single sunbeam. And he smiled at her with all his canines.

"So, Rani-beti, you have come to me for advice once again! About love?"

"You!" She turned to flee, but suddenly they were all around her, blocking out the light. Kachcha, Banyan and even the double-crossing Pehelwan.

"Ah, Rani-beti," the Professor was saying in that warm-treacle voice, "I'd like to introduce you to Swamis Kachcha, Banyan and Pehelwan. I believe you knew them before, but in a different capacity."

"Let me go, you apes, let me go! What do you want from me?" She could see the two-timing Suna Hai hovering nervously in the background.

"Of course we will let you go, Rani-beti. We can't hold you against your will. But we can only let you go to your rightful home and destiny. That is our sacred duty."

"You are going to take me back to the Ridge?" she asked incredulously.

"The Ridge is no longer your home, Rani-beti. No, you now belong to Bade Badtameez, Nawab of Badtameezgarh. Alas, you go not as his bride — but then you only have your-self to blame for that — but as his concubine. I'm afraid that is the best we can do for you under the circumstances. I'm sure you understand."

He stared at her. There was nothing he would have liked more than to escort her up those steep, narrow steps to his private quarters, and begin to do to her, in minute detail, what he had been doing all these days to Suna Hai. But she would not go willingly, gratefully — she would kick and bite and scream. And for him, the sweetness of conquest lay in the capitulation of the mind, not merely the body. Like the others, she ought to have been begging him, weeping for him to take her. But with Rani-beti he had failed, for the first time, and he felt as vicious as a just-jilted lover. Casting her amongst the concubines of the debauched Badtameez (from whom, thanks to Suna Hai, he had learned several disgusting techniques) was the only way he could get some revenge and satisfaction out of the situation.

"Take her to Badtameez immediately," he ordered, and vanished up the stairs into the darkness.

Ghungroo waited in the trees for a short while before her impatience and curiosity got the better of her. She shinned down and made her way towards the crooked bridge, before the sounds of frantic screams stopped her. She scampered up a convenient tree, her heart beating fast. There had been something terrifyingly familiar about that scream. And her eyes nearly popped out when she saw the small procession emerge from the fortress-like walls of the dark, shady garden. Rani-beti, surrounded and dragged by a gang of hirsute thugs, was kicking and screaming. In the lead was the Sanyasin Suna Hai, looking tense and annoyed.

As they struggled down the steps and came towards the trees they had left her waiting in, she heard clearly what Rani-beti was screaming.

"Run Ghungroo run! They are taking me to Badtameez! Get help, Ghungroo. Tell Altu Faltu. Help Ghungroo!"

Then one of the big swarthy fellows clouted her brutally over the head and she keeled over. The group paused beneath the trees she was meant to have been waiting in, and Suna Hai peered up into them and called out. Eventually, she shrugged and the group continued on its way and vanished amongst the trees.

Ghungroo was about to slither down from her hiding place when she caught sight of another huge simian standing on the top of the steps just outside the walls of the garden. A familiar figure, wearing a familiar paternal smile. Professor Guruganthalji, alias Swami Palang Tode, was watching with evident satisfaction.

She made it back to the Villa Lantana in record time. She scampered up the driveway, in the last stages of exhuastion, sobbing with grief and relief. Altu Faltu and the Chalta Phurta twins were lounging on the rickety verandah, lazing away the exertions of their night on the town. She collapsed weeping into the arms of the astounded twins.

"Altu Faltu," she wailed, huge sobs wracking her body. "Rani-beti's been kidnapped. She's been taken to Badtameez!" And then, echoing the cretin princess Chamkili at the Battle of the Nicholson Cemetery, she wept, "Do something, do something!"

Chapter 10

A WEDDING GIFT FOR BADTAMEEZ

Nawab Bade Badtameez sprawled in princely abandon as four of his peachy concubines groomed, kneaded and massaged him. But in spite of their expert ministrations, he was not in the best of moods. It had been days since his Chief Concubine, Suna Hai, had gone off on her mysterious errand — allegedly in connection with his forthcoming wedding. It was not as though the housekeeping at the fort was falling apart because of her absence as she had left well-trained substitutes; it was just the idea that she was no longer in the range of his direct control that galled Badtameez. He could not, had not, for days, been able to direct her every waking, breathing moment, and God knew what she might get up to after inhaling the first few lungfuls of freedom. The only liberties she was allowed to take were with him, with his permission, of course.

He was, however, looking forward to his forthcoming wedding. Word had come from the Northern Ridge —

accompanied by profuse apologies — that matters there had settled down, and that Chamkili of the glittering smile eagerly awaited her royal lord and master to-be. The wedding itself was to be a grand affair and would take place at the historic Flagstaff Tower, the seat of power of the clan. Badtameez grinned brutally. Yes, he would marry Chamkili and her glittering smile, and then demand the abdication of the Chaudhury in favour of himself, in compensation for the inconvenience and disrespect caused to him, first by the Rani-beti fiasco, then the delay and uncertainty caused by the civil war. If the Chaudhury refused to hand over power, the barat of one thousand fighting bandars would see to it that he did. He knew that the Chaudhury's forces had been under considerable strain over the last several months, after their recent humiliation in the Battle of the Nicholson Cemetery and the subsequent siege and struggle on the Ridge. They would be a pushover. Indeed, he would push for the entire Northern Ridge, for even the Chaudhury's opponents were likely to be in a weakend, enervated condition after so many months of conflict. There was nothing like a civil war to assist easy third party intervention.

It would be a marriage followed by a massacre. What more could any self-respecting feudal chieftain ask for?

One of his pretty little concubines came up to him and lowered her eyes. "Madam Suna Hai presents her compliments and begs permission to see His Highness," she announced formally.

He sat up. "High time she returned," he grunted. "She had better have a valid explanation for her long absence. Send her over at once."

She came at once and immediately offered her posterior

as a mark of respect. There was a strange, expectant look in her eyes.

"So you have decided to come back?" he said and cuffed her. "I nearly got myself another Chief Concubine."

"Forgive me, Your Highness. But the nature of my assignation required me to travel great distances."

"You have been very secretive about this so called assignation of yours, Suna Hai. And you know I do not like secrets. No one keeps secrets from Badtameez."

She came to him and began grooming him in that tingling way that had him squirming with ecstasy like a jungle babbler.

"You know, there is no one happier than myself that the Nawab is getting married at last," she lied valiantly, her heart beating fast.

"So?"

"So, as Chief Keeper of your Concubines, I found it was my duty to look for a gift for the Nawab that would befit the great occasion. I had to search high and low, travel far and wide, before I found one befitting enough."

"A wedding gift? For me?" He laughed, pleased. "What is it, Suna Hai, and why is there that glint in your eye?"

It was the shine of tears but she went on bravely. "Huzoor, no one knows more than I do how disappointed you were, how heartbroken and desolate, when your engagement to the fair Rani-beti was broken..."

He stiffened and began bristling. "Yes," he said shortly, "and the Flagstaffers shall pay dearly for it. But what has that got to do with your gift, Suna Hai?"

"Huzoor, it is not merely a matter of a broken engagement!" She was indignant. "It's the despicable, specious grounds upon which it was broken. We all know the fair Rani-beti was seduced by a drunken awara bandar and ran away, and was not injured in any fall as claimed by the Flagstaffers."

"Suna Hai, I do not want to hear about Rani-beti any-more..."

"Huzoor, just listen to what I have to say. Under the present circumstances, it's out of the question that you ever marry Rani-beti now, even if she regrets her misguided affair and returns chastised, even if you desire her more than anything else in the world." She paused significantly and took his hand. "As I know you still do," she added softly, gently.

This was perfectly true. And Badtameez's anger boiled over. "I've told you Suna Hai, I will marry this Chamkili creature. Then I shall take over the Northern Ridge. And then I shall scour the area until I find Rani-beti and her bekar seducer. That's when the wedding celebrations will really begin."

And Suna Hai smiled like a happy gharial, even though inside, she felt as though she was in the jaws of one. "Huzoor, you won't have to search high and low for Rani-beti," she said sweetly, shaking her head.

"What do you mean?"

"I have brought her here for you, as a concubine. A wedding gift from myself."

"What?!"

"Yes. I sought her out. And persuaded her with the help of friends, philosophers and holy men to agree that it would be in her best interests to accept a position as one of your honourable, prestigious concubines. Alas, she is young, impressionable and very silly and has gotten herself extremely pregnant. So we will have to wait for the baby's birth before she can be formally presented to you." Suna Hai had, in fact, abandoned her diabolical plan to force Rani-beti to abort — it was too late and too risky. She didn't want to lose the princess now that she had her in her possession. The Nawab was gabbling with excitement.

"Where is she? I don't believe you have got her! How did you do it, Suna Hai?"

"I have my methods, huzoor." She gave his ear a nibble. "Do you wish to see her? A preview perhaps?" She slipped behind a rough stone wall and reappeared in a moment. And then, to the clarion fanfare of trumpets, Rani-beti was dragged before the bestial, feudal hulk who was to have become her husband, by the revered Swamis Kachcha and Banyan. He swaggered up to her and took her face in his huge, rough hands.

"Rani-beti!" he mocked. "You have come to me at last, my beloved bride!" And laughed coarsely, as she flinched and shut her eyes, expecting a slap.

"Tsk, tsk," he went on, pointing at her stomach. "Naughty, naughty! To present yourself in front of your betrothed in a state of such flourishing pregnancy!" Again he laughed and pinched her cheek hard enough to make tears spurt out. "We shall have to do something about that, Rani-beti, shan't we? We can't possibly have a little bastard bandar scuttling about Badtameezgarh. What will everyone think?"

"Keep away from me, you hairy bully," she screamed suddenly, half-hysterical.

He shoved her away so roughly that she reeled, causing Kachcha and Banyan to stagger. Then he put his face close to hers. "I don't like the idea of that fat... thing in your stomach coming between us, Rani-beti." he hissed. "I think we need to get rid of it."

"You bastard! Don't you dare lay a finger on me or my

baby!"

This time he roared with laughter, and pointed at her stomach again. "Just look at who she is calling a bastard! My dear, may I point out that you happen to be carrying the genuine article yourself?"

"Perhaps if Rani-beti rested awhile, she might be in a more congenial state of mind," intervened Suna Hai smoothy, knowing that Badtameez was quite capable of making Rani-beti abort then and there and to hell with the conseqences. "Take her to the cellars," she ordered quickly.

They dragged her down some incredibly steep steps, and cast her into a dark mossy cell, with just a narrow slit for an entrance. Two enormous eunuchs squatted by the entrance, silent and omnipresent.

Up on the battlements, Suna Hai was cuddling up frantically to the Nawab, doing unmentionable things with her hands. She had seen the ravenous glint in the Nawab's eyes as he had baited Rani-beti and knew its meaning. It was impossible not to feel jealous, as Swami Palang Tode had urged her, though God knows, she tried.

"I hope you liked her," she purred, "even if she is a little foolish and immature as yet."

"Yes, I liked her. And I want her. Now!"

"Huzoor, you will have to wait for the baby to be born. Especially if you wish to do with her what you do to the other concubines and myself."

"Get rid of the baby then, can't you?"

"It is too late, unfortunately. If we get rid of it now, we will almost certainly lose Rani-beti too."

"How long before the bastard chuhe ka lendi is born?"

"A week. Not more."

"Too long. I am getting married in a week. I want her now. Get rid of that baby Suna Hai. It's your job."

She wrapped her arms around him. "Nawab sahib," she purred. "I have an even better idea..."

"Tell me, Suna Hai. Tell me and then go get rid of that baby."

"You really do want to humiliate this Chaudhury, don't you?"

"Of course. Almost as much I desire his daughter."

"And to take over the Ridge?"

"I intend to. And that is just the beginning."

"Well, huzoor, listen to me. I suggest we take dear pregnant Rani-beti along with us, as part of the barat, back to her home on the Ridge. Secretly and incognito, of course. After you and the cretin Chamkili are irrevocably wed, you request, out of the goodness of your heart, to meet the ailing Rani-beti. Such a noble gesture, no? You wish to meet her, to wish her a speedy recovery, to give her strength, encouragement and your blessing. The Flagstaffers will, of course, get very flustered and make several excuses. They may say that Rani-beti has contracted something infectious or perhaps even that she has expired. That's when we pull our rabbit out of the hat as it were — Rani-beti from our midst. The Flagstaffers' humiliation will be complete. To satisfy your honour, you demand immediate control of all territories on the Northern Ridge held by the Chaudhury who, following this public disgrace, will have no choice but to comply. They will capitulate without a murmur and their degradation will be total. Those opposing them will seize this chance and be ready to join issue with us."

Badtameez looked at Suna Hai with wonder. It was a

masterpiece of strategic plotting. This was cutting-edge psychological warfare. This was far better than his own plan: he was big enough to acknowledge that. With Rani-beti in his custody, and pregnant by some awara, he, her outraged ex-fiance, virtually had a divine right to the Ridge. He gloated over what would happen: the smug Chaudhury and his three fat wives would first fuss and hover all over him, heaping platitudes and delicacies on his head. Chamkili's mother would be in proud tears. And then, the ceremony over, he would make his gallant request. Ah, the guests would sigh, if only the silly princess had not gone branch-swinging like a tomboy... They would murmur in approval. There would be consternation and confusion amongst the Flagstaffers. Then the excuses. And then the final denouement as he produced the pregnant princess for all to see. For the Flagstaffers, there would be no comebacks after this. He would righteously demand the Ridge in honourable compensation. And if Rani-beti had her baby then, he could even present her oaf of a father with a bastard grandchild. Of such things were legends made!

And all thanks to wonderful Suna Hai. It made him wince to look at her sometimes these days; perhaps he could leave her in charge of the Northern Ridge after the takeover, as he proceeded on his conquests further into the city. It would be a great way to pension her off and enable him to have a free hand with any of the damsels that caught his fancy during the course of his campaigns. He had noticed of late that she had disqualified all the more beautiful bandaris that had come his way on grounds of health. But yes, Suna Hai was proving to be better as a military strategist than a Chief Concubine. She was smiling at him again, adoration in her eyes.

"And guess who I have lined up to officiate at your wedding?" she said, tickling his ribs.

"Who?" He was agog.

"The great, revered Swami Palang Todeji himself! Of the world-famous Harbandar Ashram. What's more, he has very kindly offered to let the barat halt overnight at the Ashram en route to the Ridge. All arrangements will be made."

He grinned at her. "My darling Suna Hai! What would I do without you? You are truly brilliant! And in appreciation of your wonderful gift and ideas, I am pleased to tell you that I too have something special for you."

"What's that Nawab sahib?" she asked, delighted, clapping her hands and thanking Swami Palang Tode from the bottom of her heart for all his sound advice. "What's that?"

"A surprise," he answered, taking her hand and dancing clumsily around the couryard. "You will get it at the right time and right place. Not before."

"I can hardly wait," she murmured, pulling him close.

"Nor can I," he said. "But now it's time for my orgy Suna Hai, time for my orgy."

Three mornings later, Badtameez was once again disturbed in the midst of merry-making. This time by a frantic messenger from the postern gate.

"For... forgive me, sir," he stuttered, averting his eyes, as Suna Hai (who had been choreographing the orgy) shot him black looks, "but there is a monkey at the postern gate who claims his name is Altu Faltu Sherkhanewala, and that he has come to collect the princess Rani-beti."

Badtameez continued to do what he had been doing, but fixed a bloodshot eye on the messenger.

"Why are you telling me all this bakwas?" he inquired thickly. "Why haven't you killed the bastard yet and brought me his head?"

"Sir," quavered the messenger, backing off, "he has threatened to do to the guards what he did to the tigers at the Delhi zoo — you must have heard about the terrible disembowelling incident? He gutted three tigers singlehandedly, they say. He says he will leave peaceably if the princess Rani-beti is handed over to him unharmed."

"Tell him to get lost. Tell the guards to kill him if he causes any trouble. Now go! I have other plans for Rani-beti."

Suna Hai took the Nawab by his battle-scarred ear and pulled him gently towards her. "Once moment huzoor," she whispered. "Suna hai this Altu Faltu fellow can be a dangerous creature. Too dangerous to be running around loose. And what he did to those tigers is true — I've seen the tiger-hair bracelet he gave Rani-beti myself. I think we should invite him in and um... arrange a little accident." She put her mouth to his ear and continued whispering. Badtameez's eyes gleamed. Once again, his Suna Hai had shown what a shrewd strategist she could be.

"Send that Altu Faltu bandar over immediately," he commanded. "With a guard detail of course."

And so it came to be that Altu Faltu (Sherkhanewala) found himself face to face with his arch rival and enemy for the first time ever. He had been astonished by the respect and courtesy that had been extended to him by the fort guards; evidentally his reputation as a tiger-slayer had created awe even here.

Actually he had almost gone to pieces (yet again) when Ghungroo had brought the devastating news; he had very nearly rushed off to the Willingdon Hospital to get blind drunk. This time it had been the Chalta Phurta twins who had restrained him.

"You can't do that!" Langoti had exclaimed, horrified. "You're Altu Faltu Sherkhanewala, remember? You disembowel tigers singlehandedly."

"Langoti, you know that's all bullshit! Now let me go." Suddenly he was weary of the charade. "You know it's all fraud. I can't even remember what happened in the tiger's enclosure. And I certainly didn't slaughter, let alone disembowel, it!" He gave a piteous hollow laugh. "Sherkhanewala my arse! How do you think of these names Langoti? Now let me go!"

Instead the twins grabbed him and held him down firmly, as Ghungroo looked on anxiously.

"Listen Altu Faltu, and listen carefully. The whole world believes you killed tigers at the Delhi zoo in order to rescue Rani-beti. That means you did. Even if you didn't. What's important is what everyone else believes. You have a glorious reputation — most clan leaders tremble when they hear your name. Altu Faltu Sherkhanewala! Wah! You have to take advantage of this. Because it is the only way you have a ghost of a chance of rescuing Rani-beti from Badtameez. For real, this time."

"What do you mean," he countered bitterly, "I just walk up to Badtameez and say, 'My name is Altu Faltu Sherkhanewala and will you kindly hand over Rani-beti to me on a silver platter, or else...' He'll kill both of us, then and there!"

"No, he won't! They'll all be so unnerved to see you and

hear your demands, that you may actually get away with it."

"And what happens if it comes to the crunch? If that Badtameez monster challenges me to a duel? Do you know how big and heavy he is? Do you know how ruthless and underhand these feudal chieftains are?"

"The tiger was bigger, more ruthless."

"The tiger was a hoax."

"Only you know that. Not Badtameez. He thinks you fought the tiger. So he won't be too eager to come to grips with you. Nor will his guards or lieutenants. You see, you've become invincible. Only you have to believe it."

"All right, then! Let's go!" Altu Faltu's eyes glittered as the mad passion to flirt with the suicidal suddenly surged through him again. An even more harebrained idea took shape in his silly, swollen head. He would first recue Rani-beti. Then he would challenge Badtameez to a duel. And would fight and disembowel him, just as he had done to a troika of tigers at the zoo. And then he would take over the giant fortress of Badtameezgarh. Dare anyone call him a useless, bekar bandar after that!

Now the four of them eyed the burly massif of the fort apprehensively — Badtameezgarh was certainly no place for the faint-hearted.

"You keep watch," Altu Faltu instructed the Chalta Phurta twins who had accompanied him (to ensure he didn't go off elsewhere to get drunk) as they approached the grim citadel. The twins and Ghungroo disappeared gratefully up a thick neem tree a short distance away from the postern gate. They watched, breathlessly, as Altu Faltu sauntered up to the guards, cool as an ice-cream. And then saw with awe, that amidst much saluting and genuflecting, he was escorted up the steep narrow pathway into the formidable fort.

"**Y**ou wished an audience with me?" Nawab Bade Badtameez enquired, forcing a smile that looked more like a snarl and clenching his fists. Altu Faltu stared at the hulking monstrosity in front of him, hoping no one could hear the drumming of his heart. The lunatic adrenalin had suddenly (as was its wont) drained out of his system.

"I have come to collect Rani-beti," he said courageously.

"Rani-beti? Really, I ought to take strong objection to that statement of yours. Rani-beti is my property, I think."

"Rani-beti belongs to me!"

Rani-beti would, of course, have been appalled to hear herself being argued over like a plot of land. She loved Altu Faltu but was no one's clod of earth.

"Altu Faltu," the Nawab said through gritted teeth, doing his best to keep his rage under control. "I happen to have been engaged to Rani-beti before all these... er, unfortunate developments took place. Rani-beti, after much introspection and soul-searching has finally come to her senses. She has come here to Badtameezgarh, where she belongs, of her own free will."

"She was kidnapped!"

The Nawab raised an arm and both Suna Hai and Altu Faltu thought he was about to strike. Instead he continued with dangerous calm. "If you will kindly let me finish... Rani-beti has come to me of her own free will, and begged forgiveness. Unfortunately — and thanks to some irresponsibility on your part — she is in a state that renders her incapable of ever becoming my wife. However, out of the kindness of my heart, and pity for her condition, and on recommendation of my Chief Concubine, Suna Hai, I have agreed to appoint her as one of my Executive Concubines with all privileges and perks pertaining to thereof. The little... er, bastard, when it is born, will be duly looked after communally."

"You lying bastard! Rani-beti will never go to you..." He was shrieking now.

Suna Hai raised an eyebrow. "Begging your pardon, sir," she interrupted smoothly, "then why did Rani-beti come rushing to the Harbandar Ashram in a state of collapse and remorse, and fall at the feet of Swami Palang Tode begging for advice and forgiveness?" Her tone implied that Altu Faltu was fairly and squarely to blame for the princess' distress.

It gave him time to collect and remind himself of his reputation. "Madam," he countered levelly, "Rani-beti was upset over a personal family matter. Now if you will kindly bring her to me, we will be on our way."

The Nawab nodded complacently. "By all means, you can see her. Perhaps Rani-beti ought to inform you herself of her choice. Perhaps you will believe what I am telling you when you hear it personally from her."

That took the wind out of his sails completely. His mouth fell open. The Nawab went on with astounding reasonableness. "You see, Altu Faltu, I, we, have only Rani-beti's happiness and well-being in mind. Everything else is secondary. If she wants to go with you, she is absolutely free to do so." He was talking like a bloody liberal father!

"What? You will let her go? Just like that?" He was incredulous. And then, because he was still a rabidly jealous little monkey, evil suspicions rose and hung over him like a scorpion's tail. The Nawab was nodding slowly, even smiling. Suna Hai was looking radiantly confident. Was it possible, even remotely possible, that Rani-beti had indeed changed her mind about him? And that she had decided to chose Badtameez after all? Even if only to make peace with her family and be able to have her baby on the Ridge? Had she forsaken his love for her baby? Or for Badtameez? Or for both? The great lout Badtameez was still smiling at him.

"Yes," he reiterated, "I will let her go, if that's what she wants." He shrugged self-deprecatingly. "Besides it would not be prudent for us to tangle with a monkey of your reputation and calibre. A Sherkhanewala no less! We are a simple, peace-loving, vegetarian clan."

The foolish awara bandar could almost feel his head swell, and stuck out his skinny chest. The scorpion tail of suspicion wavered and then withdrew. Surely Rani-beti would be delighted to see him? To be rescued by him a second time? Surely Badtameez had realised the folly of trying to cross swords with him and was now trying to wriggle out of a nasty situation as honourably as he could?

"Bring Rani-beti to me," he commanded grandly, as though he owned the fort, nearly causing Badtameez a stroke.

"It would be better if we went to her, oh Sherkhanewala," said Suna Hai milkily, getting into the act. "She is a princess after all and can't be ordered around."

"Very well. Take me to her then!"

Badtameez shambled off the great rock he had been squatting on, his eyes slits of anger. "As you wish," he said, and Altu Faltu felt as though he were lord and master of Badtameezgarh (which he would rename Altu Faltunagar). Accompanied by Suna Hai and the usual retinue of bodyguards, they set off.

"Rani-beti is residing in the Royal Quarters, in the western wing of the ruins," Suna Hai informed him unctuously. "It is dark and cool and quiet in there. In her condition, she needs all the rest she can get." She giggled musically.

Altu Faltu nodded graciously. He was still amazed, (and oh, so flattered!) by the obsequious attitude of the Badtameezgarhis. It was true after all — as the twins had predicted — his reputation had reduced the opposition to quivering jelly. As they made their way across the tumbled rocks and fallen bastions, he thought he would drive the point home, just in case Badtameez was trying to pull a fast one.

"You don't have any big cats here, do you?" he asked the feudal chieftain nonchalantly.

"Eh?" Badtameez turned in surprise. "No. Very rarely the vagrant leopard. Wildcats perhaps."

"A pity," sighed Altu Faltu. "You can't get good hunting anywhere these days. I'm getting out of practice. Perhaps we could do some tiger-baiting at the zoo together sometime, now that we have settled our differences." So confident of his victory was he, even before the event, that he failed to notice Suna Hai lay a strong, restraining arm on the bristling Badtameez, who now looked as though he was suffering from simultaneous attacks of constipation and apoplexy.

They scrambled down the sheer sides of an enormous crater-like depression in the ground, which might have originally been a reservoir, but which now was overgrown with acacia and lantana. They cut across its tangled thorny floor, littered with garbage and the bones of small animals (including condemned monkeys); the light filtered down, bronze green, and it was suddenly silent and still. Then they clambered up the opposite side, along a steep narrow pathway. Halfway up, they entered the mouth of a cave built into the rock, which led into a stone corridor honeycombed with small damp cells where the fug of bats hung thickly. Altu Faltu wrinkled his nose in the curdled air, as Suna Hai began talking once more, brightly and a little too breathlessly.

"We go down here," she indicated, as they entered one of the small cells at the end of the corridor. Deep steps were sunk into the floor. "These lead down to the cellars which we have converted into the Private Royal Quarters," she explained. The steps led down to a large vault-like chamber, almost pitch dark but for faint wisps of light filtering through the cracks in its roof. At one end of the chamber, a large circular stone slab lay on the ground, rather like a modern manhole cover. Purposefully Badtameez approached this, and gave a signal to the guards. Grunting, they hoisted it up and turned it over, letting it fall with a thunderous echoing report and cloud of dust that lit up the slanting sunbeams and sent the bats flickering out in high-pitched panic. Suna Hai sneezed like a bomb going off and Altu Faltu jumped with a stricken yelp. From the floor, the gaping black hole invited a closer look...

"You have her in there?" asked Altu Faltu, his voice rising in horror. He knew in a flash that mischief was afoot.

"No," said Badtameez, unexpectedly close to his ear. "Of course not. As you can see, there are no steps leading down to it."

"No steps?"

"No. Obviously it is a chute of some kind."

"A chute? But... but why are you showing this to me? And where's Rani-beti?" The panic welled suddenly; now he was Altu Faltu again, not Sherkhanewala.

"Oh no, Rani-beti's not there!" Suna Hai sounded horrified. "You can check if you like..."

They were crowding him now, but still smiling. Involuntarily he took a step forward. And then, once again, propelled by that manic surging perversion of his, he stood up on his hind legs and craned over, peering into the circular blackness.

Badtameez's vicious shunt in the small of his back, aided by Suna Hai's vice-like grip on his elbow ensured he had no chance. He staggered forward and then hung suspended over the gaping black hole for an interminable moment. Then he was falling, sliding actually, his arms upraised, his mouth open and his stomach fluttering crazily, as he gathered speed.

Free falling in black, empty space.

He braced himself instinctively for the final crunching thud. But instead of splattering messily on granite, he landed with a soft thump in what appeared to be fine sand. He lay spreadeagled, fighting to get his breath back. It took some minutes for his eyes to adjust to the almost pitch darkness. Fifteen feet above him, he could faintly discern the round black hole he had fallen through. Still gasping, he sat up. He could make out, just barely, that he was in a small underground room of some kind. Half filled with sand. He took a fistful and trickled it slowly through his fingers, close to his face. It glimmered dimly. Reminding him of the flecks in Rani-beti's eyes... He let it pour through his fingers again, and his heart began to thump. This was not sand. This was pure gold dust. A great abandoned treasure of the past. He heard a faint metallic clang echo down from the chute and the vault dimmed further. He knew the chute had been sealed.

He staggered around his golden prison, wrenched by sobs.

"Rani-beti? Rani-beti, are you here? Can you hear me?"

But there was no reply. Only the gold dust shimmered softly in the light it had trapped for so many hundreds of years.

Desperately, irrationally, Altu Faltu began to dig.

Had they buried his beloved Rani-beti in bullion dust?

Chapter 11

BANDARO
KI
BARAT

They set out from their burly rock citadel, two hundred and fifty cavorting, bouncing bandars — the barat of the great feudal chieftain Nawab Bade Badtameez. It was his Pathani boast that a single of his muscle-bound hulks was worth at least four of the best macaques anywhere else — in their ability to eat, drink, fornicate and fight. Hence, he had sent word to the effete Flagstaffers to be prepared to welcome a barat one thousand strong.

Towards the rear of the procession, and guarded by a phalanx of enunchs, was Suna Hai, the other concubines, and in their midst, a devastated Rani-beti who was hardly aware of what was going on. The raucous, shrieking horde passed beneath the leafy neem tree up which Ghungroo and the Chalta Phurta twins had vanished, and where, with undying faithfulness, they still waited for Altu Faltu. They watched goggle-eyed and then Ghungroo clutched Langoti by the arm.

"Look," she whispered, "there, in the middle of all those amazons — Rani-beti!"

But there was no way they could rescue the little princess; no way they could leap out of the trees and carry her off to safety as Altu Faltu Sherkhanewala might have done.

The baratis reached the main gates of the Harbandar Ashram early that evening where they were made welcome by a serene, smiling Swami Palang Tode. As he stepped off the shady path onto the undulating lawns, Badtameez looked around him in awe. He, and the others of his barbarian tribe, had never seen such magnificent gardens before. They were Delhizens from a different, harsher time and place. They were used to the rough-hewn contours of their grim rock fortress, with its sudden-death shafts, its cunning labyrinths, its deep slitted windows, its taloned acacias and derelict forecourts. They were familiar with the ghastly flyblown small towns of Haryana and Uttar Pradesh, mired in sewage and garbage.

But this! Here the lawns were lush, velevety and inviting even to the iron-calloused bottom of the most bolshie bandar. Here, immense flower beds dazzled the eye and made them dizzy with intoxicating fragrances. Here, the monuments stood with grave dignity, neither battered nor crumbling. Here, obliging vendors criss-crossed the lawns bearing freshly roasted gram and peanuts, and cold bottles of cola, while others delved into striped carts and produced heavenly ice-creams, cool and silky to the touch.

Badtameez stuffed his cheek pouches till they hurt, his eyes alight with avarice. Every tribal warlord, every feudal chief-tain, every great conqueror needed a pleasure resort... Some place he could come to after a tiresome campaign or bloody conquest for some much deserved rest and recreation... And wresting the ashram from Palang Tode would be no problem: no Swamiji could refuse his offer of providing protection. But that would have to wait until after his wedding and the conquest of the Northern Ridge. Perhaps he could bring his bride here, for a few days then.

They feasted well that night, the baratis did, as guests of the ashramites. While in a small stone alcove in the wall of Sikandar Lodhi's tomb, Rani-beti clutched her swollen stomach and whimpered. The six implacable eunuchs guarding her stared stonily at the moths whirring dizzily around the lights that blazed upon that noble monument.

They arrived at their final destination — the Khyber Pass Gate of the Northern Ridge — late the following evening after a raucous procession through the city and a much deserved interlude (they thought) at Majnu Ka Tila and the Khyber Pass Massage Parlour (the brainwave of a jolly veteran who had spent his youth in the area).

At the Khyber Pass Gate, Chaudhury Charbi Raisahib, his three wives and Chamkili, the cretin bride, waited tensely as the sounds of revelry drew closer. Of course, it was a bit of a pity that his own respected father, Chaudhury Taza Raisahib, would not be attending the wedding. The grizzled old soak had simply disappeared from his akhara one evening; he had last been seen sitting on the prow of his red and sky blue boat, and it was believed that he had fallen into the river while in a drunken stupour and drowned.

"They're coming!" Bibi-Teen exclaimed excitedly, her eyes glowing. Tail stiff, the Chaudhury paced up and down, bristling with tension. All the arrangements were in perfect order; he was sure of that. The baratis were to be accommodated in a specially prepared area (until recently illegally occupied by an outstation Police batallion, evicted on court orders), just off the tarred private road that linked the Khyber Pass Gate to the Flagstaff Tower. After the traditional welcome of the barat, there was to be a grand banquet that night at the Tower. The actual wedding ceremony was to take place the following morning, also at the Tower, the rest of the day naturally being spent in feasting, dancing and celebration. Another grand reception would be held that evening, and on the morning after, the baratis would depart, taking Chamkili with them, but hopefully forever linking the two great clans. The Chaudhury was only too aware that Haramisahib might well try to embarrass him during this sensitive occasion and the ever gallant General Mushtanda had offered to go on special patrol duty to forestall any potential trouble. There had also been disquieting rumours from the Nicholson Cemetery — reports that the Nicholsonites were conducting rigorous military exercises, as through preparing to go to war. It was no wonder then that Chaudhury Charbi Raisahib was tense and worried, and hoping fervently that the wedding, so long delayed, would take place uneventfully. After that, he would be ready to tackle any crisis, no matter how unpleasant.

At last, some three hours behind schedule, (which was respectable by any standards) the baratis arrived at the Khyber Pass Gate — a screeching, cavorting, fornicating mob of monkeys, reeking of liquor and lust. Characteristically stoic, the Flagstaffers greeted them with stiff upper lips and glazed smiles, bidding them welcome. A reeling, drunk Badtameez was propped up by an inanely grinning Suna Hai and Swami

Palang Tode, murmuring "khamosh ho jao puttar, khamosh!" to no effect.

But Chamkili, whose smile no longer glittered, went as wan as wax and recoiled with horror, sobbing and yearning for the iron biceps of 'Muscles' Mushtanda. "Don't worry," Bibi-Do hissed at her, astoundingly hypocritical, "they always get drunk at this time. It's a sort of male privilege thing."

"I don't like his thing!" Chamkili squawked loudly, shockingly, rebelliously, as though to reiterate her cretin status. Thankfully she was drowned by Badtameez's raucous rabble.

"Hush Chamkili," Bibi-Teen admonished, giggling. "There will be plenty of time for you to make up your mind about that." Bibi-Do shot her a venomous look and Bibi-Ek pursed her lips and looked away.

To the Chaudhury's considerable relief, the banquet that night went off splendidly. The catering was magnificent, and the naughty nautch bandaris from the Walled City had the baratis on their feet, cheering and hooting, in much the same manner as Rani-beti and Ghungroo had the crowds at the zoo during their heyday. All said and done however, especially after their earlier antics, the baratis now behaved impeccably, and there were no unpleasant feudal incidents or brawls. They were guests of the Chaudhury after all, even if they were here to take away his daughter and overrun his fiefdom. Never must it be whispered that Badtameezgarhis had abused the hospitality extended to them.

So they cheered and whistled but otherwise restrained themselves as the bandaris twirled to the rhythm of the drums in the forecourt of the Tower, bathed eerily in the yellow sodium-vapour glow.

Badtameez reclined in Mughlai manner, his mouth slightly

open, his eyes bloodshot and roving, settling leeringly on the beautiful Bibi-do. Her duffer daughter, whom he was to marry, was not bad looking either, he thought, especially when viewed through a haze of chhang, as he had experienced earlier that evening. (Now she was confined within the round walls of the Tower, crying her eyes out.) But what he was really looking forward to was the expression on the old Chaudhury's face when Rani-beti was produced before him, and with her, the demand for control of the Northern Ridge.

Meanwhile, Swami Palang Tode nursed his own thoughts. The lush Suna Hai had never looked so voluptuously desirable before, as on that auspicious evening. He had of course, earlier on, blessed Chamkili and immediately noted her upset demeanour. "If you are in any way troubled, beti," he had told her in that warm, beguiling voice, "you may come to me at any time, and I will try and help you." Preparing the ground for opening yet another cushy little private account.

Chaudhury Charbi Raisahib ensured that his guests were comfortable and tried to enjoy the evening's entertainment. He sat now, with his powerful son-in-law to-be at his right, the suave Swami Palang Tode to his left, and his three bibis in a row behind him with the gushing Chief Concubine.

About two hundred and fifty metres down the road, bound, gagged, blindfolded, and surrounded by her bristling guards, his once-favourite daugher Rani-beti was too tired to figure out whether she was dead or alive. The long journey, the heat, tumult and bustle, the screams and shouts of the great public orgy had unnerved her badly. But with a survivor's instinct, she had clutched her rotund tummy and cushioned it from the jostling and prodding she had been subjected to all of that long, exhausting day. Now, in brief moments of lucidity, she realised that there was something heart-rendingly familiar about her surroundings; about the tone and roar of traffic, the distant barking of dogs, the scent of eucalyptus leaves, and the fresh neem coolness of the air itself.

For Ghungroo and the Chalta Phurta twins however, there was nothing familiar about these surroundings. Over the last two days, they had warily but steadfastly trailed the noisy barat; Rani-beti, they knew, was alive. Altu Faltu had disappeared inside that grim fortress and not reappeared; he was probably dead. They had lain in wait outside Sikandar Lodhi's tomb the previous night but had no chance to rescue the princess. The six, swarthy viragos guarding her hadn't twitched a muscle. Even now, they squatted like rock sphinxes around the trussed-up princess, their stony eyes expressionless, their breath free of the faintest whiff of celebration (but horribly foetid, nonetheless).

High up on the eucalyptus bough, the twins and Ghungroo kept watch, still hoping and waiting, for there was nothing else for them to do. The staccato beat of drums and the jingle of bells carried clearly from the Flagstaff Tower, and filled them with strange, haunting nostalgia.

At the Tower, Swami Palang Tode found Suna Hai's paw and squeezed it, causing Bibi-Teen's ever-quick eyes to nearly leap out of their sockets. A few moments later, as the cabaret reached its climax, Swami Palang Tode rose, excused himself benignly and slipped down the moon-soaked road leading to the barati's campsite. A few decent minutes later, Suna Hai bade goodnight to the Chaudhury's three wives, claiming a headache. Bibi-Teen's eyes attained their hubcap dimensions and she echoed incredulously, "You have a headache, my dear?" And squeezed her hand knowingly.

Sprawled on her eucalyptus eyrie, Ghungroo, whose watch it was, stared down at the barati's deserted (except for Rani-beti and her guards) campsite, and then stiffened. Two monkeys, well entwined, had rather furtively entered the camp and were stumbling towards the little stone lodge that on the following night was to serve as the honeymoon suite for Badtameez and his bride. From the moans and squeals that soon emerged from within it, Ghungroo had no doubt that an extremely torrid honeymoon was under way already. Gleefully she awoke the Chalta Phurta twins.

Inside the lodge, Swami Palang Tode was well on his way to living up to his name with the lush Suna Hai. Unknown to the Chief Concubine however, the Swamiji's mind was not entirely on her, even if the rest of him was. For he was already plotting a strategy to seduce the pretty cretin Chamkili and the bewitching Bibi-Do, as he had done so many others.

"Oh, Swamiji," moaned Suna Hai blissfully, naive to the end, "In time, you must teach the bride Chamkili about selfless love. Just as you have taught me..."

Soon, they fell asleep, exhausted and clamped inextricably in each others' arms. Which alas, is how Nawab Bade Badtameez found them when he returned after the evening's entertainment, pulling a dishy little thing from the Khyber Pass Massage Parlour along with him.

"Suna Hai!" he roared, sending the dogs yelping down the street and the peacocks into paroxyms of panic.

"What... what?" she stuttered, waking with a start and

clutching the entwined Swami even more tightly.

"What the hell do you think you are doing? Are you out of your mind?"

Palang Tode too had awoken and was trying desperately to extricate himself.

"Selfless love!" squeaked Suna Hai dismally. "The Swami's only trying to teach me about selfless love." Suddenly knowing that this would not go down at all well with the obtuse Badtameez. "It's only yoga!" she added, somewhat desperate now.

"Badtameez puttar! Shant ho jao! Be calm, son!" Swami Palang Tode had extricated himself at last and quickly retreated into the path of the single moonbeam slanting through the window. "She is a wonderful lover, I mean learner. So gentle, so passionate, so bright — like this moonbeam!" He emitted his self-effacing little laugh and went on. "So jealous she was, your little Suna Hai, when she learnt you were getting married. I taught her how to get over it."

But Badtameez was shaking with rage. His hair stood erect, his tail was up and his eyes glittered. But admirably, he controlled his temper.

"Do you know who I am, Swamiji?" he asked dangerously.

Again, that incredible, sniggering little laugh. "Of course, Badtameez beta! But I have only taught your dear Suna Hai divine selfless love. As you your goodself practise it!"

"I practise it? Are you drunk or mad or both?" Badtameez took a menacing step forwards.

A whinging, sanctimonious note mixed with wheedling admiration entered the Swamiji's voice. "Yes, you know, giving your divine, benign benediction and love to one and all."

"You took Suna Hai..."

The Chief Concubine stepped in. "Huzoor, listen to me! Please! He taught me to give my love selflessly, to anyone who might desire it. Here, there, everywhere! Truly he is amazing..." She was tripping over her tongue and gazing earnestly at Badtameez. Perhaps... perhaps he would see the point after all. The Swamiji joined her, in his most unctuous, sermonising manner.

"Surely you cannot, must not, do not mind Suna Hai giving her love to others just as you have been doing. Selflessly, nobly of course..."

But Badtameez had bunched himself up into a bristling hairy ball of fury and flattened his ears. Suna Hai held out her arms in front of her, pleadingly, and Palang Tode backed away towards the window, which was now crowded with the faces of the astounded baratis.

"Badtameez beta! Shant ho jao! There is no point in losing your temper."

But it was too late. In a great growling blur, Badtameez was on him, fastening his huge dirty canines on that part of him after which he had so proudly christened himself. Palang Tode screamed, and wrenching himself free, fled, bouncing over the shoulders of the appalled baratis. Blubbering in one corner of the honeymoon suite, Suna Hai suddenly realised what the good Swami had been doing to her all along, and what she had to do now. She flung herself at Badtameez's feet. "He tricked me!" she wailed. "With his sweet words and hypnotic spells. He used black magic and ravished me while I lay help-less! Forgive me huzoor, for I have done great wrong, but innocently so!" She rolled about the floor and beat her breasts, giving vent to a first-rate show of hysterics. She knew she was fighting for her life.

"Get up, Suna Hai and stop blubbering!" Badtameez kicked her and spat out the last traces of Swami Palang Tode. Then he grabbed her by the head and thrashed her soundly, as the baratis at the window began to stomp and cheer and whistle. They liked justice to be dispensed swiftly. At last Badtameez flung her to the floor and towered over her.

"Let that be a brief lesson to you, Suna Hai. Now get out of here. I will deal with you properly after the wedding when we get back to Badtameezgarh."

And Suna Hai knew, that thanks to the devious Swami Palang Tode, she was no longer Chief Concubine at Badtameezgarh. She would be banished from the fort and have to spend the rest of her days wandering forlornly about in the sexual wilderness. And as Swami Palang Tode had once told her, she also now knew that love (proper love, selfish love) and hate were really one and the same thing. A burning, blowtorch rage ignited within her, directed first towards Palang Tode and Badtameez, and later, more effectively, towards every adult male rhesus that lived. She slunk out onto the Ridge that night, and vanished. But for months afterwards, the area was rocked by a string of serial castrations. Young, handsome single rhesus were ferociously attacked by night and incapacitated for life. And thus, in her own terrible way, the voluptuous Suna Hai did much to slow down the galloping birth rate on the Northern Ridge. An even greater service she rendered was the swift balls-off job she performed on the crazed Leechad out on the Hindu Rao Ridge. (He tried to get fresh, and that was that.) And in her anonymous honour, for they never knew who she was, the dishy little bandaris at the Khyber Pass Massage Parlour instituted an annual award for the bandari who had done the most for the cause of their emancipation.

Ideally of course, Suna Hai would have dearly loved her first victim to be Palang Tode himself. But she had been too wrought up that night to follow him. And, ironically, Badtameez himself had already done half the job. Palang Tode fled the Ridge that night and drifted around the Walled City for a while. Going back to the Harbandar Ashram, he knew, was out of the question — that would be the first place Badtameez would look for him. Instead, he eventually fetched up at the Presidential Estate, and making good use of his skill and techniques, became godmonkey to the clan. (Quite influential now, he is, however, sometimes irreverently referred to by the younger generation as "Ek Khajur" Palang Tode.)

The brawl in the honeymoon suite that night riveted the attention of every single barati. And as Badtameez let loose with his flood of biological invective, the six sphinxes guarding Rani-beti stirred restively for the first time. When the cause of the quarrel became obvious, they rose noiselessly and made for the little oblong window, already jam-packed with onlookers. Trussed and blindfolded, Rani-beti lay alone, breathing irregularly, but asleep out of sheer exhaustion.

Like oil on glass, Ghungroo and the Chalta Phurta twins slid down the smooth eucalyptus column. They untied the princess and gently shook her awake. "Come on, Rani-beti," Ghungroo urged. "We've got to get out of here." The twins hoisted her to her feet and supporting her from either side, staggered out of the campsite, across the moon-bright road and into the forest beyond. They floundered helplessly in the bewildering prickly thickets. They knew they had to put as much distance between themselves and the campsite but had no idea in which direction to head. Rani-beti lurched along and then looked at Ghungroo.

"Altu Faltu?" she asked, simply.

"We...we don't know what happened to him..." Ghungroo squeezed her hand and looked away.

They knew.

Rani-beti took a deep, shuddering breath and clutched her swollen stomach, as Langoti and Yaar supported her tenderly. Then she opened her eyes and started.

There, right ahead, glimmering in the dappled moonlight, but rock solid as ever, stood the burly Flagstaff Tower. She was home, even if not quite sure she was dead or alive. But Altu Faltu, she knew, was dead. She had seen her home, and now that they had eventually killed him, had no desire to meet her family. Now she could die properly too, once and for all, and in the time-honoured manner of her kind.

"We are on the Ridge, aren't we?" she asked, her strength flooding back because she knew what had to be done.

"Er... if you say so," Langoti ventured, in his laconic way. "We've never been here ourselves."

"Yes," she confirmed. "This is the Northern Ridge. That's the Flagstaff Tower. My home. Where I first met Altu Faltu." And then pleadingly, cunningly, sentimentally. "Come on. Let me show you where Altu Faltu proposed to me."

"Rani-beti, we all know how you feel. But we have to get away from here as quickly as possible. They'll be after us."

"Don't worry, Langoti," she replied, her face serene and calm. "No one will ever look for us there. Because they wouldn't know why. They'll never understand why."

And clutching the Chalta Phurta twins, with Ghungroo following worriedly, Rani-beti headed unsteadily towards the polished granite waters of the Khooni Khan Jheel.

Back at the barati's campsite, the six, stony-eyed eunuchs returned to their captive — and found her gone. Silently they exchanged glances and began drifting towards the thickets. They travelled like smoke through the tangled undergrowth and picked up the bloody trail left by the fleeing Palang Tode. They sniffed it deeply and their eyes gleamed. Here was one half of their kind... Purposefully they set off. But they never caught up with him. Sometime later, they caught up with the demented Leechad instead, who was twice as good. Today, this gang of seven (along with Suna Hai of course, who operates independently) terrorises lovers on the Hindu Rao Ridge and have prevented many a foolish, simpering couple from fooling about with drugs and cough syrups (as Altu Faltu had done) and worse, from getting married.

Immensely relieved that the banquet had gone off so well, the Flagstaffers slept soundly inside their burly castle that night. Their old sleeping quarters near the Rajpur Road nursery was still in the hands of Haramisahib. All, except Chamkili, who still stifled the occasional sob, and Bibi-Ek who tossed and turned and mumbled to herself.

At last, Bibi-Ek appeared to have dropped off. Chamkili rose silently from her place next to her mother and drifted towards the iron-barred gate. She got it open with the barest clink and slipped out into the cool perfumed night. Disturbed by the sound, Bibi-Ek opened one eye and caught a glimpse of Chamkili's slim silhouette in the bright moonlight. She closed her eyes and turned her face to the wall but did nothing more. All that evening, she had been grieving afresh the tragic loss of Rani-beti, whose wedding this ought to have been. Now, if Chamkili wanted a last fling with some virile young stud or even to elope, she — Bibi-Ek — was not going to interfere. She had been painfully lectured on the subject by the liberal-minded Bibi-Do, who now at last, hopefully, was about to get a dose of her own medicine. Bibi-Ek was beyond caring what a second elopement would do to the Flagstaffers' reputation, and how the Badtameezgarhis might react to this second monumental insult. It was, she knew, totally uncharacteristic of her, but she shrugged. It was time her feelings were no longer taken for granted.

But Chamkili, alas, was not seeking out the iron-bound biceps of 'Muscles' Mushtanda. His allegiance, she had learnt from bitter experience, was to her father, not to her. If she went to him, he would simply escort her back to the Tower. Instead she headed down the winding road that led to the Rajpur Road Gate and turned right towards the Bada Nashta Khana, sentimentally wanting one last walk through her home, before making for her final destination. The dreadful, haunted waters of the Khooni Khan Jheel — tonight living up to its terrible reputation as never before. (Two princesses in one night!) But it was a foolish route to take, for the Bada Nashta Khana lay in enemy hands. It wasn't long before Chamkili was apprehended by a roving patrol and dragged before her uncle Haramisahib, still lording it over at the Serpentine arbour.

"Well, well, well!" he gloated, the moon glancing off his canines. "Look what we have here! The blushing bride herself! Last time my dear, your three very clever mothers managed to escape. This time I'm afraid, I'm not going to let you follow their example. Tedi Poonch, I know it's the middle of the night, but take a ransom letter to Charbi…"

Rani-beti stepped out onto the moonlit bridge at last, and turned to her companions. "This is the place," she whispered huskily. "Where Altu Faltu came to me for the first time. Where we eloped from too. Isn't it beautiful Ghungroo?"

To Ghungroo, it looked terrifying and sinister, but she could hardly say so. "Yes, Rani-beti," she whispered back. "It is beautiful. And so romantic."

"But let's move on, shall we?" Langoti urged restlessly. The place gave him the creeps.

"You go on," Rani-beti said calmly. "I have to finish here what was started here." She stared down intensely at the black and silver water.

"What do you mean?" asked Ghungroo, puzzled. But the golden eyed princess had already hoisted herself up on to the curved black railing and now sat upon it composedly.

"Goodbye Ghungroo. And Langoti and Yaar. Thank you for everything. I will never forget you."

"Rani-beti! Wait! Don't jump!"

"Whyever not Ghungroo?" the princess countered gently. "Altu Faltu is dead. Badtameez can't wait to rape me. My family will kill me if they find me."

"You have us, Rani-beti."

"I know that Ghungroo, I know that. But you three belong to each other really."

"Please, Rani-beti…"

"Goodbye. And good luck. And look after yourselves."

She braced herself and turned to face the water again, her face utterly at peace. Ghungroo buried her face in Yaar's shoulder. The Chalta Phurta twins stared dumbstruck; for once even Langoti's quick wits appeared to have deserted him.

Just then, Rani-beti's face suddenly crumpled in pain and she slid from the railing onto the floor of the bridge. She was heaving and clutching her football tummy.

"Ghungroo!" she gasped. "The baby! I think it's coming! Help me!"

Chapter 12

STANDOFF
AT
KHOONI KHAN
JHEEL

"Chamkilee!"

Bibi-Do's banshee shriek bounced off the circular walls of the Flagstaff Tower like a locomotive sounding off in a tunnel, rousing the clan from deep slumber to gibbering panic in a trice.

"Chamkileee!" screamed Bibi-Do again, spinning around wildly, "Where is she? She's gone!"

Bibi-Ek put a hand over her wildly thumping heart and took several slow, deep breaths. "Calm down, Bibi-Do, calm down! She must have gone to get some fresh air, that's all!" And much more of course, if she was still not back, only she wasn't telling.

The Chaudhury was up too, bristling. "I told her explicitly not to leave the Tower," he growled furiously, glaring around as though expecting his disobedient daughter to chastely appear through its thick walls in deference to his command.

Bibi-Teen's eyes had attained their usual saucer-like dimen-

309

sions and her jaw dropped as she realised what everyone was thinking. "Oh my God!" she moaned, "Oh no! Not again!"

Bibi-Do lay crouched in a corner sobbing inconsolably, as though she was the first and only one to have suffered such a calamity. "She's eloped!" she wailed, "I know she has! Oh, what can we do?"

"Nonsense!" snapped the Chaudhury with the assertion of one who has complete faith in the fidelity of his generals. "I specifically ordered Mushtanda to stay away from her."

"Then where is she?" Bibi-Do wailed loudly.

"Come on," said Bibi-Ek sensibly, still not feeling the slightest sympathy for Bibi-Do. "Let's organise a search party."

Revenge was sweet.

But after an hour's thrashing about in the surrounding jungle, including the terrifying reservoir where Bibi-Do had gone looking for Rani-beti, there was still no sign of Chamkili. It did indeed, look as though she had followed her half-sister's example. And the hour of her wedding was fast drawing close.

"I'll have to go and inform Badtameez," the Chaudhury growled at last. "Tell him that there will be a slight delay..." He looked troubled and had aged visibly during these last tumultuous months. "I don't know how the Nawab is going to take the news, but I think we ought to be prepared for the worst."

"What do you mean?" Bibi-Do asked fearfully.

"I mean that Chamkili's wedding might well be cancelled. Not merely put off until we can find her." He made it sound as though it were all her fault. And grimaced. "Frankly, I wouldn't blame the Nawab if he does call the whole thing off. If I were in his place, I'd probably do the same thing."

Bibi-Ek felt a sudden shaft of guilt pierce her but the pain was gone as quickly as it had come. "I'll come along with you," she offered nonetheless, but he shook his head.

"No," he said decisively. "This is man's work. There may be some unpleasantness."

He took a small force of bodyguards and stalked regally down the metalled road towards the barati's campsite.

A strange, undulating, rattling sound greeted him at the entrance, and for a brief moment he was puzzled. Then he relaxed: the Badtameezgarhis were still sleeping off the effects of two days of travel and wanton celebration, and one night of live soap opera.

"What is it, Chaudhury Sahib?" Badtameez inquired thickly, emerging at last, irritated at being prised loose from the arms of his dishy little companion.

"I'm afraid I have grave news," the Chaudhury intoned sepulchrally. "It looks as though we might have to postpone the wedding by a bit. The priests and astrologers have declared this to be a highly inauspicious time. There were, apparently, some unexplained, er... celestial phenomena observed last night which bode ill for the wedding. We hope you understand."

Badtameez stared at him. He remembered the unexpected phenomena he had discovered in his honeymoon suite the previous night and his blood pressure began to climb.

"I do mind very much, Chaudhury Sahib," he began truculently. "And I don't give a damn about what your astrologers say. I'm sick to the back teeth with your eternal postponements and delays. The wedding shall take place at the appointed hour or not at all." He turned on his heel, as though to indicate the end of the discussion, then stopped and looked over his shoulder. "Ah, there is one more thing. Swami Palang Tode is no longer in my employment. You will have to make suitable arrangements."

"Badtameez, I'm afraid it's not possible for the wedding to take place at the appointed hour."

"Why? I've just told you that I'm not interested in what your astrologers say. My own astrologers have confirmed that this is the most auspicious time. And that's final."

The Chaudhury took a deep breath. "Well, you see, it's a bit more complicated than that. Chamkili seems to have gone off somewhere. She's er... missing. Possibly abducted. We've organised search parties of course, but they haven't found her as yet."

Badtameez glared at his father-in-law to-be and bobbed his head incredulously. "You can't find her? You can't find your daughter on her wedding day? I must say you have very peculiar daughters, Chaudhury Sahib. First Rani-beti falls down and injures herself shortly before her wedding, and now this one runs away on the night before hers!"

"I'm sorry Badtameez, that this sort of thing has had to happen. Every effort is being made to track down Chamkili. We are confident she will be found by the end of the day."

"I'm sorry Chaudhury Sahib, but that won't do. I'm not prepared to wait any longer. Have you — and your precious daughters — forgotten who I am? I am Nawab Bade Badtameez of the mighty citadel Badtameezgarh, not some two-bit bazaari-bandar you can fart around with. The wedding shall take place at the appointed hour, or not at all."

"But Chamkili is not here."

"Then I will not marry her."

"But..."

"But..." A strange, predatory gleam had entered the Nawab's eye. "But I am ready to take Rani-beti as a concubine," he finished, in a peculiar, crafty tone.

"Rani-beti? Rani-beti! Did you say Rani-beti? But you know that Rani-beti is very ill. What are you talking about? There is not much hope of her surviving the summer."

Badtameez drew himself up and prepared for his big moment. It had come a little prematurely, and not quite in the manner he had envisaged, but his blood pressure had built up dangerously and he could hold back no further. The Chaudhury was looking stunned. Badtameez unveiled his big guns.

"You know as well as I do Chaudhury Sahib, that Rani-beti was never injured in any fall. No, she is not injured, but very pregnant. Pregnant, Chaudhury Sahib, and not by me. Do you get my drift?"

"Wha... what on earth are you talking about, Badtameez? You know well that Rani-beti was tragically paralysed in a fall..."

Let him run, Badtameez urged himself, reining his temper in with great difficulty. Let him run, then pull him in slowly. Give him enough rope to hang himself. It will be so much more enjoyable. He stared the Chaudhury straight in the eye.

"Then I would like to see Rani-beti, if you don't mind," he declared with ominous calm.

"See her?" echoed the Chaudhury, clearly floundering, and wishing he had brought Bibi-Ek with him after all. She would have been so much more adept at handling these awkward questions. "But... but that would hardly be propitious at a time like this. And er... actually Badtameez, Rani-beti is no longer at the Ridge." When pushed, the Chaudhury was discovering, even he could fabricate wildly on the spur of the moment (surely Bibi-Teen would have been proud of him). "Her plight was noticed by some animal lovers who took her away for treatment. We're hoping they will release her back here when she is well again."

"Wah, Chaudhury Sahib, wah wah! Shabash!"

"Wha... what for?" Charbi Raisahib was puzzled and steadily growing wary.

"Are you trying to make a fool of me, Chaudhury Sahib?" Badtameez hissed with soft, deadly menace.

"No, no, no; of course not!" Charbi Raisahib spluttered, suddenly feeling that Badtameez, somehow, had him by the short hairs.

"Then are you calling me, Nawab Bade Badtameez, a liar?" the prince inquired like a snake about to strike.

"Of course not, Badtameez, how can you say such a thing?"

"I, just now, categorically told you that Rani-beti was not injured, but pregnant. And you are insisting on telling me that she is paralysed and being looked after by animal lovers. So am I lying, or are you?"

This was wonderful, thought Badtameez. Nail him down, and hammer, hammer, hammer! He had to hang on to his temper of course, which was the toughest part. But this was intoxicating stuff all right.

"Badtameez..." blustered the Chaudhury, suddenly realising that the game was up. "We're all very upset..."

"You're fucking right we're upset!" snarled Badtameez. "Now shut up and listen to me and stop lying. Your slut of a daughter is alive. Would you like to meet her perhaps?"

"Wha... what?" That really had him on the ropes, flabber-gasted.

"You old fool! Rani-beti is here, in this very camp, under your nose!"

"Badtameez!" The Chaudhury was trying desperately to regain lost ground and self-respect. "If this is some kind of joke, it is in very poor taste indeed!" He spoke with righteous indignation.

"Joke? You lie to my face, first thing in the morning, and dare accuse me, Nawab Bade Badtameez of making jokes? By God, sir, you will pay dearly for this monumental insult. Just keep in mind what the great Nadir Shah did to the inhabitants of this wretched city when he was slighted!" He was jumping up and down now, the bottled-up rage bubbling over. But was missing too, the comforting, encouraging arms of Suna Hai around him, and becoming even more enraged as he remembered why she was not here now with him. He collared an eavesdropping barati, and barked an order at him. Then he turned again to the hapless Chaudhury. "I warn you sir, you shall pay a very heavy price for your deception and treachery. No one tries to make a fool of Badtameez and gets away with it. Rani-beti will join us shortly and confirm that for you."

But the messenger returned alone, panic-stricken, and was sent hurtling across the dust when Badtameez received the news.

"What?" he screamed. "Escaped? No! It can't be possible!" He charged off and returned within minutes, his eyes rolling crazily. "Suna Hai!" he hissed furiously to himself. "Suna Hai and that Palang Tode! They're behind this!"

"So where's Rani-beti?" ventured the Chaudhury, sensing that somehow the tables had been turned and that he ought to take advantage of the situation. "Or is this, indeed, some kind of joke?" Even so, a doubt still snagged at the back of his mind. Had Badtameez somehow got hold of Rani-beti? And now been double-crosssed in the course of some internecine family quarrel? You couldn't put it past these feuding tribal families, what with their lifetime vendettas. Anyway he had to make the most of it. "So where's Rani-beti?" he asked unctuously again.

"Fuck off Chaudhury!" Badtameez bellowed, blowing all his gaskets simultaneously. "We're here to take the Northern Ridge! Surrender unconditionally or face instant annhilation!"

"What? You're drunk, Badtameez!"

"You thick old cock! Do you seriously think that I, Nawab Bade Badtameez, would be only interested in your halfwit daughter? We're here to take the Ridge! We're here for war. For glorious conquest!"

Frankly, at that moment, glorious conquest seemed highly improbable. Most of the 'warrior' baratis still lounged about indolently where they had collapsed the previous night, after witnessing the wonderful fracas in the honeymoon suite. A few were now taking a desultory interest in the proceedings. After two days of continuous song, dance and fornication, and one night of high melodrama, they were hardly in any condition to launch a major offensive. Even if that was what their great feudal chief was ordering them to do.

"Get up!" he screeched hysterically, bouncing with rage and pelting them with stones to get them on their feet. "Attack! Kill! Rape! Plunder! Take the Flagstaff Tower! Kill the Chaudhury! Molest his wives!"

But alas! Collectively assaulted by the mother of all hangovers, the Badtameezgarhis could only plug their ears and hobble clumsily out of the way as their demented chieftain continued to rave and rant and split their ringing skulls.

Chaudhury Charbi Raisahib however was rapidly swelling up with righteous anger, and his bodyguards bunched tightly around him with flattened ears and bared canines. The past months of conflict had honed his military instincts until they sang like keen steel, and he immediately realised what Badtameez had been really after. Of course, he could have captured and killed the rogue prince then and there and would have been entirely justified in doing so, but he had just had a wild, but brilliant idea...

"Badtameez," he said, in his most belittling voice. "You and the drunken members of your clan came here as our honoured guests. And, unlike Badtameezgarhis who turn on their hosts, it is not the custom of Flagstaffers to attack those to whom they have extended hospitality. In the light of what you have just said however, a declaration of war no less, I would like to make it clear that you no longer have my permission to marry my daughter Chamkili of the glittering smile. The wedding stands cancelled. You and your clan members are no longer our guests, but war-mongering trespassers on our land. Either you surrender to me here and now, forfeiting your army and all your territories, or you will meet us in battle on the historic battlefield of the Bada Nashta Khana in half an hour from now. My scouts will show you the place. And remember, if you try to flee, it will be all over Delhi that the great, cowardly Badtameez fled from the Flagstaffers after trying to attack them by subterfuge. You will be the laughing-stock of the Capital!"

He sat back on his haunches with a smirk, amazed by his astuteness. There was no way he could lose now. If Badtameez surrendered meekly, which was unlikely, he, Chaudhury Charbi Raisaib, would have pulled off the most audacious coup in simian history and become Chieftain of Badtameezgarh without having spilt a drop of blood. If Badtameez fled, it would again send his own prestige sky-rocketing. Either way, it would give Haramisahib and his rebels something to think about. In all likelihood they would flee the Ridge immediately.

But of course, it was the third option that he really hoped Badtameez would take: to accept the challenge to do battle on the 'historic battlefield' of the Bada Nashta Khana. For the 'battlefield' was in fact the large shady park where once the Flagstaffers had frolicked after being served breakfast by the pious, and which now lay in Haramisahib's control. Chaudhury Charbi Raisahib had suddenly realised how he could pay his devious brother back in his own currency and even perhaps become scion of Badtameezgarh in the bargain.

"We'll slaughter you!" Badtameez was screaming at him now, kicking his mighty warriors left and right to get them to rise and shine and prepare for battle. "I'll kill you myself and hang you from the Tower! We'll raze the Tower! Your wives will become part of my harem! Your children will be my slaves!"

There was no doubt about it. Rani-beti's escape had been the last straw. Badtameez had come completely unhinged.

"Stop raving, Badtameez," the smug Chaudhury now advised him. "Save your strength for the battle. See you on the field in half an hour."

He could have been fixing an appointment at his club.

"You've gone and done what?"

For once, all three of the Chaudhury's wives were united in their horror-stricken response. "Declared war on Badtameez because Chamkili's run away on her wedding day! Are you mad Chaudhury Sahib?"

"Quiet!" thundered the Chaudhury. "Badtameez is really here to wage war. To take our land. To conquer the Northern Ridge. Chamkili's wedding was merely a cover. I've challenged him to battle on the battlefield of the Bada Nashta Khana."

"Where? What battlefield? The Bada Nashta Khana? But that has been illegally occupied by Haramisahib..."

"Precisely my dear. And in all likelihood, Haramisahib and his thugs will come pouring down the hill from the wild flank and fling themselves on the Badtameezgarhis in defence of their ill-gotten lands."

"And what will we do?"

"We wait and watch on the spine of the Ridge. Once the battle really catches fire, we move in swiftly and reoccupy the Serpentine arbour and the nursery. Then we wait for the final outcome. And attack the victors. They will be weak, exhausted and bleeding; we'll be fresh and keen. Whoever the victor is, we will rout him. And not only will Haramisahib be vanquished, but I shall probably be Chieftain of Badtameezgarh too by the end of the day. Oh, this is better than any wedding!"

The power lust was shining in the Chaudhury's eyes and his tense, irritable manner had magically vanished. He looked so majestic, Bibi-Teen thought, with a sudden fierce tenderness.

"This was supposed to be Chamkili's wedding day," Bibi-Do wept, "and you're starting another war instead!"

"Silence, Bibi-Do! And speaking of Chamkili, any sign of her as yet?"

"No! And General Mushtanda has not returned from patrol either."

Chamkili in fact, was smack in the middle of a giddy melodrama, and was enjoying every moment to the hilt because she hadn't realised how serious matters really were. For the gallant General Mushtanda, out on solitary patrol (now that Chamkili's wedding day had dawned, he was feeling it badly), had ambushed Tedi Poonch very early that morning as the latter made his way towards the Flagstaff Tower with Haramisahib's ransom note.

"The bastard's holding Chamkili!" Mushtanda exclaimed, anger flaring in his brave bosom. "And wants the Chaudhury to hand over the Tower and all occupied territories on the Ridge, in exchange for her. Well, does he now! Bah!" He glared at Tedi Poonch. "Where is Chamkili being held?" he demanded. The courageous Tedi Poonch stared back defiantly.

"Very well," said Mushtanda, matter-of-factly. "Perhaps this will refresh your memory." He dragged the captured messenger up a tall eucalyptus tree and grabbed a vine from a neighbouring creeper. This he tied firmly to Tedi Poonch's crooked tail. "You've heard about bungee jumping, I suppose," he remarked conversationally. "Now I'm going to throw you off this tree, and let's see what happens. Either your tail will straighten out and snap off with a crack, or the vine will break and so will your head when you hit the ground."

"She's at the Serpentine arbour," whispered Tedi Poonch, ashen faced. "On the spit of land that juts out of the northern pond."

He whooped out of the giant bamboo clump like their great ancestor Tarzan himself, walloped the two dozing guards into the filthy water, gathered her up in his brawny arms, and bounded mightily back into the bamboo, in one swift movement. Now he held her close, in a dense thicket. She trembled like a new peepul leaf. And asked in a tight, bitter voice:

"You're going to take me back to my father, aren't you?"

"No, Chamkili," he answered huskily. "If that's not what you want."

"I would rather die in your arms than marry Badtameez," she declared simply. "Oh, kill me Mushtanda, now, while I am in your arms. Let them say, 'Ah, poor romantic Chamkili! She lived unhappily but died bissfully in the arms of her beloved!'"

"I cannot live without you," the mighty Mushtanda admitted, his iron biceps crushing her and turning her limbs to water. How could he ever have thought that he had become tired of her smile? "But I have disobeyed your father's orders! And there is only one penalty for that. Court martial and death."

"I am ready to die for you Mushtanda," Chamkili reiterated, gazing adoringly up at his face, and snuggling against his massive frame.

"Then will you die with me?" the iron General invited hoarsely, more maudlin than the cretin princess.

"Of course!"

"It is a pact, then!"

She nodded, and their tears flowed and mingled freely.

"We will go to the little hunchbacked bridge over the Khooni Khan Jheel," he whispered, "and make love one last and glorious time. Then we shall hold hands and jump in and let the Jheel do its work."

"Can you swim?" she asked unexpectedly.

"It hardly matters," he replied. "We go down together and

then our ghosts will haunt that place forever."

They made their way through the trees towards their date with destiny. But when they reached the little hunchbacked bridge, they stopped in astonishment.

There were four monkeys (and a baby) already on the bridge.

And one of them, without any doubt, was the prodigal princess of the Northern Ridge.

Rani-beti.

"Look!" Chamkili clutched Mushtanda's hand excitedly. "That's Rani-beti!" And then, in full-cretin mode: "She's come back to marry Badtameez! That means I won't have to marry him. I can marry you. Come on, Mushtanda, let's go and tell my father the wonderful news."

But before the lovelorn General could properly assess the situation, there was a sudden agitation in the foliage at the southern end of the bridge; a vigorous shaking and bending of branches, accompanied by the sound of heavy bodies crashing through. A ruddy, leathery face suddenly appeared out of the stricken leaves and glared at him aggressively. General Mushtanda found himself staring at a face he could never forget.

There was no doubt about it. The monkey on the other side was none other than Brigadier Ladsahib of the Nicholson Cemetery. And the expression on his face indicated clearly that he was not on a social visit.

Brigadier-General Ladsahib (he had promoted himself after his great victory) was at that moment equally surprised. And not only because of the sudden appearance of General Mushtanda on the northern end of the bridge...

All these months he had harboured a bitter grudge against the Flagstaffers; against the treacherous Haramisahib and his war-mongering brother Charbi Raisahib. True, he had been magnificently successful in defending the Cemetery from the invaders, but that was not the point. He wanted revenge. No clan could dare attack the Cemetery and not expect retaliation. He would teach these savages a lesson. He knew that the forces of the Chaudhury brothers, combined or not, far outnumbered his own. But he also knew that the brothers were at daggers drawn with each other. So he had plotted and schemed and listened to the advice of Lieutenant Hazari Kaan: to wait until the warring brothers had weakened each other to such an extent as to neutralise their advantage in numbers. In the meanwhile, he had drilled his men rigorously. His objective was simple if ambitious: to take the Northern Ridge from the Chaudhury brothers, once and for all.

And this was the time to strike; the day Chaudhury Charbi Raisahib's daughter was to be married to some primitive warlord. Intelligence reports had suggested that Haramisahib had been plotting mischief on that auspicious day too — targeted at his brother. And he had guessed, that anticipating trouble, the elder Chaudhury would be on his guard. The forces of both brothers were likely to be concentrated along the Line of Actual Control on the spine of the Ridge...

The Brigadier had planned his campaign (Operation Tripos) meticulously. An elite military commando unit under Colonel Kela would provide the spark required to start a full-fledged conflagration between the brothers along the LAC. He would, in the meanwhile, swiftly storm the

Serpentine arbour, secure it, and then head towards the Flagstaff Tower. Hopefully, it would fall; if not he was prepared to lay siege. And his batallion's relatively unhampered progress through the lower reaches of the Ridge that morning had fully vindicated his guess that Haramisahib's forces, whose territory this was, were busy elsewhere.

They had stormed in through the small side entrance near the offices of the Regional Transport Authority. They had met little resistance from the disorganised rebel princelings Haramisahib had left in charge there, as they marched north towards the strategic Serpentine arbour. The crushed-brick path along which they marched bifurcates into three as it approaches the Khooni Khan Jheel, which lies en route. The higher, rocky western path, and the lower, straighter eastern path (which runs over the gully through which Altu Faltu had crawled for his first rendezvous with Rani-beti) skirt the Jheel, while the central one leads to the bridge itself. That morning, Brigadier-General Ladsahib halted his immaculate army at the bifurcation. He was taking no chances. Taking Colonel Kela and Lt.Hazari Kaan with him, he went ahead to do a recce of the bridge. It was just as well. From the cover of the bed of spider lilies into which Leechad had once been flung by Bibi-Do's djinns, he stared with astonishment at the bridge.

There were four monkeys (and a baby) on it already.

And one of them bore a striking resemblance to the stunning little thing his useless son had brought to the Cemetery so many months ago.

His mind raced. Did this mean that Altu Faltu was somewhere in the vicinity? He was always turning up like a bad penny. And who were the other three monkeys, even if they did look harmless? And surely that was not a baby clutched to the little bandari's bosom? Was this a trick? Were they bait in a trap? He recalled bitterly Haramsahib's past treachery. Perhaps it would be better to wait and watch awhile.

And then he found General Mushtanda glaring at him suddenly from the opposite end. With a young female at his side...

"That's Chamkili!" Colonel Kela exclaimed unexpectedly. "The Chaudhury's daughter who is supposed to be getting married this morning!"

"How do you know who she is, Kela?" The Brigadier turned to him in astonishment. Colonel Kela was blushing furiously. Ever since he had seen Chamkili rush headlong into the Battle of the Nicholson Cemetery, crying, "Papa, papa, do something, papa!" he had been irrevocably smitten. He shrugged now. "I just know," he said enigmatically.

The Brigadier snorted like a suspicious stag. "Something funny is going on! I'm sure of it! This looks like a trap! We may have to replan our strategy. Perhaps we've been lulled into a false sense of security. We wait here, and see what happens."

They retreated into cover and hunkered down to wait.

On the little hunchbacked bridge, Ghungroo and the twins were trying to get an increasingly obdurate Rani-beti to relent. After her initial bout of panic, Rani-beti had gone ahead and had her baby with remarkably little fuss, noting with bitter irony that it had been born on the very bridge where she and Altu Faltu had been together for the first time. And instead of being radiant with joy and motherly love, she had turned flinty and cold, the gold in her eyes dulled and frozen with remembrances of the past. Her desire to end it all here, on this bridge, had not lessened one whit, much to the despair of her friends.

"But you can't jump in now!" Ghungroo pleaded, with tears in her eyes. "The little fellow needs you. Surely you realise that."

"Then I shall jump with him. Poor little bugger. He'll never know his father anyway. Altu Faltu! Altu Faltu Sherkhanewala!"

"You can't jump with him!" Ghungroo was appalled. "That would be murder! Worse. Infanticide!"

"So it would," murmured Rani-beti, abstractedly. And then, thrusting the twitching little creature at Ghungroo, exclaimed: "Here, you take him! Bring him up as your own son!" And turning dramatically to the Chalta Phurta twins: "Then he'll have two fathers instead of none! Won't he be lucky!"

Watching them from cover, an agog iron-General 'Muscles' Mushtanda wiped a pearly tear and swallowed a gigantic lump, while the cretin Chamkili grinned all over her glittering, pretty face.

"Calm down, Rani-beti, calm down!" Ghungroo pleaded. "You're only suffering from a case of galloping post-natal depression. It'll pass. Now let's get away from this creepy place."

"Ghungroo, you know I can't live without Altu Faltu."

"But he can!" countered Ghungroo fiercely, indicating the baby. "And he certainly can't live without you. You must live, Rani-beti, for his sake if not your own."

But Rani-beti only smiled tiredly and shook her head. "You know Ghungroo, if I don't die right now, I'll only sicken and pine away slowly. And this little fellow will suffer more. So take him now, Ghungroo. Take him to the Villa Lantana and raise him as your own. He must never know about the tragedy of his parents." She stared at the oily, black waters and added with sudden venom. "And may my spirit eternally haunt and torment all those who have brought this upon me!" She thrust the baby at Ghungroo, who clutched it protectively. And for the second time, leapt up to the curved black railing, poised to jump.

And for the second time, was thwarted.

A great frightening commotion erupted from the direction of the Serpentine arbour. A commotion that was spine-chilling in intensity, and that screamed of pain, bloodshed and terror. A commotion that came swiftly closer. The screeches of raging, biting, fighting, warring monkeys; of simians who were viciously snarling, grunting, ripping and tearing into one another; of victors in howling pursuit and the vanquished fleeing in panic. Stupefied, they turned towards the bedlam, saw the first violent agitation in the trees and caught sudden glimpses of monkeys in blinding haste. General Mushtanda grabbed Chamkili by the arm and made swiftly for the high ground on the western side of the Jheel. Brigadier-General Ladsahib signalled his troops to be ready for instant attack. Rani-beti, Ghungroo and the Chalta Phurta twins looked as though they had been turned to stone. And on the surface of the Khooni Khan Jheel, a hazy white mist, as ethereal as muslin, began to curl and twitch like a cat's tail, and the oily, black waters began to swirl and ripple.

The commotion had been triggered off by a string of events that had unfolded swiftly north of the Khooni Khan Jheel, on the 'historic battlefield' of the Bada Nashta Khana. True to his word, Chaudhury Charbi Raisahib had despatched a scout patrol to lead the Badtameezgarhis to the battlefield. But instead of taking the shortest, easiest route, which would have been over metalled roads, via the Flagstaff Tower, and therein too risky, the scouts had taken a steep, undulating, roundabout route, skirting the boundaries of the Ridge, and deliberately passing through some of its most thorny, tangled and inhospitable terrain. They called it the 'Taxi Driver Manouevre'. What was more, they had led the Badtameezgarhis this merry dance at breakneck speed, so that many of the troops, still struggling with their hangovers, had straggled behind and eventually got lost. By the time the warriors had reached the battlefield they were hot, panting, scratched and dusty; a disgraceful rag-tag army if ever there was one.

They assembled in the park in a disorderly manner, several still clutching their heads and wondering what the hell was going on. Badtameez toyed briefly with the idea that the Chaudhury had chickened out after all: the scout patrol had told him to wait and vanished in the surrounding jungle. There was no sign of any other simian activity in the area.

The battlefield of the Bada Nashta Khana comprised a large section of the landscaped park that runs along the eastern boundary of the Ridge alongside Rajpur Road. To the west, across a redbrick path, lies the wild flank, with its deep verdant gully, and the great flat rocks piled up in giant steps leading to the top. At its southern end, the park narrows, hemmed in by the road on one side and the thickly foliated Serpentine area on the other. A narrow rocky path meanders out of this cul-de-sac, meeting the broad eucalyptus shrouded pathway which climbs up the slope in a series of steps, to the

Chauburja Gate. The three paths leading to the Khooni Khan Jheel branch out from this main thoroughfare at various points along its slope, and beyond the bridge, meet again at the bifurcation where now Brigadier Ladsahib's batallion waited poised to charge.

Badtameez looked around the deserted shadowy battlefield, feeling that somehow the Chaudhury had taken the initiative away from him, and wondering where the Flagstaffers would attack from. He was about to order his army to form a large defensive circle, when something entirely unexpected happened and in fact, was not even foreseen by the brilliant Chaudhury. A group of four spotlessly-clad humans entered the park, their arms laden with bananas, mangoes, pomegranates, grapes and jaggery.

"Aaao...aaao...aaaoo..." they chanted enticingly, with expressions as pious as that of Palang Tode just before a conquest. (The daily breakfast privilege was now being enjoyed by Haramisahib and his troupe.) The warriors from Badtameezgarh suddenly realised that they had been marching on empty stomachs. With sudden vigour, and unexpected violence, they broke ranks and charged the bearers of the booty, forcing them to drop their bags and flee. As his soldiers fell upon the fruit, Badtameez glanced around yet again, still alert and uneasy. There was still no sign of the Chaudhury or his army. What was going on?

Then matters became even more bizarre. A shrill group of monkeys appeared at the northern end of the battlefield, skipping, dancing, chattering and squealing. Unknown to Charbi Raisahib, let alone Badtameez, Chaudhury Haramisahib had extended a standing breakfast invitation to the bandaris of the Khyber Pass Massage Parlour. Who were now tripping and

traipsing in delicately for their daily menu of grapes, pomegranates and mangoes. Breakfast, of course, was usually followed by luscious games of chase (there were so many trees in
the park) and cuddle, but then, what better way was there to
start one's day?

The warriors of Badtameezgarh couldn't believe their eyes
or their luck. And even Badtameez himself now began to
doubt whether he had understood the Chaudhury correctly
after all. He had been challenged to battle, and here on the
battlefield, had been offered first food, and now fornication.
And there was no sign of the enemy. Instead there were squeals
of delight as the Khyber Pass bandaris realised who their
benefactors were that morning: those very same, hairy, virile,
animal hunks who, just yesterday, had turned their knees to
water! Two of the saucy little bandaris now wriggled up to
Badtameez. "Like a massage, sweetheart?" one of them lilted,
and alas, the mighty chieftain was felled at once, by his own
most animal instincts.

But where then, was Haramisahib, and why was he not
enjoying the fruit and fornication at the Bada Nashta Khana
that morning? He was in no mood for such flippancies
actually, because he had just received the news of Chamkili's
escape (or rescue, it was all the same) from the Serpentine
arbour. And he was livid. For the second time, a female from
the Flagstaff clan had made a fool of him. (To be accurate, the
first time round, three of them had, together.) Honour had
to be satisfied or he would be the laughing stock of the Ridge,
an object of ridicule amongst the coalition of rebel princelings
he led.

As the elder Chaudhury had feared, and the Brigadier
foreseen, Haramisahib had plotted mischief for that auspicious

day. He had planned a blitzkrieg raid on the Flagstaff Tower, not during the time of the wedding, but just afterwards, when he guessed the Flagstaffers' guard would be down and most of them busy getting drunk. Chamkili's unexpected capture had made him change his plans: now he had an invaluable bargaining chip. Which he had, yet again, gone and lost. The Flatstaffer females were making a fool of him — Haramisahib, Patron-in-Chief of the Khyber Pass Massage parlour, et al. He would attack them right away; instant retaliation was what he believed in. Granted, his forces would probably not be able to take the heavily defended Tower this time, but they would certainly cause the Flagstaffers enormous embarrassment, and completely upset the wedding function. Now, at the Serpentine arbour, he was finalising his attack strategy and wondering where the hell Tedi Poonch had gone (trussed upside down on the top of the tall eucalyptus), when a guard sidled up and announced sotto voce:

"Sir, there is what appears to be a large foreign force having an orgy with the Khyber Pass bandaris in the Bada Nashta Khana."

"Are you mad? What foreign army?"

"Perhaps you'd better see for yourself, sir. But they are all pretty hefty and wild-looking fellows."

He went at once, but not before ordering his generals to redeploy their troops in the gully that ran parallel to the park. From a vantage point near the nursery, he gazed at the goings-on in the park below with increasing disbelief.

A full-fledged orgy was in progress, slowly but surely approaching its grand climax.

But who the hell were these great hairy brutes? Where had they sprung up from? And how had they dared to have an orgy

331

with the bandaris of the Khyber Pass Massage Parlour, who were under his patronage?

The answers began clicking in his shrewd brain, one by one, and his eyes glittered. Obviously the strangers were here in connection with the wedding at the Tower. Perhaps they were even the baratis. Perhaps Charbi Raisahib had organised this orgy as part of the wedding celebrations and to poke him one in the eye. Well, he would pay for his stupidity and the strangers would pay for their wantonness. Daring to screw the Khyber Pass bandaris in broad daylight under his nose!

"Inform the generals that we attack the strangers just before the orgy climaxes," he whispered to his substitute aide, who scuttled off into the gully. "I'll give the battlecry!"

Every mass orgy, he knew, eventually attained a single great rhythm and cadence of its own, wherein all taking part, somehow instinctively, synchronised their orgiastic activities; like several small waves combining to form one great tidal roller. And the moment before the great wave broke — that was it's most vulnerable one... Haramisahib waited, watching keenly.

"Screw them!" he screamed suddenly, (if rather superfluously) as the squeals and grunts in the park rose to a passionate crescendo. And charged out of the gully at the head of his troops.

Behind him, on the high ground, but well in cover, Chaudhury Charbi Raisahib and his three wives (who had refused to stay home this time) watched grimly and in silence.

The Badtameezgarhis alas, were caught en flagrante delicto en masse; not quite the ideal formation in which to go into battle. But they were warriors nonetheless. As the Khyber Pass bandaris screamed and wriggled free from beneath them, fleeing with a swiftness that bespoke of long practice, they snarled and turned to face the surprise enemy.

It had been a vicious trick after all, Badtameez thought savagely, as he tried to shake off the two louts who had descended on his back. And they had fallen for it. Under normal circumstances, it must be said, there was nothing the Badtameezgarhis liked better than to take on an unknown enemy in a hostile territory. Badtameez in fact often boasted that he enjoyed that more than chasing his concubines around the dusty forecourts of his citadel. But that morning alas, the conditions had not been normal.

For a start, the entire force had been severely hungover. Secondly they had been briefed to expect a short, if fierce, bitefight involving the bride's family just after the wedding ceremony, and not a fullblown battle in a strange, shadowy battlefield. Where only moments earlier they had been frolicking and cavorting. Worse, their great chieftain had been behaving strangely ever since the dramatic events of the previous night: he had kicked their butts and made them march hotfoot over some terrible terrain without the slightest notice. And had led them to this garden of love which had suddenly turned into a field of carnage. Where the enemy had leapt out at them at that crucial moment when they were about to achieve collective nirvana (in a manner that would have undoubtedly impressed Palang Tode).

An enemy, which now was inexorably driving them back towards the dark, glowering region, where the foliage closed in and the barbed wire stretched taut.

Suddenly, the mighty Badtameezgarhis broke and scattered helter skelter. Some fled out on to Rajpur Road and escaped into the lawns of the big houses on the other side. Others charged up the wild flank, only to confront the implacable forces of Chaudhury Charbi Raisahib waiting on the top of the hillside. Many scuttled through the twisting pathway leading out of the cul-de-sac and raced up the eucalyptus-shrouded path towards the Chauburja Gate.

Chaudhury Haramisahib had quickly identified Badtameez as the enemy chieftain and came after him relentlessly now, with a posse in tow. The battle was going wonderfully; they had caught the enemy with their pants down, literally, and had routed them within minutes. This would go down in history as one of the swiftest, most brilliant simian military operations ever.

"Screw the bastards!" he screamed exultantly, and charged at Badtameez wildly.

He would have been far less exultant had he known what his elder brother had been up to in the meanwhile. Charbi Raisahib had waited for the battle to hot up and then had recaptured the thinly guarded nursery and Serpentine arbour with consummate ease. He knew that Haramisahib had all but vanquished the Badtameezgarhis, and now waited with his wives for his victorious sibling to march triumphantly into the Serpentine arbour. His troops were in position and had been well briefed. Immediately upon Haramisahib's arrival, the bridges leading to the arbour would be sealed. The rebel chieftain would be captured. And justice would be done swiftly, before he could recover from the shock.

It worked out a little differently. Pounding across the undulating park, the fleeing Badtameez suddenly found himself heading for the deadly cul-de-sac, and failed to notice the narrow escape pathway. He jinked wildly to the right, charged through some undergrowth and thundered over a bridge, straight into the Serpentine arbour, skidding to a halt before

Chaudhury Charbi Raisahib and his three wives, waiting calmly in the Diwan-e-Khas for the arrival of Haramisahib. He dodged to the left, and was over another little bridge and out of there, before the Flagstaff guards could react.

"That's Badtameez!" Charbi Raisahib yelled, and charged off after the disappearing chieftain, quite forgetting about Haramisahib in the excitement. "He's getting away!!"

Bibi-Do however, recovered her wits swiftly. For seconds later, when Haramisahib himself came barging into the arbour in pursuit of Badtameez, her foot shot out with perfect timing. Haramisahib suddenly found himself airborne and then he was tumbling down, down, down, to land with a resounding splash in the scum-covered waters of the Serpentine. When he finally spluttered ashore, he found his elder brother's three grim wives waiting for him.

"It's all over, Haramisahib!" Bibi-Do snapped.

Justice would be done.

Even by Badtameez's primitive standards, it was turning out to be a nightmarish wedding day. He had first been tricked deviously and assaulted from the rear by an unknown enemy, and now was being chased by his father-in-law to-be, whose daughter and fiefdom he had come to take.

"Stop!" bellowed the Chaudhury, putting on a turn of speed surprising for one his age. "Surrender! You can't escape!"

"Never!" snarled the bridegroom, racing down a rocky winding path. The path suddenly went round a bend and onto yet another bridge.

There were four monkeys on the bridge.

One of them was Rani-beti.

In a flash, Badtameez was on the bridge and had her by the throat. The other three fled in blind panic. There was a newborn infant at her breast (Ghungroo had managed to hand it back, imploring Rani-beti to give it "one last drink", hoping this would make her change her mind about the suicide.) Chaudhury Charbi Raisahib hurled himself round the corner and skidded to a halt at the northern end of the bridge, not believing his eyes. His first runaway daughter, Rani-beti, appeared before him, struggling in the steely grasp of that monster Badtameez.

"Rani-beti?" he queried, bobbing his head in amazement. "Is that really you?"

"Stay back Chaudhury Sahib!" Badtameez snarled. "I told you I had Rani-beti in my custody." He tore the baby from her breast. "And she's already gone and had the little bastard!"

There was a sudden cracking and snapping of twigs from the southern end of the bridge. Brigadier-General Ladsahib, Lt. Hazari Kaan, Colonel Kela and a batallion of Nicholsonites suddenly appeared out of the bed of tiger lilies, ready to storm across.

The Chaudhury's jaw dropped further. He hardly noticed the arrival of his three dishevelled and bedraggled wives at his side. They had dispensed swift justice to Haramisahib. Then Bibi-Ek suddenly saw Rani-beti.

"Rani-beti!" she shrieked, "Oh, Rani-beti!" She would have been on the bridge in a flash had Bibi-Do and Bibi-Teen not instinctively grabbed her and held her back. For Badtameez was dangling the baby over the notorious black waters by its tail, his other arm wrapped around Rani-beti's delicate throat.

"Stand back! One more step and I'll drop it and break her neck!" he snarled. Bibi-Ek subsided in a heap, sobbing uncontrollably. "Rani-beti! Oh, my darling Rani-beti! What have they done to you? Are you all right?"

But even now, amidst all this terror and horror, Rani-beti's gold-flecked eyes were flinty and cold as frost.

"No!" she choked, and turned away, half throttled by her ex-fiancé's brutish arm.

Bibi-Ek suddenly saw the upside-down dangling infant for the first time. "Oh, Rani-beti!" she wailed. "You are a mother!" And then, collapsing in a fresh paroxym of weeping, "Hai, hai! My favourite daughter an unwed mother! What will everyone say!"

"Keep quiet and listen to me!" Badtameez roared. He dangled the baby lower as it kicked and struggled. (Bibi-Teen noted with horror that Rani-beti appeared completely indifferent to its fate.)"I'm going to do a deal with you."

"Don't talk nonsense, Badtameez!" the Chaudhury shouted back. "There's no deal here for you. You came here ostensibly to marry my daughter. Instead you declared war. Which you have lost. Surrender! It's the only honourable thing to do!"

"Honourable thing? You lying, deceiving old bastard! You informed me that Rani-beti had been paralysed in a fall. Not that she was having an illicit affair and an illegitimate baby. And you think, I, Nawab Bade Badtameez, would take such an insult lying down!"

The Chaudhury controlled his breathing with difficulty. "She disappeared," he admitted at last. "We did not know where she was." He wondered why the truth always sounded so unconvincing.

"Bah!"

"Shut up, all of you!" Rani-beti screamed suddenly. "You've all gone and killed my Altu Faltu, that's what you've done! Murderers!" Badtameez slapped a heavy hand across her mouth.

"Quiet, you little bitch, or I'll break your neck!" He glared at the Chaudhury again. "I'm going to offer you a deal. In exchange for your slut of a daughter and the little turd, I want your complete and unconditional surrender, and control of all territories of the Northern Ridge. You may take your disgusting family and get out of here."

"Your army has just been routed from the Ridge, Badtameez, and you're demanding our surrender! Are you mad?"

"Mad enough to drown the turd and break Rani-beti's neck!"

"Look here, you..." Brigadier-General Ladsahib decided it was time he entered the fray.

"And who the fuck are you?" snapped Badtameez, whirling around.

"Brigadier-General Ladsahib, of the Nicholson Cemetery, if that means anything to you. Altu Faltu is my son. Now unhand that little monkey and give her back her baby."

"You're the father of the silly prick who produced this little turd?"

"Mind your language you young toad, or I'll have to teach you some manners!"

"Quiet fatso, or I'll throw your grandson into the water. And hear this: the deal holds for you too. You surrender the Nicholson Cemetery to me, or the child drowns and the mother dies."

"He's mad!" shouted the Brigadier across the bridge to

Chaudhury Raisahib, who was suddenly wondering what Ladsahib was doing on the Ridge with a batallion in tow. The Brigadier was now addressing Rani-beti.

"Where's Altu Faltu?" he asked, because he still was his father, and Lady Ladsahib would demand an explanation. The little princess said nothing, but the three little monkeys who had suddenly turned up at his side shook their heads sadly.

"Altu Faltu's dead, sir. Badtameez captured him," one of them said quietly.

"Altu Faltu?" roared Badtameez, half-crazed with rage, confusion and frustration. "I threw him down the deepest, darkest hole in Delhi. Sherkhanewala — bah!"

Like so many great political leaders, when confronted by imminent disgrace and ruin, Badtameez had completely come apart at the seams. With his great barati army battered and scattered all over the godforsaken Ridge; with his Chief Concubine and military strategist gone and with him miles away from the security of his own citadel, he was in no position to do deals with anyone. But he was quite capable, in this maddened state of killing Rani-beti and drowning the baby.

"You have till the count of ten to surrender," he now shouted at the Chaudhury and Brigadier Ladsahib.

"Shouldn't we talk this over sensibly?" Chaudhury Charbi Raisahib offered peaceably, suddenly realising Badtameez's dangerous condition, and that it was his daughter who was out there with him, not the Brigadier's son.

"One... two... three..."

"Badtameez, come along to the Tower and we can negotiate something."

"...four...five...six...seven..."

Badtameez dangled the baby lower, till its head broke the

surface of the black water. Rani-beti struggled ineffectually in his powerful grasp.

Brigadier-General Ladsahib prepared to do exactly what Chaudhury Charbi Raisahib feared he might: he tensed his muscles, ready to spring.

"...eight... nine..."

"Look!"

It was Rani-beti who emitted the electrifying shriek. She was staring across the Jheel at the western bank where the rocks were piled steeply in great flat slabs. The oily waters rippled excitedly, and then the gossamer mist evaporated to reveal clearly what Rani-beti had seen. Raising a trembling hand, she pointed towards a dark crack between the rocks.

"Look!" she screamed again, and fainted away.

Chapter 13

BETWEEN THE LABYRINTHS OF LIFE AND DEATH

Altu Faltu tore around wildly in his bullion-dust prison, digging dementedly — here, there, everywhere; throwing up the fine gold dust in frantic fistfuls. At last, choking and coughing, he sprawled against the smooth wall of the vault and stared blankly as the shimmering dust settled. The vault now looked like a billionaire's wrestling-pit. At least Rani-beti had not been buried here and for that he was grateful.

They had given him an emperor's burial, he thought bitterly, in accordance with his status perhaps, except that only he (and they) knew it. But what had they done to Rani-beti? Was she also incarcerated alive in some other sealed vault crammed with useless treasure? And how long could a monkey last in such a chamber anyway? What would he die of — suffocation, starvation, or thirst? The world dimmed about him...

"You can hardly wait to find out, Altu Faltu, can you?" Chaudhury Taza Raisahib remarked drily, from the prow of his sea-blue and red boat.

It had been three days since Rani-beti's capture. Could a monkey in her delicate condition last three days in a tomb like this?

"It looks as though you are going to have to find her again, doesn't it?" The old Chaudhury sounded almost amused. "And heroically rescue her once more."

"Find her? Rescue her? But how? First I have to get out of this billionaire's coffin myself."

"That's obvious, I would imagine." Sometimes Taza Raisahib could sound extremely arid. "And you're beginning to talk like my cretin grand-daughter Chamkili. Hmm... perhaps she would have been a better match for you."

"But how the hell do I get out of here?" Altu Faltu cried petulantly, upset by the old Chaudhury's lack of sympathy. "How? how? how?"

"Think, Altu Faltu, think..."

"Think? I'm dying here in this golden grave, of suffocation, starvation and thirst, and you want me to think?"

"Well, you are Altu Faltu after all, with a certain awesome reputation. How about trying to live up to that now? Instead of revelling in self-induced melodrama?"

"So what do you expect me to do then? Rocket up the chute, punch a hole through the trapdoor and go sailing through the air like Altu Faltu Sherkhanewala in the tiger's enclosure?"

"Withering sarcasm will get you nowhere, foolish simian. Sit down, calm yourself, count to ten, and think."

"Of what, for God's sake? Of what they might be doing even now to Rani-beti?"

"Yes, and how you're sitting here, doing nothing except feeling sorry for yourself."

"I don't need a lecture, Chaudhury Taza Raisahib. You're beginning to sound like my mother now."

If only there had been more gold dust here; if only the vault had been chockful of it, right up to the ceiling, he could have somehow reached the hole and hoisted himself up the chute. There was always the chance that the trapdoor had not been battened down properly. Else, he could have crouched beneath it, like a trapdoor spider, and waited for them to lift it up again, to thrust in some other hapless victim or check to see whether he was dead. Whence he would leap out, devour them and rescue Rani-beti once more, like Altu Faltu Sherkhanewala, goddamnit!

"You could always try it."

"Try what? Going up the chute? But Taza Raisahib, in case it's escaped your attention, the misers who filled this chamber have left it half empty. There's fifteen feet of black space above my head."

"Too bad then, Altu Faltu. But I wonder where all this gold dust came from, don't you?"

"The loot of long dead kings. What does it matter?"

"Yes of course. The spoils of war. But how did it get inside here? In this underground chamber?"

"Poured in through the chute, of course," he replied with blistering scorn. The old fogey was becoming senile after all, imbibing chhang, rocking back and forth on his boat, and asking imbecilic questions.

"Really Altu Faltu? Ah, then, take a fistful of gold dust and let it trickle out of your fingers will you..."

"Why?"

"So that you can see what happens when you do so, you silly monkey."

"It makes a little cone-shaped hill, that's what happens. So what's the big deal?"

"Ah, yes of course, so it does. How stupid of me." Mumbling enigmatically to himself now, the toothless old fool.

Altu Faltu glanced up at the hole in the ceiling, down which he had plunged, and at the gold dust in the vault. If the gold dust had been poured down the chute, there would have been a great hill of it just beneath the hole in the ceiling, at the spot where he had landed...

"Do you see the light, now?" Still dry as gin.

But there had been no hill! The bullion-dust had been evenly spread all over the floor of the vault. Until he had messed it up while looking for Rani-beti.

"Well, what does it mean, Altu Faltu?"

"How should I know Taza Raisahib!" Mulish till the last. Refusing to think.

"Apply your mind, you bekar little bandar. Well, let's put it another way. How do you suppose they planned to remove the gold dust from here? You know, in order to pay for the dowry — or ransom — of a princess, say?"

"I don't know. They'd lower a bucket down the chute and scoop the stuff out, I guess."

"You could never even half-empty the vault that way."

"Well, they'd lower a man down then..."

"Down that drainpipe chute? Don't be foolish. He'd never get down; it's far too narrow."

"Well, maybe they trained monkeys for the job."

"Do you think humans would ever let monkeys touch their precious gold? I wouldn't blame them, actually: look at you — you've gone and piddled all over the stuff."

"Taza Raisahib? Chaudhury Taza Raisahib?" Altu Faltu

suddenly jerked and twisted like a marionette on the floor. Was he going crazy in this shimmering godforsaken chamber, yelping for Rani–beti's grandfather?

But then, how would they have emptied that vault had the need arisen?

There had to be a door. Somewhere.

Big enough for slaves with silver spades. Certainly big enough for him to pass through. Carefully, he hobbled around his prison. Its walls rose sheer, smooth as ice, made of great slabs of seamless black granite. He probed, he tapped, he scratched, he put his big flappy ears flat against them and listened. No hollows, no cracks, a wall of ebony glass. Exhausted and defeated, he lay back at last, pillowing his head against a mound of bullion. His eyes drooped and even while struggling to remain awake, he hoped he would sleep, never to wake again.

Then, high up, in one corner of the black granite wall, something glimmered. And protruded. A handle. A carved, golden handle. He scrambled beneath it and squinted up at it. He tried reaching it by leaping up and down, and then by running and jumping, but the hard black wall flung him back on his bed of gold. He tried scaling the polished stone face, for he was a monkey after all, but fell back hopelessly, his paws scraped raw and bleeding. He sat panting, glaring at the golden handle, bobbing his head in frustrated rage.

If there was a pile of gold beneath that wretched handle, at least he could climb up and reach it...

"Well, here's your chance to make your pile!" Chaudhury Taza Raisahib snorted sardonically. "You have all the gold in the world!"

Frantically, he began heaping the gold dust against the

granite wall face, just beneath the handle, slithering, sliding, but flinging fistful after fistful, one on top of the other. He made his pile slowly, until at last, its shimmering conical tip rested a couple of feet beneath the gilded handle.

Then, he scrambled to the opposite end of the vault, and beat the gold dust off his palms. He measured his distance, and crouched like a sprinter on the starting blocks. "One, two, three!" he cried, and was off, reaching the base of his golden pile in three swift bounds. He dug in his heels and sprang up the shifting golden slope, reaching the top before the unstable stuff could even register his weight. He flexed his thighs and jumped vertically, eyes fixed on the handle, arms outstretched, fingers grabbing, grabbing, grabbing, desperately. Like a collapsing stock market, his golden pile disintegrated beneath him, but it didn't really matter.

One slim, supple wrist was clamped as tightly around that golden handle as it had been around the roaring tiger's neck.

Like a mountaineer going up a sheer ice cliff, Altu Faltu planted his feet firmly against the smooth granite wall, and with both hands now, hoisted himself up till his eyes were level with the handle. He was tugging at it now, with all his strength, but to no avail. His eyes nearly popping, and gasping with the effort, he stared at the smooth surface. And suddenly, he could swear he could discern the fine straight cracks in the stone, clearly delineating a doorway.

He planted his feet firmly now, on either side of the stubborn handle, and bracing himself, tugged with all his might.

The bloody golden handle came away in his hands, and at the same time, yielding to his weight, the door swung inwards, gracefully, effortlessly, with a gentle sigh.

With a startled yelp, Altu Faltu plunged headfirst into the

black cave mouth of the doorway.

"Made it, at last!" Chaudhury Taza Raisahib snorted laconically as Altu Faltu landed with a thud on a hard stone floor, still clutching the golden handle. "Even if you did pull instead of pushing."

Altu Faltu gazed around warily. He had somersaulted into a damp, rocky chamber that appeared to lead into a tunnel of sorts. A few, very faint wisps of light filtered down, their origins mysterious. Shimmering with the gold dust adhering to him, Altu Faltu crept forward, feeling the rough rock-wall with one hand, for reassurance and guidance.

At times, the darkness pressed suffocatingly upon him, like damp black velvet against his face. He wanted to leap up and scream as the claustrophobia took hold, but dared not. There was no brickwork here, no great blocks of stones piled one on top of the other. The tunnel appeared to have been bored through a mountain of solid rock. He clung to the rough wall on his right, feeling his way along as a blind person would. Each step was measured and tentative. A faint current of air suddenly brushed across his face and hope flared. Perhaps he was near the entrance at last... He quickened his pace, but with one hand still feeling along the right hand wall. So intent and concentrated was he that he completely missed the twisting, sloping fork to the left which would have taken him to one of the great fort's long emptied 'toshakhanas' — and to freedom.

Instead, his tunnel plunged steeply now, banking eastwards, and then straightening out northwards. It grew cooler and damper and when he sneezed, he nearly shot out of his skin as a thousand echoes bounced back from every direction. But the solid rock wall had now given way to one that had obviously been constructed with blocks of stone. Rough cut, but so firmly and permanently affixed that not even the most insidious peepul root had been able to prise through.

He rounded another bend and suddenly found himself in the clamorous gullies of the Walled City again. Dodging dogs and peering through the flaps of circus tents, where elephants trumpeted and then walked on beach balls. Scuttling between remorseless traffic, then flitting over hot flat barsati-roofs. In frantic pursuit of the fading rattle of a bandarwalla's dug-duggi. The plaintive wheedling, "aaao, aaao, aaao..." of the wily sariwala, the rasping 'twang!' of the flying net, laughter, screaming, weeping, shouting... The thud of pounding simian feet, his mother's wretched scream, "No, Altu Faltu! No!"

And then, there she was, wicked, wanton thing, wriggling her hips and rotating her bottom, before being thrust still giggling into the great hairy embrace of Nawab Bade Badtameez by a smirking Suna Hai.

He darted ahead, hoping to get away from it all, but was confronted instead by the beautiful mad nymphet from the zoo. 'You've found me again,' she whispered, drawing herself across the tunnel wall like she had against the honeycomb mesh of her cage. 'This time, forever!' she exclaimed, and came into his arms. He looked over her shoulder and into the flame-flecked eyes of Rani-beti (still giggling and wriggling her hips a bit), and wrenched himself free, fleeing, with the nymphet's screams echoing in his head.

Then he was back again, in the comforting velvet blackness of his tunnel, clutching the hard rock to his bosom, gasping.

"Well done," Taza Raisaib remarked. "Well done."

"Well done? What do you mean well done! This feels like a flaming drug trip gone bad and you say well done. Am I dead or alive, Taza Raisahib? I don't even know that!"

"No need to get emotional, Altu Faltu."

"Are you dead, Taza Raisahib? What does it feel like?"

"I don't know. I expect being dead is like it was before you were born."

"Eh? How can you be dead before you were born?"

"Ah, I'd better be off now!" Suddenly jittery and nervous. "Or I will be dead for sure! Do you smell what I smell, Altu Faltu?"

There was no mistaking it. The hot rank reek of tiger, tiger, tiger! Billowing through the tunnel in great waves, so thick you could taste it. Then, two gigantic emeralds blazing out at him from the darkness beyond, eerily lighting up the gleaming ivory canines. Then... a bowel-liquidising roar, that engulfed the tunnel like some hurricane wind, flattening his ears back against his skull.

And then, that white-hot crazy adrenalin again, screaming through his veins, making his eyes bulge and electrifying his fur so that it stood up like wire-brush.

"I'm Altu Faltu Sherkhanewala!" he screamed, and charged between the burning jade eyes. And ran right through them, or what? For what was he doing, sprawled on the tunnel floor, with a fistful of tiger hairs clutched in one paw?

Carefully he stuck them behind his ear.

"Madman!" Taza Raisahib congratulated. "You're a manic, psychotic madman. Next time that tiger will have you for lunch."

"Bah! I'm Altu Faltu Sherkhanewala!" he shouted, and tossed his head imperiously.

"Ah, maybe. But you still have to find Rani-beti."

"Doesn't this tunnel ever end?" he complained. "And will I ever get out of it?" As usual, the adrenalin, or whatever it was, had evaporated as fast as it had surged.

Tired out, he sat down and held his head in his hands. Of course, there was no sign of Taza Raisahib now. "Comes and goes like a defective tubelight!" Altu Falt muttered uncharitably to himself.

But hark, what was that? The grunts and screams of warring, battling bandars! Drawing close. He flattened himself against the tunnel wall and waited, hardly daring to breathe.

A great bristling brute bounded up and halted before him, looking him up and down with evident disgust.

"The interfering bitch!" he snarled. "I nearly had the old cock, and then she jumped me from behind! Changed the course of the battle. Changed the course of history!"

"Who are you and what are you talking about?"

"General Zabardast! Of the Pehelee Behtereen Batallion!"

"And does that make me a monkey's uncle or what?" he responded cheekily, wondering whether Taza Raisahib was within earshot.

"Cheeky pup, eh? I'll teach you..."

"I'm Altu Faltu Sherkhanewala!" he screeched, like it was a magical incantation. "You must have heard about me!"

The General did not flinch, let alone baulk. Just looked more disgusted than before.

"Altu Faltu? The Nicholson Cemetery bounder? Whose pecadillos have caused a war? Do you know what you've gone and done?"

"No. Yes, I am that Altu Faltu..."

"Your mother broke my neck."

"You must have annoyed her, I suppose."

"I nearly had him. Then she jumped me from behind."

"Had who?"

"Brigadier Ladsahib."

"If you nearly had my father, I'm not surprised my mother broke your neck. What did she do to him?"

"Piss off you little twit. You have no idea how much trouble you have caused. The whole of the Northern Ridge is in turmoil."

"There's a lovely nubile nymphet further down the tunnel, General. Who will be so pleased to see you."

"You cheeky little pimp..."

"One more thing, sir."

"What?"

"Did you ever think it would be possible for someone christened Altu Faltu to be responsible for starting a war?"

"Eh?"

"Think about it General. They're having you on."

"Well done, Altu Faltu, shabash!" So Taza Raisahib had been eavesdropping again.

"Taza Raisahib, where is Rani-beti? And where does this tunnel end? I'm tired and sleepy and depressed..."

"...and whining again."

"Is Rani-beti dead?"

"I'd better be off again. You have another visitor coming up. Hectic social life you have, I must say, even down here."

It was the crazy nymphet again. "I didn't like the General," she pouted, "so I slit his throat."

"But his neck was already broken!"

"I've found you again!" She wrapped herself around him, and smothered him. "Mmm..." she moaned, "I've got you now, good and proper."

"I'm only allowing this to take place because I know that Rani-beti is dead, and I need someone to hold on to!" he said loudly, for the benefit of Taza Raisahib, who would be eavesdropping again, the dirty old voyeur. And squeezed the nymphet tightly. "I'm only doing it because this is a terrible moment in my life and I need to be comforted and to give comfort," he blabbered.

"Liar!"

"Rani-beti? Rani-beti? Where are you? I heard you!" He whirled, and cast the nymphet aside roughly. No reply, no sound. Just the mad nymphet with pain in her eyes. "Come here," he whispered cunningly, and took her back in his arms.

The tiger's hairs behind his ears began to prickle and bristle and stiffen. And then, curled around his throat, they started tightening, tightening, tightening... Above the roar of blood rushing through his ears, he caught the jingle of anklets and the throb of drums. He pushed the nymphet away from him, but gently this time. The noose loosened.

"I don't want to find you, Rani-beti!" he shouted. "You can do your cabarets to your heart's content. You can wriggle your bottom off for all I care. For your beloved Badtameez or any-one else!"

"Fool! Imbecile! Idiot!" Chaudhury Taza Raisahib was back again, and indignant. "Think, dammit, before you shout your head off. How can Rani-beti do a cabaret in her present delicate state?"

"The baby! I forgot about the baby!"

"And you jump to conclusions. And into other bandari's arms!"

Altu Faltu fiddled with his tail, pretending he had a flea, eyes averted. But only momentarily. Then he cocked his head and listened.

"Taza Raisahib, is that the sound of running water that

I hear? A babbling, bubbling brook, rushing pell-mell..."

"Changing the subject, eh, Altu Faltu?" The old swine was no fool after all.

But he was right! The air was suddenly damper. And he was thirsty, very thirsty. And there it was, running water all right. An underground stream, coursing swiftly in a south-easterly direction, towards the river no doubt. Covered here and there, by a gossamer quilt of white mist, that swirled and curled in myriad shapes. The tunnel twisted north-west here, running alongside the water, but upstream along its course.

Altu Faltu got onto his knees and bent down to drink. And for the second time, was shoved hard from behind...

"Godspeed!" shouted the old Chaudhury, as he tumbled headfirst into the swift black water. He would have emerged, no doubt, miles downstream in the filthy river, long drowned, but...

Strong, supple, simian fingers grabbed his arms and legs and tail. Spreadeagled on his back, he was pulled upstream at high speed, in the undignified manner of a stubborn demonstrator being hauled away by the police. His bottom bumped on rocks, and sent up a sheet of spray as it cleaved through the water like the prow of a speedboat. Bounced, buffeted and bruised, he was screeching like a first-time rough river rafter, out of fear and devilish excitement. Till at last, just as he was sure he was about to pass out, the stream cut sharply to the right. The hands that held him jerked to a halt, and then, swinging him, once, twice, thrice, let go. He landed with a thump on his wet bum, like a bum, in a rock puddle.

"Made it!" Taza Raisahib exclaimed, with a note of relief. "Nearly there, now Altu Faltu, nearly there."

"Nearly where? Sod off, Taza Raisahib, you pushed me into

the water!" Accusing and indignant.

"Had to hurry Altu Faltu, had to hurry! The way you were progressing — what with all that socialising — you would have taken a fortnight to get here."

"What's so great about here? And what's the hurry? When you're dead, it's forever."

But then he looked around and saw the smoky white glare of daylight. The main tunnel had swerved alongside the stream and vanished into blackness. But another, smaller tunnel, led to the left. A tunnel excavated by animals perhaps, for its walls were of earth and thickly interwoven with roots. A tunnel that climbed acutely and narrowed in places so that even he had to squeeze through. But as he progressed, the light got brighter, and soon he could distinctly make out the shapes of individual rocks and pebbles, the weave of roots, and scuttling underground creatures. And then, a blinding strip of pure light, pouring through a crack between two immense flat rocks.

The end of the tunnel at last.

Again the damp smell of water, but rank and putrid with vegetation. But so powerfully full of romantic nostalgia, he wanted to weep. And currents of delicious cool air, fragrant with bittersweet neem and eucalyptus. Strange currents actually, that brushed his cheeks like Rani-beti's kisses (oh God, not the mad nymphet again!), soft fingers of air that combed his fur, firm jets that massaged his bruised, tired muscles. Whisking off the debris of his journey, the dead vegetation and mud. Grooming him as lovingly and devotedly as Rani-beti (and the Khyber Pass bandaris) had ever done. Leaving him at last, massaged, brushed, and blow-dried, feeling fabulous. Still clad in a sheen of bullion dust that would adhere to him forever.

Screwing his eyes against the glare, he approached the blinding slit. He waited awhile, to get used to the dazzle, then wriggled through it, and into broad daylight.

He squatted, regarding the scene before him with astonished yet calm eyes. ("So... so aristocratically!" Bibi-Teen would later gush.)

Trees soaring gracefully arched to form a great elegant cathedral roof. Below, a blackish-green pond rippled and swirled; a faint white mist rose in tatters. Simian faces were everywhere: on the right bank, on the left bank; amazed, angry, frightened, bewildered; all bobbing up and down like so many jack-in-the boxes.

And on the bridge over the Khooni Khan Jheel, cast in gold (as always), and gazing at him in rapt astonishment, with one arm raised:

Rani-beti.

Screaming, "Look!" and then again, "Look!"

Then, sinking feebly back into the terrible grip of Nawab Bade Badtameez, who dangled a baby over the black water.

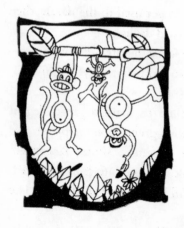

Chapter 14

DUEL AND
DENOUEMENT

They all looked.

One by one, they swivelled their heads in the direction of Rani-beti's upraised arm, their pebble eyes blinking nervously.

Chaudhury Charbi Raisahib bobbed his head several times, and his fur began to prickle and rise. "Who the hell is that?" he growled, wondering where this gold-dusted apparition had so suddenly emerged from. "And what trickery is he up to?"

Bibi-Teen nudged him disrespectfully in the ribs, unable to contain her excitement. "Chaudhury Sahib... Chaudhury Sahib..." she stuttered. "That can only be Altu Faltu! Rani-beti swooned as soon as she saw him. That's proof enough!"

"Altu Faltu? The awara Rani-beti eloped with? Impossible! What the hell is going on here?" The Chaudhury was under-standably astonished. He had never met, let alone seen the awara from the Hindu Rao Ridge — only heard about him (and that too, chiefly from Bibi-Teen). And now his worst fears were being realised: like Bibi-Do, he was not at all impressed by what he saw, golden sheen notwithstanding.

A little puzzled, Bibi-Do stared at the awara she had sworn to kill. He looked like the same no-hoper all right, but there was something different about him which she couldn't pin down.

Bibi-Ek, gulping back enormous, hiccoughing sobs, wiped her eyes and stared at the vagabond who had stolen her daughter's heart and caused her to produce the twitching, brown thingaling being dangled over the water. She turned brokenly to Bibi-Do, who was looking unmistakably sheepish.

"How could you?" she sobbed. "You cruel, cruel thing! How could you let my beautiful, precious Rani-beti elope with that emaciated junkie? His ribs stick out like the bars of a cage!"

Bibi-Teen took her arm comfortingly, as Bibi-Do turned away, ashamed. "Hush Bibi-Ek," she instructed. "Don't judge only by physique or bulk or width of shoulders. There may not be much meat on those bones, but can't you see — sona munda hai!"

Bibi-Ek blinked back a fresh flood of tears. Bibi-Teen was right. The skinny little monkey shimmered with a golden hue. She had never seen anything like that before.

"Why you're right!" Bibi-Do exclaimed, recovering her poise rapidly. "He's turned all golden! What on earth has the little bugger been up to, I wonder?"

At the other end of the bridge, Brigadier-General Ladsahib regarded the appearance of his long lost son with something akin to disgust. He knew it! He had been right! Altu Faltu had turned up like a bad (if golden) penny again. Squatting up there on that rock, like some gilded mahatma monkey, probably stoned out of his mind and wanting a handout.

Ruining all his grand military plans.

"Altu Faltu! Come down here, you little twit!" he roared. "You've caused enough trouble already."

"It's true!" whispered Lieutenant Hazari Kaan, veneration in his voice, as he clutched the Brigadier's elbow and gazed in awe at the sainted golden monkey.

"What is true?" snapped the Brigadier, jerking his arm free.

"The rumour that has been going around for months. That Altu Faltu slaughtered six tigers at the zoo with his bare hands. Look at what he's got around his neck: a necklace made out of tiger hair."

"Killed six tigers? Altu Faltu? You must be out of your mind Lieutenant. Have you been drinking?"

"No, sir! But the necklace. That's genuine tiger hair. See the fiery manner in which it catches the sunlight?"

"So what? He probably pinched it from the tiger's cage-while it was being swept or something!" the Brigadier snorted. "I know that useless little bugger." He turned towards the rock and shouted again. "Altu Faltu, get down here this instant!"

But Altu Faltu (as always) ignored him and stared down at the little hunchbacked bridge.

Badtameez had backed up against the far side railing and was staring at him with a noxious mixture of fear, rage, hate and disbelief. "You... you can't be Altu Faltu," he blurted hoarsely, "I threw you down that shaft myself! Who are you?" In his panic, he had let go of the limp Rani-beti and she slumped, still unconscious, on the bridge. He had released the baby too (fortunately not in the water) and it crawled determinedly towards its mother's breast.

Altu Faltu's eyes swivelled swiftly from Badtameez to Rani-beti, hunched so tragically there in a foetal crouch. If she had been doing cabarets (and worse) with Badtameez, he thought, trying to exorcise the demon jealousy once and for all, she would have now been clinging to the brute and glaring defiantly at him, Altu Faltu, with stony, loveless eyes, breaking his heart. Not lying like that, a castaway — like the sole survivor of some hideous mass torture.

"Go get him, Altu Faltu, go get him!" exhorted Taza Raisahib in his ear, as though cheering a wrestling bout at his akhara. And again, the foolish little monkey felt the ego-charged adrenalin begin to surge and race in his veins. He bounced on all fours, his golden fur bristling spikily, a ridiculous spectacle really, but causing Bibi-Teen to nearly swoon herself.

"I'm Altu Faltu Sherkhanewala!" he shrieked dementedly, "And I'm going to make a meal out of you Badtameez, just as I made a meal out of those poor tigers. Urrrgghh!"

"He's mad!" groaned the Brigadier. "Stoned. On a trip, or whatever it is they go on. Hallucinating. He thinks he ate six tigers. That brute will kill him."

Rani-beti shifted slightly and moaned as her baby burrowed beneath her, looking for his milk bar. She was beginning to come around at last. And this time, the quick-thinking Langoti kept his wits about him. Huddled with the other two in the bed of spider lilies where Leechad had lain, he had followed the unfolding drama keenly. And this was the moment to act, he knew — when everyone's attention was occupied elsewhere.

He darted across the bridge, grabbed Rani-beti by the arm and dragged her across to safety in a twinkling, her baby attached firmly to her breast. With a grunt of rage, Badtameez lunged after him, but was brought to a halt by the bristling Brigadier and a formidable array of veteran stormtroopers on the other side. Snarling with frustration, he withdrew to the centre of the bridge again.

"Who the hell was that?" barked the Chaudhury, craning his neck. "Not another suitor?"

And Bibi-Teen, bless her tender heart, actually began to feel sorry for the big brute Badtameez. "Poor bastard," she thought, "he came here as a bridegroom, ended up as a terrorist, is now surrounded by his enemies with his hostage kidnapped and not a hope in hell."

"Go on! Attack him you idiot! Before he recovers from the shock. You have to drive him away from here." Taza Raisahib sounded rather agitated, and Altu Faltu could have sworn he felt knuckles dig into his ribs. He sprang off the rock and landed light as a thistle on a fallen tree trunk that sprawled across the pond, just in front of the bridge — a prodigious thirty foot drop.

"Did you see that?" hissed Bibi-Teen, yanking Bibi-Do's tail. "Did you see that? A fifty foot jump and that tree trunk never even trembled when he landed on it. Not a leaf on the branches flickered. And just look at that crack he came through. No monkey could have squeezed through that, no matter how skinny. There's something terribly odd going on here, Bibi-Do."

Badtameez was glaring at Altu Faltu again, having backed up once more against the railing, his fur abristle, his tail up. He knew that this would be the fight for, and of, his life. But then, his prickly golden adversary suddenly appeared to lose all interest in him. He had turned instead towards the others gathered all around; the spellbound gathering of the clans. His dreamy brown eyes had filled with tears and his chin quivered.

"You're all horrible!" he screamed suddenly, startling them

all. "The whole lot of you. You all think that I'm useless. A wastrel. Good-for-nothing. A bekara. An altu-faltu."

"Oh God, this is not the time nor place for you to feel sorry for yourself in public, Altu Faltu," Taza Raisahib said, sotto voce. The wronged golden mahatma ignored him and swallowed a huge lump in his throat. "You all think I'm not good enough for Rani-beti," he continued shrilly, sniffing hugely, "even if I did slaughter ferocious tigers with my bare hands to save her. But that's not good enough for you. You still prefer this ugly earless thug who knows only how to rape, plunder and kill."

"Neither of you are good enough for her!" the Chaudhury roared, incensed beyond measure. "You are a drunken junkie, and he is an unprincipled freebooter. Now get the hell out of here, both of you."

"You asked for it, Altu Faltu," Taza Raisahib remarked in his arid way. "He's got a point, don't you think?"

"Shut up Taza Raisahib. This is between me and the Chaudhury and Badtameez and everyone else," Altu Faltu responded, somewhat petulantly.

He turned towards Rani-beti's formidable father, and took a deep breath, trying to control the tremor in his voice. "So you think I'm not good enough for your daughter? Is that it, sir?" he asked, injecting as much sarcasm into his voice as he could.

"I most certainly do. And don't you dare talk down to me like that, you young hoodlum or I'll have you hung publicly upside down by your tail."

"Even though Rani-beti thinks I am good enough for her?" he persisted, now trying to sound exquisitely polite.

"Rani-beti is too young to know what is good for her."

"But you know what's good for her, don't you, Chaudhury Sahib?"

"Of course I do. I am her father."

"So you think this simian pervert, this carnal cannibal, is good enough for her?" The belittling, withering note in his voice, now aided by the reckless adrenalin.

"Shut your mouth, you little pipsqueak. And apologise at once!"

Normally of course, Chaudhury Charbi Raisahib would not have wasted his time making conversation with an awara who had absconded with his favourite daughter. He would have had him slaughtered straightaway. But it appeared that the awara had brought his baap along, and the Brigadier, in turn, appeared to have a full batallion backing him up. It would have been foolish to act hastily (and the defeat from his last encounter still rankled).

Never one to be left out of a melodrama, Lady Ladsahib had got wind of the goings-on and had made it over from the Cemetery at high speed. At her husband's side now, she took in the situation with one sweeping glance.

"Altu Faltu!" she boomed. "Behave yourself. And come here at once. We're going home immediately. You have a lot of explaining to do. Vanishing off the face of the earth, just like that. Precipitating a war. And now challenging that thug to a duel. I am ashamed of you. Ever since you began mixing around with that Hindu Rao crowd..."

Rani-beti stood up unsteadily, supported on either side by Langoti and Yaar. She took a shaky step forward onto a protruding rock and gazed at Altu Faltu bemusedly, her baby clutched to her bosom. There was a sharp collective intake of breath all round, and even the formidable Lady Ladsahib paused in mid-delivery. Rani-beti extended both arms towards her beloved golden saint and gasped quiveringly: "Altu Faltu? Oh, Altu Faltu!"

Then, overcome with emotion, she fell back into the arms of Langoti and Yaar.

"Rani-beti? Rani-beti! Are you all right? Have these monsters harmed you? Have they touched a hair on your precious head? I swear I will slaughter them all..."

"Don't make an ass of yourself, Altu Faltu, for God's sake." Taza Raisahib sounded thoroughly disgusted.

"I'm all right Altu Faltu," Rani-beti called back in a wavering voice that indicated anything but that. And then added tremulously and shyly. "And look what I have for you here. A present!"

Her eyes glowing, still weak from her ordeal, she held up her squeaking, twitching baby.

He stared raptly at the tiny wizened baby, with its huge dark eyes and shell-pink elephant's ears.

"Baby Faltu," he whispered dramatically with a catch in his voice, ignoring Taza Raisahib's moan of horror. "We'll call it little Baby Faltu!"

"Actually," said Rani-beti with a wan smile, a little of her old spirit reviving. "Actually, he's a baba!"

"Then we'll call him Baba Faltu of course," he responded unhesitatingly. "Or Faltu Baba. Whichever you prefer."

Taza Raisahib sighed deeply and shudderingly. "Oh, no, no, no! Not after all I have done for you. You go and trample over everything I have ever stood for! Baba Faltu, I ask you. How will the little bugger ever live down a name like that? Call him Taza Rai Faltu, if you must. But for his sake, and mine, don't call him Baba Faltu!"

"He'll live down his name just as I have mine," replied Altu Faltu, not realising how much like the Brigadier he sounded. "By slaughtering tigers with his bare hands, like I did."

"A grandson!" squealed Bibi-Teen, nudging the stunned Chaudhury, and actually pinching Bibi-Ek. "You're the grandfather of a grandson Chaudhury Sahib. Congratulations!" Then she embraced Bibi-Ek who turned away, her head in her hands. "And you a granny," she gushed on, with just a sliver of malice. "So early in life!"

"A little bastard grandson," growled the Chaudhury, shaking his head. "Never had a son of my own and now my most precious jewel of a daughter produces an illegitimate one! How could she do this to me?"

"Arre hai! Meri beti!" lamented Bibi-Ek again, beating her breast. "The unwed mother of an illegitimate baby! Satya naas ho gaya!"

Even Lady Ladsahib's attention had been drawn to the squealing little foundling that Rani-beti was holding up. Swiftly she went over to examine the little tadpole.

"You don't seriously mean, my dear, that you and Altu Faltu actually er... produced that?" she enquired incredulously, turning the little fellow over gently.

"Yes," simpered Rani-beti proudly, her maternal instincts suddenly surging like Altu Faltu's kamikaze adrenalin. "Isn't he beautiful? Adorable?"

"How?" asked Lady Ladsahib unexpectedly.

"How? How what?" Rani-beti stared at the dowager blankly.

"How did you and Altu Faltu produce it? The baby."

"Er... I suppose... the same way that you and the Brigadier er... produced Altu Faltu," she replied nonplussed and beginning to colour.

"I should hope not!" Lady Ladsahib countered acidly. "Actually my dear, we're not quite sure how we er... did produce Altu Faltu," she admitted. "Pesonally, I feel it may have been due to something the Brigadier ate."

Rani-beti goggled. "You mean... you mean, you don't know about how..."

"Of course we do, silly. It's not that. I'm er... just not very sure that Altu Faltu knows. Um... I mean, realises the full implications of his er... actions. Actually I'm a little surprised he managed. And... er... if you did produce the baby in the same way we produced him... he might take after him. Like Altu Faltu takes after the Brigadier's family." Her logic was beginning to unravel, but Rani-beti didn't seem to notice.

"That would be wonderful!" she said dreamily. "As long as the little fellow doesn't take after my family." Her eyes filled up rapidly. "Lady Ladsahib! Altu Faltu is a wonderful, wonderful simian. So romantic. So passionate. So kind. So gentle. And when he's all charged up... why he even admitted to having created havoc amongst the Khyber Pass bandaris. That was before he so daringly rescued me, of course. He thought I was dead and was really down and out, poor fellow."

Lady Ladsahib, who had begun to feel guilty about her role in the trapping incident on the wall, pricked up her ears. "What? Altu Faltu's been messing about with the bandaris at the Khyber Pass Massage Parlour?" She staggered back a step. If it was not one thing, it was another: Altu Faltu would never change. "Ladloo!" she bellowed in a stentorian voice. "Will you get over here and hear what your good-for-nothing son has been upto now? He's been making babies at the Khyber Pass Massage Parlour, if you please."

"What?" roared the Brigadier, turning purple, blue and bulging. "Little bugger Nicholsonites running about the Massage Parlour! I won't have it. Wait till I get my hands on him!"

But it was the fear-crazed Badtameez who had decided to lay his hands around Altu Faltu's neck first. The little wimp — after daring to challenge him — had become too involved in quarrelling with his ridiculous family and had ignored him. Everyone here, in fact, had appeared to have forgotten about him — the jilted bridegroom turned terrorist. They seemed far more interested in the little chuhe-ka-lendi which he ought to have eaten for breakfast in the first place. Well, he would change all that.

In one fluid motion, he leapt onto the railing and hurled himself at Altu Faltu on the fallen tree trunk below. It juddered under the impact of his weight and he grabbed the branches wildly to save himself from falling into the water. He steadied himself, and turned to charge, grunting deep down in his belly.

And found that Altu Faltu had vanished.

Then Rani-beti screamed and the others grunted and coughed in alarm. Badtameez turned around slowly, and stared at the bridge. Altu Faltu was perched comfortably there, on the railing, tweaking his tail.

"I'll get you, you snivelling little wimp!" roared Badtameez, and with a mighty effort, leapt onto the bridge once more. And this time, succeeded in sandwiching the fragile fellow between the wire mesh and himself. "I have you, now," he gloated, and moved stiffly in for the kill, every steel muscle taut and coiled. This time there would be no escape, no matter how many tigers his adversary claimed to have killed.

Bibi-Do shut her eyes and prayed for her djinns, whoever they were, to erupt from the water one last time and prise Badtameez away like they had done Leechad. Bibi-Ek bobbed her head and screeched bloodthirstily, "Get him, smash him, pulp him!" but not quite certain which monkey she meant. Bibi-Teen slipped behind the Chaudhury's safe bulk and peeped out from there. Lady Ladsahib let off a huge shriek and would have interfered at once (yet again) in her son's affairs, had not the Brigadier and Lieutenant Hazari Kaan forcibly held her back.

"No! He's going to have to get out of this one himself," the Brigadier grunted. "Though I don't see how. He's going to get mauled."

Badtameez swung a whistling fist — and missed. Then he lowered his great bull head and charged. He never knew how Altu Faltu managed to slither away. But dodge he did, and Badtameez thwanged his head against the wire mesh so violently, the whole structure reverberated. He staggered back, momentarily dazed.

Bibi-Teen's eyes grew huge and circular. "Did you see that?" she gasped, "Did you see that? The brute appeared to charge right through Altu Faltu."

Who was now squatting peaceably on the other railing. Badtameez eyed him warily and flattened his tattered ears.

"No need to try it again," Altu Faltu advised him, in a kind, unctuous tone. "You'll only bang your head again."

But again Badtameez emitted his vicious snarl and charged. And yet again the elusive little monkey flitted away, as easily as quicksilver, and the bridge shuddered with the impact. "You'll only pound your brains to pulp," the little monkey sang cheekily, "if you have any."

"Eat him up, Altu Faltu, eat him up!" yelled Taza Raisahib, obviously carried away by the action.

"In the soft underbelly!" screeched Lady Ladsahib suddenly, jumping up and down. "Nip him in the underbelly. In-out, in-out, in-out!"

Rani-beti looked at her in horror and quickly took her baby away.

On the bridge, Badtameez reeled and paused. His chest was heaving, his head was ringing, his eyes were unfocussed, and his face was suffused with rage. There was something weird about this fight and he was becoming seriously frightened. He had struck many a vicious blow — to absolutely no effect. His scrawny opponent had struck absolutely none — with telling effect. He couldn't for the life of him understand this non-violent battle. And no matter how fast he moved, he never seemed able to sink his fangs into his quarry, who, incidentally, he had already killed once by shoving him down a chute. He could have sworn that his jackhammer punches had been right on target but each time, his massive fists had hissed through empty air and his jaws had mashed shut over nothing. He glared at his bony opponent and the baffled rage rose swiftly again. Altu Faltu was on the railing once again, watching him keenly out of his lady-killing poet-dreamer eyes.

"Get off that railing Altu Faltu," Taza Raisahib suddenly warned with a note of urgency, as though he had just been struck by a sudden foreboding. "Badtameez can't swim."

"Can't swim? Why didn't you tell me before?" A gleam entered those dreamy brown eyes and Altu Faltu slapped his knobbly knees and bobbed his head.

"Come and get me, Badtameez," he chanted, and blew a long, rude raspberry.

"No! Don't do that!" shouted Taza Raisahib. 'You'll neutralise the advantage you hold. And you'll be damning lovers here, for all times to come."

But it was too late.

With a deep rumble of rage, Badtameez bounded forward. Altu Faltu jinked deftly to the left, at the very last moment, and Badtameez sailed right over his shoulder. He landed in the water with a thunderous report, sending the spray high and wide. And vanished beneath the rippling black waters. Then the scum drew quickly over the spot, like a theatre curtain closing.

"Go!" shouted Taza Raisahib, with a ring of panic. "Get out of here Altu Faltu. With Rani-beti. Or he'll get her."

"Eh?" the dreamer exclaimed blankly. "What are you talk-ing about, Taza Raisaib?"

"No time to explain," replied the grand old simian impa-tiently. "Not now. Just go!"

Altu Faltu stared at the oily black water, suddenly becalmed once more. And a great, black fear clamped over his heart as he realised what Taza Raisahib was trying to tell him. He scuttled across the bridge over to Rani-beti and took her hand; in his haste even forgetting that this ought to have been a great reunion embrace and ignoring his first-born son. "We have to get out of here, Rani-beti," he said urgently, with all the fear and panic of old. "Let's go back to the Villa Lantana right away."

But Rani-beti was in no hurry now. She looked up at his anxious face, adoration shining from her eyes. "You brave, beautiful hero! My hero! That was the most courageous thing I have ever seen. Braver even than the slaughter of the tigers."

She took him into her arms, and then tugging him by the

hand, danced to the centre of the fateful bridge and leapt nimbly onto the railing. And addressed the spellbound clans.

"You saw that? All of you! How Altu Faltu, my Altu Faltu, dispatched that simian brontosaurus in a clean, fair fight? And so far, all you have shown him is derision and disrespect. All of you regarded him as a useless vagabond, who was only out to do mischief with me, to take my chastity, and leave me in the lurch. For shame!"

"Oh, no!" moaned Taza Raisahib. "Not her now! Shut her up, Altu Faltu, and take her away before that monster in the deep awakens. Besides, one of you is enough for me. I'm too old for such heavy, sugary doses of romance."

But the fiery princess would not be stopped. She swung around to face her parents, her eyes sparking fire.

"You both saw that too, didn't you?" she enquired, her voice loaded with sarcasm and tears. "How that humble, noble bandar won my hand and saved my honour in a fair fight? Well, what do you think of him now? I think you all owe him a very big apology. I mean, there I was, captive to that carnal Frankenstien's lust, that... that perverted baby-killing animal, that... that Delhizen you wanted me to marry! And here was Altu Faltu, captured himself by that demon, who still managed to escape somehow. And followed me undaunted, right across the city, to finally corner and challenge my abductor here, on this very same romantic bridge where he proposed to me! And rescued me from his hairy embrace and a fate far worse than death. While all of you could only look on helplessly, as that pervert threatened to have his way with me!"

"Get her off that bridge, you dolt!" Taza Raisahib hissed, "Or she'll carry on like that for the whole day. And Badtameez has been under water for over five minutes now. His lungs must be full of scum."

But Rani-beti was allowing her new found eloquence full rein. "...and so, here I am now, safe with my newborn princeling, my nanna munna baba, thanks to the courage of the bandar I love. You all saw for yourself how that great barbarian, my fiancé once, hung my newborn upside down over the murky, evil water. And how Altu Faltu, gallant Altu Faltu, swooped down and snatched him to safety and restored him to my bereft bosom..."

The murky, evil water had indeed begun to look murky and evil again. For the strange gossamer mists had reappeared — coiling and twining frantically on its turbulent surface like serpents making love. Altu Faltu appeared to be hypnotised and not by Rani-beti's flowing oratory...

He was staring into the water, staring and not believing what he was seeing. What he had first taken to be a submerged rock, greeny-yellow with sunlit slime, was beginning to take on a frightening countenance.

A fearsome simian face, with bloodshot eyes and bitten-off ears. Cruel, lipless mouth drawn back into a soundless snarl; displaying massive, jaundiced canines. Badtameez again! Badtameez, rising, rising, rising, inexorably towards the surface, looming larger even as the gossamer mists, now directly over him, spread like a trapper's net. Like a leviathan surfacing, the drowned monster broke the surface, even as the mists pressed down upon him, smothering, choking and coiling wispy simian fingers around his throat. The great fighting beast ripped and tore at the mists, but the arms and fingers formed again and again, wrapping themselves around his face, holding him down, and covering those baleful eyes, now fixed un-waveringly on Rani-beti and Rani-beti alone.

All that the others saw was the thrashing and tumult of the water and the snaking, coiling mists. But Bibi-Do knew at once that her saviour djinns were at work again, fighting a savage, invisible enemy for the cause of love and romance. "Thank you," she whispered, put her head on the Chaudhury's shoulder, and wept.

"Will you get her away from that bridge, Altu Faltu?" Taza Raisahib shouted frantically. "What sort of great hero are you? Do you know what will happen if that monster breaks free of the water?"

Altu Faltu snapped out of his trance with a jerk. He slipped a firm arm around Rani-beti's waist. (She was still waxing eloquent.)

"Come along Rani-beti, let's go. That was a very sweet speech. Thank you." And escorted her firmly over to the side where her parents and the other Flagstaffers crowded. "Say goodbye now, and let's be going."

She stopped before her great father and held out her baby. "You never had a son of your own, papa," she whispered in an emotion-choked voice, "but you now have a grandson." But the proud Chaudhury, still mortified and implacable, just blinked and looked right through his most precious jewel of a daughter.

"'Give him time, and he'll come round," Taza Raisahib chuckled toothlessly. "He's always been a pompous ass. Altu Faltu could only squeeze Rani-beti's hand comfortingly, and murmur, "Never mind, Rani-beti; he'll get over the shock eventually." But Bibi-Do and Bibi-Teen had already come round. With adoring eyes, they held out their arms and took the infant from Rani-beti. "He's beautiful," Bibi-Do crooned, as she cuddled the little thing, proud now to be at least partially responsible for its existence.

"He looks just like the Chaudhury," Bibi-Teen chimed blasphemously, clapping her hands in delight.

But Bibi-Ek, her eyes stiffly averted, had begun grooming the Chaudhury. Rani-beti went up to her, with the baby on her back now, jockey-style. "Well mama, goodbye," she said softly, knowing her mother's iron-bound bent of mind. "When you feel better about this, you can always visit us and bless the little one."

Bibi-Ek looked up at last. She saw Rani-beti, petrified Rani-beti in the grasp of that sex-maniac from Tughlakabad. She saw the infant being dangled upside down over the black water. She saw Altu Faltu now, emaciated and pale as ever, with that oafish dreamy smile fixed on his face. So wraithlike and insubstantial... Not like the solid, stolid, responsible, dependable General Mushtanda... She put her face into her hands and wept. "My beti! My Rani-beti! An unwed mother! Mistress of a drug addict! Hai!"

The agitation in the water had died down now; only a thin gauze of mist still hung low, despite the strong sunshine. Brigadier and Lady Ladsahib began stalking regally across the bridge.

"Permission to cross over and meet my son?" the Brigadier enquired frostily, ever proper with regard to protocol. The Chaudhury nodded silently. Brigadier-General Ladsahib went up to his vagabond son and looked him up and down.

"You always were an artful dodger, weren't you, Altu Faltu," he remarked sardonically. "Still, I suppose it stood you in good stead this morning. I thought that brute had you. I still don't know how you managed to elude him."

He wondered why Altu Faltu smiled back at him in that

weak, guilty way that usually indicated that all was not what it appeared to be. "Not drinking or taking those foul drugs of yours, are you?" he asked casually, just in case. His son shook his head, the strange, guilty smile still on his face.

"Ladloo! Ladloo darling!" boomed the ever exuberant Lady Ladsahib, fondling the baby once more. "Look at him! His ears stick out just as yours do!"

The little family, followed by the ever faithful Ghungroo and Chalta Phurta twins, made their way up the twisting path, and out of the Ridge via the small side entrance through which Altu Faltu had sneaked out, one full-moon night, so many months ago.

They reached their beloved Villa Lantana two days later, where Baba Faltu now frolics in the tawny grass, and Ghungroo and the twins dance and rattle the dug-duggi for him in the leaf-littered courtyard.

While Altu Faltu, more frail, pale and ethereal than ever, looks deep into the eyes of Rani-beti, and asks, puzzled and with utmost seriousness:

"You know, Rani-beti, I've always wondered how we did it..."

"Did what, Altu Faltu? We did so much!"

"I mean, produce beautiful Baba Faltu. Any ideas?"